PRAISE FOR *THE SPEED OF MERC*

"Moving, funny, and propulsive. In prose both lyrical and sharp, compassionate and wise, Christy Ann Conlin delivers a page-turner with a fierce heart at its core." —MONA AWAD, Scotiabank Giller Prize–shortlisted author of *Bunny*

"*The Speed of Mercy* is a disturbing, elliptical, powerful mystery that becomes intoxicating as the pages turn. It is a lyrical meditation on betrayal and loss, the cruel forces of ageing and confinement, and the quirkiness of memory as it recedes and rises like the salty Bay of Fundy waters that haunt this compelling novel. *The Speed of Mercy* is also a passionate testament to the resilience of those who have been wronged, and to their refusal to cave in the face of human evil. I love this novel." —LAWRENCE HILL, bestselling and award-winning author of *The Illegal* and *The Book of Negroes*

"Dark family secrets, the lore of the sea, and a tender, protective friendship between women all converge in *The Speed of Mercy*, an unusual and surprising story set in idyllic rural Nova Scotia. With subtle humour, Conlin picks the locks on the long-closed doors of two families and bares the ugly, painful skeletons everyone knew were there but chose to hide. At the end she has you wondering just what mysteries your own family might be hiding." —SYLVIA D. HAMILTON, author of *And I Alone Escaped To Tell You*

"Christy Ann Conlin is a conjurer: of place, people, and the haunting past. I was instantly caught up in the darkly mysterious wor̲   ̲t to life.
Gripping   *d of Mercy*
caught r   ̲ OHLIN,
Scotiaba̲   ̲itizens

Also by Christy Ann Conlin

Heave
The Memento
Watermark

THE
SPEED
OF
MERCY

CHRISTY ANN CONLIN

ANANSI

Published in Canada in 2021 and the USA in 2021 by House of Anansi Press Inc.
www.houseofanansi.com

Permission is gratefully acknowledged to reprint the following:

Excerpt from *The Faraway Nearby* by Rebecca Solnit, copyright © 2013 by Rebecca Solnit. Used by permission of Viking Books, an imprint of Penguin Publishing Group, a division of Penguin Random House LLC. All rights reserved.

Excerpt from "To a Young Poet" by Mahmoud Darwish, translated by Fady Joudah. Used by permission of the translator.

Excerpt from "In the Waiting Room" from *Poems* by Elizabeth Bishop. Copyright © 2011 by The Alice H. Methfessel Trust. Publisher's Note and compilation copyright © 2011 by Farrar, Straus and Giroux. Reprinted by permission of Farrar, Straus and Giroux.

Excerpt from *The Violent Bear It Away* by Flannery O'Connor. Copyright © 1960 by Flannery O'Connor. Renewed copyright © 1988 by Regina O'Connor. Reprinted by permission of Farrar, Straus and Giroux.

House of Anansi Press is committed to protecting our natural environment.
This book is made of material from well-managed FSC®-certified forests, recycled materials, and other controlled sources.

House of Anansi Press is a Global Certified Accessible™ (GCA by Benetech) publisher. The ebook version of this book meets stringent accessibility standards and is available to students and readers with print disabilities.

25 24 23 22 21   1 2 3 4 5

Library and Archives Canada Cataloguing in Publication

Title: The speed of mercy / Christy Ann Conlin.
Names: Conlin, Christy Ann, author.
Identifiers: Canadiana (print) 20200368680 | Canadiana (ebook) 20200368699 |
ISBN 9781487003401 (softcover) | ISBN 9781487003418 (EPUB) | ISBN 9781487003425 (Kindle)
Subjects: LCGFT: Novels.
Classification: LCC PS8555.O5378 S64 2021 | DDC C813/.6—dc23

Book design: Alysia Shewchuk

Canada Council   Conseil des Arts
for the Arts   du Canada

ONTARIO ARTS COUNCIL
CONSEIL DES ARTS DE L'ONTARIO
An Ontario government agency
un organisme du gouvernement de l'Ontario

We acknowledge for their financial support of our publishing program the Canada Council for the Arts, the Ontario Arts Council, and the Government of Canada.

The author acknowledges the Canada Council for the Arts for its support in the realization of this project.

Printed and bound in Canada

MIX
Paper from
responsible sources
FSC
www.fsc.org   FSC® C103567

For
Marie Louise Cameron
and Olivia Apsara Purohit

We think we tell stories, but stories often tell us, tell us to love or to hate, to see or to be blind. Often, too often, stories saddle us, ride us, whip us onward, tell us what to do, and we do it — without questioning. The task of learning to be free requires learning to hear them, to question them, to pause and hear silence, to name them, and then to become the storyteller.

—REBECCA SOLNIT,
The Faraway Nearby

Part 1

Don't ask anyone: Who am I?
You know who your mother is.
As for your father, be your own.

Truth is white, write over it
with a crow's ink.
Truth is black, write over it
with a mirage's light.

—MAHMOUD DARWISH,
translated by Fady Joudah,
"To a Young Poet"

Mercy Lake.

Now

MAL WAS COVERED IN sweat, bits of twigs and bark
sticking to her skin, bits of lichen caught in her curly
black hair. She stood at the edge of the woods looking
out at Mercy Lake, listening to a loon call from the
water, and then the honks of Canada geese floating on
the lake. Mal felt primeval, not just-turned-thirty.

The burned-out remains of the lodge were barely
visible from where she stood. Nature was slowly
purging and reclaiming the site, absorbing and
concealing what had happened there in 1980. Fireweed
in the meadow in front of the burn-out ended at a cres-
cent-shaped white sandy beach. At the other end, ten
miles across, the lake broke into estuaries and streams,
which led to a bog, from which flowed the Mercy River.
It cut through the Acadian forest for miles, then snaked
across meadows and fields, bending by the tiny town

of Seabury, widening into a bay before flowing into the Bay of Fundy and, finally, the vast Atlantic Ocean beyond. It was very different from the coastal forests at home in Northern California. A seagull cried overhead and Mal looked up at the white bird floating through the blue of the late afternoon sky, a sky that seemed closer over the short trees than above the sequoia, the soaring California redwoods.

She had never been to this far-western part of the Annapolis Valley. Her grandmother had lived two hundred miles away, outside of Bigelow Bay, on land given to Black Loyalists coming up from the American South around 1775. The Valley was dotted with these satellite communities northward off the small main towns that no one, hardly even locals, knew about. A few wealthy white Loyalists had made an effort to recreate their plantations, but winter in this northern climate destroyed that antebellum dream. Mal had visited her grandmother numerous times when she was a child, and then later when Gramma Grant was in the final years of her life in a nursing home. Mal's mother had left Nova Scotia when she was eighteen, making her way to art school, meeting Mal's father on vacation, never looking back. Except when they came to visit. They would just see Gramma Grant. Grampa Grant had died before Mal was born. He was buried in his kilt, Gramma said. The auburn glints in Mal's hair and the Grant clan motto, Stand Fast, *Craig Elachie*, were her Celtic inheritance. Mal's mother hadn't kept in touch with any of her childhood friends.

Mal began taking photos of the meadow. It was almost dinnertime and it had taken longer than she'd anticipated, hiking the overgrown road to the lake after finally locating the dirt road off another back road that connected to a secondary road she'd taken when she came off the main highway. She would have to hurry back to her car. She didn't want to be here when it got dark. Not that she knew exactly what she was supposed to do here.

If this excursion to the lake were a short story, Mal knew it would end with something popping its head through the dazzling surface and making its way towards the beach, towards Mal. There might be a canoe, previously hidden in the deep shade cast down by the woods. What moved towards her might be something that had come up from the bottom, something she couldn't quite see because the sun was in her eyes. It would be the truth coming for her, slipping towards her, a canoe in the shadows. Riding in the canoe would be the lies she'd told her mother about why she flew from California to Nova Scotia, their ancestral home.

Mercy Lake was in the centre of a vast stretch of old-growth Acadian forest owned by the Seabury Estate. The remains of the Seabury family now lived in Florida. Mal had already been down there, interviewing an old woman in a nursing home, a painter named Sarah

Windsor. Mal's mother had thought Mal was interviewing Sarah Windsor about a retrospective of her
early paintings of disturbing domestic scenes, for her
podcast. Mal had lied about that too. Her mother knew
Sarah Windsor. Not well, but they'd served on some
prize juries together. In fact, her mother had called and
talked to the nursing home staff so Mal could actually
get in. Security was tighter these days, people more
paranoid. When she got back from Florida she told
her mother the old woman wasn't able to talk. But that
wasn't true. She had managed a few words, a few senten-
ces. Enough for Mal to decide to go to Nova Scotia.

"Mal, rural Nova Scotia wasn't a place for me, and it
certainly isn't a place for you," her mother had told her.
"It's the Georgia of the north. Why do you think I left?"

"You say all the time that your inspiration for painting comes from the natural world—from all the stages
of your life. Why can't I find inspiration for my writing
and podcast through the natural world of my maternal
ancestry?" But it wasn't a spiritual pilgrimage to the
land of her mother's childhood that Mal had in mind.

Mal's mother had been quiet for a time and then
smiled. It wasn't surprising she believed Mal. She'd
always encouraged her to follow her passions. *Be the
best version of yourself*, Mal hears her mother say. When
she was younger, Mal had loved this. But by the time
she was in her early twenties, without any sort of "real"
career, she blamed her mother. Her father, before he

died, said her mother was making up for what she saw as the deficiency in her own upbringing, how Gramma Grant had always said no. Mal's father had a way of being very direct while always being kind. No judgement. They were poor. Life was hard. You had to be practical. You had to stay on the safe side. Life was dangerous. Her mother wanted Mal to know a different life, her father explained. He was the son of immigrants from Gujarat and shared her mother's desire to provide a different future for his family, the tricky business of both protecting and encouraging your daughter in a society rife with racial discrimination.

Mal wanted to prove she was more than a thirty-year-old podcaster and obscure short story writer living in her mother's garage apartment gobbling mango lassi and Doritos. This was *not* her best self. She had stumbled onto something secret—a real-life crime, a cold case—and she would break it on her podcast. But she needed a smoking gun. She needed evidence.

Her podcast was about mental health, and mostly the people she interviewed talked about how they managed theirs. They told their stories, gave tips on how to navigate depression and anxiety, how to have hope. Until she interviewed Flora, that was. The woman was in her late twenties. She was pale, winter white. Flora had a floral arranging business and talked about therapeutic gardening. It was Flora who had brought up Mercy Lake, in their off-the-record conversation after the interview. The two women found it impossible to avoiding exploring their shared Nova Scotia connections. "Oh, mercy," Mal had said, when they were talking about the East Coast, like she was a country girl. Flora, hearing that word, *mercy*, paused, and then dropped her story out of the blue. It was a confession of sorts. *Mercy* seemed a code word and Flora's story was sealed inside her, waiting for the right person to call it out of hiding. Mal was that person. Flora's tone was matter-of-fact but her voice was hushed, and Mal's unease grew with every detail, her breath quickening. What had happened to Flora when she was fifteen? Flora claimed there was a link between a place called Mercy Lake in Nova Scotia and a group in New York that hid under a cloak of business, billions and blackmail — money and power providing an impenetrable shield for traditions, beliefs and rituals going back hundreds of years. A company called Cineris International. An old family named Jessome, in New York. Mal remembered how Flora's voice trembled as she spoke, trailed into a whisper. The woman was terrified. What they did to her went way back. There were others, lost in time.

Two days after she spoke with Flora, Mal got a phone call. It was from a private number. She answered anyway. A low male voice. He knew her name. *Malmuria, don't stick your nose where it doesn't belong.* Mal reached in her shorts pocket and pulled out her copy of a 1980 article about a Seabury Summer Barbeque, with a photo of Franklin Seabury and William Sprague, arms around shoulders: *Fellows United*, read the head-line. And their daughters, Stella Sprague, twelve, and Cynthia Seabury, thirteen, holding hands, with bright smiles—Cynthia half a foot taller, teased wild hair, and Stella in her old-fashioned dress with a pixie cut. Mal had made copies from the microfiche at the archives in Halifax before driving out to Mercy Lake. But it had been a mistake to stop at the Jericho County Care Centre on her way, to try to speak to Stella so soon. Mal was never going to get near her again with the crazy old lady guarding her. It was so much more complicated than she had ever imagined. She folded up the article and put it back in the pocket of her stylish but practical hiking shorts.

The confidence that had billowed through her while travelling from San Francisco to Halifax, and then all the way through the forested trail to the lake, was sagging. Mal was alone, deep in the woods in a strange place. There was no signal on her phone, and the GPS had been useless once she turned off the main highway. The fire roads and dirt roads were obscure, lost in the past. She had a paper road atlas that did have the small roads marked, tiny thin lines, almost unbelievable.

When Mal had stopped at the Jericho Centre just after lunch, before driving west to find Mercy Lake, the first thing she'd done was hand her business card to the tall old lady outside smoking on a bench and ask

if she knew Stella Sprague. The old lady had bolted up
with such speed that Mal jumped.

"Why are you looking for Stella?"

Mal had tried to think of a smart answer, but nothing came.

The old woman had no shortage of words. "Why
do you want to talk to Stella? Do you know her? Are
you some cousin?"

"I just want to talk to her."

The woman was obviously a resident. A loon called
from the lake. Mal couldn't believe how naive she
was — she should have assumed the old woman was
a resident. She had clicked her dentures and globs of
white spit dotted the corners of her thin lips.

"About what?" The woman's voice had been so suspi-
cious, her eyes so narrowed.

"About something that happened way back." Mal
hadn't been prepared for what the lady asked next.

"Is danger coming?"

It was such a strange question that Mal had nodded
before she could catch herself, before she could stop the
words pouring out of her mouth. "Yes. Danger is coming.
Danger is already here. I think people are looking for me,
and probably because I'm looking for her. Does Stella
have something that might incriminate someone?"

The loon called again, and Mal remembered how
she'd immediately wished she could take back what
she'd said.

The old woman had shut her eyes for a moment and then opened them again. "You go away from here. They don't want visitors coming 'round unannounced. Didn't you see them signs inside? You go away. Don't bring any trouble here. I'm late for yoga." The old woman had then marched in through the main doors.

Mal had hurried to her car, aware that security guards might come out to ask her what the hell she was doing. She was lucky no one else had been outside. She didn't have journalistic instincts—that was very clear now she had come all the way to the lake alone.

Mal was already making a mess of this trip she never should have come on in the first place. She walked around the site of the old lodge, holding up her phone, taking a video as she circled the area before walking back to the north side, just to the east of the trail. There was a patch of mint near the tree line, pungent in the heat. And just beyond, rosemary spiked out from the overgrown grass, the heat amplifying the sharp aroma. It was strange, this wild herb garden. She took pictures of the unexpected plants. There was nothing intentional about it. Maybe someone many years ago had tossed a bouquet that had rotted and decayed and seeded. In the high meadow grass to the side of the trail were tiny true-blue star-flowers. Borage. Mal knew all of these from her mother's garden in Los Gatos. And about ten feet to the south of this, in the bright sun and sandy soil, were lavender plants growing up through the weeds, purple flowers bright in the pale green grass near the beach.

If this were a short story, Mal would know it was a story that started with deceit, a lie that led to all her problems. It was the truth of how her trip from California to Nova Scotia had begun, with deceit. Her mother was a famous oil painter, brilliant and beautiful. She was just emerging from her grief over her husband's death, and Mal was living with her. Mal's mother had decided she'd spend the end of the summer on a painting retreat in Big Sur—she was doing a series of paintings on grief for a show at the Triton Museum.

Mal told her mother she too was going on retreat, a pilgrimage to the place her mother was from: *the backwoods hick land*, as her mother called it, of rural Nova Scotia—a place of primal beauty, of seafood and fecund fields and orchards, a place where racism ran like an eternal current just below the polite surface. It might not be as blatant as it was in other parts of the world, but it was more durable in its disguise, embedded in the society of polite. Her mother said that Silicon Valley used to be much like the Annapolis Valley, a place of traditional farming, rural communities, but it changed and became a place of innovation and reinvention. Mal could hear her mother's voice in her head now.

The Annapolis Valley isn't a woke place, as you say, my darling. It's sort of lost in time, and that's not always a good thing, you know, a place where there is a lot of misremembering.

Mal knew there were Black people, multiracial people, addressing racial inequities in Nova Scotia. She had read online about Black Lives Matter protests and Gamechanger 902, a Black activist group. Her mother made it sound like a place where no one was doing anything. Mal put it down to her mother's age, being old and resigned.

"All the more reason to go to Nova Scotia to find my roots, Mom." But Mal didn't actually care about her roots. She wanted to figure out the mystery of Mercy Lake. When she researched Nova Scotia — the seascape, the lakes, the forests — it seemed welcoming. No massive forest fires. "Canada's Ocean Playground," they called it. Compared to California, it was a haven. Except for Mercy Lake. Mal knew her mother would have worried if she'd told her the truth, what Flora had said. She would have made her call the police, as scared as her mother was of the police.

A series of sharp snaps and cracks rang out from the woods behind the ruins of the lodge. Mal was still, holding her breath. Had someone been watching her? A loon called out again and the geese honked. Another crackle and another. Something, or someone, was coming through the tangled trees.

Yoga Monday.
Dianne's Unfortunate Teeth.

Now

THE CLOCK TICKED.

Dianne was late.

It was Yoga Monday.

Yoga at 1 p.m.

On the bookshelf, Stella Sprague's antique wind-up clock showed 12:55. Stella's uncle Isaiah had given it to her to help her keep track of time. Every morning the alarm went off at 7 a.m., and every morning Stella would wind the clock.

At bedtime she crossed off each day on her wall calendar with a thick X.

The clock was from the shop he'd had for years, called Isaiah Antiques. Stella needed only the seasons and the sky to keep track of the days, but the clock was helpful in the morning. Stella wanted to see Isaiah. He and Stella's mother had grown up over on the Mountain, and while Stella's mother had left Nova Scotia when she was young, Isaiah stayed. He had worked on the family farm on the Flying Squirrel Road, and then he inherited a house just outside of Bigelow Bay, down east in the Valley. It had an old carriage house attached, in which he opened up an antique shop he ran for ages. Every object holds a story, he had taught Stella.

Stella had lived with Isaiah years ago. Those years were dim in her mind. She had lived in different kinds of hospitals and group homes, and there were therapies and drugs, and efforts to get her to talk, to live on her own. Eventually, when they realized she would never be able to live *independently*, she was placed in the Jericho County Care Centre. Stella detested group homes, partially residential but with closed-in stairwells for fire safety, and glowing red exit signs — a house where the staff still had jangling key rings, where the adults living in the homes were all paid staff, not family. Stella could not stand the facade.

Dianne had been transferred to the Willow Unit back when Stella was forty. Stella had seen her before, from the window. She had watched Dianne walking, seen her sitting on benches, talking, telling her stories to anyone and no one. She had once had a violent streak but that had subsided.

She and Dianne would both be late for yoga by the time they made it down the three flights of stairs from the Willow Unit to the Vitality Room where the class was held on Monday afternoons. Stella didn't take elevators. She worried about being trapped. It was problematic for some of her appointments. That wasn't of concern to her, being problematic.

Stella's room was sparsely furnished, with a bed and an armchair in the corner by the wide window, a bookshelf against the wall. The Jericho Centre didn't have air conditioning but the windows partially opened, enough to let air in and keep people from jumping out. The ward cat sat on Stella's lap. It was a therapy animal known simply as Cat. Or CAT by residents who had no volume control, seeing the feline every time anew. But Cat's way of rubbing at Stella's ankles, jumping on her bed in the morning, bred a familiarity that ingrained the creature in Stella's mind, moved the cat to her long-term memory. Cat had come after Stella arrived, but Cat was old now too.

Footsteps in the hall. At last. One determined bang at the door. Nurse Calvin at the threshold.

"Stella, you'll be late for yoga. If you're waiting for your sidekick, Dianne's outside having her after-dinner smoke and talking to a visitor, a Black woman in an expensive yellow linen dress. And the hair!" Nurse Calvin held her hands out beside her ears. "Dianne will talk to anyone."

Stella knew Nurse Calvin was wrong. Dianne was very careful about who she talked to. Everyone was always underestimating the old ladies, Dianne said.

Nurse Calvin was the senior nurse on the Willow Unit — she still wore her original white nursing uniform from 1960, complete with vintage headpiece bobby-pinned to her dyed brown hair.

"Well? What do you have to say for yourself?"

Cat opened its eyes.

Nurse Calvin was retiring at the end of August. Stella knew this would be an overall improvement for most residents. Nurse Calvin had no time for the latest research. Medicine and disease, especially mental illness, were about common sense and practicality, she informed the workers in a voice loud enough for the residents to overhear. Nurse Calvin made it her mission to remind Stella just how things might have been if she'd been born in another time, when people like Stella — mute, or *dumb,* as they were called back then — weren't *indulged.* When they worked in the fields. When they were buried in cemeteries with unmarked graves.

"Fine, have it your way. If you don't speak up, others will make decisions for you." Nurse Calvin waited.

The latest neurologist said what the last one had said, and the one before that: *to repeat, to maintain routine, to see each task as a ritual.* Stella did this. It was in her nature to adhere to routine and schedules. Now she was fifty-four, she worried about a future as an old lady with dementia. Stella felt she'd already lived most of her adult life as an old woman, but she was changing now.

She had been an old lady in a young woman's form, but more and more, her body was suiting her mind. It didn't matter—young or old, she had spent years as an institutionalized woman with unpredictable memory problems. She worried now about disease taking the last of her good brain matter. Stella knew also that her medication had been cut back and that last week she hadn't taken any at all. The new neurologist said the less medication, the better. She was only to take what was necessary, and that would be determined through trial and, perhaps, error.

When the consulting psychiatrist came from the city for her monthly round in July, she'd agreed with the neurologist about cutting back Stella's medication. They could anticipate some confusion, memory loss but perhaps also memory gain, perhaps more sleep, perhaps less, maybe more appetite, or a diminishment. Stella had seen Nurse Calvin roll her eyes at the term, *chronic treatment-resistant mental illness*. As if it were a moral failing. Self-indulgence.

Grace, on the other hand, said Stella was just a variation of normal. Grace was a therapist at the centre who, in her *other life*, as Grace called it, was a poet. She had one son, at university. Grace had a picture of him on her desk in her office. Grace was a single parent.

Stella's uncle Isaiah came every Sunday afternoon to see her. He was here last week. Or maybe it was yesterday? Stella *thought* he had been here yesterday.

Stella wasn't sure. It was August. They would have sat outside on a bench in the shade. (Did they?) Dianne may have been with them, talking to Isaiah about the migration of birds, a particular preoccupation of hers. Maybe he hadn't been feeling well. He was old now. He didn't drive in the night or heavy rain anymore because of his eyesight. She hadn't seen him during the Covid. Stella couldn't recall when the antique shop closed. At least a decade ago. Isaiah was eighty years old, four years younger than Dianne. Stella knew he had given her the alarm clock at the same time he had given her the antique bookshelf, when she first came to live at the Jericho Centre. When she started wandering off, like an old lady with Alzheimer's disease, except she was twenty-five.

STELLA COULDN'T REMEMBER THE moment she stopped talking. She could not vocalize much more than a grunt or a groan or a squeak. She had been mute long enough for the diagnosis to change from *elective* to *selective* mutism. But a diagnosis, Stella knew, didn't assist recovery. Stella accepted that she didn't talk in the same capacity most people accepted their inability to fly. She had occasionally tried to speak when alone in her room, opening her mouth wide in front of the mirror, but the language of sound and vibration was lost to her. Sometimes she would hear herself humming, but another self, and as soon as she listened—silence.

Her vocal cords had retired when she was thirteen, so even when she wanted to talk, she could not. But there had been very few times she had wanted to speak. Stella knew that sometimes she muttered in the night. They had sent her to a sleep lab. They had played a recording for her. It was unintelligible.

Stella looked at the groomed grounds from her window, a wall of thick blue firs jutting into the sky. Sweet silence filled the room. When Stella looked back at the doorway, it was empty.

Stella would wait for Dianne. It was Yoga Monday at the Jericho Centre. Today. Yoga followed lunch, as Stella called it. Dinner, as most residents and staff called it. There was a weekly cafeteria menu and activity schedule posted every Sunday night and copies of both given to residents with individual appointments and activities for the coming week. Stella pinned these to the corkboard beside her bookshelf. She needed her routine. The only variation she could easily abide was in nature, the capriciousness of the seasons, and yet even in that, the seasons were always predictable. Daylight savings time always threw her for at least a month.

Strolling on the extensive paths of the Jericho Care Centre property was Stella and Dianne's main activity. Dianne and Stella had seen different programming come and go over the years. The Covid came and for a long time they weren't allowed to walk alone. Just short walks, always with a worker. There was constant hand-washing. The activity room had become a temporary hospital ward. A storeroom at the far end of the building was converted into a morgue. It was a hard year at the Care Centre. Many of the residents had died. Stella's anxiety medication and sedatives had been increased so much she was not able to do much more than sit in a chair.

Stella's mind was jumbled with time. Her hands were sweaty and she wanted to chew her nails but she was not supposed to have her hands near her face. She remembered this. Also that Dianne had not come by for their Sunday bedtime walk last night. Stella had waited in the resident lounge at the other end of the hall, sketching a daisy in a white vase, lifting her eyes at every footstep until it was bedtime.

Dianne was eighty-four, Stella reminded herself. She could be napping. *No.* Nurse Calvin said she was outside talking to someone. Stella's body knew when the time was for Dianne to appear and Dianne *always* appeared with her grey ponytail hanging down her back, her thin shrivelled lips turned down in a half moon through which she hurled wheezy belts of laughter. Dianne told Stella stories during their daily walking ritual, *walking and talking,* her observations about this person and that person, about what the sky was telling her, what her bones were telling her, if a storm was coming, her opinions on flowers, on the quality of the food.

Stella knew Dianne was born at home on the North Mountain on the Flying Squirrel Road, and went to live in the Valley in Kingsport on the Minas Basin with Sorcha, her distant cousin, when she was a teenager. Stella had gone to Kingsport on a weekend pass a number of years ago to visit with Dianne and her cousin in the early summer. Dianne had told Stella she once fell on her head on the rocky beach and was never the same. Dianne could remember when she was different, when her thoughts were different, when she was somebody else. Someone she once missed but eventually forgot. Stella knew that she was different too, from many years ago when she was a child, when her mother was alive. But that was another lifetime. And you couldn't live for other lifetimes.

Footsteps in the hall—Dianne in the doorway, her slate-grey hair in a braid.

"Get up, Stella. Don't want to keep the hippies waiting." Dianne clapped her hands together and her silver necklace flew into the air before landing back on its perch on her breast. Dianne resembled an ornament from an antique shop, one of those strange memento mori objects Isaiah kept on a shelf, with her lined face and her dark skin hanging over her cheekbones. Dianne had lost her teeth. She snorted when people said that. *Pulled out. Didn't lose them. Not a set of keys.*

Dianne looked over her right shoulder. Then the left. Back at Stella. Then down the hall. Again back at

Stella, smiling, trying not to alarm her. This was new and strange. Dianne was not paranoid.

"Let's go." Dianne hoisted the corners of her mouth but her lips fell down as quickly as they had lifted, a flag raised but not tied off, the collapsing smile Stella knew Dianne reserved for the nurses and workers, the people who took care of them. Dianne didn't mention a visitor, a Black woman in a beautiful yellow dress.

Dianne played with her necklace with her left hand. "How are you managing without all them pills? Remember? That new psychiatrist wound back your meds to nothing. I still got my pills every morning. Never getting off those. For my ticker." Dianne patted her chest as she glanced around.

If Dianne kept behaving this way, Stella worried they'd reassess her. *Paranoid. Neurotic.* They would insist Dianne was losing her proverbial marbles when Stella knew Dianne's head was full of fine marbles, marbles made from the finest stone.

Stella remembered she wasn't taking much medication anymore. Maybe none. She couldn't quite recall. A nurse had always come to Stella's room each morning after breakfast with a plastic container of pills. It had been this way for years. But she wasn't coming these days. This was why Stella felt clearer-headed, but the clear-headedness was disorienting in itself. She recalled the brain zap, the feeling of electricity in her head as they cut the dosage down. But that was gone now.

There was no weather in her head, just the calm blue sea and empty sky of her memory.

"Got waylaid by Nurse Calvin. She's going on about my cousin Sorcha. Says she's too old to have me over on weekends. What does that old bag know? Can't wait till she retires. One more month and we'll be free."

"Hurry up, quickity-quick." Dianne shuffled back and forth in her white running shoes and put her hands into the pockets of her blue house dress. She only wore blue dresses and always wore running shoes now to help with her back. She hated bare feet, and sandals were for hippies, Jesus and Pontius Pilate. Stella wore dresses and running shoes as well. She walked over to the door, picked up her knapsack and slung it over her shoulder.

Dianne called Stella's routines a form of *dead reckoning* her way through life — figuring out where you're headed based on where you are now. Every morning Stella reviewed the items on the top of her bookshelf, including a shell and a framed photo of Isaiah, Dianne and Stella on the beach by Periwinkle Cottage. The cottage belonged to Isaiah. It had been in Stella's family for generations. The photo was from an outing on a weekend pass, Stella and Isaiah sitting on a log by a fire, Dianne playing her banjo and with her head thrown back singing. The date was written on the photo. Stella didn't actually remember this outing. Still, she treasured the picture, the family cottage, painted periwinkle blue, named after both the creeping flower and the snails on the basalt beach rocks at low tide.

The word came from the Latin, from *pina*, and *wincel* from Old English, a *pinawincel*. (How did she know this? Who told her? Granny Scotia? She hadn't thought of her in many years. Perhaps her mother? Isaiah? Had she always known?) Stella was a placid lake. Most of her life memories were far offshore, lost in the horizon, where she wanted them to stay. But it was at the cost of a different type of memory, the minutiae, the curios, the details — things that were boats to that remote region.

Stella never knew what would live in her short-term memory long enough to make it to the part of her brain that stored long-term memory. The doctors said it was the hippocampus (the small seahorse-shaped part of the brain, they said — the vessel of short-term memory — damaged in a childhood car accident). Layers of trauma blended with time; her memories shifted and faded and reappeared again, popping back to the surface from the deep currents below, her brain living by its own seasons. The brain was fat and water, with salt, Stella remembered the neurologist saying, the specialist who also said that really, they had very, *very* little comprehension of the brain, the last great biological mystery, the realm of memory a mystical terrain. Some people wanted to travel to the moon. He wanted to travel through neuropathways. Now, when Stella closed her eyes and pictured her head, inside was a sea of mind, strange things living and swimming in it, shells on the ocean floor, the broken seahorse. She knew that before the Horrible Accident, she had a normal mind. And after the Horrible *Accident* and then the Horrific *Affliction* it all went dark.

THEY WALKED DOWN THE flights of stairs to the Vitality Room — tall, thin Dianne and short, stocky Stella, her little knapsack over her shoulder with her sketchbook and pencil inside. Dianne's brain was reliable and firm, even with age. Her memories were well-polished souvenirs. She moved more slowly every year. She had paced the halls like a caged animal when they were locked down by the pandemic, muttering and shaking her head. Dianne's philosophy was that life was about movement and forward motion — when the movement stopped, you were in trouble. For example, the meditation part of yoga. The surest way to die early was to meditate, Dianne enjoyed proclaiming.

Stella appreciated meditation. If a thought strayed through her head, she pictured an opened shell and tucked it away. Her mind matched the bookshelf in her room, except without end, the shelves stretching into a white haze, shell after shell lined up. She didn't open the shells.

Stella rarely thought of the years behind her or the years before her. She knew something terrible had happened the summer she was almost thirteen, the summer her father took her from Athens, Ohio, to his childhood home of Seabury. She knew there had been a car accident in the spring. That was the *Horrible Accident*, the HA. And then in August they had gone to Seabury, Nova Scotia, and something else had happened, in early September, as summer ended, the second HA — the *Horrific Affliction*. She avoided, at all costs, remembering the HAHAs. And she was so successful she forgot she ever had a childhood.

It was cool and damp on the lower level in the Vitality Room. Stella put her backpack in the white cubed shelving unit at the end of the room. She watched Dianne take her cigarettes and lighter from her deep dress pocket and put them in the next cubby. The staff were always taking lighters from Dianne and she was always finding new ones.

They picked up mats from beside the shelf and went to their spot at the back. Today Dianne put her mat by the wall on an angle, watching the door. She saw Stella watching her. "Just keeping an eye on the door. Can't be too careful these days."

Stella kept watching Dianne.

"Don't look at me so, Stellie. Nurse Calvin might come barging in, see how much she can piss us off before she's gone."

Stella shrugged. Karen would never allow Nurse Calvin to barge in. Karen had been teaching yoga for

ten years and working as a casual when the centre had
staff shortages.

They were waiting for Fred and Bob. The class was
tiny, only a few other residents at the front, stretched
out on their mats, quiet, maybe dozing.

Dianne wore her false teeth today and clicked along
to the music. Dianne could barely tolerate yoga music.
"Bluegrass is what we sang when I was a girl, that
and the gospel music. Sang in the choir in the North
Mountain Mission. We lived not far from the pastor's
family, the Swindelles. Used to sing down on the beach
'round a driftwood fire, down on the Fundy shore with
my grandmother. Did I tell you that?"

She had, over and over and over. But Dianne
repeated the stories for a reason. For Stella, so she
would remember. Dianne knew about Stella's memory
problems, or what Dianne called a *memory that resembled the ocean*, coming and going, dead calm and then a
North Atlantic storm, sometimes still water, sometimes
lost in the doldrums.

Fred came into the room in navy blue track pants
and flip-flops. He walked by Stella, shaking his finger
at her, a wide smile on his face, reciting facts. He was
obsessed with Russian history. He spent a lot of time in
the east wing where the Learning Annex was located.
Fred worshipped computers. *Mind thieves*, Dianne called
them. Stella wasn't sure how old Fred was, if he was in
his thirties or forties. He pranced when he walked and

his face was smooth and unlined—he seemed perpetu-
ally young.

"Rasputin was a hard one to kill," Fred murmured.
"Didn't wanna die. Not good, being poisoned.
Poisoned...shot at. And beaten. Then drowned. No
dignity in that kind of death. No sir. Those Romanovs.
Shot up like a bunch of targets...Charlotte's coming
on a plane. Charlotte Pacific will be here soon." Fred
clapped his hands together and smiled. Stella didn't
know what his official diagnosis was. Some people had
lived there for years and their stories were still secret.

Fred's grandfather came from Lebanon. Fred had
black hair, lots of black hair, but no family alive now
except an older distant cousin in Vancouver, Charlotte
Pacific, who came every summer to visit. Charlotte was
a retired social worker and always brought presents
for Dianne and Stella. Charlotte would glide into the
lounge with her pearls, a sapphire ring, and a vast hand-
bag, her soft hair that was always light brown even
though she was in her seventies. Stella remembered
one Charlotte visit. She couldn't remember which
summer. What Stella remembered was Charlotte
beside her when everyone else had gone outside for
an afternoon birthday party. Stella was upset that day.
They had changed her medication. Or maybe they had
said she couldn't go outside. Stella didn't remember.
Charlotte had held her hand as she spoke with Stella.
"I had a different life when I was younger, Stella. My

name was Bertram and I was a cartoonist. I don't tell many people this." Stella had squeezed Charlotte's hand and Charlotte squeezed back. Fred was Charlotte's only remaining family. She wanted to move him to the West Coast but didn't want to disturb his routine.

Bob came into the Lifestyle Room. Bob looked entirely normal. He was from Cape Breton. Or maybe Cape Sable Island. One of them. Or Ecum Secum. Stella couldn't remember exactly. He was new. The same age, give or take, as Fred. He also had been hit on his head. Or hit in his head. He was beaten up. With a baseball bat. Yes, that was it, Stella remembered... beaten on his head. He repeated words. Once he started speaking he got stuck, the way old records used to skip. His memory still worked well but he could not pay attention unless it was an action movie.

"Stella, we went to the drive drive-drive-drive drive-in last night. Why didn't you come, Stella? It was John Wick. John Wick. John Wick. Chapter Three Three Three. Parabellum. Bang Bang Bang. Fred, why didn't you come to the drive-in?"

"Too much killing. You never know when you'll get killed, Bob."

"But John Wick's a good guy."

"Bang bang. On your way out. Lights out. Lights down. House is dark."

"But he's an actor. Keanu Reeves."

"No drive-in for me."

"Bye, Stella," Fred yelled. Stella waved as he spread his mat out at the front of the room.

There were new floor fans in the four corners of the room. The Jericho Centre was built in the 1960s to replace a previously existing cottage hospital, the lunatic asylum, built in the 1920s. It was a *modern* hospital and then converted to a long-term-care facility. It was state of the art in the 1960s, but now old and worn. Stella enjoyed this about the centre, how the past and present wove together with no fixed time period, a world that existed only in the institution.

Sometimes Stella and Dianne would try to follow Karen's instructions for the entire class, and sometimes they rested on the mats and forgot Karen was even in the room. Today Stella and Dianne were participating. Stella watched Dianne attempt downward dog. Her silver necklace dangled from her neck, the intricate filigree rectangle hanging from the chain, banging on her chin as she stuck her butt in the air and relaxed her neck.

Karen came over to check their form. "Awesome. Must be all that walking you girls are doing again. When you sit down all day, it signals your brain to shut off the lower part of your body. Dianne, why don't you leave your jewellery in your room?"

"I can't do that, Karen. Family heirloom. Won't take it off 'til the day I die," Dianne said, still bent over, the delicate silver rectangle resting between her eyes.

Karen laughed. "Dianne, I think you just might live forever."

Karen put her head to the side as she watched Dianne wiggling her buttocks.

"JohnWick-JohnWick-JohnWick," Bob yelled from the front, jumping up and down. Stella lifted her head, straightening her neck and glancing through the wobbling downward dog triangles of the class. Fred's arms stretched up in the air, his fingers fully extended, as he yelled out that Charlotte would soon arrive.

Dianne's teeth fell out. She reached for them with opened fingers but fell forward a bit and knocked them. The teeth scuttled over the floor. Dianne's dress fell down over her head, her old lady green cotton panties exposed as she balanced on one hand, the other hand trying to pull her dress down. "Goddamn yoga."

Stella wobbled after the wayward teeth, still in downward dog. She stopped and took a deep breath, her eyes closed. She inhaled and mooed, as Karen had shown them over and over again, flapping her lips. Stella reached for the false teeth. She handed them to Dianne, who now sat on the mat with her legs out straight. Her knee joints were often stiff and she called herself the Tin Lady. Dianne wiped her dentures with the hem of her dress and popped them back in.

"Thanks, Stella, my girl. Damn things." Dianne chomped down on her teeth, wiggling her tongue, settling them into place.

They did a few more poses, wobbling mountains, quivering trees, felled trees giving up and collapsing to the mats for savasana, the meditation part of Yoga Monday.

Dianne farted. Stella laughed but laughing made her abdomen hurt. She felt something warm between her legs. Maybe pee. Stella worried there would be a stain on her dress. She wanted to leave before the other residents got jammed in the door. She was comforted knowing she had an exit, free passage. It's why she was fond of life at the centre. There were walking trails and gardens and it was close to town. It was an institution with many halls. If there was a blizzard they could walk the halls and corridors. The power never went out. The Jericho Centre was on a generator and a back-up generator. It was a spaceship, the Starship *Enterprise*, Bob called it, never stopping, its passengers lost in time.

Stella shuffled over to the cubby to get her knapsack. She slung it over her shoulder and her sketchbook fell out behind her onto the damp tile floor. There was nothing in the sketchbook except for her few drawings of flowers and woods and leaves with a pencil or ink, but it still felt very intimate, private. But something new was on the floor beside the book—a postcard of two girls in a canoe, muted pastels, a vintage postcard. Stella squatted down and picked up the sketchbook and put it in her bag, all the while looking at the postcard. It was as though a voice was coming from it, a feathery whisper, words she couldn't make out. A voice from her past.

Stella flipped over the postcard. She recognized the handwriting. Years ago the girl it belonged to had told Stella to hide. And now this girl, *this woman*, was coming.

Seabury.
Little Bear.
The Nature of Love.
Then

STELLA'S FATHER FANS HIS hand out at the view as they approach Seabury. Stella looks at his other hand gripping the steering wheel. She had felt safer in the airplane, before they'd landed in Halifax and rented the car for the long drive to his childhood village.

"Take it in! Almost home." He says *home* as if he wants to imprint it upon her. It would be impossible *not* to notice the incandescence as they drive to the tiny seaside village on this mid-August evening, the blushing sky radiant at the horizon, streaks of colour shooting up into a pale gold, a fantastical shimmering on the ocean, and, high above, a navy sky, darkening as Stella looks north where the deep blue fades into black and stars glimmer overhead.

On the plane from Columbus, Ohio, Stella had tried to read the book left on her mother's bedside table, the book she had been reading before the car accident. Her mother's place had been marked with a pressed-flower bookmark. *The Violent Bear It Away* was upsetting. Stella's head and eyes hurt, she thought from the quiet violence, but then she remembered the doctor's orders NOT to read. She kept reading, rubbing her eyes. Then her father finally remembered Stella wasn't supposed to read and told her to put the book down. They were an unlikely pair, and her father had never expected to be on his own with her. Forever. He couldn't even pretend he knew what to do.

Stella notices it's not nearly as warm as back home in Athens, Ohio, where her father, Professor William Sprague, as the plaque on his office door reads, has his cross appointment in the History and Sociology Departments at Athens University. They have lived there for seven years. *Had* lived, Stella reminds herself. They aren't going back. Their belongings, including all Stella's books, will follow in the moving van when the house is packed up by professionals. Her father didn't have the stomach for it. They both brought suitcases, mostly with clothes. It had been a quick decision, made when Frank, her father's childhood friend, had called. Frank suggested they start fresh in Seabury. Not that he lived there year-round. He had resided in New York for most of his adult life, where his business was head-quartered, but every summer Frank brought his wife and daughter back to Seabury, where Frank's mother still lived. Frank had invited them before but Stella's mother had refused to go.

After the Horrible Accident, Frank had invited them again, this time suggesting it be a permanent move. He would use his contacts and get Stella's father a job at the Lord Bishop University in Bigelow Bay. Frank was on the board of governors. But the true tantal-izing lure, Stella understood, was the suggestion that Frank might be able to fund her father's project, an intentional community where the mentally ill could live, inspired by what her father always described as the *much-misunderstood* Kirkbride Plan, the nineteenth-century idea of moral treatment developed by Dr. Kirkbride — his idea being that architecture and land-scape could heal and restore sanity. Her father had been working with a group back in Ohio for the last few years. Frank had told her father they could discuss the project, and possible funding for it. Stella's father was hopeful. Frank's family had always been very gener-ous financially, first with Stella's grandfather when he almost lost his insurance business to bankruptcy, and then with her father, paying for him to go to boarding school and university. He's told Stella more than once that the Seaburys have never hesitated to help out the Spragues.

Stella was shocked when her father announced the move, the new beginning—she was still numb from the car crash, disoriented from her concussion, the weeks she had been in a coma, the two months in the hospital. And coming home to the quiet and dirty Sunnyside Drive house without her mother, Catriona, was strangest of all. Stella waited for the delicious smell of muffins and cookies baking in the oven.

Instead, the kitchen smelled sour. In the backyard Stella looked at the empty clothesline. Her father used the dryer. She listened for her mother's footsteps. Instead, she and her father walked along the river every day. They lunched at cafés. He heated up frozen pizza and opened cans of peas and beans. Stella would wait to hear her mother read to her, to call to her from the kitchen about a poem she was reading. Stella's mother had always wanted to go to university, she confided to her daughter, to study and write poetry. But she was from the wrong time.

"I knew I wouldn't need a map, Little Bear." Stella's father smiles and glances over at her.

"That's great, Dad."

He pushes his straggly hair back from his face and scratches the top of his head, the bald spot. "Hair today and gone tomorrow."

She manages a groan. This Stella does not want to humour her father. The previous Stella, she recalls, would laugh at things, tease her dad, who would then chuckle and tilt his head to the side, which her mother had once described, during one of their *quiet arguments*, as his *contrived bashfulness*.

Since Stella was little, her father had always told her he'd never return to Nova Scotia, but in the aftermath of the accident, he was lost. His childhood home is an anchor in his mind, a place where he has a history, for better or for worse. All Stella knows is that her grandmother died when her father was sixteen and home from boarding school. And only his father, Stella's grandfather, had been alive, but they had fallen out years ago, when her father was eighteen. He had gone from boarding school to university and never looked back.

Before Ohio, they lived in Cambridge, Massachusetts, where her father did his post-doctorate at Harvard, where he had done his Ph.D. Stella's mother always described his work as an *arcane specialty* in the history of hospitals. Stella doesn't remember much of Cambridge or Boston. The library her mother took her to. The walks on neighbourhood streets lined with brick houses. The gardens in the summer. She had always been home-schooled. Her mother had a horrible time in the public school system in Nova Scotia, where she was also from, but much further east. Her parents had met by chance in Boston where her mother was training as a nurse, finding an instant comfort in their shared childhood geography.

Stella's father has talked about the Kirkbride hospital model, going on about the extraordinary Danvers State Hospital in Massachusetts, for most of the drive from the airport. Stella knows he's pushing the silence away. He doesn't enjoy the new, quiet Stella. Before the car accident, Stella was a chatty child, comfortable with both her parents and with meeting new people. Four months can change a person at this age. She might have a head injury, she may be *marbled with trauma*, as the doctor says, she may not remember the accident, and she may never remember it, but she does remember the past, life in Athens, the university town the Hocking River bends through.

From both parents Stella has inherited her brain, her high IQ. She always remembered what her mother told her to do when she was small, to put her problems in some sturdy shells, nothing fancy, and keep them tucked away in her mind until she felt ready and able to open them, to encounter what lived inside.

Stella's father fiddles with the radio. "The Wall" by Pink Floyd blasts out. Fiddle, static, fiddle. Christopher Cross singing "Ride Like the Wind." She cringes as her father tries to sing along, lost on some stage in his mind.

She rolls her eyes. Since the Horrible Accident she is not herself. So her father says. Gone is his sparkle of a child. She resembles her mother now, quiet. Like her mother *was*.

Stella feels like herself, to herself. This Stella appreciates how she is more like her mother. It keeps her mother alive. She is her mother's daughter. The chatty girl her father keeps mentioning is a fantasy Stella. She can't imagine ever being that girl again, the girl her father has her in competition with now.

Her father says her mother home-schooled her *not* because Stella was painfully shy but because Catriona was. Stella's *mother* didn't want to deal with teachers and other parents. Stella didn't particularly enjoy other children, so it was fine with her. She didn't feel left out. Her mother and she were a society unto themselves. The Stella who chattered away about flowers and birds, who danced around the room — this Stella was the dream Stella, as her mother now was a phantom mother. The accident was just over four months ago.

"Little Bear, I'm driving with a ghost," Stella's father says, looking out the windshield at the sky. At first she thinks he means her dead mother, but then Stella realizes he wants her to make small talk. Right now her silence frightens him.

"Mom couldn't stand rock music."

Her father slams on the rental car brakes and Stella lurches forward, the seat belt locking. In front of the car looms a buck with antlers, immobile. "Jesus Christ," he exclaims. He turns the car lights off and the music blasts from the radio, the silhouette of this beast still in front of them. "I forgot about the deer."

Stella's heart seems to be beating in her head. She turns the radio off. She's hyperventilating, and her neck is sore from where her head has hit the back of the seat. The dark shape on the road prances into the woods. Her father bangs his hands on the steering wheel, turns the car lights back on and starts driving again. He sighs. "Sorry, Stella. I got lost in my head."

Silence sits again between them, silence holding Stella's hand, a soft whisper of touch that soothes Stella's ears, as much as the deep bruised twilight comforts her eyes.

There is a sign that says *Mercy River* and they drive over the bridge and into the village down the deserted Main Street with old-fashioned storefronts from a time Stella can't place, but not the 1980 world they are in. It's tiny compared to Athens, but in Athens there is no ocean for the Hocking River to empty into. Both places have winding rivers, though. The Mercy River flows into the inner bay, which empties into the outer bay, which flows into the Atlantic Ocean. The water is still and shiny in the moonlight, glittering black. "Did you ever hear about what lies at the bottom of the ocean and twitches?"

Stella shakes her head.

"A nervous wreck." Her father bangs his hand on the steering wheel and laughs. Stella says nothing. "You know, you used to think I was the funniest guy alive."

She lets the silence continue to speak for her.

"Your grandmother always called this the purple hour, Stella, when night has not fully revealed herself." Her father reminisces as he drives through the downtown, then up the hill and to the left. A few more turns on the maze of residential streets until they pull into the driveway of an old house. It's plain, medium sized, bigger than their house in Athens, but without a wide verandah at the front of the house looking out on the street. As her father drives in and parks, the front windows gleam.

They stand in the driveway with their bags, the two of them. She's not sure what he's waiting for. Stella is tired from the travel. She's hopeful for a bed. Stella shivers and buttons up her yellow cashmere cardigan — it was her mother's. An outdoor light casts a soft glow at the back of the house, the rest of the yard lost in darkness. Pebbles crunch under Stella's feet as she walks closer to the door on the closed-in back storm porch. Her father looks startled, surprised to see his daughter approaching the door of his childhood home. He doesn't move. "There's a magnificent sugar maple in the backyard. I used to climb it. I had a tree fort. And we had a swing on it too. Sure is cold. The temperature can drop down at night — but not always. The weather here is unpredictable."

Stella knows how home to him was never truly in Athens. She knows home for him was never with her mother, or with her, his daughter. They were merely an island this restless man was stranded on. Stella looks up at the night sky while her father talks about the weather, while he stalls at moving them inside the house. It's a sea of black now, winking stars in the north. She finds the Big Dipper and follows the pointer stars to Stella Polaris, the North Star. She lifts her arm up and with her finger traces the Little Dipper, the constellation her father calls *Little Bear*, Ursa Minor.

Stella jumps as her father puts his arm around her. He takes a deep breath and walks to the rickety screen door, opening it to the solid wooden door behind it. He opens this heavy inside door and beckons to Stella. He leans down and pulls a house key from underneath a wooden statue carving of a fisherman standing on a table to the left by another inner door, also with a screen door. Hat pegs dot the wall to the right, a sole small-brimmed straw hat hangs from one.

"We always kept the spare key here, Stella," her father says. "Frank had the house cleaned and the beds made up. And fresh towels. It's been years since anyone lived here. Now it's just you and me."

Stella's father beckons to her from the kitchen doorway. "Come, Little Bear." She takes his hand, holding her breath as she steps onto the linoleum floor, the old-fashioned kitchen cozy with soft lamplight. There is a note from Frank on the table with a colossal vase of daisies, roses and lilies. A welcome card for Stella, mauve flowers hand-painted in watercolour.

August 1980

*Welcome! I'm so glad you're here, Stella. I hope you like
this card I've made for you. We've also left a bicycle for
you in the garage.*

Your new friend,
Cynthia

Her handwriting is not a normal teenaged girl's
writing. It's calligraphy, perfectly sculpted letters, black
ink on thick linen paper.

Stella's father peers over her shoulder at the note.
"Wait until you meet the Seaburys. Mrs. Seabury's family
descends from a noble clan in Ireland, the O'Clearys.
Made it big here as shipbuilders and such. But time
passes. They ran out of money. Aoifa was married off to
Frank's father in order to keep their mansion running...
you'll get to see it when you meet Cynthia because Frank
says she's living with her grandmother for the summer.
She wants to be home-schooled, as you are."

There is a faint scent of lemon and lavender
veneering over a deeper smell of old wood and books.
Homemade bread and strawberry jam and butter on
the counter. Milk and juice in the fridge. A basket full
of blueberries. The freezer is filled with meat loaves and
casseroles and stews Stella assumes Sally Seabury and
Old Mrs. Seabury, Frank's mother, have made.

Down the hallway off the kitchen there is an old black rotary phone on a vintage phone table. The dim kitchen light falls halfway down the hall—beyond that, the hall stretches into darkness.

"You would have adored my mother. Morgana. That was her name. Did I ever tell you that?"

Stella shakes her head.

A garbled sound comes from her father's mouth and dies, a stillborn word. He sniffs and rubs at his eyes. "I remember how light my mother was on the stairs. You could hardly hear her coming and then she'd be in the kitchen with her gentle smile."

Her father had flown home when his father died, but not for the funeral. There was no funeral. He had come back to Seabury on his own. Stella wasn't even born then. He had gone to the graveyard for his father's burial. Her mother told her that her father had donated all of the clothing and much of the furniture to the Salvation Army. There are few personal touches in the house now.

Her father carries their suitcases upstairs and Stella follows him. She's exhausted. There is a light on at the end of the hall in a room on the right where her father will sleep. Stella peeks into the room on her left. There is a white lamp by the side of the bed, a vase with a flower. Stella tries to open the door beside her room. She peeks through the keyhole and sees only darkness. For a moment she hears waves, as though she has a seashell to her ear, and can smell sharp sea water.

"Stella."

She jumps and screams.

Stella's father says, "Sorry. I didn't mean to scare you. You need to get to bed."

But Stella is wide awake now. "Why is this door locked?" She touches the wide wooden door casing.

He doesn't say anything.

Boom, boom behind her eyes.

"Dad? What's the deal with the door?"

"You need to get to bed," he repeats.

The Feckless Sky.

Now

MAL STOPPED AND HELD her breath. Another snap in the woods, a branch breaking. And then more. Mal was panting now, drooling. She wanted to run. To scream. To be back in Los Gatos in the apartment eating sour cream and onion ripple chips and watching Netflix. She closed her eyes. Opened them. Out from the woods came a herd of deer, first two adults emerging, then several fawns. Mal bent over. She vomited on her running shoes. She had never felt more alone. More of an idiot.

She'd told the man at the airport rental car desk that she was a journalist, the rental guy with a name tag on his shirt that said *Ron*. She had waited for him to look up from his computer and smirk. But he didn't. He didn't even look up. He just bobbed his head as he completed the paperwork. She could have said she was a brain surgeon. He didn't care. He didn't know she was lying. At first she had told him what she had told her mother, that she was on a sightseeing trip, heading out in a southwestern direction toward Seabury.

"Not much there besides nature," he had said. "It's pretty remote once you get past Bigelow Bay. Beautiful countryside though."

Then Mal had tried out her story on him. "Awesome. Actually, I'm on a working holiday. I'm a journalist. I'm doing a story on the area, the history."

Her face got hot as she waited for him to laugh or roll his eyes, but he smiled.

"Great." Bored, not caring either way why she was here, for holiday or work. It was all small talk.

She looked out at the beach, to the stretch of meadow and grass where the sprawling old lodge had once stood. She pulled her phone out of her pocket and crouched down as she took another photo. To one side, in the shade of the forest, were brilliant orange flowers with fat green seed pods. They burst open as she brushed her fingers against them. Touch-me-nots, or jewelweed. The air was a fragrant blend of pine and hemlocks, towering maples with a few leaves just starting to turn red at the edges, the sweetness of lake water, and the heady smell of late-summer flowers and deep forest floor moss, all starting to settle down into end-of-season decay.

There was a dramatic stretch of fireweed, a brilliant fuchsia in the sun on this very hot August afternoon. A great black cloud of starlings lifted out of the treetops, a murmuration travelling through the feckless blue sky reflected in the calm of the lake.

Mal laughed out loud from sheer relief, tugged her backpack over her shoulders and slowly walked back to the trail.

She'd spent the previous year doing nothing but watching television and eating chips, lost in a depression she didn't understand. Yes, her father had died, but the melancholy had been there before. Her parents described it as her artistic side.

Live life like it's a novel and not a short story, Malmuria Grant-Patel. The problem with a short story is that it never really concludes. Your life will conclude, at some point. Live life as though you're in a novel. You'll put yourself in a position of having to make choices, of living knowing there is an ending. Famous last words, famous last ironic words from her father in the hospital bed, shrivelled like a mummy days before his death, every word from his hacking lungs a treasure, every word a gift. She was glad she and her mother had been able to be there with him, every day, right until the end. She was angry, was still angry, that he died of lung cancer, when he'd never smoked. He had been more sanguine about it. They had lived in Silicon Valley. Air pollution came for everybody. Of course they had relocated to Los Gatos where the air was a bit better, but not better enough.

Mal took a deep aromatic breath and exhaled, her body suddenly full of grief and longing for her father, who always knew what to do. She could go to him with anything. Her yellow shorts were covered in splotches where she had fallen in potholes full of swampy green water on the way in. She was hot and sweaty from the bushwhacking exertion needed to get this far. When her grandmother said there was a road to Mercy Lake, Mal had expected *a road*. And forty years ago it had been a road for sturdy vehicles making their way to the lodge.

She had called her grandmother in the spring, after she interviewed that young woman, Flora, for her podcast. Flora. Wasn't her real name. Mal did the interview over Zoom. They had talked about how to survive in a world under lockdown, how to survive in a world where people thought you were broken. She had some interesting ideas about wabi-sabi, a Japanese aesthetic that embraced imperfection and impermanence. And Kintsugi, Japanese pottery made with broken pieces, beauty made from what was broken, from remnants, the resiliency in what survives, what comes together in a new form. It was after they finished the interview that the woman told her about Mercy Lake, after Mal said her mother was from Nova Scotia originally. It was that word, *mercy*, that triggered this whole situation.

"Have you ever been to Mercy Lake?" the young woman had asked her.

"Never heard of it," Mal said.

"Good," Flora had said. That's where it started. Flora said she'd overheard it when she was younger and in some trouble. There was a company, Cineris International. It was the link. To something called Sodality. And those who belonged to Sodality met every few years in Nova Scotia, at Mercy Lake. And then Mal had remembered — Sarah Windsor had done a series of paintings of a river, the Mercy River Study. Dark, creepy paintings.

Mal had called her grandmother in the nursing home. She was ninety years old and didn't enjoy talking on the phone. When Mal asked her about Mercy Lake, her grandmother had said, "What do you want to know about that place for? Way back we were related to the people who owned most of the land in that direction. But that was way back."

Mal had explained as much as she could. There had been a lot of silence on the phone, but her grandmother was ancient and hard of hearing. It wasn't that though. Mal listened to her breathing. And then clucking.

"You stay away from that place."

Mal had pushed and her grandmother had changed the subject.

A few days later Gramma Grant called, leaving a message on her cellphone, telling her to go to the Flying

Squirrel Road, to the house with the fountain in the front yard—Mal would get answers there. *The Offing Society. Find Lucretia. Lucretia will appear.* And then the next week she developed pneumonia and passed so quickly. Gramma Grant's ashes were shipped to Los Gatos, where they sat on a bookshelf.

MAL HAD DONE RESEARCH the way she figured an investigative journalist would, but she knew it was meagre, at best. Her primary research nothing more than a bit of distracted googling and the purchase of a specialized geographic map book of Nova Scotia. And even with that, it took her forever but she found the side roads, the back roads, the obscure location. But the paper map was more helpful than her phone because on Google Maps it showed the lake but no road to it. When Mal called Flora to follow up on her interview, she couldn't find out anything more because Flora was dead. Not from the coronavirus—she'd jumped off her balcony. "Depression from the sheltering in place," the landlord said. "From social isolation." But Mal found that hard to believe. When she'd spoken to Flora the week before she had sounded normal, worried but calm.

A few days later Mal received a package in the mail from Flora. With papers. Photos. She was shocked. She didn't know why Flora had sent these to her. Was it the Nova Scotia connection? Surely she didn't think Mal was a real journalist? And then the creepy phone call telling her to mind her own business.

It was Mal's mother who had suggested she do a podcast in the first place. Her mother loved podcasts, especially *On Being*. That was the extent of it. Do that sort of thing, her mother said. At that point in Mal's life, she had published some short stories in impressive journals, although she had dropped out of the creative writing program at the University of British Columbia in Vancouver. She had published a few art photos. She had a nervous breakdown. And she had a podcast. But no one took her seriously. Well, she didn't take herself seriously. This trip was supposed to change everything.

Mal took a photo of the ruins of the lodge, now a pile of scorched rock, from the mammoth fireplace, she supposed. There was a fresh path through the ruins; brush pushed back, grasses trampled down. Sweat crept out over her skin, her bamboo T-shirt sticking to her flesh. She was far from her car parked out on the road by the trail. The tourist information clerk in Middleton, where she had pulled off the highway and stopped to use the restroom, had said there was the odd black bear and coyote, but they wouldn't be out in the day. He told her to sing and talk on the trail if she was worried. Mal had only noticed how anxious she was when she realized she had stopped singing a pop song and had unconsciously switched to an old hymn Gramma Grant had taught her. Mal thought about the envelope she had found just before she left California. On the landing outside the door to her apartment over her mother's garage. *Malmuria* typed in the centre, old-school. More from Flora? But inside there was one piece of paper with one sentence typed. *Mind your own business. We're watching you.* Someone knew where she lived. That was all Mal needed to finalize her plans to go to Nova Scotia, to get out of Dodge, as her father would have said. But this was Nova Scotia. This was the north. She should be safe here. The *Atlantic Bubble*, they once called it during the pandemic.

Rustling, this time at the edge of the woods on the south side of the clearing. Mal turned around. A crackling of branches, the swishing of leaves, as something, or someone, made its way to the edge of the forest. Mal waited for more deer to come out, but the sound stopped. All was silent except for the wind picking up now, rippling over the water and whispering through the meadow near the side of the beach. She kept her eyes on the far side of the forest to the north. The Canada geese began honking urgently, then flapping their wings as the family lifted off Mercy Lake and circled in the sky. Had someone been on the other side of the clearing the whole time, watching her? Mal turned and headed back into the woodland, her skin covered in goosebumps, hurrying on the trail to her car.

She came barrelling out of the trees, panting from her mad dash. She leaned on the hood of her rental car to catch her breath. There was no wind here and the sun had moved around in the sky. As Mal opened the car door, the faint smell of cigarette smoke curled in through her nostrils. There was a butt in the dirt right by the driver's-side door, as if someone had been leaning against it smoking, and then had crushed the cigarette butt with a heavy shoe, ashes mixing with the powdery dirt.

A Chorus of Frogs.

Now

STELLA AMBLED BESIDE DIANNE under the lovely after-noon sky. She was confused. The morning felt a week ago. Summer afternoons evaporated one's sense of time, Stella thought, and not just for people like her and Dianne. No one was safe from the bewitchment of a summer afternoon. As they walked, Dianne mumbled on about the beach and the moon, how many butter-flies were about this August, and then her voice faded away, as though she were just a cricket in the afternoon meadow.

Stella still held the postcard in her sweaty hand, and when she glanced at it she could hear a faint whispering.

Wish you were here. But don't worry because I'll be visit-ing soon. Just like I said I would. When the boat can't come to the sea, the sea will come to the shore. Love, your long-lost friend, Cynthia.

That unforgettable handwriting, calligraphy in the black ink of a fountain pen. Handwriting like a birthmark.

No date on the card. Why was Cynthia coming? It had been years. So many years. *She had said to hide. Silence would protect them. They would find each other again. Cynthia had proof. She would keep it safe until the right time. For now they would hide.*

Age moves forward, a tsunami of a thing, pulling moments with it, days and weeks and years.

It was a vintage card, with pale colours, a photograph of two girls in a wooden boat. *Rowing on the Mercy River at High Tide.* It must have been taken not far from where Stella's father grew up, his childhood home in Seabury where he took her that summer in 1980. After the car accident. Her mother driving. Her mother in the seat. Her mother outside. Her mother in pieces. Stella smelled salt water. Surf on a rocky beach. The wind whistling through the pines in the night.

HA

HA

Must not think of the HAHAs.

Stella was hyperventilating. A panic attack. She needed to be back on her meds. The ocean in her mind was swelling now, rising and falling, the shells rattling. She rubbed the sides of her head above her ears, listening for the hippocampi, the seahorses in her skull. Cynthia said she would come if there was trouble. *Hide.* Cynthia said this—Stella is sure she said to HIDE. The years had passed. It could only mean danger. Stella's eyes teared up, drops rolling down her cheeks, salty over her lips, falling on the postcard.

The postcard girls wore white dresses. The girl in the middle held the oars, her face turned away, looking at the girl in the bow who faced the camera.

There was a moment, a slack tide, when Stella's breath stopped and her mind emptied. The beating of her heart, a rush in her ears, sound simultaneously amplified and muffled. The moment turned. Sweat crept over her skin, rivulets coursing down from her hairline and over her spine.

"Stella, the postcard came a long time ago. Do you remember? Years ago. Isaiah said you might start to remember. We just had to be patient," she heard Dianne say.

Cynthia was swimming up in the dark waters, ripples on the surface of her mind. Stella tried to push Cynthia down to the bottom, to quiet the rocking seahorse, to tuck Cynthia into a shell, to close the shell, Cynthia banging inside.

Stella wanted to see Isaiah. Where was he? Had he visited yesterday? He used a cane and was driving less and less. Stella wanted to go to her room, to sit in her chair and look out the window, to have Cat jump on her lap, soft fur, quiet purr.

Stella's father floated into her mind. He looked as he did that long-ago summer, fifty-five, shaggy dirty-blond hair in need of a cut, a rumpled white cotton shirt, a coffee stain he hadn't noticed on the pocket, unshaven. Those shells Stella collected in her mind, those shells where she had stored her memories, were opening, this oyster shell lifting and her father tumbling out.

The postcard reminded Stella of her father's album of postcards about her father's hero, a man named Dr. Thomas Story Kirkbride, famous for the Kirkbride Plan for mental institutions built in the Victorian era. Kirkbride believed the building, as well as the setting, had healing properties. Kirkbride had written a discourse, *On the Construction, Organization, and General Arrangements of Hospitals for the Insane*. Stella's father had been writing a paper that last summer of his life on the healing power of architecture.

Her father's history lessons had stayed with her. His gifts to her, she supposed. The problem, he had said repeatedly, was the drastic funding cuts, the overcrowding, where a room intended for one person housed fifteen — the staff shortages and the resulting return to inhumane treatment. The Kirkbride hospitals were set in the country on stretches of land. They had farms where patients worked. Her father had postcards of asylums from all over North America, from when people would visit and send a card of the asylum to a family member. There were postcards of the French Devil's Island, the Australian French Island. In Vietnam the French shipped dissidents to Con Son, where thousands of Vietnamese suffered and died. The Riverside Hospital had been put on North Brother Island, in the East River in New York, for isolating people with infectious diseases. *People do well in community, Stella*, her father would always tell her. Intentional community, accidental community, a place where they are with like-minded people, where they are not alone.

But Stella knew any community could be corrupted. And the most unlikely place could provide sanctuary.

The Nova Scotia Hospital, the NS, was where patients worried they'd get sent if they acted out. It was originally a Kirkbride hospital and still existed, although the main building — which was called the DeWolfe building when Stella had spent time there — was torn down in 1996, and the rest of it renovated beyond recognition. There was one postcard of the main building and a black-and-white photo taken from Citadel Hill looking across the Halifax Harbour to Dartmouth. With a magnifying glass you could see the hallmark "batwing wards" of the hospital stretched out. That architecture and setting had an enormous impact on health, her father said. Stella's mother had told her that Elizabeth Bishop's mother had been in the Nova Scotia Hospital, when it was called Mount Hope, and had died there, back before the city of Dartmouth had grown around it, before the government had started clawing away the sprawling grounds.

I don't want to think about my mother. Or my father.

This was Stella's mind's voice.

Dianne sat on the bench by the river with her eyes closed. Stella looked over at the graveyard. It must be getting later in the afternoon. The sun wasn't as bright. The modest graveyard was abandoned, only numbered stone markers for the buried. Once there had been a lecturer in the Community Room who had talked about the history of the County Home Road the Jericho Centre was located on. He said that the tombstones were unmarked to respect privacy, that families had been ashamed to have a relative so poor or disabled that they ended up in the poor farm. There were records in the municipal offices, he said, the records from the poor farm — every farm had had to report to the super-intendent of the poor. It sounded evil and inhumane, he said, but it was an improvement over the insane and poor being abandoned on islands with lighthouse keepers, or being left to beg and die in the streets. No one remembered the poor farms, he said, not anymore. After the war, when social services and social welfare had been introduced, a federal old age pension, govern-ment security, the poor farms were only remembered by historians and the elderly.

Queen Anne's lace quivered in the breeze. Queen Anne's lace was not a native flower. Stella remembered this. Something she learned from Granny Scotia. Tall blue flowers grew next to the Queen Anne's lace. The shells in Stella's mind rattled. The seahorses let out a few bubbles. She put her fingers to her temples and pressed.

Blue petals. Borage. This was a flower that grew in Granny Scotia's garden. *Ego borago, gaudia semper ago.*

I, borage, always bring courage.

"Did you say something, Stella? No, course you didn't." Dianne swivelled her head around, her eyes narrowed and shining. She jerked upright. "Dozed off there for a bit. Getting old, Stella, my girl. Must almost be time to head back. Got to see Gracie. Let's go. I need a cuppa tea."

She may have spoken out loud. Stella didn't know. She licked her lips, watching Dianne as she studied Stella's face, and then looked at the postcard in one of Stella's hands and the flowers in her other. Stella didn't realize she had picked them. "Ain't those pretty."

Why hadn't Isaiah come to visit? Was it that she just couldn't remember? He usually called on Sunday nights. Had he called this week? Which day was it? Stella had a cramp in her belly, a dull ache that might have been with her for many years. She wasn't sure. This afternoon Stella's head was full of whispers and rustles. Bits of memory seeping out now, since the postcard—lurking danger and lost threads.

They headed to the back door of the Jericho Centre,

stopping at the resident garden where Dianne snapped off some sprigs of rosemary and put them in Stella's hand with the blue borage.

AFTER SUPPER, DIANNE AND Stella walked out behind the centre to the bench to watch the late-summer sunset. Dianne wasn't wearing her teeth and she talked with the cigarette in her mouth, puffing and speaking at the same time. She had a flashlight. She had never brought one before. This was new, Stella noted.

"God, I miss them spring peepers. I do love a chorus of frogs."

Stella stood up. She took the postcard out of her pocket.

"Just put that away, Stellie."

Stella turned the postcard over and back, over and back, forty times, hoping this might break the spell, what she couldn't remember. It was as if this was a calling card from her past, a cryptic calling card sent to her from a childhood she had tried to forget. It was her one success. She tore the postcard into two. And then into pieces, hurrying over to the river, ignoring Dianne's protests as she threw the pieces into the water. Stella didn't want to remember. She wanted things how they had been for years now, the quiet familiarity of days and seasons.

There was a snap in the line of trees to the west. The sun had set and a thick mauve dusk coated all. Dianne beamed the flashlight on the evergreens. She moved the light in a circle, all around, and then on the ground by Stella's feet. They listened. Silence.

"What's on your leg?" Dianne bent over and shone the light on the inside of Stella's calf where a thin trickle of blood ran all the way down into her white sock in her running shoe. Dianne took a hanky from her pocket and, with great effort, leaned over and wiped at Stella's skin. "Let's go back and get you cleaned up. Bit late in life for the monthlies to start up again. Don't you worry, Stellie. Old Dianne is keeping guard, just as she promised."

Back at the centre most of the other residents were in bed, doors closed. The duty nurse was marking something in a book. Stella didn't recognize her and hurried off towards the bathroom, Dianne following. Dianne stood outside the bathroom while Stella wiped herself with toilet paper. This bleeding was bizarre. Her underwear was ruined, covered in a red-wine-coloured stain. It was thick and sticky. Dianne opened the door and took the underpants. "I'll get rid of them, don't you worry."

Later, as Stella lay in her bed, there was a quiet sound at the edges of her mind, a sniffing, a dog in the distance on the scent of something alive, hidden. Through the open window the crickets still sang and a night bird called out. Far off, a lone coyote howled and then the rest of the pack joined in.

The Original Stella.

Then

"Why is the door locked? Why won't you tell me, Dad?"

"Well...that was my sister's room."

"Your *sister*?"

Stella wonders if she knew he had a sister, a memory taken by the car accident. But she knows there were no photographs of a sister, no *mention* of an aunt.

"She was thirteen when she died."

"But you always said you were an only child. Just like me."

Stella and her father stand in the hallway. He looks at the shiny hardwood floor as though it's the most fascinating thing he's ever seen.

"Dad, come on. Why didn't you tell me about her? Did Mom know?"

"Of course your mother knew, Stella. What kind of a question is that?"

Stella thinks it's a reasonable question. Her mother never mentioned an aunt. Her father has hardly talked about his past and now he's thrust them both back into the central nervous system of it. He cocks his head, as if he hears something coming from the room. Stella thinks he hears his memories. She listens to the quiet of the house, the grandfather clock downstairs in the hallway tick-tocking.

"What was her name?" Stella forces herself to ask this question, to break his trance. She wants to go to bed and escape from this strange night, with Ohio a dream in the past and Seabury the nightmare of the present.

"Her name was . . . Stella. You're Stella Maris — or Stella Polaris, as I think of you. She was Stella Violette, the original Stella."

Stella watches his blue eyes darting left and right, up and down, as though he's following the flight path of an insect. *Two Stellas.* She swallows and tries to speak, croaking out the words from her dry throat: "We have the same name? My name?"

Her father taps his index finger on his chin. "Well, *her* name. Yes, you were named after my sister. We almost named you after my mother, Morgana Llewellyn. She was born out on an island in the Bay of Fundy. Her father was Welsh. Her mother was Scottish."

"You never told me I had an aunt." Stella's voice is hoarse, the skin in her mouth and throat drying out as she sucks in one shallow breath after another.

"Stella! Don't speak to me that way. You used to be so polite. The only reason I didn't tell you was because it was so long ago. She had an accident. I can't stand talking about it. And now with your mother gone . . ."

The implication hangs in the air between them, a toxic vapour that had come with the night air — it was Stella's fault *her mother* and *his sister* and *his mother* had died.

He hasn't come out and said how much he hates Stella's new personality — the one that came with the head injury from the car accident. But his resentment is a living, breathing thing that follows Stella wherever she goes.

Her father raps on the locked door of Stella Violette's room, maybe hoping the knob will turn, that his sister will appear, all grown up, and assume responsibility for her niece so her brother, the widower, can hide in his research, can prepare for his job that starts in two weeks. Stella's father clears his throat. "It was locked after my sister died. I expect it's been locked ever since."

Stella shivers. "Well, that seems really crazy weird, doesn't it, Dad?" Her anger recedes as quickly as it surged.

"It might to you. Children don't understand grief any more than an animal does. It's not uncommon for the living to just seal up a room." He presses his hands together.

"How you did with this house?" Stella can't help but point out the similarity.

Her father's face collapses, his eyes perched over what her mother called jowls. "My father wasn't sentimental. He was superstitious though. He didn't go near Stella Violette's room. They always despised each other. We all despised my father. There wasn't an ounce of mercy in his blood. Too diluted with whiskey."

Stella's father slaps his hand against the plaster wall, clearly thinking he has made a mistake in talking about his dead sister. "It will be good for you to meet Sally, Frank's wife. We'll see her tomorrow. Do you need me to read you a story or anything? I guess you're a bit too old for bedtime stories now."

He clearly doesn't understand bedtime or bedtime stories. He points to the cozy room across the hall with the lamp and vase on the nightstand. "It's all ready for you, Stella."

And then a loud clang from downstairs, the old phone ringing. He turns and thuds down the stairs and Stella pads into her new room.

The bed is turned down, a just-opening yellow rose in the bud vase beside the light. Cynthia and her mother must have done all this work of getting the house ready together. Stella looks in the bathroom mirror as she brushes her teeth. She is pale with dark circles under her eyes. Her hair is short now, cut to match the side of her shaved head where the stitches were, from the deep cuts on her scalp where the glass dug in. She was wearing a seat belt. She remembers buckling up before they backed out of the driveway. There was thunder. She knows this.

There is a little grate in the floor in her bedroom. Stella's mother had told her about these, how they had heat registers in the house in Nova Scotia she had lived in when she was little, for air circulation, and in the winter for warm air rising from the wood stove. Stella can remember her mother's voice, but since she woke up in the hospital she can't picture her mother's face. When she looks at a photo she sees her mother, her dark hair, her gentle smile, the crinkles at the corners of her eyes, but as soon as she looks away, she can't hold her mother's face in her mind. All the photos are back in Ohio, being packed with the rest of their belongings and sent in the moving van.

She hears her father's voice on the phone coming through the floor so she closes the register. She opens the window and props it up with a wooden stick that's been left on the ledge. It's quiet outside except for a few crickets. She tucks herself into the squishy old spool bed.

Stella drifts off but a creak on the stairs calls her back. Her father opens the door and the hall light falls in.

"Stella?" he whispers.

"Yes, Dad?"

Only the floor creaking as her father comes to her bed and bends down, kissing her good night on her forehead, something he hasn't done since she was very small. His dry lips brush over her scar.

Stella's stitches were taken out before she left the hospital, now a red scar running from her temple around the side of her head and down the back. It's been four months since the accident. She was in the hospital for two months after the crash, for April and May, unconscious for April. She kept asking for her mother when she woke up and her father avoided telling her the truth. When Stella was discharged in June her father drove her home, looking straight ahead at the road as he told Stella they were moving to Nova Scotia.

Stella realizes her father isn't in her bedroom anymore. The door is closed and the room is dark. She remembers a summer night when she was nine years old, in her nightie in bare feet on the warm sidewalk in Athens, looking up at the night sky. It was warm, not the usual muggy hot, when the scorching temperatures and humidity turned the night sky into a cloudy dark ocean. It was, as it is here this raven night in Seabury, untainted by nocturnal clouds. Her father had taken her from her bed. He smelled of whiskey and smoke as he crouched beside her. Her mother was away, on a trip to Kentucky, to Pleasant Hill, the restored Shaker village that her people, the Settles, came from during the American Civil War. Stella's mother had told her stories of how the Settles moved up to Nova Scotia.

They were standing on the sidewalk so her father could show her Stella Polaris, the North Star, which does not rise or set but stays in the same spot, the axis of the Earth pointed almost directly at it. "You'll never lose your way if you can find the North Star. That's your homing. I wanted to name you Stella Polaris, but your mother insisted on Stella Maris, her tribute to the ocean. It wasn't worth arguing about."

Stella can smell the rosebud in the crystal vase. It comforts her knowing the flower is there. Crickets sing into the night. *Crickets, crickets, crickets*, Stella repeats, although in her mind what she sees are the fireflies on their front lawn that she watched with her mother on hot summer nights when she couldn't sleep, sitting on the verandah in Athens. Stella tumbles into a heavy slumber where the lullabies of insects become soft gusts of *mother voice*, carrying her away into trembling black.

The Fundy Waves Motel.

Now

THE SMELL OF ACRID cigarette smoke lingered in Mal's nose as she drove east on the highway, the early evening sky bright behind her. Phantom smoke. She knew it wasn't in the car. The car had been locked. But the stale odour painted itself onto her sinuses, her mouth. Her stomach kept clenching and no matter how much deep breathing she did, she couldn't relax or get the idea out of her head that maybe someone *knew* she was bumbling around, pretending to be a journalist, asking questions, trying to make connections. Her throat was sore. It couldn't just be from a whiff of smoke hanging in hot, humid August air. A summer flu or traveller's cold, the kind her mother said looked for exhausted, vulnerable bodies where it could lodge. In the back of her mind she was convinced that as soon as she had finally tried to take control of her life the coronavirus was ambushing her. But maybe it was just a cold. Her muscles were sore from the bush whack on that overgrown trail and from being "under the weather," although Mal thought of it as the weather over the body, pressing down, pressing in, flattening out the person and then inflating the head with mucous, boggy eyes like seeping pools.

After Flora had confided in Mal about Mercy Lake, Mal had tried to casually find out more from her mother. They were having dinner, one of her father's family recipes for curried lamb that they'd cooked together. Mal brought up the Mercy River paintings by Sarah Windsor. Her mother said it was in Nova Scotia, a river that led to a lake with the same name. All she recalled from her childhood, she said, was that a group of tourists on a backwoods hunting expedition had perished in a fire. She was just a girl then, so she hadn't paid much attention to the news. And it was two hundred miles away from Bigelow Bay, where she lived. Mal's mother did remember how her mother had turned the radio off whenever it was mentioned. And at school, she and her best friend talked about how two girls, twelve and thirteen, were the only survivors found at the site. They were never identified by name but they were the same age, and that's why they'd talked about it at school. Mal's mother had then abruptly changed the subject, switching to groceries and menu planning in a firm voice that signalled the conversation was closed. It was out of character for her. She had never mentioned any of her childhood friends before, for sure not a best friend.

Mal exited the highway in Middleton and pulled over on the side of the road. She glanced in the side mirrors, the rear-view mirror. There were no other cars. But there was still her mounting anxiety that someone had been in the woods. Had been near her car. Was it a tourist, a backwoods hunter? She remembered the threatening call and note before she left California. Was someone looking for her? Wanting to find her? Or just scare her? Before she left, she had googled the place for racial issues. Mal knew there had been BLM rallies in the province. There still were. She was surprised by this, the large size of the Black population, especially in the capital city. But the countryside seemed so serene. She always thought the North was a haven.

She never should have come here. She was being reckless. Paranoid, even. Neurotic. All the things her ex had found a turn-off in women. The right thing to do would be to change her flight, go back to California. She had cancellation insurance because her mother insisted on that. Mal would tell her mother the truth. If only her father were alive. He would know what she should do. She put her head on the steering wheel, feeling the vibration of the running engine in her skull, the cold air from the vent blasting on her face, and her eyes starting to leak tears. Her instincts were good when it came to that clench in her gut — the one that told her she'd made a mistake or was in something way too deep. There were backstage politicians in this story, powerful people—if her feelings about the depth of this were correct, the slightest whisper of inquiry or whiff of curiosity could awaken a depraved monster she couldn't even imagine. She shuddered as she thought about Flora's so-called suicide. And that fire so many years ago.

The air conditioning was irritating her sinuses, making her eyes bulge. She put the windows down and turned the car off. There was staggered traffic on the highway behind her, a few birds singing. Mal was not the sort who scared easily. Unfortunately, she was usually oblivious to fear when she should be fleeing. Fear always came too late. When she felt resistance, it mustered intrigue and temporary fortitude. Challenge summoned momentary courage. And then her confidence shattered and the truth would stand before her, a taunting demon that would crawl into her head and beat on her brain, making her temples throb as they were now. She would find a hotel for the night. See how she felt in the morning, maybe find a doctor. And then she would reassess.

Just then she heard a car behind her. It was a police car. Pulling up beside her. Stopping. Drops of sweat trickled into Mal's eye and stung but she kept her hands on the steering wheel. The police officer put his window down. He was young, with short blond hair and dark sunglasses. "Everything okay, Miss? Car troubles?"

"Everything's fine. Just pulled over to take a call my from mother," Mal lied, hands shaking on the steering wheel. She wanted to grab her phone, but her mother spoke in her head. *Mal, hands on the steering wheel.* Was he going to make her get out of the car?

The cop nodded. "Beautiful day. If you pull over again, you might want to do it right on the shoulder, so your car's fully off the road. You never know when some yahoo is going to come roaring along in some jacked-up truck." He drove off, glancing back in his rear-view mirror. Mal watched his car until it disappeared around the bend in the road ahead, trembling as she rubbed her burning eyes.

The Fundy Waves Motel was conveniently across the street from the Soldier's Memorial Hospital. There was a neon-red *Vacant* sign. Mal parked at the motel and went to the hospital. The doctor in emergency peered in her mouth. Strep throat. He put her on antibiotics and told her to drink fluids and get some rest. After a quick stop at the pharmacy, Mal crossed the street to the motel's reception desk, which was in a convenience store attached to the old motel.

"It's so hot out," Mal said to the clerk, fanning herself, hoping the old woman wouldn't notice her symptoms.

The clerk squinted at Mal and then handed her an old-fashioned key. She pumped the hand sanitizer on the counter into her palms and rubbed her hands together as though wringing out a towel. "Well, the heat won't last. We're well into August and summer's gone, even if it doesn't seem so. That's some tan on you. Looks like the heat shouldn't bother you."

Mal shivered as she walked back to her room with a bottle of orange juice and some acetaminophen. Thinking she would blend in here was ridiculous.

The room was dated, with wood panelling and 1980s light fixtures, but it was clean and spacious. The entire motel, this strip off the highway, felt left over from another time. A fever. She was so cold. There was a framed picture over the bed of happy children canoeing on a lake. It was old, Norman Rockwell–esque. Mal remembered when she was twelve and went to a goddess camp with her mother in the Santa Cruz mountains, a rite-of-passage sort of place for girls becoming women, with innocent moonlight rituals and canoeing on the lake surrounded by redwoods. They banged on drums and learned about undines, drew anatomically correct mermaids. It seemed eons ago, a simpler and much less complicated time in her life. Here, in this strange rural world, they would think those young girls and their mothers witches or New Age flakes. Dripping with sweat, Mal turned the air conditioning on high and crawled into bed, the loud roar of the old machine blasting away her adult worries.

Cynthia Aoifa Seabury.
Cedar Grove.

Then

A CRASH FROM DOWNSTAIRS, under the bedroom floor. Stella jolts awake. Sun pours in through the lacy sheers in the east-facing window. Stella didn't pull the blind down last night. She isn't sure why there is now a blind in the window. She only has curtains in her bedroom. Stella doesn't know where she is. Her bedroom faces west. There shouldn't be sun in the morning. Then it comes to her. Stella is not in Ohio. She is in Nova Scotia, her first morning in her grandparents' house. Her stomach growls. There is a dull ache behind her eye. Another bang from downstairs, from the kitchen. Her father is an early riser, getting up at what he calls *first light*.

Stella pads down the stairs and through the hallway. She opens the kitchen door and her father turns his head at the loud creak. "Good morning, Little Bear," he calls out. He's at the stove cooking bacon, wearing an old flowered apron over a wrinkled white short-sleeved shirt.

"Hope I didn't wake you up. Just knocked that old bookcase over." Books are sloppily shoved back on the shelves, a few still on the floor. "Thought I'd whip up a breakfast for us. Then we can go out for a walk to orient you. I'll need to start preparing for work soon, finishing up my paper." Her father turns back to the stove, whistling.

Stella sits at the table. Everything is strange. Her father never cooks. He makes coffee in the morning but Stella's mother does all the cooking. *Did* all the cooking. There are four chairs at the round wooden table. The round blue wall clock ticks. It's almost ten. She wonders if the clock has been ticking for all the years the house has been empty or if Frank or Sally Seabury put new batteries in. From what her father has told her of Frank, he is a high-flying international businessman who only comes home to Seabury in the summers and at Christmas. Stella doubts he's person-ally done anything in the house. Rather, that he has instructed others to do these things for him.

"Dad, why didn't you get along with your father?"

The whistling stops. The clock ticks. She's always fatigued, no matter how much she sleeps. "Well? Dad?"

"It's not a simple thing to explain, Stella."

"I'm not going anywhere."

Her father opens and shuts his mouth like a fish. Puts his head to the side and sticks out his bottom lip, drums his index finger on his chin, as he always does when he's trying to come up with an answer. He can hardly tell a bedtime story let alone his own.

"Well, Stella, your grandfather was a nasty man. It's that simple. My mother was very young when they married. She was a saint. Your grandfather worried about money. He sold insurance. He was always out at meetings. After my sister died, I was sent off to boarding school. I was done with him. He wanted me to be his clone."

Her father puts the bacon on a plate, on top of a piece of paper towel, and pours the hot bacon fat into a tin can on the counter. "But that's ancient history, Stella. We'll let it drift out to sea. We won't be just keeping it at bay anymore, get it? Get it?"

Stella groans.

"No one appreciates my humour now that your mother is gone." He cracks four eggs, which sizzle in the cast iron pan, egg white dripping onto the stovetop and down the oven door.

Stella wonders if her parents would have stayed together if her mother had lived. Her mother got her driver's licence six months before the accident. She wanted to be independent, she said, to be able to take Stella on trips, to drive her places in the bad weather.

Her parents didn't have screaming matches but it was constant bickering, separate lives.

Stella's throat feels thick and stiff now. She tries to swallow as her father puts a plate of bacon and a rock-hard egg mass in front of her. She doesn't want to cry. He'll be upset. He hates tears. Stella wants to hide. She wants to read but she can't because it hurts her head and it reminds her of her other self, the Stella who always read.

The counter is cluttered with bowls and pots. Her father is cooking for an entire family. She sees beer cans on the counter as well. Stella knows he'll leave the kitchen a mess as he did in Ohio. He blames it on his years spent in university, living in residences and faculty accommodations, eating in cafeterias and in restaurants. Her father sits down at the table with his plate heaped with eggs and bacon.

The back doorbell rings out, an old-fashioned grinding sound, and then the kitchen door flies open. There stands a girl a bit older than Stella, but with teased black hair, a nose ring, and wearing black sandals, all of which contrasts with her red sundress, her pale blue eyes. She's holding a basket with flowers sticking out one end and sets it on the table, oblivious to Stella's and her father's shocked faces. She opens the basket to reveal blueberry muffins.

"Success! Still warm," she cries. "Welcome to Seabury. I'm Cynthia. Granny Scotia said we should make sure you feel welcome, so I got up early." She puts her hands on her hips and looks at the bookcase, the few books and magazines still lying on the floor. She's thirteen but she has the confidence of a seasoned adult tour guide arriving to orient them.

Stella watches her father's sallow cheeks turn red. He wipes his hands on his pants and then grabs his napkin and wipes his face and looks down bashfully, pushing his glasses up, as though he's a teenager again. He gives Cynthia a slow, awkward smile. "Well, hello. I'm William Sprague. And this—"

"Like, I know who you are, Mr. Sprague. And this is Stella, Stella Maris," Cynthia says as she puts a muffin on his plate. "That's a totally excellent name, by the way. I've been waiting and waiting for you to come. Seabury is *so* boring in the summer. My parents live in New York during the year. That's where my father's company is. We come here every year, or at least my mother and I do. Daddy never really takes a holiday, even though Mom says it would be good for him. He's good at giving orders but not taking them." Cynthia giggles like this is hilarious. "I've been at a boarding school in New Hampshire but this year I'm living with Granny Scotia. She's getting older. Daddy says she has a heart problem. And he worries she has a memory problem. *He* has the memory problem." Cynthia rolls her eyes.

Stella and her father stare at the girl.

"I love your white shirt, Mr. Sprague," Cynthia says. "Is it Irish linen?"

Stella's father nods, impressed.

"That's so nice. My father always wears a big tie. And pin-striped shirts. He's so formal. Or if he isn't wearing a shirt and tie he wears a golf shirt. He's all business and sideburns."

"Frank was always all business, although I don't know if I'd call him formal. Maybe a traditionalist."

Cynthia laughs. Stella's father smiles and points at Stella. "Well, my daughter here is in good hands." As though Stella is a child and Cynthia is the sitter he's arranged.

"Stella, why don't you come with me to Granny's. She's so excited to meet you. And wait until you see her house. My dad says you're a historian, Mr. Sprague."

Stella's father does a funny back and forth with his head, blushing again.

"Well, yes I am, although I'm not a specialist in Georgian manor homes. My specialty is medical architecture."

"Oh, I see. Wow. That's fascinating."

Stella can't believe Cynthia is serious, but she looks totally serious. "Well, my grandmother's house isn't technically a Georgian manor home."

"Yes, that's right. It burned down."

"All but—"

"—the stone walls."

Cynthia smiles. "And it was rebuilt inside as an Edwardian home, with only the old kitchen in the cavernous cellar left intact."

Her dad and Cynthia grin at each other.

"I see you appreciate history, Cynthia," he chuckles.

"It's hard not to with Granny. My mother just wants to paint. It started out as a hobby but it's all she does now. She has a studio in the carriage house at Granny's. She has what she calls an *open studio policy* for me. She never stays at the new house up on the Mountain near Seabury Gorge. She stays with Granny Scotia and me." Cynthia reaches for the basket and takes out a muffin. She picks up Stella's knife and butters the muffin and puts it on Stella's plate.

Stella looks at the muffin and then at Cynthia and then at her father. They are smiling at each other, gabbing away now about mental hospitals. She can't figure out if Cynthia really is that interested in her father's work as he goes on about Kirkbride hospitals and their bat-like wings staggering out on each side, the curative effects of architecture. What Stella has heard over and over again. Imprinted on her memory. But it seems impossible Cynthia can fake this sort of enthusiasm.

Stella picks up the muffin and takes a bite. It's moist and delicious. Her cheeks are hot. It's the nasty sting of jealousy pricking her flesh. Her father never looks this way when he talks to her.

"Stella." Cynthia's voice echoes in the kitchen.

Stella jumps.

"Sorry. I didn't mean to scare you."

"Don't worry, Cynthia," Stella's father says while buttering another blueberry muffin. "She spaces out. Right, Stella? A result of the accident. A different girl came out of that car."

Stella is shocked he would say this in front of a stranger.

Cynthia doesn't allow a moment of graceless silence. "Whatever," she says. "I love this Stella right here. Why don't we go to Granny Scotia's? Lots more muffins there. We can ride bikes. Did you see the one I left for you? It's all tuned up. Granny got me one for my birthday and so did my mother, so I have two bicycles. The moral of the story is that adults should discuss presents before buying them."

"Great! Why don't you girls go off and I'll do some work." Stella's father leans back in his chair. "Cynthia, do you know anything about Dorothea Dix?"

Stella gets up from the table.

"Dix was a Quaker from Maine, a trailblazer for *moral treatment* of the insane, a treatment that provided compassionate care rather than locking up the mentally ill in jails and poorhouses. Dorothea Dix even visited Sable Island, the shipwreck island, her father called it, where it was rumoured desperate families had abandoned the insane."

"I have to brush my teeth," Stella announces.

Stella's father and Cynthia don't even stop talking. The older girl's laugh and her father's booming voice follow her up the stairs. She closes the bathroom door and leans her head against the cool white wall and takes a deep breath. Then she splashes water on her face in the old porcelain sink. Stella looks at herself in the mirror, at her thin, drawn face, her lips drooping downward as though she's already an old woman, her short hair, shaved on one side, her saucer eyes in her face resembling strange pools of water. She wishes she could cry, but since her mother died she's been empty. She turns on the tap. And then Stella starts shaking— it's as if grief is attacking her from inside, pounding and kicking her, tears now gushing from her eyes as she hyperventilates.

When Stella goes downstairs and into the kitchen, she sees Cynthia has placed the flowers in a vase on the centre of the table and is kneeling on the floor putting books neatly back in the bookcase while her father stands at the antique sink, filling it with water, squeezing a yellow plastic bottle of lemony dish soap. He keeps squeezing and the sink fills with bubbles and more bubbles. Soon they will overflow onto the floor. Stella hears a snort and it's Cynthia, with her hand over her mouth. "Okay, see you soon, Mr. Sprague," she sings, gone before Stella's father turns around.

Stella waits until her father notices her. He holds up

his hand, covered in bubbles, and blows. A glob falls to the floor. "Have fun. I'll catch up with you later today," he says, staring at the mess on the linoleum just as the sink water starts to overflow. Stella runs out into the porch and then through the screen door.

Outside, Cynthia leans on her bike. Stella smiles and takes a deep breath. They both explode with laughter.

Cynthia runs her fingers under her eyes and dabs at her tears of hilarity. "I guess your dad doesn't do much cleanup. Mine either. The only way I can deal with parents is by laughing. Mine are fighting all the time. It's one of the reasons I'm staying with Granny, not just because she's old. And *feeble*. That's what my dad says. That word makes me sick. I'll never be feeble." Cynthia speaks in the way you do with old friends, in a way Stella has read about in books, books she used to read before her head hurt all the time, stories in which girls became best friends in the blink of an eye.

"I think your dad wants to put on a good show, that's all. I've had that kind of teacher, at my school. In New Hampshire. I thought it would be weird staying here in Seabury all year, but it's probably, like, way weirder for you. Granny says it's a hard time for you guys."

Stella's mouth and throat feel dry and scratchy, as though she's been licking sand.

"I love your eyes, Stella. One's green and one's dark brown. Granny Scotia says your aunt Stella's eyes were the same as yours, and your grandmother's. Gemstone eyes, that's what it's called. It runs in the family, Granny Scotia says. I'm sorry about your mother, Stella." Cynthia pats Stella's forearm in an adult way. "It's weird, but it will be okay."

Cynthia really means it, Stella thinks, sniffing the air. "What's the smell?"

"Oh, that's my perfume. Anaïs Anaïs. Like it?"

Stella does. It smells of enchantment. She's heard the name Anaïs before, a French poet her mother talked about, who her father called the *naughty poet*. Stella has never had a friend, let alone a friend who wears French perfume.

They ride at an easy pace down the street, past wooden houses painted bright colours. They ride slowly and Stella is surprised at how good her balance is. She's a bit wobbly but only a bit. She knows her father will be impressed when he sees her keeping up with Cynthia, just like a normal girl.

They come to a crossroads with a stop sign. The sidewalks are very old, made of cobblestone and slate. At each corner there are faded grey paving stones with worn carvings of the odd bird and curious flowers. They ride onto a boardwalk where the blue river flows into the basin so wide it seems more of a sea, a sea dolloped with whitecaps. A faint breeze. Boats bobbing on the water, a hazy blue beyond.

"It's what they call a continental climate, snowy and cold in the winter and warm in the summer," Cynthia explains as they ride side by side. She flicks her hand and, as though she commanded it, a fog comes in on a wet chilled breeze. Seagulls bicker in the mists overhead.

"You'll get used to the fog. It's good for your complexion. That's what my mother says."

They ride off the boardwalk and onto another quiet street with old homes and leafy trees, each one emerging out of the murk and then disappearing behind them. It seems as though everyone has vanished and they are the only two girls on Earth.

Cynthia smiles and hums a peculiar melody Stella doesn't recognize, almost chanting, letting Stella set the bike pace. The fog is behind them now. Only a few cars and old trucks pass them on the road. Stella feels they are in a moving postcard, two friends on a dirt road riding bicycles, the North Mountain rising up, covered in deep green trees brushing against a sapphire sky, the river a startling blue ribbon curving through the pastures and meadows, the South Mountain on the other side, a few white clouds throughout the blue, angels looking down. Stella thinks she's landed in a normal childhood, for the first time.

They turn onto a path that runs on top of the dikes built up around the tidal river. It's low tide and the banks are a shining red mud. They ride single file, Cynthia in the front. Daisies and goldenrod and fireweed fill the meadow by the dikes. Cattle moo and sheep bleat. The path leaves the dikes and connects to a dirt road lined with trees, leading away from the water. One pickup truck passes them, honking. Cynthia waves. Stella can't imagine taking a hand off the handlebars. Through the trees, she spies a white mansion. Down a tree-lined lane. And then the colossal house before them. Cynthia rides through two imposing stone columns and an arch with a tarnished brass plaque: *Cedar Grove 1813*. Ahead Stella sees a circular drive and they ride into it and stop at the front of the house. Cynthia looks at the trees, smiling, as though they are her friends of old. "White cedars," she says. "My grandmother's people planted them. The O'Clearys. Clan O'Cleary. Poets and historians in the Old World. The house was in Granny Scotia's family. She inherited it. She says my grandfather was uncomfortable living here. He wasn't an O'Cleary, that's why."

A solitary wooden swing hangs from an oak at the far side of the house, the rope grey and frayed. The white paint is peeling, and some shingles are missing off the roof. The grass in the front needs to be mowed and the shrubs haven't been trimmed in what must have been years, giving the front grounds the look of a place where deformed botanicals came to live out their final days.

They ride around back and prop up their bikes against a tree trunk. There is a faint squeaking sound but Cynthia doesn't seem to notice. She points at a meadow with a broken fence and gate, where livestock once were kept. To the south side, a carriage house also in need of paint and a new roof with a metal weather vane. Fixed black arrows point in the cardinal directions, above a tarnished greeny-brass figure in a swimming position, wobbling and squeaking as the breeze blows from the west.

Cynthia takes Stella out back to the carriage house and up the stairs. She opens the door and leads the way into a stuffy, dusty room. "This is where my mother works."

There is a record player to the side of the door. *The Kick Inside*, Kate Bush, an album on the top of the player. A beautiful woman with sweeping brown hair and red socks. Cynthia picks it up, pointing at the cover. "My mother loves Kate Bush. Do you?"

"She's pretty. But I haven't heard her music."

Cynthia puts the record on. She picks up a paint brush, holds it to her lips pretending it's a microphone. She seems to know all the words; she twirls, singing about rolling, falling and roaming in the night. Stella read Emily Brontë's *Wuthering Heights*, out loud with her mother, over Christmas last year.

Cynthia picks up the needle and the music stops. "I'm my mother's favourite subject. She taught me how to use a camera." Cynthia points at the photos and paintings of herself everywhere in the studio, and a few of Sally that Cynthia took. Cynthia opens a window to let some fresh air into the warm space, a bit of sea breeze mixing into the faint linseed oil scent. Pictures of Cynthia when she was a baby, a toddler, a little girl, school photos from when she had gone to actual school. Pictures of the two of them in Paris and Toronto and New York and Florida, Hawaii and Alaska and Vancouver. Photos of the two of them skiing. Photos of Cynthia playing a trumpet, at the piano, at a harp, Cynthia in her running clothes holding medals. It seems either Frank or Sally had taken most of the photos. Hardly any with all three of them.

A wall cabinet full of volumes on painting. Stella looks at a book about Egon Schiele, pages of nudes, erotic poses. Cynthia is at her shoulder. They giggle. The people seem to be melting, made of wax, left in the sun, buttocks drooping, bodies draping over each other.

"My mother started taking art classes when I went away to school. Here's her artist statement." Cynthia hands it to Stella.

SARAH WINDSOR

My earlier work was romantic and gentle, but then I began to explore deeper themes in the everyday, substantial archetypes and elements present at a core level in both object and setting, which were dominant in a sense of light and natural arrangement. Elements that challenge us to understand inherent danger in everyday moments, the juxtaposition of tender and harsh, a reflection of the destructive forces inherent in nature, in humanity — that a simple flower can also be deadly.

"I thought her name was Sally?"

"It's the old-fashioned nickname for Sarah," Cynthia explains. "She uses her real name for her artwork. Windsor is her maiden name. It made my dad so totally mad."

Stella can't imagine having a mother who thinks these things. Stella now wonders if her own mother thought this way, if this was why she was drawn to poetry, if it was a place for her to compare all the beauty in her life with all the disappointment. Stella hands the artist statement back to Cynthia and looks at the wall covered with paintings — elaborate botanical paintings, six square canvases of giant peony heads, with a watery background, faces in the flowers and in the water, but if you look again, it seems to be only texture. Paintings of a kitchen and laundry room, a playroom, but in every painting a disturbing aspect — shears left on the floor beside the toddler playing with the stuffed panda. A candle burning perilously low on the wooden bedside table beside the sleeping child.

Stella smiles. "I can't wait to meet your mom."

"My dad doesn't really approve of Mom's work." Cynthia faces the southern window, the sun pouring in, and then she turns and runs out the door and down the stairs, calling to Stella as she flies. Stella waits a few moments, breathing in Sally Seabury.

"STELLA, ARE YOU COMING?" Cynthia stands outside the carriage house with her hands on her hips as Stella carefully comes down the stairs.

Stella follows Cynthia towards the house. The weather vane on the top of the carriage house squeaks. Cynthia looks up. "That's a mermaid up there. Pretty far from home, don't you think? Everything around here needs to be fixed. Come on, Stella."

The girls skip to the rear of the mansion, where Cynthia stops and clears her throat, and becomes a strange goth tour guide:

"Please note that this mansion was built eons ago by some forefather of Cynthia's, a lady apple farmer and her husband who came over from Ireland. The gentleman enjoyed his wife's love of the agrarian life and her fanciful fixation on the old ways. The house is rundown, inside and out, because the scion, Franklin Seabury IV, hasn't hired groundskeepers for the last two years. Sheep used to graze out back but they were sold off three years ago, too much, Franklin thinks, for his elderly mother, Mrs. Aoifa O'Cleary Seabury, the grand dame of the property who still resides here at the age of ninety-three, with her grand-daughter, Cynthia Aoifa Seabury, who has refused to go back to boarding school, abandoned by her mother.

"Note the heritage plaque by the front door. Champlain explored this area, the famous French explorer, who you may or may not have heard of. Probably you have because you're a nerd and I mean that as a compliment . . . anyway, Champlain was friendly with the Acadian settlers and the Mi'kmaq who called the Valley Kespukwik." Cynthia inhales, holds her breath and then lets out a puff of air. "Like, my father would want me to be a tour guide. As if."

"Wow, you know so much history."

"From Granny Scotia. But these days she has some trouble remembering things, more day-to-day stuff, like what year it is and who's who, the seasons and stuff. Sometimes. Not all the time. She never used to but now she does. Don't tell anyone. Dad doesn't have patience with old people. My mother says it's how he deals with his emotions. He says she reads too many self-help books.

"The house was in Granny Scotia's family. Matrilineal, left to the daughters. Granny says it was unusual then and it still is now. It will be mine someday, not my dad's. He's not happy about that. There's a lot of land, my mother says. That's what's valuable, or will be someday. My father's the investor but my mother can sort of see the future, he says. That's why he needs her to spend time with him. I'm sorry. I don't mean to keep talking about my mother."

They come around the corner of the house and Stella sees an old lady sitting on an old-fashioned lawn chair on the garden-level terrace at the side of the house. A sweet breeze brushes Stella's face and shakes the tree branches. The sea is visible to the west from where Granny sits in the throne-like wicker chair under a wide faded awning. As Stella and Cynthia walk towards the old lady, Stella sees Granny Scotia's summer dress is at once antique and classic, her silver hair in a perfect bun, pearl earrings in wrinkled lobes. Her hands covered in thick blue veins. She flutters her fingers at Stella, who flutters back as though she's at a parade and Granny is on a float passing by.

Stella is enthralled with the trees.

Granny lets out a cackle. "Those, darling, are eastern white cedars. They can live to be three hundred years old. *Arborvitae.*"

"That's Latin for 'tree of life,'" Cynthia adds.

"Yes, Cinder, darling, it certainly is. Stella, dear heart. What a pleasure to have you here."

Granny Scotia pushes herself up with her cane. "That over there is our herb garden, although it's dreadfully neglected. It's a bit harder for me to garden than it used to be. But see the borage, for courage, of which we will need plenty, an herb that also opens up the mind and eyes. The mint and lavender for purification, the rosemary for protection. We'll show you how to pick it, to use it, won't we, Cinder? And do you see those day lilies? We just planted those a few years ago. *Stella d'oro*, that's their name. And those dandelions? They're called the two-flowered Cynthia. If you want birds about, you better have flowers and berries. My grandmother used to say birds were messengers who could move through time."

Granny gently pokes her cane at the flowers, as though they are listening.

"I know your uncle, Isaiah Settles, although I haven't seen him in years. He's an antique dealer way down east in the Valley. I've only met him on a few occasions. He's bought a few pieces of furniture from me."

"I don't think my dad likes him . . . I mean . . . even knows him."

Granny Scotia takes a step forward. "That doesn't surprise me either." She hugs Stella and then takes a slow step back, giving her the eye. "We are simply so delighted to finally have you in Seabury, Miss Stella Maris. Your grandmother was a dear, dear friend of mine. I'm sure your father told you that already. He's probably filled you in on everything and hasn't left us any stories at all to tell."

Stella doesn't say that he has hardly ever mentioned Seabury, let alone the Seaburys, his childhood or the people in it. She has a feeling the old lady probably already knows.

Jericho County Courthouse Museum.
Under the Arbor.

Now

MAL FELT MUCH BETTER after three days of sleep at the Fundy Waves Motel. Weak but much revived, her fever gone and her throat just a bit sore now, not raw. The last three days she had dreamed of Mercy Lake, standing at the edge of the water, the burned-out ruin of the building, of Flora and her stories of what had happened to her when she was fifteen. Mal had barely eaten and felt shaky, but she had a renewed conviction to at least see what she could uncover.

From what Flora had told her, what her mother had revealed, and the way her grandmother bristled at the very mention of the area, Mal had determined Mercy Lake was used as a secret retreat for a fellowship, some sort of offshoot of a sect, with the religion part dying away but other rituals remaining. Mal was still shocked by the connection between this shadowy group in the United States and the area of Nova Scotia her mother was from. And that this group they called Sodality had existed not just in the eighties but was generational, going back at least as far as the late eighteenth century, morphing to hide in the open of whatever society it existed in at the time.

Mal had invested too much to give up so easily. Maybe, if she uncovered something, she could contact a real investigative journalist, make sure the story got out into the world. She didn't trust herself to be able to do the job that would need to be done. And it was probably her feverish imagination that had her thinking she was being followed. Yes, there'd been the smell of smoke, the cigarette butt, but maybe it had been some local, a sportsman out fishing or something, wondering why a rental car was parked on the road in the middle of nowhere. Anyone would wonder, right?

Moving forward, it was about being careful. She had two weeks left on her "retreat," two weeks before she was supposed to fly home to Los Gatos — her mother would be back from Big Sur by then, wanting to compare notes. Going deep into the woods at Mercy Lake had been risky, and it wasn't Mal's courage that had propelled her. No, it was the sheer adrenaline of discovering what was hiding behind this company called Cineris International, what Sodality was, this exhilarating feeling that she was in a suspense story. That feeling was gone now, replaced by a sobering reality. Turing thirty had spiralled her into a life crisis and made her reckless. Mal understood now the need for caution and discretion. But in this sort of rural area, a brown-skinned woman asking questions — discretion wasn't possible. Saying she was a podcaster... it wasn't something most people around here would understand. It sounded made up. It would be easier to say she had her own radio show in California. The more Mal thought about trying to explain what she actually did, the fluffier her podcast seemed.

Her mother had come up with the name of Mal's show: *Under the Arbor*. Her mother worked in a studio in their backyard that was designed to evoke the ambience of a Victorian garden house. When she looked out the window, she looked through arches of roses. Mal thought it was a good name, that it implied she was low, that she was depressed, but all around her was life and beauty — they were inseparable. And Mal's task was to find balance. She had started the podcast to make her mother happy, her mother who wanted her to have a focus, but Mal grew to enjoy it. People opened up to her because she was interested in their stories. And she wasn't afraid to share her own story with them. Her ex thought it was silly, and that was part of the problem — worrying about what other people thought, wanting to be taken seriously in the way her parents were.

BIGELOW BAY WAS A large town compared to Middleton. Mal had left the Fundy Waves Motel for her new "base of operation" at the Sun Valley Motel, equally as dated and shabby. Bigelow Bay was the area's regional centre, with a hospital, the municipal offices, the law courts. And next to the law courts, in the old courthouse, was the Jericho County Courthouse Museum. Inside the museum the air was heavy and still, musty with the scent of old oak and paper. Mal had to wait when she arrived. A woman in hiking boots and a dirty sundress was shouting at the museum manager standing at the landing at top of the stairs, listening patiently to this woman with black braids streaked with silver who was stamping her boots on the old hardwood floor. At first Mal thought she was angry, but she realized the woman was just speaking at a high volume, full-on with passion, oblivious.

"Why don't you have more information on the Flying Squirrel Road? Or the Offing Society? Or Lucretia? She's not just a myth, you know. Is this or is it not a historical society? Jillian said she'd do some research and call me. I hope she does. I'm not crazy, you know."

Maybe the manager didn't think this woman was crazy, but Mal did. Except she'd mentioned the Flying

Squirrel Road, where Gramma Grant had said to go. The manager's arms were crossed and she seemed very patient, giving Mal the feeling that this skinny middle-aged woman was a frequent visitor. *Kate*, the manager's name tag said. Kate looked over at Mal and apologized that there was no air conditioning, no central air, no cross breeze. The Jericho Historical Society owned the old courthouse and they had only enough money to keep the building running as it was.

The woman in hiking boots turned to come down the stairs to the front door and stopped as she saw Mal. Then she pinched herself and kept staring. The manager hurried down and took Mal to the lower level. "Don't mind her. That's Seraphina. She's researching the same things you are. Well, I don't know if you can call it research. She's not making much sense these days."

Kate took Mal to the archives room where the only paid archivist was waiting for her, papers spread out on the table. Jillian was in her fifties, due to retire soon so she could travel with her husband. She told Mal how she had been married for just one year, joking that she'd been married to history before that. Jillian's light brown hair was streaked with grey and her eyes were such a pale green they almost glowed. She didn't have a lot of information for Mal, mostly a few stories and anecdotes she'd heard over the years from some of the older historical society members.

Jillian held a photocopy of the same *Fellows United* newspaper article Mal had with her in her file. She'd left the rest of the paperwork Flora had sent back in California for safekeeping. Mal now wished she was more prepared, that she had scanned the documents and had digital files she could access. Jillian pointed out the photo of Franklin Seabury IV with the article. His company had changed names several times, had been bought up by a bigger company. It was complicated — that's all Jillian knew, and that his business had been centred in New York. His family had come from here but he had lived primarily in the United States. His mother, Aoifa O'Cleary Seabury, was a different story. She had lived her life in Nova Scotia, had died in 1982 at the age of ninety-five. Well, she'd been in a nursing home and went missing. They never found her body, and assumed she'd drowned. She was an old woman, and no one paid much attention to that sort of thing back then. Her granddaughter Cynthia Aoifa Seabury had inherited her estate. She lived in Florida with her mother.

Mal didn't say anything. She had already figured this out when she'd gone to Florida. It was why she was in Nova Scotia now.

Cedar Grove itself was privately owned now, a vacation house for someone from Europe, but Mercy Lake and the trails were owned by the Nature Trust. No one visited the lake anymore except local adventurers and fishermen who would come up the Mercy River.

The lodge at Mercy Lake had been built by a rural sect, connected to some other chapters throughout the eastern and southern seaboards, a revivalist sort of charismatic religion. But it had died out and the lodge on the lake became a deep-woods retreat for wealthy sportsmen. Jillian had another newspaper article, about the local fire department's response to the fire, how they worked to contain it to the cleared area around the lodge. It had not spread into the woods. Fifteen people were charred beyond recognition. There wasn't a guest list. They had been identified through dental records: tourists, foreigners from the United States and England, from France, men on a wilderness holiday with Sodality. It was before DNA testing and such. When travel over borders and by air was much simpler. A few locals had drowned in the lake, what was left of their bodies found weeks later, washed from the lake to the river and then out into the Gulf of Maine. To Mal, the whole thing seemed like a creepy religious version of Outward Bound. It was a closed case. The two girls found there after the fire were never identified by name in the news.

No one really remembered this fire, Jillian explained. It was over forty years ago, and it had happened in a different part of the province. "You need to understand, today it might not seem far away, but in 1980, Seabury — a three-hour drive from Bigelow Bay — was a place unto itself. People didn't have much interest in the world outside their own towns. It's still somewhat the same today. And certainly back then, Seabury was distant enough for those in Bigelow Bay to consider it a different region. I've heard that one person who knows the story ended up as a long-term resident at the Jericho County Care Centre. It's a place for adults of all ages who can't live independently. It's in Blossomdale on the County Home Road, about twenty minutes west of here."

Mal didn't bother explaining she had already tried to talk to the resident.

"Well, what about the Offing Society? Do you know anything about it?"

Jillian shrugged. "Not much. Some people say it was a secret society of women who lived by the ocean. Magical. It's more of a legend. We don't have any letters or books that mention it. The story seems to have been passed down only through the oral tradition, as many stories are." Jillian escorted Mal out. On her way to the exit Kate handed her a flyer for a poetry reading at the museum in two days. She recognized the poet, Grace Belliveau, who had been popular with her UBC classmates. She shared that with Jillian, who wasn't surprised to hear it. "She's an acclaimed international poet, but that's no way to make a living. She actually works at the Jericho Centre as her day job. Maybe she could help you."

Mal went to the parking lot behind the courthouse and took out her phone to take a picture. The woman in the hiking boots and sundress was smoking, leaning against an old green pickup truck.

"I thought you were an apparition," she said. "And those phones are nothing but bad news. It's how they track you."

A local conspiracy theory lunatic. Mal opened the car door.

"I heard what you and Jillian were talking about."

Mal looked at her, this Seraphina woman. "You were eavesdropping?"

"Yes."

"Seriously?

"Danger is coming," Seraphina said flatly.

Mal tossed her purse and jacket onto the passenger seat. The woman was frightening her. For a moment, Mal felt as if she were in some weird mashup of *Game of Thrones* and *Twin Peaks*.

"They're looking for Stella. Things got stirred up. I think you stirred things up. They think she might be hiding something that went missing. But Stella doesn't remember anything. That won't stop them from trying to find her though. They'll go the whole wide world. I heard your name. I knew your mother. And your Gramma Grant."

Mal didn't know what to say.

"Your mother left and she was smart to do that.

Your grandmother kept her safe, unlike my mother. My mother didn't approve of the Offing Society."

Mal crossed her arms and stared at this strange woman. She decided to press her, see what she could find out. "What exactly do you know about the Offing Society. And the Flying Squirrel Road. And a woman named Lucretia?"

Seraphina stared at her, her dark brown eyes watering. "We might be safer at the shore—"

Seraphina stopped talking and tilted her head, listening to something Mal couldn't hear. "Okay, I got to go and have my blood work done. And find my own daughter. To keep her safe. You should leave, Malmuria. It's not safe for any of us here." She jerked the truck door open and leapt up into the seat. The engine roared to life and Seraphina zoomed away.

Mal got into her rental car and put her head on the steering wheel. She was exhausted. And afraid. How did this woman know who she was? And how was Mal going to find her again? Maybe it was time to call her mother in Big Sur. Maybe not. She drove out of the parking lot and headed to the other side of town.

As she parked in front of her cabin at the Sun Valley Motel, she half expected to see a black car parked nearby. Nothing. Mal relaxed. When she'd checked in last night, she hadn't been surprised by the 1950s aesthetic of the old roadside motel outside of Bigelow Bay. She was already acclimatized to the Valley. It was worn and dated, but clean. And Mal had her own tiny cabin here, with two Adirondack chairs on the small deck, looking out on the old road through a stand of tall pines. Mal put the key in the door and went inside. There was a closet of a bedroom, a bathroom and a kitchenette in the main living space. It was quaint and felt safe, making her feel that no one in the world could find her. The old man had been happy when she'd paid in cash. He wrote her name in a book. It was the one time she missed social media, not being able to share photos of this place.

There was a bookshelf beside the couch with a crisp hardcover copy of Salman Rushdie's *Midnight's Children*, some vintage Nancy Drew and Hardy Boys books, a few tattered *National Geographics*, a brand new Bible, a dated *Seashells of the World: A Guide to the Better Known Species* and a few ragged Stephen King paperbacks. Rushdie was her father's favourite writer. He would have laughed at the assortment of reading materials. *What's on a bookshelf tells you much of what you need to know, Malmuria.* She smiled as she took off her shoes and walked barefoot to the bathroom. She could hear her father's laughter in her mind. Mal felt old and worn, like a book on a shelf that no one remembered anymore.

Granny Scotia.

Then

"CALL ME GRANNY SCOTIA, Stella darling. Everybody does. I was so happy to hear your father had named you after your aunt. You take after her. Those eyes!" She pinches Stella on the cheek. "I'm sure he's told you lots of stories about her." Granny sits back.

"Well, no. He never even mentioned her, not even once."

Granny huffs. "Men can't deal with the past as well as women. They dig holes and bury things. It's been my experience that whatever you bury always claws its way back out. It was terribly upsetting for your father. His sister was only thirteen. Frankie was there as well. Frankie wasn't the same after that, and he went away to boarding school, as your father did. I never did meet your mother. We were so sorry to hear about her car accident."

Granny reaches up and strokes Stella's cheek. "Grief will run its course. It always does. Cynthia and I will take care of you. We'll just eat in the kitchen tonight. I can't bear that formal dining room."

"We haven't even had lunch yet...Granny Scotia?"

Granny shakes her head. "Of course, darlings, what was I thinking. It's still so light at suppertime it's easy to get mixed up. I always find late August especially perplexing, half summer, half autumn. Stella, did you see the periwinkle border? Such a pretty blue. The sorcerer's violet, as it's also known. It's said if you gaze upon the flower, it will aid in the restoration of memory. Perhaps I should weave myself a garland and put it on my head." Granny laughs as she stares across the gardens, at the bay offshore, her eyes on the offing, gazing at something there the girls can't see.

Stella has a moment of hesitation. She bites her lip. She wants to ask Granny Scotia more about Stella Violette and how she died.

Granny snaps back from wherever she went. "Take Stella inside and give her a tour of the house. It's not Blenheim Palace but it will do. Frank will sell it, if he has his way."

The girls go in through a rear sunroom with sofas and chairs and then into the back hall. There is a vast old kitchen to the left.

"Sorry the place is a bit dusty. Granny doesn't do much housework these days. There was a housekeeper but my dad said she up and quit in spring. Dad says it's hard to get good help around here, people who can do good work and be discreet."

They walk into the heart of the house, impressive rooms at either side — a drawing room, a receiving room, a formal dining room with ornate china and elaborate silver place settings on the table.

Stella looks at the china, the grand chandelier. The window at the side is partly opened, an old grey screen keeping out the August bugs. Cynthia beckons from the doorway and then skips down another hall that runs along the side of the house to what Cynthia tells Stella is a butler's pantry, from way back when there was a butler, maids and a cook, when Granny Scotia was very young. They make their way to the formal dining room, a gigantic portrait of her great-grandfather looms above the fireplace. "Allow me to introduce you to another Franklin Seabury. He was a lumber baron or something. And the grandfather before that was a sea captain. My father says we're related to an explorer who led the Franklin Expedition to the North where they ran out of food and started eating each other and froze to death and gross stuff like that. The painting is all my father has from his family, an old painting of some uptight old guy. An illustrious sea captain," Cynthia says. "That's how my father describes him. Whatever that means. Granny says that he was a sea captain who did a lot of bad things. They had slaves."

The girls run up the grand staircase, taking two steps at a time, flying by the oil paintings. Upstairs there are two halls off the staircase, grand bedrooms, and then a third flight of stairs. "We don't need to go up there. It was storage and where the maids slept, a sewing room and sitting room. It's all just full of antique stuff now. It's super-hot up there too, in the summer, even with the windows open. Granny Scotia sits up there in the winter by the fire," Cynthia mentions.

"Granny says the house was modernized in 1900, when they rebuilt it after the fire, and then nothing was done except the wiring. It's just like it was and Granny wants it this way. Let me show you the original kitchen." With that Cynthia pounds down the stairs singing and Stella scampers after her, singing along, trying to catch the lyrics but just making up sounds to join in. They enter into a cavernous cellar room with windows on the southern side, a colossal iron cook stove that seems almost built into the stone wall, rows of built-in cupboards.

"This is the only part of the house that didn't burn. Granny says they just left it as it was, that her fore-runners couldn't bear to do away with the hearth, the kitchen. I guess it was a sacred area."

And then they hear someone calling their names and run back up to the main floor. A man who resembles Cynthia stands at the top of the stairs. "Girls, girls, come up from that dungeon. It's a glorious day. You don't want to miss the sunshine. Summer will be over soon enough." He looks at Stella and takes in a quick shallow breath. "My, you look just like your aunt, my dear. You must be Stella. I'm Franklin Seabury, Cynthia's dad." He takes Stella's hand.

Frank has dark blue eyes and he holds her hand in his soft, dry hand, squeezing it gently. Her father's hand is always damp. Stella can't help but compare. "I hope we equipped that old house in town with everything you need to start over here." His face is serious. "It will take time to settle in and we'll help you every step of the way, won't we, Cynthia? Cynthia's had a hard time too."

Cynthia puts her arm around Stella's shoulders. Stella doesn't flinch or move away. She wonders what's been so hard for Cynthia. Stella wants the Seaburys to take care of them, the Spragues, the distracted father and the motherless girl.

"Now let's go outside. Your father's out exploring the grounds. This house is far too much for my mother but I pick my battles, girls. It's good you'll be here with Granny this year, Cynthia, with your mother gone now."

Cynthia skips ahead and takes Stella by the hand, pulling her behind, calling over her shoulder, "Daddy, I don't want to talk about the fall. Let's do what you said and enjoy the last of summer."

Stella follows, with this new information flashing in her mind. *Cynthia's mother, gone?*

The girls sit with Granny under the awning sipping lemonade. The sun is very bright now and Stella's stomach growls. Frank walks off to where her father is out in the meadow, and then they both turn and stroll back on a slate path. Stella wants to ask where Sally Seabury is, why she left everything in her studio, but to break the quiet would feel irreverent. And then the sky seems to darken, the way it would if clouds had moved in, Granny Scotia's face appears carved from stone and Cynthia's hair lifts, her hair floating around her as it would in water.

Stella blinks her eyes. Granny smiles. "Dear, you look as if you've seen an apparition. I wouldn't wonder. Just like your father's mother—*your* grandmother, Morgana. You have that way about you, as she did, with those eyes of yours. My way is in the garden. We used to meet every week, she and I, as part of the Offing Society, as it's called. We can talk about all of that another day—"

Frank calls out to them as he and William arrive, interrupting. "Why don't we all go to the diner for dinner? We can show Stella the town, Cynthia. What do you girls say? Then we can go for ice cream."

"That's right," says Granny Scotia. "It will be good for these poor motherless girls. Have you talked to Sally recently?"

"Mother, let's not talk about that." Cynthia's father frowns. "Sally isn't coming back. You have to accept that."

Cynthia's face doesn't change. Implacable, the ocean on a windless summer's day, impossible to read, to know what's underneath. No signs of what it is capable of, in other conditions.

It's too much, Stella thinks. Too many people. Too much sun. Too much history. Too many missing mothers.

But her father nods. Stella knows he doesn't want to be alone with her.

"What do you want to do, Stella? I love the diner. And ice cream." Cynthia claps her hands together. "And we can take you to the beach. It will be so much fun. I don't know any other kids in Seabury. They all seem to have jobs babysitting and stuff."

Stella's voice is almost a whisper. "It doesn't matter to me."

Granny takes a sip of lemonade. "They have jobs babysitting and working on farms, Cynthia dear, because they aren't wealthy, as we are. You do not know what it is to live in rural Nova Scotia. Now, Stella darling, you need to make up your mind. If you can't make up your mind about something as simple as luncheon, you'll grow up into a woman who can't speak her mind about anything. We don't want that, dear. It's no end of heartache."

"Granny Scotia, that's not very nice." Cynthia's hands are on her hips and the look on her face makes her appear much older. "Stella's a great listener. There's lots to be said for that. That's what Mommy says."

"Well, your mother isn't here, darling, is she? Sally isn't one who has any trouble making up her mind, so we have seen. You have to make sure your voice is heard if you are to make it through this life in one piece. Stella's grandmother was very quiet and that was her undoing."

"Mother, really. That's enough. Get a hold of yourself," Frank barks. Stella sees how tight and red Franklin Seabury's face is. He towers over Granny Scotia but she doesn't back down.

"Well, it's true," the old lady spits up at her son.

Stella's father lets out a dry, nervous cough. "Yes, it is. My mother was afraid to challenge my father on anything. But everyone was." He's slurring his words a bit, and Stella wonders how many before-lunch beers he's had.

Stella wants to go back to her grandparents' house. She wants to putter around in the backyard, any backyard. She wants an adult to be in charge. She had wanted Sally Seabury to be her new mother. But there is no mother here.

"Now girls, girls," Frank says, Granny lumped in with the children, Stella notices, "it's just a dinner invitation, that's all. We'll reschedule. And there's the town barbeque at the end of the week."

Stella's neck aches on each side — her skull feels too heavy, putting too much pressure on it. She doesn't

116 | Christy Ann Conlin

want to tell her father. She worries he'll make her lie in her bed with the blinds pulled down. He looks disappointed. His eyes slide over hers and then down to his shoes, which he addresses as if it were his two leather loafers who had invited him for lunch. "That's right," he says. "We're not going anywhere, are we, Stella? We are here for the duration."

BACK AT THE SPRAGUE house, they eat turkey casserole and fresh green beans for supper, neither of them speaking, Stella's father staring at his plate, perhaps wishing the answers to how his life has brought him to Seabury are among the rich turkey gravy, the thin carrot slices. Stella scrutinizes her father's face, his downcast eyes, his unshaven cheeks with the silver stubble, and wonders at how it has come to pass that she is alone with her father, a man she realizes she hardly knows.

The phone clangs and echoes through the hall, into the kitchen. They both jump. "Good God, that sounds like an alarm system left over from the war. My God." The ringing stops briefly and then immediately starts again. Stella's father squeaks his chair away from the table and stomps over the creaking wooden floor and down the hall.

"Hello, William Sprague speaking . . . why hello, Frank . . . yes, yes, that sounds fine. Lunch the day after tomorrow . . . yes, another try at lunch. Yes, later. That will give us some settling-in time. Fine . . . yes."

He comes back to the table and dishes out more turkey casserole. "We'll have lunch with Frankie and Cynthia in a few days, okay? If you feel better. And once I finish this paper I'm working on, for the November conference at the university, I'll take you on a road trip, just you and me."

Stella smiles as she chews. It's unlike him to suggest this. He's planning ahead. Stella swallows and puts her fork down. "Dad, where is Cynthia's mother?"

"Gone."

"Like... dead... gone?"

"May as well be. Frankie told me she left at the end of July. He didn't want to upset us, what with all we've been through. She wanted to take Cynthia with her down to Florida, but Cynthia won't leave her grandmother. Who moves to Florida in the summer? I guess she has a man-friend down there. She wasn't from here to start with. Maybe Georgia? Somewhere down south. It's a terrible thing, a woman just abandoning her family. Apparently she wants to be a painter. Poor Frank."

Poor Cynthia, Stella thinks. Cynthia who didn't even let on. It must be too painful for her to talk about. It occurs to Stella that maybe Cynthia blames herself, that she's full of shame. Stella thinks Sally left the paintings behind because they belong to another life, the life she has deserted.

LATER, LYING IN HER BED, Stella hears her father pacing. She knows he's downstairs in the front room he's using as a study, with his whiskey and beer, looking through his notes. She wants her own books placed on the bookshelf in her room — even if she can't read them without her brain hurting. In the morning, she'll ask him when the moving truck will arrive.

Wandering Wednesday.
Wayfaring Stranger.

Now

AFTER BREAKFAST, STELLA AND Dianne were herded
from the cafeteria down to the activity room to make
table decorations for Nurse Calvin's blueberry-themed
retirement party. It was late in the planning. This was
why they were doing crafts on a Wednesday and not on
a Tuesday. And Grace had cancelled their appointment
on Tuesday. It was now on Thursday. Nurse Calvin
was disrupting things. It seemed she would always be
getting ready to retire, striding down the halls with her
nurse's cap and her white dress, holding her clipboard.

"Take your jar, and you paint with these markers
that work on glass." Betsy, the head of the activities
programs, demonstrated as she talked, which made
it seem as if they were watching a television show.
Cooking shows and home reno shows were the most

popular with the residents. For a long time they didn't have any craft programs, and many residents spent hours in front of screens. The Covid had ruined the whole schedule and Stella partly blamed the virus — and not just the medication changes — for disrupting her memory. Betsy was short-staffed today due to summer vacation and people coming down with summer colds, so she was running the craft program herself. "Well, people, at least it's not the same as the last few years. It can always be so much worse." She laughed.

She was especially fond of Dianne, who sometimes joined in the concerts when Betsy brought in bands and choirs. Dianne played the banjo and could belt out gospel songs, usually "In the Sweet Bye and Bye" and "Wayfaring Stranger," and if she got on a stage, she tended to loop through them, again and again.

"We'll use these lanterns outside as table decorations for the blueberry retirement barbeque for Nurse Calvin," Betsy said. "We'll have an outdoor canopy set up, so if it's hot we'll have shade and if it rains we'll have shelter. We sure could use some rain, right, gals? Dianne, maybe you can sing your songs for her, at the barbeque. Your new banjo should arrive soon."

Dianne's banjo had been destroyed by a patient who was taken away to the institution in Dartmouth. The NS, as everyone called it. One day he not only stopped talking but stopped getting out of bed. When they lifted him out, he ran suddenly down the hall, screaming into the lounge, grabbing Dianne's banjo and hitting himself in the head with the white resonator. Dianne snatched at it but he wouldn't let go, and she hauled the banjo and the man across the room. He was sedated, although he had eaten so little he was weak and his fight was only a flare, fizzling out into weeping. He left on a stretcher and never came back. And Dianne was still waiting for a new banjo.

"Hope it comes soon. But I don't think Missus Calvin understands the Mountain music. More a Presbyterian hymn lady." Dianne snickered and then threw her head back. *"I'm just a poor wayfaring stranger, travelling through this world below,"* she crooned. *"There is no sickness, no toil, nor danger , In that bright land to which I go..."* Dianne stopped singing as abruptly as she had started. "I need a smoke. My cousin, Sorcha, is getting me a new banjo. Stella and I are visiting her this summer. Got any smokes, Betsy?"

Betsy's cheeks bulged out as she tried to swallow her laughter. "Let's get back to our lights for Nurse Calvin."

"Oh, she's some nice, Nurse Calvin is. Sure, we want to do something sweet for her like this here candle stuff, right, Stella?"

"Now, Dianne, let's be polite. We want to give Nurse Calvin a good send-off."

"Even a Gorgon gets a send-off, so it seems," Dianne muttered to Stella, who let out a whoosh of air. Betsy looked up. Whenever Stella made any sort of vocalization they stared at her, like she might break into a monologue and fill them in on all the missing years. No luck. They drew blueberries with green leaves on the glass jars.

Betsy gave them tea lights to put inside, battery-operated tea lights.

Stella rubbed her jaw. There was an ache deep inside the joints on both sides, the kind you'd get from grinding your teeth all night. On the way upstairs, Stella stopped to use the washroom, with Dianne standing outside the door. Her head was heavy and as she closed her eyes she felt a shell in her mind fall from the shelf and crack open, photos falling out as they might tumble from an old scrapbook: Stella and Dianne on their holiday weekend at Sorcha's house in Kingsport. When? The year 2005 in faded black ink at the bottom of the photo.

Sorcha at the stove with a copper maslin pan, pointing at Dianne. What had she said? "You come stir the pot." A low, deep voice that was funny coming from such a tiny old woman. An image of hot jars of blueberry jam cooling on the counter. Berries they picked in Sorcha's backyard. Stella at the counter lining up the sterilized glass jars in perfect order.

Sorcha in an armchair in her house, in the living room where Sorcha's father had lain in bed for the last six months of his life. When Sorcha couldn't cope anymore, and Dianne moved to the centre. A black-and-white photo of Sorcha's father, Wade, who had been the last lighthouse keeper in

Kingsport, when there was a wharf the train tracks went out on, when it was a shipbuilding village — all of this illuminated by the old framed pictures covering Sorcha's walls. There was gold wall-to-wall carpeting Sorcha had put down in the 1980s, a soft golden colour, faded but very clean, a china cabinet with fancy teacups.

Sorcha and Dianne and Stella holding hands, wading out in the Minas Basin as the tide came in, Stella in the middle. The piping plovers gathered in intricate clouds, weaving in and out over the water, buzzing low over their heads. Dianne in the water, her coral flowered bathing cap the only sign of her as she moved out in the water. Sorcha with wet shrivelled flesh beside Stella on the beach.

Dianne in the water, a lone blue heron, observing, feeding on the smells, the memories, pulling the sky into her, letting the sun dazzle on her face and eyes so she could take it back to the centre with her.

Words floating out now. "You're a good friend to Dianne, Stella. It broke my heart to put her there but I could hardly look after Dad. It fell to me to take care of him, being an only child. Some terrible things happened to Dianne over on the Flying Squirrel Road when her Nana died. Some cousin came to the house. I don't know exactly what he did. Dianne would never say. He disappeared. They found Dianne on the rocky beach, unconscious, soaking wet, as if she'd fallen into the water and the tide had spit her up on the shore. Dianne said Lucretia appeared with her long white hair as fine as sea mist. Pulled her from the sea. There is always a Lucretia, in *every generation, in every time. She helps women. You have but to look for her. I never saw Lucretia myself, but I believe the story. I wasn't going to turn Dianne away. We all need each other, us old ladies, don't you think, Stella?"*

Stella leans her head on Sorcha's shoulder. She smells of salt and mint and rosewater.

A bang on the door. Stella jumped. "Stella? You dead in there? You don't want to miss snack time." Dianne knocked again.

Stella wiped. There was no blood this time, in the toilet or on the toilet paper.

UPSTAIRS IN THE LOUNGE there were plates of warm oatmeal raisin cookies and glasses of frosty lemonade on the table at the side. A new young nurse came into the room. Stella couldn't remember her name.

"Stella, honey, finish up your snack. Your social worker is here." The nurse's name tag: *Susan,* LPN in black letters. No last name.

Stella stood up, still chewing her cookie. She didn't follow Susan, who pointed down the hall.

"Eugene. That's her social worker's name. Stella keeps worrying he's gone for good," Dianne said.

Stella adored Eugene. Dianne adored him. Eugene always brought flowers for her birthday. He brought her sketchbooks and pencils to draw with. He arranged for her to go to Kingsport with Dianne, to visit Cousin Sorcha. And Isaiah liked Eugene too. Isaiah always said she could trust him. Dianne said Eugene was kind and that was a rare commodity these days. Eugene was here but where was Isaiah? When would he come to visit?

"Your social worker, *Eugene Campbell*, is here," Susan said in a very loud, slow voice. Stella covered her ears with her hands.

Dianne stood beside Stella. "You need to explain to her. Explain over and over sometimes. And sometimes not. Sort of a riddle. Do you see? And we have a meeting with Grace today. I do anyway, but Stella comes and listens to my stories. We did crafts today. It threw Stella off. See?"

What Stella could see was that Susan was irritated by this timeworn resident in sneakers and a house dress explaining her job to her, explaining Stella's schedule, Dianne acting the nurse and seeing Susan as the resident.

Dianne took Stella by the shoulders. "Stella, Eugene's back. He was just on a sick leave. He broke his ankle. Remember? Not the Covid. He's healthy now. Saw him out the window when he parked his car and skipped right in like nobody's business."

Susan beckoned and Dianne walked behind her; Stella followed Dianne. "Stella thinks he went away for good. The way Isaiah did." Dianne towered over the petite blonde nurse.

"Now, Dianne, hon, this is a meeting just for Stella. Stella knows Isaiah is gone." Susan smiled at

Dianne as she might at a young child. It was a prac-
tised smile.

Suddenly Stella felt very old and tired. Where had
Isaiah gone? What did this young nurse mean? How had
all the years passed? Time had come looking for Stella,
had found her room one night, walked in through the
dark and settled down on top of her, sinking into her
flesh and rooting in her bones, into her blood and joints.
Now time was in her groin, groping around, making
things sore and out of place.

"She don't know he's gone is what I'm trying to tell
you. And if I'm not there, how will you know what
she thinks?"

Stella thought about Isaiah, about what Dianne
meant, that he was gone and not coming back. Eugene
had gone, but they said he was back now. Isaiah would
be back.

"Well, then how do you think you can help, Dianne,
when she doesn't talk to you either?" Susan replied.

Stella watched Dianne cross her arms and lean back,
looking at Susan. Stella knew Dianne thought this new
nurse was the biggest idiot she'd ever encountered. "I
can tell by her face. Isn't that right, Stella? She talks with
her body. That's how I hear her."

Stella patted Dianne on the shoulder as she turned
and followed Nurse Susan down the hall to a meeting
room. Nurse Calvin came in. Stella tried to remember
just when Nurse Calvin would retire. In a few weeks?

It was summer. It was August, Stella saw by looking at the bank calendar on the wall.

Stella heard Eugene's voice as she came into the room, his bright coppery hair flecked through with silver, and his green eyes that bulged out in a reptilian way Stella found both disconcerting and reassuring. He had been her social worker for more than two decades, since he was a young single man—now he was the father of triplet boys, all at university. He stood up, smiling as he pulled out a chair for her. "Stella, how are you? It's good to see you. I was off on sick leave for a while but I'm back now. I broke my ankle playing soccer, my old man's league. But all better, nothing serious. Grace told me you were asking for me a few weeks ago. I know they sent someone different each time. Sorry about that. Anyway, it's good to see you, Stella. I'm sorry I couldn't go to the funeral."

Stella didn't know which funeral he was speaking about. Emily, an elderly resident who had still managed to go to yoga, doing it in her wheelchair, had died when the lilacs were out. And before her so many died that they had one memorial service.

"Stella, a space has come open in one of the group homes, remember? You could try independent living again. I know you hated it, but maybe this time you might enjoy living in a home environment. This one is called Mountain Top, up on the South Mountain."

This was the last thing Stella might enjoy. It wasn't a real home. Her home was at the centre. They had kept her safe all these years, even when the Covid came. And now this postcard—that Cynthia was coming. It was at the Jericho Centre Stella knew she would be protected. Everything needed to stay in order, in place. It was how Stella felt safe, here, where she had been for years, with her daily routines, with familiar faces, with the seasons, the wide windows, the walking paths, the old poor-farm cemetery, with old purring Cat, Fred and Bob. Dianne. Stella refused to be trapped deep inland, on a country road, knowing it would take her days to walk to town.

Stella rocked back and forth. Nurse Calvin leaned forward in her chair, letting out a dramatic sigh.

Stella saw Eugene give Nurse Calvin a quick hard glance. He smiled at Stella. "It's okay, Stella. It was just an idea we thought we'd run by you."

Nurse Calvin persisted. "It's not *just* an idea. There's no need for you to have a bed here. You know there's a shortage in these facilities. Wouldn't it be nice to be in the country, Stella? In a real house? I mean, it's still institutional, but homier."

The more agitated Stella became, the more entrenched Nurse Calvin was. "It says right here in the brochure it's located on the highest elevation. You can see almost all the way down the Valley to Seabury on a clear day. You can see the sun glinting off the Mercy River, it says."

Stella crumpled in her chair and put her hands on the top of her head.

"I think we've talked about this enough, Mrs. Calvin." Eugene squeezed Stella's shoulder ever so gently, as he always had, even when he was a young social worker, checking to see if she was real or a figment of his imagination, Stella thought. "Why don't you go outside and get some fresh air? Grace says you and Dianne are coming to see her late this afternoon. A bit of fresh air beforehand will do you good."

Stella stopped in the hall. Nurse Calvin spoke very loudly. Dianne waited halfway down the hall. Stella couldn't tell if Dianne could hear Nurse Calvin hold forth in her argument with Eugene.

"Dianne has to take the placement in the old folks' home. I mean, how much longer will she last? She's eighty-four. We can give her bed here to someone younger."

Stella heard Eugene's sigh and then his deep breath before he spoke.

"Dianne won't want to go to the nursing home. She won't leave Stella. Grace and I both think it's a mistake to split them up. We've both told you this, Mrs. Calvin. Stella needs Dianne. Dianne needs Stella. And I don't even know if it's a good idea for Stella to go to Mountain Top. This is her home. She doesn't even remember Isaiah is gone."

Stella glanced down the hall at Dianne — she was in the same position, not moving.

"That's because everyone keeps tippy-toeing around Stella like she's made of shell and perched on a knick-knack shelf. We *need* to keep reminding her. Stella must realize there are other people in this world and that Dianne's an old lady. She won't live forever. We just have to convince Dianne. Or we can just wait it out, for her cousin Sorcha to die. That old lady's in the hospital anyway, and if you ask me, she's not coming out. I can't believe the Covid didn't kill her. But she's ninety-five. Someone needs to tell Dianne, if you ask me."

Stella rubbed her temples. She wanted to go for a walk with Dianne. Sorcha couldn't be in the hospital without Dianne knowing, could she? It was confusing. Stella wanted to see Isaiah. She wanted to talk to Eugene without Nurse Calvin there. Nurse Calvin was in the hall now, her voice hurtling out behind Stella. "That Stella doesn't fool me with her deaf-and-dumb show."

"Okay, this is out of line, Nurse Calvin. I know, because you constantly remind me, how you happen to be from another time in health care. I *know* you think it was a better, more practical time. But this is really inappropriate. She's mentally ill."

"Oh mentally-shmentally. No one cut her throat. *Trauma this and trauma that.* Neuroplasticity and all that silly talk. Stella's only fifty-four. She could still do an honest day's work. What worked back then still has a place now."

"She has worked in the greenhouse in the spring. I know you have a lot on your plate, Nurse Calvin, and I know you've worked hard all of these years, but this sort of conversation is unprofessional...Pauline. Please. You know better."

Stella had never heard Eugene use her first name before. She didn't even know Nurse Calvin *had* a first name. *Please* was spoken as an order.

"I've got to get back to the office. Let me know as soon as Stella's tests results come back. She has the medical appointment tomorrow."

Stella realized her eyes were closed. As she opened them, she saw Dianne walking to her, taking her hand, leading her away from the nurse's station, leading her outside where the soft, dappled light fell down through the old chestnut trees.

The Flying Squirrel Road.
Just Going Over Yonder.
Who Killed Laura Palmer?

Now

MAL DROVE DOWN YET another dirt road on the North Mountain. She'd been driving for almost two hours now, trying to find the Flying Squirrel Road. Once she'd come up the Mountain, her phone hadn't been able to pick up a signal. Her grandmother had mentioned this location and this mysterious woman named Lucretia, but she hadn't given Mal very sensible directions. She'd said to look for the house with a fountain in the front yard, on a dirt road. And Seraphina had torn out of the museum parking lot so quickly Mal hadn't been able to ask her where the road was, or who Lucretia was. Mal was still finding it hard to believe Seraphina knew her mother. She would have called her mother, if she wasn't supposed to be on a retreat. For sure she would have called her father. Tears poured down her cheeks. Her grief had been waiting there right behind her eyes. It was still hard to believe he was dead and that she would only ever hear his voice in her mind. He would have known what to do, but he wasn't here to ask. Still, Mal knew he would tell her to call her mother. But she wasn't willing to confess the false pretenses of her trip. Not yet.

Mal turned back onto the main road and headed north. There seemed to be only abandoned old farms set way back from the roads, and deep, thick forest. She could now see the bay. She glanced in her rear-view mirror. There was a black car behind her. Not a police car. She turned right onto the next dirt road she came to. The car turned and drove behind her, a bit faster now. There was no way it was an unmarked police car. It was too obvious, too shiny. If someone was following her, they sure weren't being discreet. Maybe it was all in her head. Mal pulled over to wait for the black car to pass but it pulled over as well.

Mal started driving again, the car following. She came to a crossroads and turned left, and then another crossroads with a signpost on the left, almost obscured in the alder bushes. A sudden fog was rolling in, quickly blocking out the blue sky. There was no black car in her mirror now. It was possible it had been a local. Or perhaps the changing sky had disoriented the driver.

She drove down the road and, sure enough, there was a house with a fountain in the front yard, just as Gramma Grant had said. But she'd also said there would be an old lady, Lucretia. The place looked abandoned. The lawn was now more of a meadow of high grasses and wild-flowers. An old swing hung from a tree. The haze had blown away and the blue sky hitting the blue bay gave the place an oddly monochromatic look. Even the fir trees were an unearthly pale blue.

Mal sat on the verandah of the abandoned house. Her phone was now dead. The rocking chair was rickety and she creaked back and forth on it, trying not to fall asleep. She was still on antibiotics. She hadn't had any appetite since she arrived in Nova Scotia. That was six days ago — first jetlagged one in Halifax, the day trip to Mercy Lake, and three days in the motel. The day at the museum in Bigelow Bay with the historian and then with the crazy lady, Seraphina, saying she knew Mal's mother, telling her to leave.

Mal took a sip of water from her bottle. Not a single vehicle had passed and she guessed she'd been in the rocking chair for more than half an hour, probably longer. She was light-headed, probably because she was dehydrated. She would have to be more careful. Or maybe she should just drive to the airport and fly home. That would be the sensible thing to do. She could give her research (although she felt like an idiot even thinking of her papers and notes and emails as research) to a real journalist. What if someone had hacked her email? She hadn't even checked it since she'd been here. Before she left, she'd deleted all her unanswered mail, unsubscribed from newsletters and blogs, all the things that were eating up her focus and concentration. Set auto-reply on her email. Deactivated her social media. A full-on digital detox. She would try life old-school.

Mal closed her eyes. What to do next? Back down to the Valley to the Jericho Centre to try to find the girl? The *woman*, she reminded herself. The at least *middle-aged* woman by now. Or find the poet the historian had told her about? Or drive to the airport and fly back to California and get some proper rest, shake the strep throat and figure out a way to—

"You there."

Mal opened her eyes. A very old woman with a thick wooden walking stick was coming up the driveway, almost at the steps to the verandah. Mal stood up. Her face was a mosaic of intricate wrinkles and her hair was dyed raven black. At least Mal thought it was dyed. "Hi there. I'm looking for Lucretia," she said casually, the way she would if she had an appointment. Mal cleared her throat, feeling ridiculous.

The old lady pounded her stick into the ground and then she cradled the top of it. The cane was rough-hewn, still with bark. "Well, aren't we all. She left some years back. Went over yonder. I don't expect we'll see her again here. Maybe she'll appear eastward, down by

Lupin Cove. She was a distant relation of mine. And yours. We're all from the same family line, you understand. So the story goes. But no one remembers the old ways anymore."

Mal did not understand. But at that, the old lady turned, done talking, and headed back down the driveway and right onto the road, past the old swing, and then disappeared behind the line of trees. Mal closed her eyes and rubbed her temples. It was all so bizarre. She wouldn't be surprised if the Log Lady jumped out from behind a tree and shouted, "Who killed Laura Palmer?" Mal hurried down the driveway and ran past her car onto the dirt road. The old woman had vanished. "Wait," she called out, but the word just echoed back, a strange foreboding sound dangling on the hot air of the lonesome dirt road.

A Walking Tour of Seabury
by the Sea.

Sisterhood.

Then

THEY ARE BOTH AWAKE at first light, her father
downstairs with his coffee and research and teaching
preparations, Stella lying in bed thinking about *Charlotte
Sometimes*, a book she read last year. She brought it with
her but she knows better than to try to read it now,
bringing on a headache. Instead, she rests in bed, the
soft light coming in through the sheers. Stella pictures
the book in her mind, but when she imagines a page,
it is blank. All the pages are blank. It was a Christmas
gift from her mother, a book about a girl who was a
reluctant time traveller—from postwar England to
Second World War England and even further back, to
the Great War, almost trapped in these layers of time,

returning, trading places with a girl from the wartime, a girl she later understands died, which was the only reason she could travel in time. Stella feels tears in her eyes for this fictional character, trapped forever in a paperback, living her life over and over again, unable to escape the sad truth at the end.

She stays in bed listening to the birds outside until she hears her father coming up the creaky stairs, knocking softly on her door. "Awake, Little Bear?"

They eat toast and blueberries together at the kitchen table before heading outside.

It is only a five-minute walk to the harbour. There are two wharves where fishing boats are tied. "Lobster and scallop boats, Stella. They head out from the harbour into the inner bay, the outer bay, and then into the Bay of Fundy herself," her father says as they walk through Seabury's downtown, if it can be called that. The village nestles on the side of a wide bend in the Mercy River, a tidal river that expands as it flows into a huge bay, now obscured by the fog bank. Main Street runs through the village and then weaves and slopes up into what her father tells her is "inland Nova Scotia," a landscape of lakes and rivers, forests and glens.

"That's the enchantment of Nova Scotia, Stella. It's pocket-sized but so diverse."

Thin residential streets spiral outward from the downtown like waving octopus legs, the streets lined with curious old houses with wraparound front verandahs and soaring trees. The weather is peculiar. At first it is sunny and warm, and then a cool breeze blows in with mist that drapes over the tops of the quaint buildings as moss hangs on branches — then the mist clears, leaving a sky smudged with white clouds.

"Frank tells me the village doubles in size now in the summer from all the tourists. It's still early in the day but just you watch."

Two old men with beards smoke pipes on a bench. They wear caps and nod at Stella and her father as they walk by. "Beautiful day," her father says. The plumper man puffs on his pipe and speaks in a cloud of smoke: "Don't let that fool you. The weather can turn in the time it takes to have a piss." Stella's father raises his eyebrows. *He's such a prude*, Stella thinks.

Up ahead, a young family walks to a car laden with suitcases, the man clean shaven and the woman with teased poufy hair. The man stops them and pulls out a map from his back pocket. "We can't figure out how to get out of this place. We got here in the dark last night and got lost just trying to get to the inn. And the directions they gave us at the diner where we had breakfast didn't make a lot of sense."

Stella's father points at the one-way street sign.

"Oh right, another one of those one-way streets. This place was designed to disorient you." The man laughs as he shakes his map.

Stella watches her father play local historian. "It actually *was* designed to disorient you. The story goes that the streets were laid out this way so the devil would have trouble coming into town. And so that the good townsfolk would have trouble leaving into the evil outside world."

Stella sees how carefully the man studies her father. "I thought you were tourists too."

"We're locals," her father says tersely, obviously surprised the man had taken them for visitors. Her father's reaction is the only surprise to Stella, considering how they are dressed — Stella's father in his tweed jacket, Stella in her smocked green sundress.

At the end of the street a cobblestone path leads through a black iron arch into the fenced graveyard. They walk under the rusty old arch, which has an elaborate iron bird at its centre, wings outspread and flowers and berries clutched in its beak.

The stones in the back of the graveyard are mossy and worn. Stella finds the family plot, the tombstones an old style, a border carved in the marble, a weeping willow cut into the centre. Fingers pointing upward. *Gone home* chiselled into the stone.

Stella sees that her grandmother died the year after Violette, leaving just her father and his father, the stern Mr. Sprague. "They died years ago," Stella's father says. "Poor Stella Violette." He wipes at his eyes and tugs Stella's hand away from the stones. "It wasn't right that

Violette died so young. She was only thirteen. It was a tragedy. She drowned, Stella. She couldn't swim."

As they walk home, Stella lets him hold her hand for the first time in forever.

STELLA'S FATHER COMES OUTSIDE into the back verandah where she's sketching some of the flowers in the wildness of the garden. "You want your brain to rest. You don't need to fire up your brain to draw pictures out of nothing. Have a look at these, ready-made."

He hands her an album of old postcards from the days of hospitals in the country, of tuberculosis sanatoriums. Stella finds it odd her father doesn't consider that looking at postcards and photos of hospitals might hurt her brain more than sketching or reading. Probably he just wants to talk to her about his work. It's always easier for him to use his work as a bridge to intimacy, even with her, not even a teenager. Stella sighs as her father comes back with a cold beer and a glass of water for Stella.

Stella drinks the water. She's parched. Her father doesn't notice how she guzzles it down. He is lost in history again.

"Hospitals today are generic, designed with industrial efficiency, places with no humanity. But the buildings we live in are what we leave behind. Look at the pyramids, mysterious, perplexing. Look at the Victorian brick buildings, gothic and stern. These old buildings are ripped down. We're being robbed not just of our history but our heart and soul, Little Bear."

As Stella flips through the postcard album, her father sits close beside her, lovingly running his fingers over the pictures. She can smell his aftershave, spicy and sweet on his warm summer skin. The sun has come around as it's near noon, and it beams in on her head and casts her father in a hazy illumination. The scent from the jasmine growing up the trellis at the side of the verandah is cloying. She sees golden wax inside her father's ear and, outside on the edge, crystals of shaving cream, how the dried foam resembles coral, as though tiny bits of the sea have clung to him, that his ears are shells. His eyebrows are thick and wiry and hair sprouts from his ears — Stella thinks he looks like a creature that has stumbled from the Mercy River, something that's swum in all the way from the Bay of Fundy.

Stella remembers her mother trimming his hair, his eyebrows, clipping the straggly hairs on his ears that sprouted when he was nearing fifty. But her mother is gone now and this is what Stella is left with, this father in a rumpled cotton shirt with coffee and ink stains on the breast pocket. This father has lived a life apart from his daughter, and their new proximity has jarred him, set him off kilter. He has dark circles under his eyes. Stella thinks maybe his judgement is affected by his lack of sleep, his chronic lack of sleep the last number of months, and his beer, his suppers of whiskey and cigarettes.

She puts her head down on the verandah table, feeling its coolness on her cheek, the room spinning. She has a headache again, just a quiet one, but throbbing every few minutes, reminding her of the car accident. Reminding her of her mother. She notices her father is gone. His talk of hospitals and institutions, of the dead in the graveyard, her aunt buried so young—Stella wants to scream and run away. He is making her old before her time. She feels her father isn't in charge, and if something bad happens, he will be helpless. Worse, he won't even know something bad is happening.

LATER IN THE DAY Stella heads back outside, the screen door slamming behind her. She picks some of the soaring purple and orange flowers growing in the weedy old garden at the back of the yard. The sun has moved over in the sky and the yard is in partial shade.

Her father comes to the door and talks to her through the screen. "Old Mrs. Seabury knows a lot about gardening. She and my mother were great friends. They belonged to a women's club called the Offing Society, a sisterhood, I guess you could call it—a bunch of women who had roots in Ireland and Scotland and Wales, all those old countries, who told each other tales of the sea. I think Aoife, or Granny Scotia, as you girls call her, is the only one left who remembers the

Offing, and she isn't making a lot of sense these days. It was harmless—not that I knew much about it. No men allowed, you know." Her father giggles as a young boy would.

"My sister—God, she was headstrong. I remember her standing right there with her arms full of flowers, so many they covered her face. Brown-eyed Susans, I think they were."

Stella doesn't know why her father is suddenly talking about his sister, apropos of nothing, as her mother would have described this turn in the conversation. For most of her childhood he's hardly ever talked about his family, *Stella's* family, and now he can't stop.

"She always had to be the centre of attention and then my father would get angry. My mother had to calm him down. We used to fight all the time, you know, my sister and me."

Her father points to the front of the house. "My mother planted some mountain ash out there. The berries turn red in the autumn. They were purported to keep evil spirits away. My father cut them down. He said it was witchcraft." He pauses before speaking again. "I'm sorry, Stella. It's just so strange being home. I don't mean to babble away."

Stella thinks about how this isn't *her* home. That she has *no* home. But she doesn't say this. She can see in her father's face that he doesn't want to hear it, the way his lips turn down. He wants her to giggle, to sing and take his hand and lead him outside and show him cloud formations, or just read a book, as she did before the accident.

Her father regroups and lights a cigarette. The smoke blows out through the screen in the door. "Why don't we go for ice cream? Because I scream, you scream, we all scream for ice cream," he chants as he holds the screen door for Stella, who comes in and puts her flowers in a green china vase.

IT'S A SHORT WALK to the ice cream parlour, which was here when her father was a child, up the street from the diner, near the top of the hill. All the way there her father muses out loud. "Frank bailed me out of numerous childhood escapades. How do you ever repay all that? I don't know what we would have done without him stepping in, helping me get this job, suggesting we come home, with the house waiting for us. It's a fresh start for us, Stella. You need a quiet year, to rest and heal."

"Dad, look, there it is. Right here." Stella grabs his hand so he won't stride right by.

Keep It Sweet.

"And so it is. You'd think they'd change the name."

"What's wrong with the name?"

"That's what it was called in the old days."

"I thought you were all about the old days."

Stella rubs her temples. He's hurting her head. He's

floating back and forth between two shores, one of nostalgia and one of reality.

"*Parts* of the old days, Stella. 'Keep it sweet' is what people used to say to the girls, telling them to be lady-like, always smiling, never complaining. It made my sister furious when my father would say that to her . . . I want a double-scoop chocolate!"

Her father opens the door and as a brass bell jingles he stops in the doorway. "Well, would you look at that!"

The ice cream parlour has new owners and is not quite as her father remembers. Old-style fans in the ceiling whirl around, filling the shop with a sweetness of vanilla and peaches. It's not modernized so much as restored to a more modern version of what it had been when it first opened. Old-time black-and-white photos line the walls—of young girls with bows in their hair eating ice cream and boys in white shirts and bow ties smiling, elderly people sipping milkshakes.

She and her father get ice cream cones to go and head down to the wharf near the diner. Her father holds her hand and weaves through the crowd. Stella feels claus-trophobic as they make their way through this flood of tourists holding maps and fancy cameras. A group of women come at them wearing cork-soled wedge sandals, high-waisted shorts and giant sunglasses. They smoke menthol cigarettes and blow dirty mint smoke in front of them. Stella coughs and looks at the bright red lipstick smeared on the filters as her father pulls her through the sea of the women, smoke billowing and mixing with their strong perfume and sweat. A group of children coming now, holding three-scoop cones and rocket Popsicles. They giggle and shove past Stella, who then sees four girls who look about nine years old, in terry-cloth shorts and with high ponytails in blue tartan scrunchies. Her father pulls her to the side as the girls skip by arguing: *I told you so. You did not. Like, yes, I did. No, you didn't.*

Stella feels she is neither tourist nor local but some nether creature caught between. Some sort of event for very young children is just finishing at the park near the boardwalk by the river as Stella and her father walk by. Stella's chest feels tight, her breath simmering, almost at a rolling boil, and she wants to scream along with the sugared toddlers passing them, children overstimulated and ready for a nap. Four party clowns walk down the street, two on either sidewalk, smoking cigarettes now that their work is done. If she has to breathe in any more smoke she worries she'll throw up. Cars are parked on either side of the road and the traffic is steady, people looking for parking, people in cars and trucks just passing through. There are no stoplights and the traffic streams one way, weaving into the centre, then onward and outward.

They are finally at the other side of the village, on a side street. Birdsong fills the air, and the smell of some sort of flower. A gust lifts Stella's hair and her stomach slowly relaxes, her boiling-hot breath settling back down deeper in her body. Her father lets go of her hand and points up at the sky where a flock of large birds fly in silence. They look familiar to Stella but she can't place them.

"Those are turkey vultures, Stella. They're only interested in carcasses. Flying, they're called a *kettle*. When eating something dead, we call them a *wake*. But don't worry. They can't hurt you because you're alive."

He takes her hand and they continue walking slowly down the sidewalk.

Thinking Thursday.
The Lonely Road.

Now

DIANNE SAT IN A poufy armchair in the corner of Grace's office used for meeting. Stella perched by the window. The room was transformed by a woven rug of deep blues and greens. Comfortable armchairs, a round oak table in the corner for *therapeutic* writing or drawing, or *tactile* activities. Potted ferns on the floor. The walls were a very pale blue and when the light from the south shone in, the room had a soft, soothing glow. There were floor and table lamps throughout, and Grace only used the overhead fluorescent lighting if they were doing crafts or activities. It was a popular room with residents, and Grace was a favourite staff member.

When Grace announced that she would be on holiday again next week, Dianne said, "Oh yes, that's nice. Where you going? The beach?"

Grace laughed. "I'm having a staycation. I'm doing a poetry reading at the Courthouse Museum too. And trying to get some things done around the house. I want to sell it."

Stella stiffened.

"I want to downsize, that's all, now my son is at university. Don't worry, Stella, I'm not going anywhere."

It was always difficult for Stella when Grace went on summer vacation. She could manage the weekends, but weeks were disorienting. Stella and Dianne normally met with Grace on Tuesdays. Today was Thursday. But it should have been Tuesday. The schedule changes were chopping up her continuity. Sometimes they talked with Grace. Sometimes they listened to music and drew pictures in response to different poems, to books and pictures and objects. Grace called the experience *deep listening* and *authentic response*.

Nurse Calvin disapproved of Grace as much as she disapproved of Stella. *Flakey Gracie,* Nurse Calvin called her. *Woowoo Grace.* Stella knew how Nurse Calvin disapproved of Grace being a single parent, being a poet who wrote poetry that didn't rhyme, for letting her red hair go grey, for being in her forties with a pierced nose and tattoos, for encouraging the residents to embrace their eccentricities, for her bond with the residents. Grace *indulged* them. Grace was *part of the problem*, not the solution.

"Maybe we should tell Stella what we're doing," Grace said to Dianne.

"Just talking."

They knew Stella could hear them — that she might listen, or might let her mind drift.

"That's right, telling stories. It's called *narrative therapy*, Stella."

Stella considered an antique art deco Czech Bohemian crystal perfume bottle with an etched Japanese pagoda design on Grace's bookshelf. She wasn't interested in any sort of therapy today. She would rather think about Isaiah, who had given this bottle to Grace as a Christmas present. Stella didn't know which Christmas exactly. Grace had had the bottle for years. It was *always* on the window ledge, where the ornate crystal stopper refracted the sun and threw rainbows on the parquet floor at the edge of the carpet. But Grace had moved it. Stella saw a miniature green and red cactus in its window spot. This bothered her, the bottle on the dark shelf, that cactus in the sun. Where was Isaiah? She didn't want to think about Mountain Top. Or Dianne in a nursing home. Sorcha in the hospital. Or narrative therapy. What she wanted was to see Isaiah, to know where he had gone. Eugene had been sick. She understood that. Isaiah had been away. He had gone on holiday before and there were times she forgot until he gave her a souvenir. Or sent her a postcard. (*Cynthia sent you a postcard. Remember?)* Maybe he was on vacation.

Grace was taking vacation. On a writing retreat. No, she *had gone* on a writing retreat, to Elizabeth Bishop's childhood home in Great Village. That was in the past. She would have a staycation in her own home. (*Your mother loved Elizabeth Bishop. Her favourite poems were "The Moose" and "Sestina."*) Why was Stella still thinking about her mother? Someone else seemed to be in her head, thinking about Catriona Sprague. Stella's breath quickened. She made fists. All these changes, to her medication, to the schedule, holidays and appointments, were mixing everything up, the changes sending out sound waves, rattling her head, a persistent vibration spreading through her mind, down through her skeleton. She stamped her feet and shook her legs, trying to get the tremors out of her body.

"Stella's out of sorts. Right out of sorts. Nurse Calvin was at her again about God knows what. That thing loves to spread suffering the way a farmer loves spreading cow shit on a field."

"Well, she'll be retiring soon."

"Can't be soon enough."

Stella, light travels faster than sound, which explains why some people appear bright until you hear them speak. (Who said that? *Her father.* William. Why is Stella hearing him?)

The bottle was empty, now just a decoration, no perfume in it. Stella closed her eyes and tried to visualize an empty shell and put Nurse Calvin and her plans in it. But no shell appeared. There was no beach, no ocean in her mind, the watery floor covered in closed seashells, all the bad things hidden away, guarded by the seahorses. But in her mind's eye she saw Isaiah standing at the top of the beach near Periwinkle, the cottage that had been in their family, a craftsman bungalow, with an oversized stone chimney and covered front verandah to sit and look out at the sea. He was leaning on a driftwood cane. He wasn't smiling. He wasn't angry. He was looking out over the bay. But what was he looking at? Stella didn't know. She kept her eyes closed as Dianne and Grace talked.

"So, Dianne, the last time we talked you were telling me about your grandmother."

"Yes, I was born in her house up on the Mountain. On the Flying Squirrel Road. My mother was only fourteen when I was born and she died having me."

"That's very sad, Dianne."

"Yes, it is sad. My cousin Sorcha, she's got the family photo albums and you can see pictures of my mother when she was a girl. And there are a few with me in them."

Dianne let out a wheezy boom of a laugh and then drummed on her chest a few times. Stella heard the smack of the heel of her hand on her sternum. Dianne had a pot-belly but she was overall thin, and the bone sounded hollow. Stella knew she found it hard to be without a cigarette. But Dianne was nothing if not a good sport.

"My grandmother raised me for a spell. She was a widow. Her husband was a fisherman and he drowned out in the bay as so many of them did, fishing when a sudden storm come up. They didn't have the weather forecasting, you see, not like they got now, although how reliable it is, I always wonder. Right, Stella?"

Stella shrugged her shoulders but she didn't turn around. She looked at the antique wall map. She knew the Flying Squirrel Road, which ran for miles across the North Mountain until it ended at the Lonely Road, far west on the mountain near Cape Blomidon. She saw where the road ran—where Periwinkle cottage was in Lupin Cove; the island her grandmother came from.

Kingsport was on the map, perched on the Minas Basin, so different from the rocky basalt cliffs and beaches along the Bay of Fundy. In Kingsport, low tide revealed miles of red mud and sand, the tide that turned came in so quickly, where you could stand in bare feet on the sand and the wavelets would flow over your toes, surrounding you in a matter of minutes. She turned and saw both Dianne and Grace were looking at her. She had gone to Kingsport with Sorcha and Dianne. Sorcha was much older now and rarely drove. And she was in the hospital, Stella remembered Nurse Calvin saying. Sorcha was sick. But Dianne didn't know. Did Grace know? Sorcha was a nurse and never married, living with her father until he died and then staying on in the house, the only child. Stella went to the bookshelves on the wall. She touched the crystal perfume bottle. *Isaiah.*

Dianne continued. "Nana never gave me any advice. It was more she gave me her philosophies. When my grandfather died my grandmother kept doing the things they did together, trapping and skinning racoons and the things he did alone. It always seemed he was there with her but I just couldn't see him. Who knows? Maybe he was.

"Nana was odd about words. *Be careful what you speak out loud, Dianne.* Maybe she thought talking about it would make it happen. All I have now are the words and stories she left me with."

"Do you think that's wise advice?"

"What now?"

"To be careful what you say?"

"'Course I do, Gracie. Words have power. Silence has power. Ain't nothing we do that don't have some sort a power over what comes next. I remember we once come across a raccoon, hit by a car in the night, lying on the dirt shoulder, moving a bit. It was dawn, the light was blue and gold. It was gravely struck. And in the middle of the road were three of its kits, all crushed by a car. They were dead but not the mamma. Nana had a shovel in the back of the truck and she moved those babies and put them in the ditch. She left me in the truck right in the road. There wasn't any traffic of course, it being the country. And then she turned the truck around and we went home and she got her gun.

"When we came back Nana put the gun to the creature's head. Then she looked out over the flowers for an instant and closed her eyes. Her finger was easy on the trigger. This was before she had that tremor. And in that moment when she was looking away the light got brighter and there was a slight breeze that come up so quick. And then Nana pulled the trigger. You always think a gun makes a great boom and I suppose you can hear the crack of a shotgun ringing through the trees. But Nana's .22 made only a pop and the animal jerked once, and then it was still. That's all it took, just a little pop and the thing ceased to be, and the air went still and the light soft. The ditches were full of lupins. Nana rolled the dead animal down to the bottom of the ditch where the dead babies were. There's worse ways to be left than there among the flowers and the green grasses and the daisies. They would rot and the turkey vultures would come and they would go back to the earth.

"Nana died just after that. I was only about thirteen or so. I was left with an uncle and a cousin and that didn't go well. I ended up in the hospital, as you already know. They never found my cousin. I don't suspect they ever will. I went to live with Sorcha, until I had some episodes, which I don't recollect. She kept me home while she looked after her daddy. Then they put me here. I don't blame her. Now Sorcha swims every day and she's gardening, and gave up smoking. I don't think I ever will. Sorcha's ten years older than me and her life wasn't easy neither. But I do enjoy the holidays over to Kingsport. Right, Stella?

"My nanna only drank tea out of her apple blossom pot. I don't know who give it to her but she was some attached to it. I got it in my room, with my boxes. Nana would make her concoctions and put them in glass jars on the shelf in the pantry. Right pretty to look at. Some tasted pretty too. Some tasted like the urge. Gracie, *my bones* are telling me now a storm is coming this summer. There's signs. Maybe it's my time."

Stella heard a change in Dianne's voice, how slowly she was speaking now.

"A Black girl came looking for Stella the other day but I sent her away."

Dianne's voice was amplifying with every word. It wasn't like Dianne was doing it—more like someone was turning up the volume, forcing Stella to listen. She put her hands over her ears and rubbed to make the words stop. Why was a woman looking for her? There was a resident who lived on the first floor of the Jericho Centre. She was African Nova Scotian. That's how Grace described her. The Valley was not a friendly place for young women. *Who had told her that?* Her head hurt. Dianne's voice was even louder now.

"And now it's time for supper, Gracie. Not getting nothing else from me today."

Stella took a notepad out of her bag, the first time in many months. She wrote, *I want to see my uncle.*

Grace put her hands on the back of her head and looked up at the ceiling. Dianne closed her eyes as she spoke. "'Course you do, Stellie. 'Course you do."

Grace sighed. "Oh Stella, I'll talk to you tomorrow about that. I've got to get home now. The dog hasn't been out all day."

Dianne stretched her neck and rubbed her shoulders, turning at the doorway, beckoning to Stella, who followed her like a cygnet.

Commonplace Book of the Offing Society.

Then

STELLA WAKES TO THE sound of her father typing.

He is busy in the front room he's using as an office, or *his study*, as he prefers to call it. He doesn't want to talk, shuffling through his papers when she finally comes downstairs. "Good morning," he mumbles, briefly glancing up at her and then looking back at the old typewriter, talking to it instead of Stella. She can't tell if he even went to bed.

"I have to make more headway on this paper. We'll do a fun trip, just as soon as I get this done. A father-daughter extravaganza. Why don't you go explore on your bike? That way you'll feel more confident when you go biking with Cynthia again. Frank says Cynthia got called in to volunteer at the library. You could volunteer there too, Stella.

It's just a few blocks from here. Just head west."

Stella takes a deep breath. She has a horrible sense of direction. Her father knows this. She watches him put his hands on the desk, probably readying himself for her refusal. Stella doesn't say anything. She decides he can keep waiting. He doesn't even seem worried she might fall and hit her head.

"Just find the North Mountain. And to the left of that is west, and to the right, it is east. Which means the mountain on the opposite side is south. Surely that will work?" Her father exhales through his lips, like a motorboat.

Stella makes toast in the kitchen and spreads jam on it. She hopes she can make jam with Granny Scotia and Cynthia, do something fun, something normal. After she's dressed, she brushes her teeth. She goes back to her father's study. The door is closed. She can smell the cigarette smoke coming from under the door. Stella knocks. At first he doesn't answer and she wonders if he's gone out. When he opens the door she sees the beer on the desk behind him. He has the blinds pulled halfway down and a lamp on.

"I'm going for a bike ride. Maybe I'll check out the library."

He smiles and rubs the stubble on his cheeks. It's getting scruffy. It's easier for him than shaving. An inertia beard. "Well, that's wonderful. Let's see how you do. You'll be as good as Cynthia in no time, Stella.

Remember, head west to get to Main Street. Look for the mountain. Even you can't miss it."

Stella heads out through the back porch and through the screen door, letting it slam shut, her father's comments about her biking churning in her gut. But the garage smells of linseed oil and turpentine and she finds it comforting. Her mother used to occasionally refinish antique furniture. Stella would help her sand and paint. Her father isn't handy. He hasn't been out in the garage once. There is an old cedarstrip canoe in the rafters, paddles hanging from the walls. It is very tidy and warm, some old dried herbs hanging from the rafters, faded grey. Against a wall there is a wooden work table nailed to the side of the garage and a row of empty glass jars.

Stella pulls up her dress above her knees so it won't get caught in the chain and heads west. She's wobbly but definitely faster than on her first ride with Cynthia. Her father hasn't even seen her ride her bike and he's judging her. She stops at Main Street. To the north Stella sees the dark green mountain trimming the edge of the Valley. And the red brick library across the street, to the west.

Stella stands up on the pedals and leans forward over the handlebars. She'll show her father how fast she can go. She feels her dress slip and she looks down. Tires screeching, a horn wailing. The car barely touches her but she falls to the ground anyway, her balance so precarious, the dress hauled up and caught in the chain. She can't win. Her hip burns. She touches it and sees blood on her finger. She's scraped the skin off her elbow too.

"God almighty, missy. Look both ways! I could have killed you." A man looms over Stella, blocking the sun. It's hard to make out his face. The sun gleams on his bald head. "Are you okay?"

Stella pushes herself up to her knees. She's gasping, weeping, and the man holds out his hand. "Let's get you up."

But Stella doesn't want to touch his hand so she gets up herself and pulls her dress free and down. "Sorry," she says, trying not to sob, wondering why she's apologizing.

He picks her bike up and leans it towards her, looking it over. "Bike's okay."

She looks at him and he stares back at her eyes. "You got off lucky, Stella Sprague."

She looks down, self-conscious, her eyes marking her as some sort of freak. But how does he know her name? She quickly thanks him and then walks her bike across the street to the library. She hears him get in his car and drive off. She leans the bike against a tree.

The library is comforting, the universal soothing smell of dry books and polished wood filling her with a terrible melancholy. This is one library she'll never explore with her mother. Her mother will never visit

Seabury. Her mother has been turned into ash and shipped to this Uncle Isaiah whom Stella has never met. Her father had mentioned this was what her mother had always said she wanted, for her ashes to go home to her brother. She was superstitious that way, her father said, about returning to whence you came, and that sort of thing.

The library is almost empty, except for a woman who is busy at the card catalogue. Stella looks around but she doesn't see Cynthia. The woman smiles at Stella. "If you need any help, just let me know, dear." Then she goes back to her cards. Stella sits at a table by the window and looks at the giant bend in the river, now covered with whitecaps. A wind has come up. Stella takes out her notebook and tries to draw the waves but her heart pounds, alive in her chest, trying to get out, realizing it's trapped. Stella understands how close she came to being hurt out in the street, hurt *again*. She closes her eyes and remembers how loud it was when they hit the tree, the rain, a smashing sound and glass breaking, her mother's voice calling, then blackness, then her head heavy, too heavy, a bird chirping, as if there had been no crash, then blackness again. A month later in the hospital, her father coming in when she was finally conscious, her eyes stinging, her splitting headache, the medication, the nausea, the catheter because she couldn't walk without barfing and falling over, her father by her bed, whispering that her mother was gone, Stella thinking he meant on a trip, her father bawling, Stella dozing off and waking up in a darkened hospital room with an empty chair by the bed, the doctor making it clear her mother was not on a trip.

She can't tell her father about the near miss or he'll never let her ride the bike again. Then she'll be stuck in the house with him and the dense misery bulging between the two of them.

Just then, the library door opens. A man's voice asks, "Mrs. MacLean, have you seen Cynthia?"

The librarian comes out of a back room. "Hello, Frank. You just missed her. She's gone back to Granny Scotia's, she said, to change before dinner at the diner."

It's Cynthia's father. Stella has forgotten they are supposed to have the noon meal at the diner with the Seaburys. That's what the locals call *dinner*. And they call dinner *supper*. Stella's learning. Today is a diner dinner. Her father must have forgotten they were supposed to meet the Seaburys. He didn't mention it when she left on her bike.

"I see . . . Stella?" Cynthia's father walks over to the table. "My goodness, are you okay? You're so pale, dear. I can give you a ride home and then just bring you and your father to the diner."

"It's okay, I have my bike, the one you gave me. My dad will want to walk."

He studies Stella's face. Stella sees he is trying to

decide if he should push the issue or leave Stella alone. "Are you sure?"

Stella bobs her head.

"He's all-out with preparations for the new position. Your father was always that way, putting his head down, lost in his studies. We'll see you soon, Stella."

He pauses and then speaks in a hushed voice. "Be patient with your father. He's had to make some important decisions very quickly." His concern is almost palpable, a deep tenderness that encircles Stella.

"And remind your father about the barbeque tomorrow at suppertime. My company sponsors it. A nice way to say goodbye to summer." And then the brass bell by the door jingles as Frank leaves.

Mrs. MacLean smiles at Stella, who blushes. She wishes this kindly looking old lady was her grandmother. That she had a normal life. A normal father. Her eyes sting. Too much sunlight. She's sitting in a library, surrounded by books but not reading, doing nothing but sitting. It's hard to keep track of time. But she's hungry. She didn't eat enough for breakfast and it's still an hour until lunchtime. *Dinnertime.*

"How about a drink of water?"

Stella shakes her head and the librarian heads back to her card catalogue.

WHEN SHE GETS BACK to the house, Stella feels her muscles releasing, her headache abating. The car is in the driveway but her father is not home; he has left a note saying he's gone out for a walk before lunch. The house smells of lemon oil and old wood and dried flowers. Stella wonders if her grandmother smelled like this. *Morgana*. That was her name. Not just *Mother*. Or *Grandmother*. Stella's stomach rumbles. The house feels infinite, full of echoes, every creak amplified. Stella thinks she hears a thump coming from above as she limps up the stairs to tend to her hip and wash her hands. It's just noise in her head, Stella tells herself as she takes the dress off and sees she's sheered a good three inches of skin off her hip and her elbow is scraped raw. It's not deep, but it's throbbing sore. She dabs at it with wet tissues and then flushes them. She opens the medicine cabinet but there aren't any bandages. Stella walks back to her room, covering her chest as she walks, alone in the house but still feeling exposed.

She stops. A swishing coming from her aunt's locked room? But when Stella stands by the door, there isn't a sound. It must be her brain. Auditory hallucinations. What she remembers most from the hospital is the neurologist saying how mysterious memory is — it's hard to predict the future of how her brain will work, how it will process grief, how it will encode, store and retrieve memory. If memory will come back, if it will form, if it will stay, or if it will be flirtatious, coming and going, coy. Her high level of intelligence will help her adapt. Stella doubts this. Her father waiting for her to be vivacious has failure flushing through her, a toilet inside that has a broken handle. Her introversion, which feels normal, is also a leash, holding her back, protecting her from danger while at the same time robbing her of life, of experience. It is a conundrum. The girl Stella is a watercolour memory, static memory. Her previous life is a series of photo albums she can sometimes find and at other times cannot locate. And Stella's mother, always from behind, or the side, a mother without a face. Only changing the past would help and she feels a pang of despair that this isn't possible. She is not Charlotte Sometimes. She is Stella All the Time and None of the Time.

It must have been the wind. Or maybe it was the sound of her longing, Stella thinks, the wry Stella inside the stiff, formal, twelve-year-old body at the top of the stairs with her hand on the glass doorknob. She turns it. Locked. The air is cool in the hall. Stella holds her breath and looks in the keyhole. She only sees a wooden floor—a wooden floor, illuminated by yellow sunlight.

In her room she puts a tissue on the wound and attaches it to her skin with some tape she finds in the writing table in the corner. Stella balls up her blue dress with the red stain and puts it on the floor in the back of the closet. She recalls when her mother bought her the dress. It has smocking on it and Stella knows it's too young for her now; she's almost a teenager. She's so scrawny it still fits but it's a dress from her past. Seabury is showing her this.

Stella makes a cheese and tomato sandwich and pours a glass of milk from a glass bottle. She looks at the bookcase near the table where she imagines her grandmother did her cooking, rolled out her pie dough, as Stella's mother did. She misses her home cooking and wishes she had learned to cook too. She feels she has so little left from her mother other than her adoration of flowers and nature and literature. She forgot to ask her father when the moving truck will come, when she can open up boxes and the scent of her mother will waft out.

The kitchen bookcase has roll-up glass covers on each shelf. And if you take the handle and pull, the glass will tip back and then slide inside, just over top of the books. Only the middle two shelves hold books, recipe and cookbooks. Her father's lucky the glass didn't break when he knocked it over. Just before she pulls the glass door down again, she notices a long book with a tarnished silver flower running down the spine, a ledger-style book. There is nothing on the hard cover but a larger version of the same flower. Inside, on the title page, it says *Commonplace Book of the Offing Society*. She shuffles through it but all the yellowed pages are blank.

Just then she hears her father's footsteps crunching on the driveway, and as he gets closer she hears him whistling. He isn't very good at it but she would never tell him so. She pushes the book back and pulls the glass door down just as he comes into the kitchen through the back porch, the screen door slamming behind him.

Seraphina Sullivan.
The Secret Language of Flowers.
Valley Regional Hospital.

Now

STELLA STOOD BEHIND GRACE near the registration desk at the hospital. It was very busy and everyone was sitting in chairs, two chairs between them for the safety of distance, circles on the floor to space out waiting lines. Grace got Stella registered and took some hand sanitizer from the pump on the counter. It was early Friday afternoon, the last lurch to the weekend. Grace took a number and they sat down to wait. Stella was woozy from the pill Nurse Calvin had given her before they left. She was pleased about the tranquillizer. Hospitals disturbed her. Dianne had been insisting on coming with them. Stella didn't mind but Nurse Calvin did. The two were still arguing when she left with Grace.

Grace wrote in a notebook, looking away and then back, carefully writing a few lines. Her handwriting was elegant, each letter carefully created, each word intentional, each word summoned. Grace knew Stella was watching her, that she didn't want to draw. Every day she was sketching less and less, thinking more and more. Grace's handwriting reminded Stella of Cynthia, of the postcard. Cynthia floated about in her mind now, that seashell Stella had stored her in open, whatever else was tucked away inside slow to come out.

Grace smiled. She spoke to Stella without looking up from her page. "Maybe you should write some poetry, Stella."

Stella thought about her mother and the poems that died with her. Stella would rather read poetry, see the poetry around her. And in this place, the sad poems, the elegies, the ballads, the sonnets, were all walking about.

There was a hum. It was in Stella's throat. Grace's hand stopped moving, suspended in mid-air, the writing incomplete. She didn't mention Stella's humming, and when the sound stopped, Grace continued writing. She had told Stella that most of her poems were about her only child, her son. About life as a single parent, how this changes you. Also, poems about being exhausted. A few times she had read poems at the centre, during open mic nights, when residents who wrote poetry read their work, or their favourite poems by famous poets. Stella and Dianne enjoyed these evenings.

Right now, Stella was tired, tired and sore. There was a loud beating. It was a vein in her temple. Her hands went clammy. Grace patted her arm. "You're here for some tests, Stella. They were scheduled for you a few weeks ago. To find out what's going on. Do you remember? I know tapering off the medication has been problematic."

Did someone call her name? Stella looked around. Grace looked up and watched Stella. But there were only people sitting on chairs, sad people, fat people, tired people, angry children, sick children. Stella heard her mother's voice, calling her name, reading to her, Elizabeth Bishop:

The waiting room was bright
and too hot. It was sliding
beneath a big black wave,
another and another.

Stella touched a page of Grace's notebook; there were scribbles where she had crossed out words. She was sketching now, some delicate flowers in a vase. Violets.

"Violets symbolized everlasting love and remembrance to the Victorians. And mysticism. A diminutive flower that packs a punch, hey? Want me to read a bit?"

Stella touched Grace's hand. Grace began:

There was so much you let go of, for the next day.
But all those next days chained
in a garland
of lost days around your neck,
the relentless routine of each day
kept you captive.

Grace paused, took a sip of the stuffy waiting room air
and held it for a few seconds, then exhaled the words:

These violets are for you, standing
on the bus,
biting your lip,
wondering how time vanished,
leaving small lines beside your eyes and mouth,
A story etched into flesh.

Grace licked her lips and continued:

You were so busy taking
care of people while
the relentless routine of each day
kept you captive.

Deep breath in. Grace inhaling the waiting room.
Exhaling living words:

Now you see life was drawing
a story on your body the entire time,
your skin and bone and muscle remembering
all those days,
all your wishes and dreams.

Pause.

These violets are for you, so you'll remember:
the shape of days can change.

Yelling.

The stories you read on your face are
stories without endings.
May these small flowers remind you how
the shape of days can change
How the stories you read on your face are
stories without endings.

Hollering.

These flowers are for you to hold
when you cast the garland from your neck
and find how easily it breaks.

The poetry died.

There was shouting and fuss near the main entrance as a woman barged in, skinny as a stick of uncooked spaghetti, black braids flying. She wore muddy hiking boots and a flowery sundress. It was a strange combination. The woman looked familiar to Stella. She didn't get a ticket, a number, to wait her turn.

"Listen to me. How many times do I have to say I don't have time to sit here and wait all day for goddamn blood tests. I washed my hands so many times I got skeleton hands. You're making me into the living dead. My truck's been parked out there for two hours. I have places to be. Have you ever heard of the three sisters? Or Lucretia rising misty from the foam?" Then a horrible mewling sobbing.

Grace put her pen down on her notebook in her lap. "Oh Seraphina, she must be having a hard time. I heard they put her daughter in foster care. I think she's about thirteen now."

Thirteen, a magic age when life collapses, Stella thought. When you realize life is not the rhapsody your mother talked about, that there never will be a rhapsody.

Seraphina, railing in front of them, seemed to be living proof there was constant tragedy. Stella knew this name. She knew Seraphina. Seraphina with bipolar disorder. Hypomanic right now. Yes, that was correct, from the centre. Seraphina had come there to visit before. *When she's steady, she's salt of the earth,*

Dianne has remarked more than once. Seraphina attended the weekly Alcoholics Anonymous meeting held every Thursday, what some of the residents called Thirsty Thursdays. Some of the other residents called it Thriving Thursdays. It was about perspective and experience. Some of the residents attended. And people from the community, like Seraphina.

"Oh, that Seraphina," Grace said. "She believes in the losers. She believes that she can save them, that's what she says. But through her upheavals, she never drinks."

When Seraphina had her episodes they would take her to the city hospital, the one Stella's father had told her about, the one that dated back to the days of moral treatment. Stella rubbed her temples. Her head was filling up now, and hurting, from these shells beginning to float about, banging against her skull, insisting on dislodging themselves from the murky floor of her mind, jostling themselves open. She knew Seraphina from somewhere else.

Seraphina spied Stella from across the waiting room, as though she'd heard her thoughts. She held out a thin arm and pointed as she bellowed: "They're looking for you, Stella. Run. You better hide. Don't you remember? They didn't all go up in flames. Don't let them find you. They know. They know what you have and they want it. I saw them in the cove. They asked me if I knew your whereabouts. I told them you were one of the ones at the Jericho Centre who died last year, but I don't know if they believed me."

Grace reached over and put her hand on Stella's arm. "Stella, don't pay attention. She's sick. She's not well."

Stella knew this but she also knew that sick people wove truth into fantasy, or their truth was just a heightened version of reality, and that sometimes their reality was what was real, not the deadened society they were trapped in. Seraphina was still calling her name, loud, desperate. *StellaMarisStellaMarisStellaMaris.*

Two security guards came over to Seraphina. They spoke in low voices so it was impossible to make out what they were saying, especially over her shouts and cries. She wasn't making sense now. Sadness swelled up in Stella. Her groin tightened, so sore — ripples of melancholy rolling up, shades of lilac and pale blue, dull green in her mind, tears trickling from her eyes. Grace dabbed at Stella's cheeks with a tissue.

"It's okay, Stella. This is the last thing you need to see. Seraphina was doing so well, I heard, but I guess not. Maybe she has started drinking again."

Stella doubted that. It wasn't about alcohol or its absence but the angels and demons inside of her, warring, each demanding her voice, her thought, her time. Stella took Grace's hand and she squeezed back as they watched a squirming Seraphina carried out the door towards emergency.

As the doors closed and the dull murmur of the

waiting room came back, Stella continued to think about Seraphina. She was sure she knew her from another time, but where and when, she wasn't sure. Her head was feeling heavy. From the sedative. What did Seraphina want her to remember? What did Seraphina think Stella was in possession of that people wanted? She had nothing. Who could be looking for her? No one even knew Stella was alive, except for Isaiah. But he wasn't looking for her. He hadn't been to visit in a long time. Stella couldn't remember how long a long time was. But since the last season. She had not seen him in the summer. She was sure of it. Pretty sure. Almost sure.

The Diner.
The Help.
Chocolate Milkshakes.

Then

STELLA AND HER FATHER don't pass many people on the way to the diner for dinner with Frank and Cynthia. Stella's hip hurts where she scraped it, but she doesn't want her father to know. She'll have to wash the stain out of the dress crumpled in her closet or throw it away. She can rip it and tell him she caught it on a nail in the garage. But then he might want her to have a tetanus shot. She doesn't ever want to go back to a hospital. Maybe she had a shot after the car accident? She doesn't know. Or maybe he wouldn't even think of a tetanus shot.

She expects her father to be waving at familiar faces. She thinks maybe everyone is old now, so he doesn't know who they are, friends from the past erased by time, or maybe moved away, dead, all those things Stella now knows happen.

As if reading her mind, he says, "I don't recognize anyone, not that there are many people around right now. So many people moved away, as your mother and I did, for education or work. I suspect these people are tourists, Stella, with their hats and walking shoes and cameras. It's a myth about towns, how people are friendly and walk everywhere. That went out of fashion in the 1950s when everyone got cars. Small-town people are just that—small-minded, closed-minded, narrow-minded. They play their cards close to their chest and don't bother with outsiders."

Stella wonders why he insisted on moving back here if he hates Seabury so much.

"Excuse me," a man says, his voice coming from his sinuses. He wears a maroon velour track suit. "Do you know how to get to Seabury Marsh? We want to see the birds. We just keep going in circles." He holds out a map to Stella's father. Three middle-aged women peer from behind him, all shoulder-length feathered hair and gigantic sunglasses.

Stella's father points. "Just head west. You can't miss it."

"You're sure it's that direction?" The man narrows his eyes as he scans Stella and her father. His eyes linger too long on her budding breasts. She crosses her arms and his eyes flit away to her father's. "You don't have the local accent. Are you sure you know your way?"

"Of course I know the way. Do you want me to write out the instructions?"

"No, just double-checking. We're on a bus tour. We have an hour to wander. It's my wife and her sisters who want these tours." He holds his hand up to shade his eyes as he gazes to the west.

A woman in fuchsia sunglasses looks west as well. "That's right, it's always the wife's fault." The other two women laugh. "If the man says it's west, it's west." Their voices trail behind as they head to the marsh.

Her father chuckles and rolls his eyes at Stella. Stella knows he thinks they are in on a joke together.

They walk through the glass door into the diner and the brass bell at the top rings. There is a jukebox in the corner, and an old-fashioned *Please wait to be seated* sign with faded lettering. A waitress comes over. "Well, look what the dog dragged in. Frank said you were coming home. Now, you must be Stella. Frankie told us that Billy had a girl with those magic eyes. I have a booth reserved back here, the best one in the house."

Stella and her father follow the short, plump woman to a booth. "I'll be right back, folks."

Stella looks at the framed pictures on the walls, most in black and white and some in colour, of boating on the river, apple orchards covered in blossoms, horse-and-wagons loaded with barrels, like in the ice cream parlour. A wooden-framed poster hangs on the wall by the pictures of the old days. *May you never forget what is worth remembering nor ever remember what is best forgotten. Keep it sweet.*

The waitress comes back with menus. "This here diner's been in my family for four generations. Did your father tell you that?" She smiles at Stella. She pronounces *father* with an *r, far-ther*. It's almost a southern accent. The local accent the tourist mentioned.

"No, he didn't . . ."

Stella sees her *far-ther* has no idea who this is, from how he keeps nodding, the neutral look he had in Ohio when his students would come up to him in public. *Hi, Dr. Sprague. How are you? Off exploring the lunatic asylum, the abandoned buildings?* He would always smile, pleased they recognized him. He looks at her name tag. "Stella, this is Cheryl."

Cheryl laughs. "Pity about Frankie's mother, living all alone out there at Cedar Grove. My cousin's girlfriend was cleaning house there and cooking, but Frank fired her, out of the blue. She worked there for over ten years. She's all afraid of him now. Frank's just like his father, people say. He let the landscaping company go too. That lawn's a mess. I guess we all turn out to be our parents. Sorry to hear about the car accident and all. What a sin. Frank told me when he made the reservation."

Stella sees her father's face go pale.

Stella thinks about this maid or cleaner/house-keeper, whoever she was. Cynthia said she had up and quit. Why would she lie about that? Maybe Cheryl was mixed up, got it wrong... or maybe Cynthia didn't know. Cheryl now goes on about the special, fresh fried Digby scallops, which came in on the fish truck early this morning, *so fresh they don't even know they're dead but you can't go wrong with the clubhouse because we bake our own bread, nothing out of a bag, no sir.* The bell jingles again and a stream of people flow in. To Stella's great relief, Cheryl rushes away, leaving menus on the table. Her father studies the menu as though it's a missing historical document he's found in the archives. It's always awkward now, when he's alone with Stella, his stiff efforts to make small talk. Stella knows that she reminds him not of her mother or his sister, the first Stella — she reminds him only that they are dead.

The bell jingles once more and Frank fills up the doorway. Stella watches him look around the diner, smiling at people. She sees Cynthia behind him, look-ing bored. Frank proceeds down the aisle, shaking hands, patting people on the back, scanning the room at the same time, smiling when he locates Stella's father, winking at Stella. He seems to know she has been observing him. She blushes.

"As I live and breathe. Billy, my dear old friend, I *still* can't believe you're back."

Stella's father stands up and Frank clasps his hand, pumping his arm as he squeezes his shoulder.

Stella and her father move over to make room for them. Stella's hip burns where the skin is raw, the make-shift bandage rubbing on it.

"Mr. Sprague, how are you finding your old home?" Cynthia asks, sitting down beside Stella. "Are you coming to the barbeque tomorrow?"

Stella's father can't hide his delight at seeing Cynthia. It doesn't occur to him to hide it. "Well, it's much the same as it was when I was a boy, Cynthia. You'll have to come over and visit again. Right, Stella?"

Stella clutches the menu and fans herself. Her father reaches out and stops her, embarrassed, that Stella's a psycho with strange behaviours, and he's the normal one, in his rumpled, stained shirt, with his scruffy face the colour of dirty dishwater.

Cheryl comes back and takes their order. She double-checks and then points her pencil at Frank. "You hardly ever come into the diner anymore. You're a summer visitor yourself, Mister. Look, I'm sorry to hear about Sally. And how is Granny Scotia? It must be hard with her getting on in years now. My sister-in-law works at the nursing home and it's a nice place—"

Cynthia interrupts. "Granny Scotia is just fine on her own."

A bell from the grill dings and Cheryl sways away. Stella isn't hungry after having her cheese and tomato sandwich, but she doesn't want to be rude — or worse, have them think she's sick. The food comes quickly. The girls have chocolate milkshakes in glasses with the metal canisters between them. Frank ordered them with whipped cream and cherries on top.

"We want to see if we can convince the old bird to finally sell the house. It would make a first-rate hotel. Or maybe a museum. We could sell it to the province. The O'Clearys are worth remembering, those great old eccentrics from Ireland."

"Dad, Granny is perfectly fine. She doesn't want to move."

"It's true, Frank. Your mother does seem sharp as ever. It's remarkable how little the house has changed over the years."

"There comes a time for us all. You know old folks, especially the ladies. They get more dangerous the older they get."

Cynthia bites her lip. She knows better than to get into it with her father in public, Stella notices. Frank's smiling but his voice is measured.

Frank asks Stella's father question after question about Athens and his work and the Hocking River. Cynthia and Stella eat and listen to the men talk about the old days, about Frank's business. Stella has a hard time understanding what Frank does. He talks about investments and stocks, about buying and trading, about mining and minerals in faraway places. The girls go to the washroom together. Cynthia plays with her hair in the mirror and whispers that her father's into *gaming, hospitality and leisure, water resources, asset management and property development, investments, stocks, bonds.* Cynthia rattles these words off with the speed of an auctioneer.

"It's stupid. I don't get what he does. Your father's a historian. He has a real job."

The girls go back to the table and Cheryl comes by with the bill, which Frank insists on paying. Stella turns and her dress sticks to her scraped hip. A bit of blood soaks through the light blue fabric. Stella covers it with her hand and looks away. Cynthia says nothing as Stella puts on her sweater, which hangs down over the stain.

Cynthia stands by the booth talking about canoeing and making soap, picking blueberries and making jam, the fun things Stella can do with her and Granny Scotia. Cynthia makes endless banter so Stella can adjust her sweater. Stella watches Frank put his hand on her father's shoulder, patting him as though William is a high-backed chair and Frank wants to see how sturdy it is after all these years, if there is any give. Her father is rigid now, and the comfort of the good food, the fresh fish, the rich milkshake, is gone. Frank then claps her father on the back and gives him a look of pity.

"You always were the sensitive type, Billy. My assistant, Tommy Jessome, can help you out too. Just know how glad the Seaburys are to have you home, right, Cynthia?"

They are almost at the door now and Cynthia turns around. "See you at the barbeque, Stella."

THE REST OF THE afternoon Stella's father shrinks into himself, poring over books and papers, lining up file folders. He starts his new job the following week, the last week of August, before September classes start after Labour Day weekend. Stella thinks that because she is almost thirteen her father feels no guilt *(or less guilt . . . less shame, that's what it is)* about leaving her on her own in a village, where life is simple and safe. He's burying himself in his work. Her father brightens in the company of the Seaburys, not his own dour daughter, the itty thing with thin hair and mismatched eyes.

She realizes, for the first time, how jealous she is of these people, their bigger-than-life smiles and laughs, their health and confidence. But Stella's never had anyone want to be her friend before. She wants to see Cynthia and, of course, she also wishes she had never met her.

Temporal Displacement.

Now

STELLA'S *LADY PARTS*, as Nurse Calvin called them, were not working properly, which was why she was at the hospital. She had not slept well. She knew that poor sleep made her memory worse. Cynthia's grandmother also called them *lady parts*. *Granny Scotia*. Why was she thinking of Cynthia and Granny Scotia? Stella squeezed her hands into fists. There was a nautical picture on the wall across from her, a lobster boat in a green sea, a fisherman hauling his traps. It looked like a paint-by-number. The fisherman held a giant blue lobster, frighteningly out of proportion to the trap. The fisherman had a grey beard and red cheeks, and a crazy smile. "Ahoy, Stella," he seemed to be saying with his eyes.

"Scootch your bottom down," a nurse with wavy auburn hair said. "Don't worry, Stella."

Her name tag read *Clara*. Stella stared at it so she wouldn't forget who she was. Clara smiled encouragingly, waving Stella down a bit more, as she would if she was helping her park a car. "A little bit more," she said. "And a bit more."

Stella shuffled her hips and buttocks down the examination table, but then too far and the nurse and Grace lurched forward to grab Stella's sides so she wouldn't crash down between the stirrups, hauling her back up. Stella's feet now rested in the stirrups. She didn't want to bawl in this room with bright lights. The fisherman's smile seemed even wider now. Stella fluttered her lids together, sealing away the wall and the fisherman with his creepy lobster.

STELLA WOKE UP, PARCHED, groggy, in a sedative haze. *Memory is a mystery*—the new neurologist's summation. Why was she thinking of this? She sniffed. Hospital air. Stella opened her eyes. The doctor sat on a stool by her feet. The painted lobster loomed over his turban, the fisherman leering behind him. This was Dr. Singh. Not a doctor of the brain or the mind but a doctor of her innards. *A gynecologist.* Stella had been having her period again—dark, gruesome bits of blood. But her period stopped a number of years ago. The ache. Was this why she was here?

Dr. Singh cleared his throat. He never rushed. She remembered him from before, not from his face or his voice but the way he moved. Deliberately. Intentionally. She watched how slowly he gestured with his hand as he spoke. Nothing about him indicated a rushed personality. In an emergency he would be methodical, calm, precise, steady.

He smiled. "Ah, awake. You had a short nap. Grace was just giving me some background. Do you remember me, Stella? We're just doing a checkup. It's called a colposcopy. It won't hurt. I'll take a tissue sample. That might pinch. I'll swab you with a bit of a vinegar solution." He gave her instructions but Stella couldn't keep track of them, her heart thumping so much, her throat and eyes dry, her legs spread open like locks on a canal—what she had studied as a child in geography, when she was young—the air cold on her privates.

"Stella, Stella, you need to move your knees." It was Grace. Tapping her on the arm. "Stella."

Stella's knees pressed together. The doctor held a speculum. He smiled. She spread her knees apart and felt the metal between her legs.

"It will only take a moment. Just a peek. There we go... sorry. Just a bit more. Okay, now just tightening it a bit, so it won't slip. Just a bit of a pinch. I see you have a prolapsed vaginal wall. Anterior and posterior. Now, just putting a vinegar solution on your cervix."

The doctor and nurse now gazed at a screen, which apparently displayed her innards. She felt sick. Why hadn't they put her to sleep? That's right, Stella remembered. She had a phobia of general anesthetics. Stella would rather be conscious. Sedated consciousness. They begrudgingly respected her wishes.

"Do you play the piano?" Dr. Singh. She knew his name.

For some reason, Stella lifted up her hands and wiggled her fingers as though she were playing Chopin. He laughed. He was a nice man.

"We'll have the test results soon." Then Stella wasn't able to help herself and out came the pee she was holding. The doctor left and Grace came to her side as the nurse handed her a warm wet towel.

"There, there, Stella. It's okay. It happens to most of us ladies at one point or another, the prolapsing. And I know it's easy to put off pap smears. It's not pleasant. No one talks about it, is all. That's a problem. But it's good you're here now. Dr. Singh will find out whatever's happening... *down there*. Don't you worry a bit. That's a good girl, Stella," Clara said, smiling as if Stella were her child.

A trickle of tears ran down Stella's temples and into her hair, into the soft pillow. Grace stood beside her. The room was quiet except for the thin buzz of the fluorescent lights. Dr. Singh was back, studying the screen Stella couldn't see, which was fine because Stella did not want to see her inside world, the deep Under Land beneath her flesh. His face didn't move but it was hard to tell through his black beard flecked with bits of white, similar to someone's hair she just saw. Whose hair? Seraphina shouting in the lobby. *Who was looking for Stella?* The psychiatrist had told her years before to work on time orientation, so she could avoid *temporal displacement*. Stella felt this way now, moving in time, that she needed the North Star so she could stay fixed. But some part of her was paces ahead, orienteering with a compass, forcing the rest of her to follow.

Stella tensed up again and then it hurt inside in a remote way and she cried out, not able to make words, just sound, but the words in her mind so loud, crying for her mother, for Catriona, who died years ago. Grace patted her hand and dabbed at her face with a tissue. A fan clicked on and cool air billowed out of an overhead vent.

Seabury Barbeque.
Tommy Jessome.
The Purple Hour.

Then

STELLA IS QUIETER THAN normal before they leave for
the barbeque — the new Stella, silent, shrugging, face
blank. Her father gives her an aspirin and sends her to
her room to rest, but when she mentions staying home,
he frowns. *We'll get to see Cynthia. Won't that be fun?* Fun
for him, Stella thinks, noticing how he includes himself,
like he is part of a new club.

Stella knows he doesn't want to go alone and yet is
reluctant to drag his sick child who *obviously* should be
at home. People might judge him. Stella knows he sees
this choice he has to make as Stella's fault. Her headache
is better from the pill but her hip still throbs. She digs
deep through her toiletries bag and finds a package of

bandages her mother must have put in there a few years ago. They are still sticky and hold in a criss-cross over raw flesh. Stella asks her father again when the moving truck will come. *In a week or so.* She knows she must rest her brain, but she wants to put her books, her mother's books, on a shelf, to participate in the healing ritual of organizing books—arranging and stacking them, looking at the spines, sniffing the pages—just as her mother did. Stella wants her mother's photo albums, the framed photographs. The silver-birch china dishes. Country Roses china plates. Her mother's Depression-glass water pitcher, cake stand and bowls. She pictures the bright pink, blue and green glass on the shelf near the kitchen window in Athens. The sheets and pillowcases trimmed with her mother's meticulous embroidered flowers.

The waterfront park teems with people and there are tables set up at the southern edge of the park near the wrought-iron fence, tables with heaping paper plates of food and a handmade sign that says HELP YOUR-SELF. Her father loads up his plate with potato salad and coleslaw and a thick hamburger. Stella has some salad and a brown-bread bun. She hates barbequed food. A stout man comes over to their picnic table. He takes off his hat and Stella sees the evening sun shining on his head. It's the man who almost hit her with his car. The man who knew her name. Stella waits for him to tell her father how she'd ridden her bike straight into the road, how careless she is, that she can't be trusted. She'll never be like her mother, or her dead aunt, or her maddeningly perfect new friend, Cynthia.

"I'm Tommy Jessome. Originally from Kennebunkport, Maine, but I've lived in New York for years. Love coming to Seabury. People mind their own business. No one even knows my name."

Tommy's watery pale blue eyes remind Stella of a polluted sky. He's thick and dense all over, stocky, reminding Stella of something born out of a life-sized cookie mould, generic and primitive. His clothes look expensive. Another man walks over — thin, a baggy suit hanging on his body, thick hair standing straight up in wiry bristles. He whispers in Tommy's ear. Tommy slaps him on the back and roars with laughter. "No can do, buddy. Have a hamburger and we'll talk later."

That is how Tommy talks: *No can do. Yes can do. Will do. Could do. Might do. Would do. How do.* But it doesn't sound natural, more like he's trying to be country. He sits at their picnic table and eats his hot dog, slathered in ketchup and mustard and relish. He doesn't get a drop on his smooth yellow shirt or his pressed black pants.

"Don't you eat hot dogs, Stella? I thought all children loved hot dogs. Get some of the fruit punch. What kind of girl doesn't love a glass of fruit punch? Cynthia will take care of you. Pity her mother just abandoned her. That Sally. She was calling up Frank in New York in the middle of the day complaining. Frank's soft-hearted when it comes to family and friends." Tommy shoves the last piece of meat-stuffed bun in his mouth. He slaps Stella's dad on his shoulder and walks into the crowd.

It's very loud, with all the talking, fiddle music, and accordion and guitar. Children scream and laugh, holding blue balloons, *Seabury* in black letters. Tired young women push strollers and elderly people walk with canes. It's easy to spot the tourists with their visors and cameras and sensible footwear. Her father has crumbs in his scraggly beard and on his shirt but he doesn't notice.

A chill creeps under the warm evening air. A foghorn booms out near the river—it startles Stella's father and he spits out a mouthful of hamburger, smearing mustard on his white shirt. "Dammit," he says just as Frank calls to them from the picnic table across the path. He's standing by a group of police officers eating burgers. Crows fly overhead, on their way to roost. Seagulls squall, circling, screaming, hoping for discarded hot dogs and buns in the grass.

Frank is now at their table. It's too noisy. Overpowering. A sensory overload—the smells and sights and sounds swirling around her. Stella feels trapped in a kaleidoscope. Stella closes her eyes. Frank could talk all night. He and her father discuss Lord Bishop University, real estate in Bigelow Bay, having dinner at the Seabury house on the Mountain.

"Hey."

Stella opens her eyes. Cynthia sits beside her. They watch the sunset deepen over the river. Cynthia moves closer and speaks quietly by Stella's ear, her breath soft puffs on Stella's jaw. "My dad says you came to the library. Sorry I missed you. I'll come over tomorrow morning and we can go biking. Granny wants to go to the beach. She wants to give you the salt water cure. She thinks it will help you heal from the car accident."

Stella has no idea what Cynthia is talking about. She craves quiet. A short stick of a young man with a drooping mud-brown mustache appears with a black camera. He says he's from the local newspaper and asks Frank and Stella's father to pose for a picture. Then the reporter poses Cynthia and Stella with their arms around each other.

Tommy appears out of nowhere and Stella feels Cynthia stiffen as Tommy flicks his hand at the man with the camera, an insect to be shooed away. Frank walks off with the disgruntled reporter, his arm around his shoulder, as Tommy burps and points his finger at Cynthia. "Your father is proud of you for making old family friends feel so welcome, Cinder." He winks at Cynthia. Just then someone from the crowd calls: *Jessome. Tommy Jessome.* "I'm a wanted man, girls," Tommy says, almost run over by four young boys shooting toy pistols. *BangBangBangBang.* He thinks this is funny, and makes his hand into a gun. He points it at Cynthia. "Pow-pow, Cinder." He laughs, then turns and disappears into the crowd.

It's now well into the evening and the fading sun gilds Cynthia's dark hair. The twilight gleams in her eyes and, as strange as it is, Stella thinks Cynthia gets taller. A slant of wind comes into the park. Cynthia doesn't mention another word about the salt water or a cure. Stella isn't sure she heard correctly. Perhaps it is the tide turning, the wind sweeping in from the ocean—perhaps it is the arrival of the purple hour.

The Girl in the Yellow Dress.

Now

A BUTTERFLY FLITTED BY. The grass was dry, a strange deep green and brown. "We're needing some rain, Stella. Clouds letting loose. But it sure don't seem they're coming, not today anyway."

The sky was a dark blue. The sun was pulled around in the horizon though, a sign that August was soon leaving. They looked to the west and it was then they saw the woman walking across the grass. There was a compact silver car parked on the side of the County Home Road. No one was supposed to park there. Stella didn't remember if the car was there when they sat down.

A gorgeous young woman walked across the grass towards them. She was wearing a stylish yellow dress and sandals and carried an expensive-looking vintage leather backpack. No, it was a briefcase. Her skin was dark brown and her hair short in tight curls.

Dianne immediately stiffened.

"Stella Sprague?" The words whooshed out as the woman hurried over the dry, crunching grass. Maybe it was her fatigue and the heat, but the earth seemed to call Stella's name, echoing the words rushing out from the young woman's mouth.

Dianne peered up at her. "You got the wrong person, lady. I told you that before. Don't come around here no more." Dianne dragged on her cigarette and looked away.

Stella watched a few beads of sweat roll down the young woman's forehead. Dianne slowly pushed herself upright, looming over the interloper. The young woman hesitated, not sure what to do, as Dianne spit to the side, onto the ground, rolling her tongue in her mouth, searching for the right words, the right tone. "Jericho Centre's back that way. Visitors got to register, if you got family to see. No one right here to visit. We ain't nobody anyone knows, just two old ladies. See you."

The woman handed a business card to Dianne. "I'm Malmuria Grant-Patel. Mal, people call me." Her voice was shaky.

"I see. Nice name. You give me one of those little cards on Monday. I don't got memory problems, not me."

"Are you Stella Sprague?"

Dianne stood in front of Stella. "Never heard of anyone by that name."

"Look, I'm a journalist. Sort of. Well, I'm a researcher. Kind of. A blogger."

"Isn't that something. Good for you. I'm an old lady. Good for me. We have to go make crafts for old Nurse Calvin. I play the banjo. We're having pork chops tonight. Applesauce. Mustard pickles."

Stella knew that Dianne was pretending to be slow. She wanted the woman to go away. Stella felt removed from her body, a shadow watching from the edges, watching Dianne towering over this nervous young woman who kept rubbing her jaw.

"I'm investigating something that happened decades ago. I guess it's what you'd call a cold case. It's a cult. I've been doing research. I didn't plan on doing this. I interviewed this woman named Flora for my podcast. It was about mental health. I know this doesn't make any sense. She told me how when she was young she ended up in this . . . cult sort of thing. Oh my God, I know I'm not making much sense. Look, I think you're in danger, Stella."

Stella saw that this woman, Mal, was close to tears. She felt her heart begin to thud, a far-off drum sounding the alarm. The grass was spinning. Everything shifting, tilting, slow motion, the words drawn out, nightmare words. *Mercy Lake. The lodge. Sodality. Franklin Seabury.*

Stella closed her eyes. All words floating up. Seahorses swaying. She opened her eyes and rubbed them.

A blurry Dianne stood in front of Stella, her house dress wrinkled—Dianne a reaper, with her left arm held up in proclamation and her right arm extended, finger pointed at the main road. But the woman's words kept flowing.

Warning. Followed. Not all dead. One survived.

The woman in the yellow dress who called herself Mal reached in her bag and pulled out a piece of paper that flipped up in the breeze. Her voice came back into focus.

"Look, I'm from here originally. Well, my mother is, actually. And my grandmother. Anyway, I found some links."

Links. Connections. Grooming. Girls. Cynthia.

"I want you to help me. So I can help you. I know that's Stella sitting there. I know she doesn't talk. I tried to find her uncle but I was too late. They're watching you. Did you know that? You can't trust anybody. I want to help you."

"No, she's safe here. She don't talk. She don't know nothing about nothing. You need to go away now. You can't do no good here. Stella's got me. Time to go now, quickity-quick."

"I went to Florida before I came here. I talked to Sally Seabury. Well, sort of. She had a stroke. She's really old now. She's in a nursing home. Sally told me what her daughter said, what her daughter gave you to keep safe."

Stella's shadow-self settled over her body, anchoring into her bones, adrenaline surging through her spine, her stomach. Were they talking about the postcard? Stella heaved herself up. Dianne and Malmuria looked at her. A crow flew overhead croaking, several small birds following it, diving, attacking. And still this young woman, this Mal, would not stop.

I know who you are. You need to talk to me. You need to let me know what it is you have. We need to stop them. I'll go the whole wide world to figure this out.

Over the Mountain to Seabury Gorge.

Then

IT'S POURING RAIN IN the morning, so Cynthia does not come for the bike ride. Stella listens to the public radio station, all news and classical music and radio drama shows. She tries to sketch the garden view, but it's blurry from the rain smeared against the window. She does crossword puzzles. Her head doesn't hurt. Maybe she's pushing her luck, Stella thinks. Down in the kitchen, she looks through the old recipe books, looks at the commonplace book, empty with nothing written on the thick, yellowed paper. She sits at the kitchen table and tries to sketch on the old pages, but her pencil won't work on the paper. The lead smudges on her fingers and falls from the page in grey dust. Stella gently shakes the old book over the floor, wondering if anything will fall out but nothing does, only the whisper of the pages rubbing together.

Stella places the book back on the shelf. She knows what a commonplace book is because her mother once called her father's notebook a *scrapbook*. It was *not* a scrapbook, he proclaimed, but a *working research book*, in the grand scholarly tradition of the commonplace book, which dated back to ancient times and continued right to present day. He was a modern practitioner. Her father had said his commonplace book was a historical receptacle for knowledge gathered by an expert. Her mother said a scrapbook was the exact same thing. Stella can't remember how the fight ended. But this *Commonplace Book of the Offing Society* is a collection of nothing but empty pages.

Her father is reading for his classes. His *prep*, he calls it. Stella doesn't understand his work any more than she understands Frank's. Her father spends his prep time mostly flipping through books, making notes, typing and typing and typing. He's preparing his lectures, he says. Finishing up his paper for the conference. He's also preparing slides, and at night projects images on the wall in the living room, images of the postcards he has of old buildings and people in old-fashioned clothes and uniforms, patients in lawn chairs that remind Stella of deck chairs from the *Titanic*.

After lunch, the rain stops and the sun comes out, transforming the world into glimmering brightness. A thick rainbow stretches over Seabury like a handle, the village a miniature world in a basket. Frank calls and invites them up for an early supper. Stella hears her father offer to pick up Cynthia and Granny. But Granny isn't up for it, Stella gathers, and Frank has already arranged for Tommy to bring Cynthia.

The meadows are full of orange, yellow and purple flowers as Stella and her father drive up the Mountain to Frank's grand country home.

"It isn't really a mountain," Stella's father says, "but the tail end of the Appalachian range. The Seaburys live just beyond the highest elevation on a sprawling property of five hundred acres that includes the dramatic Seabury Gorge. I guess Frank needs his privacy when he's not working, which is not very often."

He waits for Stella to reply from the passenger seat, as he would with an adult companion. Stella resents this adult role he wishes to cast her in. Stella doesn't answer. She rolls the window all the way down and looks at the scenery. She imagines them in a postcard, the red car on a bumpy old road, an older man wearing thick glasses gripping the steering wheel, his mouth open, a girl looking out the window, serious, her short hair undulating around her face, no smile, just a direct gaze at the photographer.

The view is everything to Stella.

"Eastward down the bay, about a three-hour drive from here, you can see Parker Island, dear, where your grandmother was from, where the Llewellyns kept the light. It is abandoned now, uninhabited, with swirling mists and rugged barrier beaches, dangerous cliffs, riptides."

The ride becomes instantly smooth as they turn onto a newly paved black driveway with a grand gate, open, security cameras on either side. It's more a road wending through the trees. The house appears. Stella's father lets up on the gas and the car slows almost to a stop as they gawk at the massive modern home. He whistles and puts his head back. The car isn't moving but it seems to Stella that the concrete house looms closer, black columns on either side of the front door. She rubs her eyes, which have begun to prickle. This structure at first seems a fortress, but the more she looks at it, the more it is a castle, from the old times when a castle *was* a fortress. This is Frank's domain, his summer palace, where he conducts his business, grants favours and extols payment, delivers punishments and rewards. The house presses in upon her. Stella shakes her head and looks down at her fingernails. When did she start biting them? She looks up at the waiting house.

CYNTHIA IS TO BE the official tour guide while the men have drinks on the front deck. Stella listens as Cynthia sucks in a deep breath:

"It-was-built-by-some-rich-guy-from-Europe-who-lived-in-a-castle.He-died-in-a-mysterious-plane-crash."

She takes another breath and lets it out, and then another, and paces herself. "May I present the door to Daddy's office — off limits. And the dining room, all set for dinner; the den with the creepy black leather furniture — imported from Italy; and a wing of guest bedrooms — off limits, to keep them guest-ready. Here's the hallway lined with paintings, none by my mother because my father can't stand paintings of flowers and disturbing children. You can see why I prefer my Granny Scotia's house."

Down another hallway lined with photographs and paintings of beaches and lakes and forests in modern frames and leading back to a sweeping circular staircase with one picture at the top of the stairs watching over all, a long-time-ago man with thin severe lips and thin dark brows and strange blue eyes.

"That's another of the original Seaburys. Friendly looking, don't you think?" Cynthia claps her hands together and bends over laughing at her own joke. Stella laughs too and follows Cynthia down yet another hall. "Granny says she had to marry to keep the Cedar Grove in the family. She wasn't sad when her husband died. She only told me that this spring. Granny says that a storm is coming. She can feel it inside, that her blood is rising, her muscles are quivering. I know... like, totally strange."

Cynthia again speaks, in brochure talk. "Please note the special glass ceiling in this area and the eighteenth-century chairs, imported from England. A gift from a friend of Mr. Seabury who lives in New York. He's rich as shit. They knew each other at Columbia. Note the identical chair in the opposing alcove. And note the original Maud Lewis painting. See the blooming trees in the winter? *Who is Maud Lewis*, you might be wondering, seeing as you're from away. Well, she was a folk artist who painted with house paint, on every frigging thing in her tiny house and on boards and tins and stuff. She's dead, and her crazy husband, who my father remembers, is now dead, and her house sits empty. It's a work of art in itself, Mrs. Sarah Seabury says, but it's abandoned and falling in. Sarah Seabury, famous painter who summered in the Mercy River watershed region, was acquainted with Mrs. Lewis. Her friends and family called her Sally, just as friends and family of Mrs. Lewis called her Maudie. The two artists used to discuss painting technique, although Mrs. Lewis had a wholly unique technique due to her severe arthritis and her chain-smoking. Mrs. Sally Seabury abandoned her family, her own daughter, and went to Florida."

Cynthia curtsies perfecty and bows her head. Stella misses Cynthia's mother and she's never even met her. She misses all moms. She can't tell if Cynthia misses her own mother. She always goes along with everything.

They are in Cynthia's bedroom now. "Cynthia has an ability to *cut through the bullshit*, to call an ace an ace and not a spade, a mermaid a mermaid and not a fish, and to call a lie for what it is. Now, if you'll look over here ... see how Miss Seabury has her very own powder-pink ensuite bathroom with a tub shaped like an oyster shell. And in this closet, look at the clothes Miss Cynthia Seabury has."

"Wow. I only have this kind of stuff." Stella points at her own dress.

"It's very pretty, though you do remind me of some of the old postcards my grandmother has, of old-time girls. But that's a style statement, Stella. It's like ... stellar." Cynthia giggles. She looks pleased when Stella smiles.

"Now, please observe how Cynthia's mother, the famous artist Sally ... I mean Sarah Seabury ... I mean Windsor ... has painted an extensive mural on the walls, a garden scene here, and on the other side, a seascape, with plum and black water with hints of silver. Note the detail on the sandcastle, the exquisite blending of colours in the sunset, the Renaissance influences. You'll notice by the bed the mermaids in the sea on the rocks, a tribute to German expressionism, an early influence. Observe the young girl in the castle, how she looks out to sea."

It's Cynthia painted in the castle, in the most beautiful room Stella has ever seen.

"My mother painted the room herself. Well, I helped her. She said she couldn't have done it without me." Cynthia looks around her bedroom. "I've only ever spent about ten nights in here, if you can believe it.

"We did it when my mother came back from the nuthouse. That's what my father calls it. She went away for a while. I was at boarding school. Did you ever read *Charlotte Sometimes*?"

"Yes!" Stella can't believe Cynthia knows this book too. And that her mother was in a hospital.

"My mother cried all the time and stuff. At least whenever she called me she did. My dad got mad at her. She was scared to bawl in front of him. He hates *bawling*. That's what he calls it. He'd take the phone away and apologize to me and then hang up! 'On behalf of your mother, I apologize to you, Cynthia.' All formal, and stuff.

"My dad can be a humongous asshole, you know. Don't let him fool you. I knew he'd be mad when I dyed my hair and got tattoos. He blamed the school. He's always blaming the wrong people. In the old times, my dad's ancestors had slaves. I bet he misses those days."

Cynthia presents a photograph of her parents together when they were younger. When Frank was younger, Stella thinks. "I know, ginormous age gap. Cradle robber. That's what Granny calls it. Mom got pregnant with me so that's why they got married."

"My mom too. But she was thirty when I was born."

And almost forty-three when she died, Stella thinks.

Frank's voice rolls out of a square beige box on the wall. "Cynthia? Stella? Are you girls in your room? Time for supper...Hello?"

Cynthia crosses her arms and smirks.

"Girls? Cynthia...Stella? I don't know where they are, Billy. That's the trouble with a gigantic house."

Cynthia winks. "Let them worry a bit. We'll just show up. If you want, I can give you some of my clothes that don't fit me anymore. I love your style with those old-time dresses and all, but if you want some things in fashion, it's no problem."

Cynthia puts on a Blondie cassette and shakes her head, singing along with the song "Call Me." The intercom buzzes again and she turns up the music and sings until the song ends. Then she puts in a different cassette. Another song flares out. *Love will tear us apart,* she chants. Cynthia turns off the boom box. "Wow, I feel so much better. That's Joy Division. That song is killer. It's on a mixed tape my boyfriend sent me. Well, he wasn't really my boyfriend. We hung out. At school. Well, he was at a boys' school. My dad keeps taking the tapes away. He's keeping my mail now. It's hard to go against my father."

Back down some halls and around some corners and up and down some stairs, a maze of a house, and then into the dining room where the men are just sitting down.

"Oh, there you are, girls. Didn't you hear me calling for you? I tried every intercom in the house." Frank smiles.

"Sorry, we were having a discussion about art and music."

Frank pours everyone glasses of champagne, even the girls. Stella looks at her father but he seems oblivious, studying the flute rimmed with gold. Frank raises his glass. "Let's have a toast—to new beginnings, to the best of the good old days, to friendship, to family."

Stella's father raises his glass. "To summer in Seabury. Seas the day, get it?" Cynthia erupts in a tinkling laughter as though it's the funniest thing she's ever heard, and Stella's father blushes and tips his head to the side. The good feelings Stella has had about Cynthia drain away as quickly as her father is downing his champagne. Frank pours him another glass. Stella sips her champagne. To her the liquid tastes like rancid ginger ale. The dinner is served by two waiters who bring in food on silver trays, placing one in front of each of them. They set wine bottles on the table by Frank, who samples the wine and smiles his approval, licking his lips. Then they pour wine for everyone, for the girls as well. Stella looks around the table. Her head hurts at the base of her neck. She rubs it and then lifts the lid of the silver tray in front of her. She has no appetite, looking at the bright red lobster, looking back at her like any minute it might leap off the platter and take out her eyes.

After supper, Stella sits in the car waiting for her father to come out. She's sleepy and her mouth tastes sour, probably from the half-glass of wine she managed to sip.

"Stella." Close to her ear.

She jumps. It's Frank in the window in the lavender dusk. The sky is bright behind him but his face is in shadow. Stella can smell wine and garlic on his breath. "Your father will be right out. The chef is putting together a care package for you to take home. I know it's been hard for you two but we'll help. That's what Seaburys do. Your grandfather drank all his money away and it made it so hard on the Spragues. Did your father tell you it was my uncle who paid for him to go to university?"

Stella shakes her head.

"It's nothing to be ashamed of. He'd help me out if I needed anything. It must be déjà vu for him being back here. Maybe on Labour Day weekend I can take you girls away for a few days and give him a break. I bet he'd love to go on a solo fishing trip. Let's keep our chat to ourselves, Stella. The Seaburys are here for you, okay?" He leans into the window and Stella can smell the alcohol on his breath as he speaks in a low voice: "Put your seat belt on, Stella. We don't want you to get hurt. No car accidents or anything of that sort."

STELLA'S BODY IS RIGID as her father drives down the mountain to Seabury, weaving back and forth over the centre line. He seemed sober enough when he came out to the car, calling out to her just as Frank was about to say something else.

Drunk as a lord, Stella hears her mother say in her mind. She doesn't want to blubber and distract her father from driving. She remembers being in the car that night in the early spring. She wants to banish that memory but she can't. Her mother went to the library every Tuesday night for a book club, her alone time. But that night Stella had begged to go. She had books to return, books to take out. She would entertain herself. She loved the local library and she was twelve years old going on thirteen. Her father, oddly, didn't want her to go. He kept insisting she stay home with him. And this made her mother insist Stella go with her. Stella recollects sitting beside her mother, putting on her seat belt. Her mother had just permed her black hair — Stella recalls the chemical smell, then the sound of her mother twiddling with the radio knob. Music. It was dusk. Grey. It was raining. *Stella's fault for wanting to go to the library.* She thinks her father said this sometime after the accident. Maybe Stella had said it to herself. She closes her eyes and doesn't open them until they stop in their own driveway.

That night Stella brushes her teeth and looks in the mirror. She thinks about déjà vu. The doctor told her it can happen after a brain injury, that it isn't magic. It doesn't mean she's crazy. He didn't use that word. He said it doesn't mean she's *losing her mind*. But she hasn't had déjà vu. Her father never seems to have been in complete possession of his mind. Rather, his mind seems to possess him. Stella's face tenses. Her cheeks and jaws twitch. Grief attacking her, taking possession of her bones and flesh, squeezing her heart. Her mouth fills with spit and the room spins. Like father like daughter. Her shoulders ache from bracing herself in the car. Her father shouldn't have driven home. He had too much to drink but so did everybody. Whenever he talked to Stella, he would look at her and then steer in that direction.

She leans on the sink and catches her breath. Stella looks at her thin face, her red eyes, her straggly short hair. She needs a trim to even it out. She needs a mother. She washes her face with cold water. Then she notices a few drops of dark brownish-red blood on the floor. Stella pulls up her nightie, but the bandage is still on. There is blood dripping down her leg. She spreads her legs and bends over, and pulls her panties to the side, trying to see, but then she is dizzy and grabs at the wall. She balls up some toilet paper and wipes gingerly between her legs. It's coming from inside her. From her vagina. Stella has started her period.

Stella cleans herself with more toilet paper, so she can flush the evidence away. She has no idea how she can talk to her father about this. She'll have to talk to Cynthia or Granny. Stella folds up a face cloth and puts it in a clean pair of underwear. It seems to be staying put. She puts her soiled panties at the back of the closet with her stained dress. She doesn't know how to use a washing machine. She doesn't even know if there is a washing machine. She realizes she hasn't looked in the cellar yet. She'll offer to do their laundry. She's sure her father will agree.

She slips downstairs and her father is in his study with a beer. He's staring at an old map of Nova Scotia. He's also smoking, something he gave up years ago, but has been doing more and more since they came to Seabury.

"Dad, how about I do some laundry?" She realizes her father knows nothing about her wardrobe or her underwear situation. He has no idea of what a twelve-almost-thirteen-year-old needs.

He blinks slowly a few times. Stella sees he's still drunk. "That's a good idea. I'll get some laundry soap. There's a washer in the cellar but no dryer. You'll have to use the clothesline. We'll have to get you a winter coat, and some boots."

"When the moving truck comes, I'll have my winter clothes, Dad. They'll still fit me. Mom always bought things a size up. And Cynthia says she'll give me some of her clothes. You should see her closet. It's packed. She doesn't even wear most of it, she says."

Stella's father is grateful for the small talk. "I'm sorry about tonight. I guess we got carried away. I'll be up to tuck you in."

Stella hovers by the door.

"Yes, Stella? What is it?"

"Can you call the moving company again?"

He sips his beer. "Sure, Little Bear. I'll do that first thing tomorrow. Now get to bed."

Stella falls asleep waiting for her father to tuck her in. She dreams she is in a boat on a placid sea, the surface reflecting the sky. She runs her fingers through the clouds in the water but they aren't a reflection and they come out of the water on her fingers, strange seaweed, clouds that exist in the sky and in the water. There is a splash and she looks to the horizon, where the sky and the water merge. The ocean sky ripples in the distance and the undulating clouds reach the boat. Stella sees something, someone, in the water, swimming, someone down deep but coming up. The surface breaks and through the sky and clouds of the water pops out a wet head, closed eyes — and the eyes open. It is her mother, and she smiles at Stella, who starts weeping and reaches for her. Catriona cries but her tears are black pearls. She reaches out to Stella and their fingers almost touch, but Catriona slips below the surface and Stella is alone in the boat that floats on the rippling sky.

The Poet and the Podcaster.

Now

THIS TIME MAL WALKED through the front doors of the Jericho County Care Centre and went to the front desk. She pumped the hand sanitizer on the counter as she waited by the Plexiglas screen. Not that there had been anyone outside when she arrived—the bench where the old lady was sitting last time, empty. She asked for Grace Belliveau. It was simple, and Mal wished she had done this the first time, instead of acting on her nerves and speaking to the old lady. The young guy at the desk put the phone down. "I can't reach her. Do you want me to page her?"

"Yes, that would be awesome." Mal smiled, waiting for him to ask her name but he didn't.

He pressed a button on the phone and Grace's name came out over the loudspeaker. Mal wondered what it would be like to live in a place where there were announcements and pages. She couldn't imagine. There was a sign reminding visitors not to shake hands or hug, and not to take photos or videos anywhere on the premises.

Then Grace was at the desk, smiling as she came over to Mal. They didn't shake hands. Grace was friendly but reserved, her smile thin but sincere. Grace, unlike Mal, was not reckless.

"Hi. You were looking for me?"

"Yes, I'm doing some research. Jillian at the historical society said you worked here. I'm hoping you can help me. I was driving by and just thought I'd . . . stop in." Mal knew this sounded ludicrous. But she hadn't called for fear Grace would refuse to speak to her. Mal didn't mention meeting the old lady with the clicking teeth, or her encounter with Dianne or Stella. She had the good sense to keep this from Grace. It would look like she was interrogating the residents without having gone through the official channels—exactly what she had done.

"My name is Mal. I'm a journalist and I'm working on a story about an international company with ties to rural Nova Scotia. I was hoping you could help put me in touch with Stella Sprague. I believe she lives here."

Grace stopped smiling. "I can't discuss residents, Mal. And in order to speak to Stella you would have to talk to her guardian. And that would involve contacting the Department of Community Services."

"But doesn't she have any relatives?" Mal realized she hadn't even given this woman her full name, or said where she was working. "I was talking to a friend of hers, Seraphina?"

Grace laughed and then quickly composed herself. "Ah, yes, Seraphina. Well, I would take everything she says right now with a grain of salt. How do you know her?"

It came out of her mouth before she could think of something professional to say. "Her mother was friends with my mother . . . when they were kids . . . a long time ago."

"Oh, so you're from here?" Grace's voice was professional and controlled, but curious.

"No, but my mother was, from outside of Bigelow Bay. Look, I just need to talk to Stella, to figure out her connection to Mercy Lake. I found an article in the paper."

"I guess you should do more research, if you're a journalist." Grace's tone was more maternal now, patient, with Mal so obviously unsure of what she was doing.

"I'm not literally a journalist." Mal handed Grace a business card. And as soon as she did, she wanted to take it back. *Under the Arbor*, it said. *Stories of Mental Health. Malmuria Grant-Patel.*

Grace glanced at the card and put it in her pocket. She smiled as Mal poured out her story, how she wanted to talk to Stella Sprague, and hoped to speak to Stella about her father, because he was in the *Fellows United* newspaper article with Franklin Seabury.

"People are a tad paranoid about visitors, from the whole COVID-19 thing. I'm sure you understand. If you want to speak with Stella, you would need to talk to the head nurse, and her social worker. But it would probably be hard. And I'm not sure Stella can help you. She doesn't even talk." Grace put her hand to her mouth as if to stop the words. "Look, I can't discuss her, okay, Mal?" Her voice was guarded, but still kind.

Mountain Top.

Now

IT WAS SUNNY AS Eugene drove Stella across the Valley and up the South Mountain, the ditches full of asters and brown-eyed Susans.

The road was bendy, rolling up and down. Eugene did most of the talking on the drive. He told Stella about various living options. Staying at the Jericho Centre, of course. And group homes such as Mountain Top. Or an alternative family support program, where a person could live in a private family home, as Dianne had done with Sorcha. Stella's stomach lifted up and then down as Eugene finally turned left into the drive-way of an old home painted green with white trim. There was a sign, *Mountain Top*, and off to the side in the lawn, a circular garden with a glider swing in the middle with two tired-looking middle-aged ladies sitting on it, rocking back and forth, back and forth.

Stella thought of Dianne at the centre, sleeping in her chair.

Dianne had been wandering the halls at night, on lookout, she explained to the staff. Stella knew this was because the woman had come and terrified them on the lawn. Yesterday? Last week?

Stella had been at work on the English country garden puzzle after lunch, putting together an elegant gazebo beside a rose garden. She had an eye for colour and patterns, and enjoyed puzzles. This one had two thousand pieces. Stella had just put another piece of the puzzle in place when Nurse Calvin summoned her with a snap of her fingers. She stood up and looked at the clock over the door. It was 1:45 p.m. She lost track of time when she did puzzles, and her mind emptied out. She thought about the riddle of Isaiah, wondering where he was, why no one would tell her. And the woman who had appeared on the lawn the day before. It was hard to remember. Cat padded into the room and jumped up onto a chair beside Dianne where it sat, flicking its tail.

Eugene had fiddled with his watch, as he always did when he was frustrated. They went into the meeting room behind the nurse's station and sat down, Stella at one side of the table, Eugene across from her, and Nurse Calvin beside him. He told her Mountain Top had called and there was a room available she could see today.

Stella had watched Nurse Calvin cross her arms.

"You don't have to make a decision. We'll be the ones to decide that."

"That's not how patient rights work, Pauline." Stella could tell Eugene didn't want another confrontation.

"If you ask me, not that you bother, it's all about rights these days. She can't make a decision to help herself. She can hardly remember what day it is. But she has *rights*."

STELLA AND EUGENE WENT in the front door. It looked like a house but the staircase was closed in and it smelled of institution, like the Jericho Centre — cleaning fluids, floor polish, air freshener. But it was supposed to be a home. The smell was all wrong here. A glowing exit sign stuck out from the wall, like at the centre. A framed list of fire escape procedures was on the wall beside a fire extinguisher in a case beside pictures of cats and sunsets, the smell of banana bread coming from the kitchen. She wanted to go back to the centre, walk with Dianne out to the river. To check her room, the bookshelf, to find Cat. These people didn't understand what home was to her — it was Dianne. Dianne was her family. And her routine.

Stella rubbed her hands together as they waited. A lady with dyed red hair and grey roots came to the office door and shook Stella's hand. "I'm Lenore," she said, smiling. "It's nice to meet you, Stella. I think you'll enjoy living here."

Eugene patted Stella's shoulder. "If you want to. We're just taking a look, right, Stella?"

They took Stella upstairs to see the room, with a western exposure. Lenore pointed at the beds. "You would only have one roommate, Stella. Her name's Ruth. She's away visiting her brother for a few days."

Ruth's side of the room was very neat. She had a bed with a quilt made of different blue fabrics and a bedside table and a rocking chair. There was a bookshelf full of books on embroidery and the wall by her bed was covered in framed embroidered pictures of country houses and gardens and seaside views.

Lenore spread her arms out. "You should see this view on a clear day. All the way down the Valley to Mercy River, almost to Seabury by the Sea."

Stella started panting. She needed to get back to Dianne. Dianne might have woken up. Maybe Nurse Calvin would spirit her away to the old folks' home while Stella was out, no goodbyes. And maybe the woman in the yellow dress was right, that someone was watching them. *You are being watched. Be careful.* Stella rocked from one foot to the other and back again, wringing her hands, looking up at the ceiling and down at the floor. She wanted her brain to work now, for all the shells to open up, for the memories to spill out, dark pearls each with a story. She must remember. It was imperative. Her body was telling her it was. She believed her body. Her brain had to co-operate. The hippocampus on either side of her head had to work. The seahorses needed to swim— they had to guide her.

Lenore tapped her on the shoulder and Stella jumped back.

"Oh, sorry, dear. I didn't mean to startle you. Why don't we go down to the kitchen and have a piece of banana bread, Stella. A few of our residents made it this morning. We do a lot of home cooking here. Everyone has chores. It's quite independent. I think you'll enjoy it."

In the kitchen, Eugene took a piece of banana bread. Stella shook her head.

A thin man came in and he patted his hands together. His head was balding on the top and his pants were pulled up very high, right up to his ribs, and held there with a tightly cinched thin black belt with a silver buckle. He was wearing a green bow tie.

"This is Charlie. He's lived here for ten years. He dresses up every day." Charlie paid no attention to Stella. He wanted some banana bread. A worker came in behind him.

"This is Stella. Stella, this is David Jessome. He just started here last week. He's a brand-new volunteer. He's working with Charlie mostly in the evenings, on literacy. Charlie goes out most mornings to work at the wood shop in the community."

David was older and short, with watery blue eyes. He put his hand out to shake Stella's but she looked down at her banana bread, her feet cold and tingling.

"Nice to meet you, Stella. We've all been looking forward to meeting you. I hear you appreciate nature."

She wondered who had told him this. Jessome. She knew this name. From Seabury. Her eyes shut, and then opened. David Jessome still there, holding out his hand. She closed and opened her eyes again. He was still there. "Stella, are you okay." David looked concerned. "Would you like a drink? Some fruit juice?"

Eugene assumed Stella needed a washroom. "Lenore, where's the washroom?"

Lenore pointed down the hall.

An automatic fan screeched on in the bathroom with the light. A framed *mandatory hand-washing* sign hung by the mirror. Stella sat on the toilet. Her stomach was hard. She needed to eat prunes. To eat broccoli. Some blood on her panties. Stella balled up toilet paper and put it in her underwear, washing her bloody hands in the sink.

Laughter from the kitchen. Stella walked the other way, to the exit sign at the side door. In the back garden, which sprawled into the woods, she found only one person in a gazebo, a withered woman with wiry carmel hair. She smiled at Stella. "Hello, dear. Ruth's roommate passed away. One day she was up and then the next day she was down for good. It was the coronavirus, that's what I think. I'm Delores. Have a seat. Lots of cardinals this year."

A bird shrilled out. Stella jumped.

"I used to be at the centre. They put me here so I wouldn't run away. David Jessome just started. He doesn't seem to have much experience. Says he wants to work at the Jericho Centre. He's from California. Listen to the birds."

The woman almost seemed normal, except that her conversation just looped around and around. Dianne would be so worried. Maybe they could go live with Sorcha. But Sorcha was not at home. That's right, she was in the hospital, Stella remembered. She decided to call Isaiah when she got home but she couldn't even talk to him on the phone. He would know from the silence who it was. She could tap.

Stella hurried down the gazebo steps and her sandal caught. She fell down and the bloody toilet paper squished out from her underpants. Stella lay there weeping in the sweet-smelling grass dense with late-summer clover.

The Fellowship.
Inscrutable Houses.
The Last of the Bohemians.
Then

WHEN CYNTHIA BOUNCES IN the door in the morning, Stella is shocked to see her father hurry out from his study. He is all smiles as he greets Cynthia. "Cynthia, so good to see you. Stella's so happy to have you here."

Stella knows her father is the happy one. Her fingers curl into fists. She doesn't want to share Cynthia with her father, and she doesn't want to share her father with Cynthia. She needs them both. But separately.

As they ride their bikes towards Cedar Grove, Stella thinks about how Cynthia must be used to people, including her friends' fathers, fawning over her. She doesn't blush or giggle. At thirteen Cynthia looks more like sixteen, with breasts. Even her teased goth hair shimmers, the opposite of Stella's short dull wisps. It would be easy to believe Cynthia is trying to diminish her, but Stella knows this isn't true. Stella's spirit just *ebbs* so quickly — it is her natural state of being now.

They stop because Cynthia says she's out of breath but she's not winded at all. She's being kind. Stella is the winded one. Stella hates Cynthia for being kind. She wants her to be mean so she can feel justified in hating her. Stella's hip burns and her elbow stings. The face cloth between her legs is heavy now, her crotch itchy. Stella sees Cynthia watching her wiggling, shifting from foot to foot, blushing. Stella heaves out her words: "It's the bike seat. I'm not used to this sort of bike seat. And my mother and I mostly walked."

"Well, we can walk, if you want to. It doesn't matter to me, Stella. We have all the time in the world." It's true — she doesn't mind either way. She's always so accommodating. And they do have all the time in the world. Home-schooling will start with Granny in September, no formal routines, no mothers to report to. No mothers to keep a cautious eye. Cynthia seems to know what Stella is thinking without Stella even having to ask. For a moment Stella thinks this is what it is to have a sister. Stella is conscious of how her teeny breasts poke out of her T-shirt as she pants. She doesn't even need clothes anymore, covered as she is in a cloak of self-consciousness, shame and regret. Stella also knows

232 | Christy Ann Conlin

that her intelligence is as much a curse as it is a blessing. Stella should *keep it sweet*.

Stella points to the sidewalk at the stones. "What are those?"

Cynthia kneels down by the paving stones, her bike leaning against the stop-sign post. She traces the stone markers with her finger. "I don't know exactly. They've been here since forever. Street markers or something, before they had street signs. We can ask Granny. They're left over from the old days. There were lots of freaky things in those days." Cynthia is now whispering. "Our forefathers all went to this old-time men's club—a fellowship, is what Granny says they called it. First it was religious: the Sodality of Fire and Mercy. Now they just say *Sodality*. It's some weird men's group. You know how they like to get together and talk about all that man stuff. That's how my father knows Tommy Jessome and those guys from out of town. I know your dad's a historian and all, but maybe he didn't tell you. There was someone associated with it who took people's money. For business favours or something. And he wouldn't let people get vaccinations and a lot of the children died. He sold them what my grandmother calls snake oil. He used to preach down by the harbour on the Main Street on Friday nights. Granny Scotia said his personality was the size of Texas. He squandered their money and killed their children with his quackery. He made people beholden to him. That was the problem. Granny says he ruined my grandfather and your grandfather, that they were around him too much when they were younger, that he brainwashed them, poured rum into them. The men's group was kind of like the Masons or the Rosicrucians. Did you have those in Ohio?"

"There was a Masonic Temple. My father said it was stupid."

"Well, it's all gone now. My dad's a member of a men's group, but they raise money for charity and stuff like that."

THE HOUSE SMELLS DELICIOUS inside. The girls hear faint music down the hallway, in the back parlour. There is a dark rectangular cake on the kitchen table, cooling. They find Granny sleeping in the parlour, the music loud now, Handel's *Messiah*, the room partially decorated for Christmas. *Yule.* Cynthia's voice is a whisper. "That's what Granny Scotia calls it. *Yule.*" Cynthia presses her lips together, her eyes azure pools, a gust of something over the surface, stirring the water, a tear trickling down her cheek. They take down the decorations and turn the music off. Granny doesn't wake up.

In the kitchen, Stella helps Cynthia make sandwiches. While they're eating they hear Granny coming down the hall. She stands in the doorway. "Goodness me, I dozed off. I was going to make you girls dinner and I sat down to wait, and next thing you know, it's a hundred years later, and here I am, an old lame crone of a woman." Granny seems normal. She doesn't mention the Christmas decorations. She gives a snort and crosses the room to put the kettle on for tea. Stella clears the table and takes the china plates across to the old sink. Granny gasps. "Did you hurt yourself, Stella?"

Stella looks down. Coming out from under her dress is a trickle of blood. She leans over the sink and a tear smacks down on the worn porcelain. She's sore and sticky. Her hip still burns. Granny puts her hand on her back. "My dear, I think you've started your cycle. The Red Lady. Not to worry, my dear, not to worry. You'll get to know her and miss her when she eventually leaves you. Cynthia, do you have anything she can use?"

Outside the downstairs washroom Cynthia hands Stella a black washcloth and a pad and a clean pair of purple underpants. "Use these. Just hang the cloth on the towel rack. Don't worry, okay? It happens to us all. I got my period when I was almost twelve, last year. I was swimming. It was totally embarrassing and so grody and I almost barfed. Total humiliation."

When Stella comes outside they don't say anything to her about it. Granny rubs her head and gives her a glass of frosty lemonade.

They go for a walk through the marsh, over a footpath to a sandy beach. They stop by a plaque on a post, which Cynthia reads out loud:

Seabury Marsh: A Restored Wetland
*This pathway stands on an old dike built by French
saulniers, or salt marsh workers, in the early 1600s.
The marsh was later drained and used for pastures and
hayfield. The land was donated to the Town of Seabury
in 1970 through the generosity of the Seabury Family and
Cineris International.*

Then Cynthia leads them to the beach. Stella takes off her shoes. Granny Scotia is already barefoot and she's standing out in the water.

Cynthia waits for Stella.

"Is this the salt water cure, Cynthia?"

She giggles. "No, we're just standing in the water. You'll know the salt water cure when it happens."

It's all very cryptic. Stella thinks of when she was a child at the beach with her mother. A group of adults with tie-dye T-shirts and beads and long hair were smoking by the food stand. "The last of the hippies," her mother said. "I was a bohemian, not a hippie. There is a difference. Hippies aren't intellectuals." Stella hadn't known what her mother was talking about except that her mother told her she'd spent a year in Paris. Stella thought Paris must be full of bohemians.

Cynthia takes Stella's hand and they walk out in the water to join Granny, who stands with her face raised and her eyes closed, the warm sun soaking her old skin.

The sea is surprisingly warm and the sand under Stella's feet oddly firm.

"You see, Stella, life is about cycles. You've changed now, even though you might not know it. But I think you do. No girl should have to lose her mother so young. And now here you are, in a strange land with strange people, and your body is releasing blood. We women have to teach each other these things. You have us now, my dear. You've come home. This means you're a woman even though you are still very much a girl, both things at once, as we all are . . . as we all were. And you must be very careful, my dear. It's a strange magic that comes about when we bleed, when we come to that time. You're just at the beginning and I'm at the end, my cycle now completing." Granny opens her eyes and gazes out over the sea.

Stella glances at Cynthia but she too is looking out over the water. Stella isn't afraid, but she observes that they are not like anyone else she has ever known. They talk like people in a storybook. And just thinking about a book brings on a headache, or maybe it's the sun, or not enough water. Stella doesn't know. Granny turns to her. "We need to keep this between us. We don't want your father to feel uncomfortable. God help the man, but he has no idea. Or maybe he does. That's the problem — I'm unable to discern."

STELLA PUTS HERSELF TO bed. She wakes up in the dark. She can't have been asleep for long. She's not sure. Stella's body wants her to go back to sleep, but her mind wants her to wake up. Her head is so heavy as she turns it on the pillow. A slant of light falls in on the floor through her slightly opened bedroom door, the pale green floor seeming to glow. Stella hears her father's voice. The cast iron register in the floor is open, the louvres flicked back for ventilation. Is her father on the hall phone? Or maybe he's talking to someone in the house... that's it, he's talking to someone in the kitchen... a low voice, "I see, yes, yes, I see, I hear you, I understand, it's so hard, okay, yes... so difficult being a father." The low voice reassures her father that it will get easier, that they'll all help, that Cynthia and Granny will all help, and time will pass and things will get better, once he's started his new job. He should go on a trip for Labour Day weekend. They can take care of Stella. He should think about it.

Violette. Stella thinks of flowers in her sleepy mind. *Violette drowned.* Stella sees rippling ebony water. *Mercy Lake. Merciless...* Her father's voice. Frank's voice. *You can't blame me, William. You aren't an innocent. I'm sorry for your loss but you can't change the past. Or reimagine it. Old pal, you need to toughen up. It's a lot of money but we can work something out.* Frank's voice, firm. Her father sobbing now but Stella still not able to wake up, not able to surface in her room. Below her exhaustion her brain hurts and insists she let it slip away into the darkness.

An owl hoots and the wind blows. Stella thinks of "Sestina," the poem her mother used to recite to her and she drifts off thinking of inscrutable houses and old-fashioned stoves and the little girl she used to be.

Charlotte Pacific.
The Art Gallery of Nova Scotia.

Now

THEY WERE ON THEIR way to Halifax in the Jericho Centre minibus. Dianne sat in the very back with Stella, looking out the window the whole way there, reaching out her hand and feeling Stella beside her, patting her and then pulling her hand away, reassured. Stella knew Dianne was happy to be away from the centre. If anyone was watching them, it might trick them. Grace wasn't there because it was her staycation.

Fred was of course sitting in the middle, beside Charlotte Pacific, who had arrived the day before. Bob was on Fred's other side, looking out the window. Karen, the yoga teacher, drove, the passenger seat beside her empty. She was picking up extra work because of staff vacations. No other residents had wanted to go to the city on a hot summer afternoon. Fred was bouncing on his seat. "Charlotte Pacific is here. She's here. Here, here here."

Charlotte patted him on the cheek and Fred settled, putting his head on her shoulder.

Stella found it hard to keep track of the days now that the Unscheduled Outing had bumped the weekly schedule. She turned her hands over and over and over, water wheels. *Where was Isaiah? Who was watching them? What did that young woman in the yellow dress want? Why did her head hurt all the time now, whenever she tried to think about the past? Why was her brain not helping her?*

Karen and Charlotte let them wander through the gallery at their own pace. It was air-conditioned inside and Stella wished she had brought her yellow sweater.

The number of paintings was overwhelming. Stella worried she might see something by Sally Seabury. Or rather, *Sarah Windsor.* Maybe a series of paintings that explored her guilt at having left her daughter behind, at how her own mid-life crisis had blocked out the danger awaiting young girls. Stella rubbed her ears. A rattle in her head, a sloshing sound. She stopped looking at the walls and followed Dianne, who looked left and right, and left and right, on the watch as they walked through the gallery. Dianne led them to the lower level, to the Maud Lewis House. Stella stopped. Shivers rippled up her neck. She knew this house. A soft click in her mind, the gentle rattle of a shell as it opened a fraction. She did know this house. But not like this. Here it was rebuilt and on display, not faded and rotting as when Stella first glimpsed it from a car window when she was almost thirteen years old.

Stella rubbed her neck and her temples. She recalled passing this house, when it was an *abandoned* house, standing shakily where it was built, a shack surrounded by weeds, not this perfect restoration without a hint of the decay or sadness that it encapsulated all those years ago on the drive to Mercy Lake.

Stella needed to sit down. She was trembling, shaking, her mouth filled with drool. This house had come to life. It had been saved. Restored. Vibrant once more. People had remembered Maud—not just her art, but where she lived and worked.

Charlotte came into the room and sat beside her. She took Stella's small cold hand. Charlotte's sapphire ring sparkled in the precise gallery lighting. "There, there, Stella," she said. "Oh, my dear girl, we all get older, and the days come back to us as they were. All we can do now is try to make sense of them, of what was. I know it's so hard for you with your memory, a whole life closed away. Why don't you show me your sketchbook? I used to draw myself. Did Fred tell you that?"

Stella took her sketchbook from her backpack. Only Grace and Dianne had ever looked at it before. She held it out and Charlotte carefully took it in her hands. "Oh, Stella, what an honour. I know what it's like to show sketches and doodles to someone. Dear, I can't tell you how much this means to me."

Charlotte's voice was low and quiet. She spoke slowly as she turned the pages. Stella hadn't realized how many pages were blank, how often she sketched only with her fingertip, drawing flowers and birds, rivers and skies only she could see. But Charlotte lingered over even the blank pages. "Yes, Stella, sometimes it's the spaces in between, isn't it? That's where we say the most."

Stella smiled and rested her head on Charlotte's shoulder. Charlotte briefly stroked Stella's hair and turned the page. "Now, look at these roses. They are absolutely baroque. You do have an eye, my dear. Look at these waves. Something just below the surface? What is it, we ask? Does the artist know? Has she left us guessing, or was she herself not sure what resided beneath the gleaming surface?"

Stella sat up and leaned her head back against the wall. She was calmer now, her breathing slow, the drool swallowed down, her mouth dry. Charlotte was absorbed in Stella's ferns and petals, the night sky, the sea in starlight, people around a beach fire. Stella didn't remember drawing this, these people on the shore.

The gallery was quiet. The air reminded Stella of libraries, the scent of wood and oil. She could hear an etching, the soft sound of lead on paper. Charlotte was drawing. It was Stella on the page, her head against the wall, her eyes closed, hands folded in her lap.

"I haven't drawn a single line, Stella, not since I became Charlotte. It's as though the cartoonist I was, when I was living as a man, hasn't joined me. Or if she has, that she hasn't made herself known." Charlotte kept drawing, shading, capturing Stella's face in repose. "Just a few simple lines show it all, dear. Especially eyebrows. See how beautifully arched yours are? Always looking a bit surprised, a bit wonderstruck, those marvellous eyes of yours. One dark. One light." There were lines by Stella's eyes, by her mouth. "It's much better to have an expressive face, dear. We carry life with us. Beauty lines, they really are."

Stella was much older on paper than she was in her mind. It was startling. Occasionally Charlotte would reach out and pat Stella's hand, humming as she sketched in Maud's tiny home in the background, the flowers on the walls of the house. And in front of the house was a bench, with an old lady and a middle-aged lady, the old one drawing and the younger one staring straight ahead.

Part 2

The offing was barred by a black bank of clouds, and the tranquil waterway leading to the uttermost ends of the earth flowed sombre under an overcast sky — seemed to lead into the heart of an immense darkness.

—JOSEPH CONRAD,
Heart of Darkness

Aviator Glasses and the Salt Water Cure.

Then

STELLA SOARS OVER THE road beside the marsh on her way to Cedar Grove. She's wearing her father's aviator sunglasses to shield her eyes and brain from .the sun. And for extra protection, an old sunhat. The lenses colour the world a pale violet. On the inside rim of the sunhat was an embroidered name tag, carefully sewn to the straw, the coral satin yellowed now from oil and sweat. *Stella.* Her aunt's. It fit her perfectly. She'd tied it under her chin so it wouldn't blow off. It occurs to Stella that while the straw hat keeps the sun off, it would do nothing if she fell. She feels a gush of anger that her father would point out her lack of athleticism but not even consider the risk she was taking. She wishes she could be more like Cynthia.

She's wearing Cynthia's shorts and T-shirt, and her old training bra. It's easier to ride a bike in modern clothes, easier with her sprouting breasts confined. Stella can't believe she thinks of the clothes as modern, that her parents have shaped her in this way. She giggles. The Stella she is now, the post–Horrible Accident Stella, has a private sense of humour. She doesn't even need Cynthia in front of her leading the way.

And she doesn't need her father, smoking and preparing for his job, the only thing that seems to interest him. This morning when she'd asked him again about the moving truck he admitted he'd forgotten his promise to call and check. He flicked his fingers on his chin. For a second she had wanted to throw up on her father's face, putting all her sadness and disappointment right in his eyes, dripping off his nose.

Stella is tired. The phone had clanged in the middle of the night, waking her. Her father had spoken loudly, oblivious to his sleeping daughter upstairs. Then he had lowered his voice to an absurd almost-shouted whisper. *You have to take her to the hospital? Yes, makes sense to have her checked out . . . hopefully just a spell or some such thing . . . Yes, I'll have Stella go keep Cynthia company in the morning. Yes, yes, I understand. She's old now. No, no, you don't want her going around talking that way, Frankie. I understand.*

As Stella pedals she wonders what it was her father understood. He didn't seem to understand anything but his damn work or where the liquor store was. Stella is braver on her bike outside of town, where there's no traffic. The fields are covered in Queen Anne's lace and purple clover, such a contrast to the stale air of the Sprague house. She hopes her period never comes back. Granny Scotia told her it might come and go for the first year or so, before settling into a cycle. She hopes it simply goes. She doesn't want to be a member of this club, a woman, a grown-up. She doesn't want to be let in on the secrets. Canada geese honk out in the middle of the marsh water. The late-summer goslings are indistinguishable from their parents in appearance now, full grown in body but without any survival skills. They'll migrate in the autumn, Cynthia has said, but right now their parents are teaching them how to fly, life skills. They mate for life, Stella remembers Cynthia saying.

Stella rides down the lane, to the back near the carriage house, and leans her bicycle against the copper beech. To the side of the carriage house there's an expensive-looking black car. It's that Jessome man from the barbeque, the same car that almost ran her over. Stella takes the straw hat off and hangs it on the handlebars. She walks to the house and from the open dining room window she hears loud muffled voices. Stella stands beside the window.

"I told you to go." It's Cynthia, yelling.

"You can't tell me what to do. Who do you think you are, with the disgusting hair? Dressing like a tramp."

Cynthia whimpers. It's Cynthia...whimpering... shrieking.

Stella creeps closer to the window and peers through the heavy grey screen. She can see nothing so she takes off the sunglasses and looks through the screen again, smelling the old house through it, so different than the outside, the smell of goldenrod and asters and clover, the tangy air meandering in off the marsh, from the bay beyond.

Cynthia runs to the back of the dining room but Tommy Jessome is fast behind her, surprisingly nimble for a man with a gut. She almost escapes him but not quite. Her hair is messy. Her face is streaked and smudged with runny black eyeliner. He pushes Cynthia up against the wall and a chair falls over, the crash covering up Stella's gasp. Neither Cynthia nor Tommy move for a second, and then Cynthia starts yelling at him to let her go. Her fear is now rage. She spits in his eyes. He slaps her face, his thick hand thudding and smacking on her young skin, Cynthia screeching. This seems to further enrage him and he pushes her harder against the wall, with his hand around her neck, pushing his body against hers, his stomach keeping a bit of distance between them. Tommy whispers in Cynthia's ear. Stella can't hear what he's saying. The hushed tone ominous, slithering into a hiss. Cynthia lunges to the right but Tommy Jessome pulls on her arm, twisting. She falls and a crystal water glass crashes down behind her. Some bumps and bangs and then Cynthia lurches up. Stella sees bright red blood smeared on Cynthia's arm and watches her pick up a linen napkin from the table.

Tommy pants and puffs. Stella hopes he has a heart attack, that something will intervene and strike him down, but he looms over Cynthia, wheezing and huffing. "Think you're tough, like your old grandmother? Don't you think about telling your father. He'll never believe you. He's busy trying to deal with that senile old woman and your slut of a mother. You say one word, one word, and your dear old Granny Scotia might not do so well, if you get my meaning. She's old now, forgetful. Worrying your father with her goings on. Her mind's out of balance and so is that old, twisted body."

Stella is frozen at the window, her fingers tense on the ledge, as though she's some strange lawn ornament the O'Clearys brought over from Ireland and propped up against the house, some fairy from a thorn tree spying on the humans. Neither of them are talking now, just breathing heavily, Tommy grunting, Cynthia whimpering. Stella wants to run and get her bike but she doesn't want them to hear her. She wants to be back on Sunnyside Drive sitting on a chair on the wide wraparound front verandah with her mother on a summer evening counting fireflies. Stella knows she should start yelling but she's paralyzed. She should ride home as fast as she can and get her father. He'll help Cynthia.

Stella's mouth opens — her body is taking over, her body knowing the moral thing to do, but her mind is not co-operating. Her mind says to run. She pants through her open mouth. She can't make a sound. No words. Nothing but shaking all over.

There is a crash outside from back near the carriage house. Tommy and Cynthia both look towards the window. Stella ducks down. She doesn't know if they've seen her. She runs and grabs her bike and rides around the back way, takes the path to the marsh and then sits on a bench near the water, watching the geese, hiding behind the line of birches and the rustling elephant grass. She's hysterical, gasping for air. She waits on the bench until she sees the geese are missing. When she climbs back on her bike, she sees the hat is still tied to the handlebar, but the aviators are gone. She crams the straw hat on her head and races off. There is a breeze she must lean into and it takes all her energy to keep the bike upright.

The quiet of her grandmother's kitchen calms her, despite the dirty dishes on the counter and the unswept floor, the empty beer cans stacked by the overflowing trash can. She takes her grandmother's apron from the hook in the pantry and puts it on, starts washing the dishes. She doesn't want to be still. Her mother would want her to clean up. Her mother would want her to do the right thing. She will tell her father. Maybe Mr. Jessome is ill...that's it. Maybe sick in the head...like all those people her father obsesses over. But bad sick. Not sad sick. Mean sick. Evil sick. Or just plain bad. Bone that is bad. Bad in his blood. Merciless blood. Not mad but wicked. A brutal monster.

She dries her hands on the apron and knocks on the door to her father's study. No answer. Knocks again. Angry now, she flings open the door. The room is disgusting. The blinds are down, but she can make out overflowing ashtrays, his papers spread out on the desk, a typewriter in the middle, a blank piece of paper in it. Her head is achy. Stella is still wearing the old straw hat and she's so angry with herself. She wants her father to snap out of it, to see she is still Stella, just a different version who has a head injury and has to wear sunglasses to reset her brain but still *his daughter* and that he has to, *he must*, be her father, that she's not even thirteen.

In the kitchen she looks everywhere for a note but he hasn't even bothered. He thinks she's at Cynthia's for the day. He's probably buying more beer. Stella is suffocating on her own fear. She runs upstairs and splashes cold water on her face, looks in the mirror. "Mommy," she cries, seeing only her own face, her strange eyes, the eyes of an aunt she never knew. She cannot imagine the face of either of these women and she can't stop bawling, trembling, these inherited eyes welling with salty tears that drizzle down her cheeks, her nose running. Blood on her lips where she has bitten right through the skin.

STELLA RIDES HER BIKE back to Cedar Grove, taking the marsh trail all the way, avoiding the road. Tommy Jessome's car is gone, but Frank's car is in the driveway close to the house. Her first stop is by the dining room window. The glasses are gone. She looks everywhere. She runs to the back of the house, where she sees her father's rental car.

Stella comes in the side door and up the few stairs, and then down the hall and into the kitchen where Granny is, back home, making tea. She doesn't hear Stella come in. Stella clears her throat and Granny slowly turns. She has a blank face. She blinks. "Stella, darling. You're back. I was so worried. I know you were going to Mercy Lake."

Stella blinks this time. They weren't going to the lake. Granny is confused. Granny's face moves, a current passing through. She rubs her eyes and smiles. "Stella Maris, it's so good to see you. I just had some dizzy spells. Nothing to worry about. Frankie took me to see the doctor. All is well. You go into the front room and see Cynthia. She's lying down. She had her own dizzy spell and took a tumble. She'll be happy to see her best friend."

Stella walks down the hallway to the formal parlour on the north side of the house, shielded by the copper beech outside. Her father stands by a window.

Cynthia rests on a daybed, with a face cloth on her forehead and a white bandage on her arm. Frank sits by

Cynthia, holding her hand. "Stella, we were worried," he says.

Stella's father turns from the window. "Stella," her father says in a stern voice, "I thought I told you to come over and keep Cynthia company. She called Frank's assistant after she fell and cut her arm. Tommy drove all the way out and took her to the hospital. He called Frank. And Frank called me from the hospital. Cynthia was asking for you." He keeps lecturing her in front of everyone. Stella bites her sore lip and it starts bleeding again.

"If you want me to trust you, you have to do what I say. You need to take some responsibility here, Stella. You're not a little girl anymore."

Stella is speechless. She can't tell them what she saw, because clearly Cynthia is hiding the truth. She is afraid of Jessome, of what he'll do.

"Why don't you go help my mother, Billy?" Frank kisses Cynthia's hand. Stella's father leaves the room.

Cynthia is relaxed. She's even smiling. They gave her painkillers. "I am so clumsy these days. And I broke a piece of Granny's good crystal, in the family for generations, and then I smash it . . . just like that. I was rushing."

It shocks Stella how utterly convincing Cynthia's deception is. She even wonders if what she saw was real, if maybe her head injury has affected her more than she thought. But she knows what she saw, what she heard. What Tommy did to Cynthia. *Raped*. The word makes Stella feel sick. She is overcome with shame for not saying anything, for not rushing into the house to help. For not rushing to the closest house and calling the police. Stella wants to believe Cynthia's made-up tale so she can excuse her own cowardice.

Granny comes in with a tray. "Have some iced tea, dear. And it's just a glass...just a glass. Our precious girl. You people, you have to pay more attention, all of you. We should have brought you with us, Cynthia. Although I didn't need to go to the hospital in the first place. Frank, you're just as bad as Sally, so don't go blaming her. Who will keep these girls safe?"

Frank's face changes ever so slightly, his lips shifting a bit to the left, and then creeping back, but no one seems to notice but Stella.

"Stella, be a dear and bring in the cookies. I left them in the kitchen." Granny has set the tray down and pats her cheek. "It's terribly upsetting for you, all of this. We need a quiet summer for the girls, for everybody."

Stella's father sits in the kitchen fiddling with his sunglasses and absentmindedly flicking his chin, as though a fly keeps landing on it. He looks up as Stella comes in and picks up the plate of cookies. "I'm sorry I was harsh, Stella. I just couldn't believe you weren't here. Where were you?"

It's her opportunity. She will tell her father the truth. He will fix everything. He will deal with Tommy

Jessome. She licks her lips, tastes the blood, feels the swelling in the middle of her bottom lip and rubs it with her tongue. But her father speaks first, as he hands her the sunglasses. "Take these. You should be wearing sunglasses when you're outside. The doctor told you that. You can use mine for now. I must have left them here. Cynthia said she found them out in the grass." He shakes the aviator glasses at Stella, impatient. She takes them and puts them in the back pocket of her shorts and carries the cookies to the front room.

Stella stands by the window while Granny and Frank fuss over Cynthia. Stella studies Cynthia's blank face, wondering about what Cynthia saw, if she saw anything. And then Cynthia opens her dark eyes and smiles as she focuses on Stella, Cynthia's eyes shining still waters, whatever she knows hidden in the depths.

Outside, Stella retrieves her bike, wanting to get a head start as her father finishes up his visit. He wants her to go home and put on a casserole, or fix something for dinner. When she mounts her bike she notices the weather vane mermaid has plunged off the carriage house and crashed onto the grass—the sound that had disturbed Tommy's assault on Cynthia.

THE NEXT DAY THE girls help Granny in the garden, putting early September roses in vases, filling the sunroom and parlour with rich fragrance and shocking colour. They cook supper for Granny. They go for a walk after because it's been an unseasonably warm day and the evening is warm too. Summer has gone into reverse and come back. Cynthia is quieter than usual but doesn't seem depressed or upset. She links arms with Stella, as though nothing has happened and it's still her job to take care of her. Stella wonders why Cynthia is hiding what Tommy Jessome did to her. Is she afraid of what else he might do? Has this happened before? She is afraid for Cynthia but she is also afraid of Cynthia.

They walk through the marsh to the beach. It's a glorious sunset, a serenade to the day, to the summer that has passed, but they are a sombre lot in the face of such beauty and wildness. Granny tells them about sea glass and precious gems, how these have powers. When Stella and Cynthia ask what the powers are, Granny points to the water, out across the breakers where the water disappears in the far horizon, whatever might be there lost in the distance.

"There is much I need to teach you girls, although there isn't much time. It's September. The moon is changing. We all were sisters in the Offing Society. It goes back to the Old World, the old ways, when we came over the water originally, coming to settle on land we shouldn't be on, leaving our homes, creating a cycle of shame. But we understood the connection between the land and the sea in the olden days. And the women kept those ways, my people — the O'Clearys — and your grandmother Morgana. She was very strong. We have it written in our book, *The Commonplace Book*. But it's been missing for years. You must find it. It's in your blood, Stella, in your tears, your inheritance, this power, and it will save you. But I must teach you. I'm the last one now. You must not go to Mercy Lake. Do you understand? I had a dream. A vision. They will try to divide you. You must not let them."

Stella is afraid. Granny sounds crazy, and Stella worries that Frank is correct, that she's lost now in a briny wash of dementia, that Cynthia is protecting her, that she's trying to stop the future from arriving. Stella doesn't want to tell Granny she has found the book but the pages are blank.

"We'll take the salt water cure, girls. Stella Violette, we'll keep you safe. You must not go to Mercy Lake."

Cynthia and Stella don't correct her.

Cynthia clearly knows what they are doing, and has done it before. They create a triangle, each at a point, and facing the sea. Granny is at the front. She lifts up her arms. The sky is hysterically orange and red. Granny calls out and Cynthia answers. They make strange noises, singing, wailing, grunting. They stop, waiting for Stella, who lets out a howl. It's pure grief, not any words or incantations, the misery pouring out in a call to her mother who is gone. They walk forward into the water, holding the triangle, waist deep into the swells splashing against Stella's chest, breaking onto her face. She can taste the salt in her mouth, and it stings her eyes. The wind has picked up and she cannot hear Granny and Cynthia. It's the purple hour now and Stella watches the iridescent water cascade from their hands to their hair as they hold their cupped palms up into the twilight, the water gushing over their upturned faces. Stella does the same thing, imitating them.

They don't talk on the way back to Cedar Grove, shaking and shuddering the entire way home. Cynthia brings towels for them, drying Granny off. She opens a cupboard and makes a tea from herbs in copper containers, Granny sitting in a rocking chair calling out instructions. Cynthia serves them cups of the mysterious brew. At first it tastes bitter, and then salty like the sea, with a sweet lingering aftertaste of roses and honey. What magic does the tea have? Stella thinks about the power Granny mentioned, how her grandmother Morgana was very strong. And the *Commonplace Book of the Offing Society* with its blank, yellowed pages. Stella shivers as she hears Granny in her mind saying it was in her blood, her tears. Just *what* is in her blood and tears?

On the Road.
Goodbye, Isaiah Settles.

Now

TODAY STELLA TRIED TO sneak away from the centre without Dianne. But she always seemed to know what Stella was thinking, especially now that she was on high alert after the brave young woman in the yellow dress and her disturbing warnings.

"Oh, Stella, you're walking so fast a person can hardly keep up." Stella was grateful for Dianne's company but worried she might get worn out. It was one thing to loop endlessly around the centre grounds but another to go on the trail all the way to the Bigelow Bay Cemetery. But then there was the worry that Dianne might be removed to a seniors' home while Stella was away, that Nurse Calvin would use that as an opportunity, thinking Stella might have forgotten it was even the plan. But this new Stella, this Stella driven by a brooding fear, by the past rolling out of the mind shells, this Stella hoped if she could solve the mystery of Isaiah, then she could stop this plan of moving to a group home, of Dianne in a nursing home. Whenever Stella looked down at her ageing hands she heard a clock ticking—life was moving forward, years had passed, and she had missed so many of them. The luxury of hiding at the centre was gone. Her mind was working differently now. She needed to remember.

Late morning and a chill in the August air. It would warm up very soon. Stella buttoned up her old moth-eaten yellow cashmere cardigan—her mother's favourite, which Stella had taken when they moved here in 1980. Her father gave away almost all of her mother's clothes without telling her. But she still had the sweater after all these years, thin elbows, a few holes, matted and thick from washing, but warm and comforting nonetheless. How could it be Stella's mother had died when she was much younger than Stella was now? How could time move so quickly and so slowly, with holes filled by memories from another time, memories that didn't belong in the places they were inserting themselves?

Stella wore a small backpack that held some nuts and crackers and muffins she had taken from breakfast. But she had forgotten water. With every crackle in the woods, Dianne looked about, a geriatric sentinel.

Stella had to know about Isaiah. There was still a regular phone at the centre, for local outgoing calls and any calls coming in. Isaiah's number was disconnected. Three times she had tried, to make sure she wasn't pushing the wrong buttons.

They hurried over the old train tracks, both grateful for their walking regimen. A few dragonflies darted about as the heat came on.

The tracks would come out near the graveyard. Stella hoped it was a weekday, when people would be at work. If they were caught, they would be shipped out, dispersed like dated, worn furniture, shoved into back rooms.

Dianne was not talking. She was listening, on guard. They stopped for a few rests in the shade, catching their breath. The railway ties had been ripped out years earlier. They came to what used to be a railway crossing and Stella leaned on a poplar tree. She looked out over the beginning of a strawberry field, berries harvested, leaves turning red now. A shack for weighing fruit stood at the edge of the field. They sat on the bench in the shade. The town's graveyard was down the farm lane and across the road behind a row of pine trees. They were very close now to solving the mystery of who was dead and who was alive.

"Well, let's go. They'll be looking for us soon enough, Stella."

The red, dry dust floated up with each step. Stella

heard Dianne smacking, thirsty, her voice cracking as she spoke. "Now, Stella, you got to know that they never told you Isaiah died. It's not you forgetting. They thought it might send you over the bend. They was planning to tell you. I know because I overheard them. They thought I was sleeping. People think whenever an old lady's leaning back with her eyes shut and breathing heavy that she's dozed off. If I said it once, I'll say it again... never underestimate an old lady."

Even in her good running shoes, Stella's feet hurt. Her head hurt. She felt crusty and old, worthy of being underestimated. There was nothing she could do except hide. Stella stepped back into the shade of a maple, crushing the wild mint growing around the trunk, the peppery oils permeating the warm air.

"The Covid came? Remember? It took him away. Isaiah was some old. Back in the autumn. Don't you remember, Stella, not even a bit?"

Sure enough, in the graveyard by her mother's tombstone, one of red granite, Isaiah's. *Beloved brother to Catriona Settles Sprague, uncle to Stella Maris Settles Sprague.* Stella had a memory of coming here with Isaiah when they buried her mother's ashes, after Stella had gone to live with him. But she had no memory of coming here to put Isaiah to rest. Not a postcard memory, not a movie memory, not a set of mind slides. Nothing.

The grass was sparse and thin on his grave, planted in the spring. Lavender and rosemary grown all around the other gravestones. They heard a lawn mower, maybe at the other end of the graveyard. It was hard to tell. The graveyard was just before the town line. There was a row of high shrubs, lilacs, Stella guessed, blooms over, just bushy now, with a single black crow on the top. It looked at her and then glided down and landed on the ground at her feet. It leaned forward and cawed, flying off.

Stella dropped to her knees at Isaiah's grave, a dull pain in her knees as tears trickled from the corners of her eyes. He wouldn't be coming to get her. Dianne scuffled up behind her.

"Oh dear, Stella, dear, oh dear, oh dear, oh dear. He was some old. Why, look how old he was! He had a good life. At least Isaiah had you. That's the problem—you left behind. You should rest, Stella. You're looking so sallow, all parched and dried up."

Stella's hands were red from the dust, bits of pine needles stuck to her palms, sweat mixing with the dust, making a paste in the fate lines, tidal rivers on her hands. Nurse Calvin was right. Isaiah had died. Stella just didn't remember.

"Stellie, my girl, even if you didn't know he was dead, you knew he wasn't coming 'round. You missed him. You figured it out now. That's different than before, Stella. That's a good sign. That's a good omen."

Stella didn't share Dianne's strange optimism. Her mind was sore, if that was possible, a soreness spreading in ferny tendrils, a noxious, filmy seaweed in a tidal pool. Each undulation a sting. And her body, her aching body. Perhaps, Stella thought, memory had gotten lodged in her body. Bad memory. Rancid memory. Maybe this was why she felt so raw, her pain puffed and gaseous, a swamp of sorrow in this stiff body, her flesh and bone nothing more than a vessel carrying a spoiled life.

Dianne's knees didn't bend much even when she moved her legs quickly. She strode up and down between the rows of graves, jerking her legs out, to and fro, her ponytail bouncing on her spine, the silver locket trembling on her breasts.

"Time to go back, Stella. Stay safe."

Stella saw another grave marker, newer, behind all the rest, off to the side by a flowering orange bush. It was shiny grey granite. Stella crawled towards it and ran her fingers over the etchings in the smooth stone, feeling the chiselled hard grooves that form the words written here in the Bigelow Bay Cemetery. She stroked the stone wave carved underneath the inscription:

Cynthia Aoife Seabury
1967 New York, New York
2010 New Smyrna Beach, Florida
Seaward

Stella remembered something Isaiah used to say, that you could feel a story by just touching a stone. If you closed your eyes the stone became a face and your fingertips could feel the past in the grooves and ridges, or in the smoothness, the sleekness of a pebble tossed by the sea. Stella rubbed her palms over the granite — it was speaking but not telling a story. It was warning Stella. She was in peril. She had to hide.

A Liar and a Thief.
Lures.

Then

IT'S VERY WARM AND Stella finds it hard to believe summer is almost over. Or to even remember when it began. There are a few leaves already tinged in yellow and red. The flowers in the garden have begun their die down, Granny Scotia had explained, except for the asters and the goldenrod, the kind in the vase on the kitchen table, these flowers that span seasons, flowers that adapt to change. As Stella stands in the kitchen she wishes she was one of those sturdy flowers.

Stella quietly pads down the hall in her running shoes and into her father's study, which reeks of smoke. There are empty beer bottles lined up on the window-sill, and the wastepaper basket is overflowing with crumpled balls of paper and crinkled potato chip bags and candy bar wrappers. The sun is brilliant outside but you would never know it in here where the venetian blinds are still closed, the walls sallow from the dim desk lamp her father has forgotten to turn off.

He's just left, for a walk around town to clear his head. He was up for most of the night typing. Stella doesn't think he's even going to bed anymore. He is typing non-stop, always shooing Stella out of the house, telling her to go see Cynthia, to entertain herself, to enjoy the splendour of the countryside. He finds it annoying, this *typing business*, as he calls it. Stella's mother always typed his papers because he can only peck with two fingers. There's a history conference at the university in November and he's doing a keynote, as he reminds Stella every day. The theme is medical architecture. It's his grand entrance, he says — and he wants it to be an unforgettable entrance. The dawning of a new sun in his field of expertise. Those are the words he uses. *Splendid. Dawning.* He's also been promising they'd go on a day trip as soon as he finishes. And this morning when Stella slips into his study, she sees that he has typed "the end" on the paper in the typewriter. *The end!!!* Not that he bothered to tell her.

She wishes her father could buy a house in Bigelow Bay and they could move away. Have a real fresh start. This isn't fresh. It's stale. Old. Used. They are forcing a shroud of worn-out life over the maimed body of what's left of their family. And the Seaburys don't even seem to know they're doing the same thing. Stella doesn't want to spend time with Cynthia anymore. Whenever she looks into her dark blue eyes she sees herself reflected in them, in the window, looking in, watching Tommy Jessome slam Cynthia against a wall. Stella feels she is in Cynthia's eyes, looking at the side window, the dark screen, seeing a head on the other side, watching but staying silent—Stella, doing nothing, nothing but running away as only a coward does. Stella doesn't have a clue if Cynthia did see her there, if she suspects someone was at the window. Cynthia is impervious. She is a tomb, silent and closed. And she's still so friendly. Every time Cynthia does something nice, Stella feels sick.

When Stella arrives at Cedar Grove, Granny and Cynthia are already outside waiting to go blueberry picking, so she leans her bike against the carriage house and hurries into the car.

They park near the weigh-'n'-pay shack. The U-Pick is an old farm by the river about twenty minutes away, with the North and South Mountains soaring on either side of the rows of high bushes that are loaded with berries. Granny wants lots of fruit for freezing and for jam. It was cool when they started, but by mid-morning it's roasting. Granny Scotia is only able to pick for the first half an hour and then she sits in the car drinking ice water out of a Thermos. Her blood pressure is low, she says. She needs some salt because it raises the pressure.

Cynthia and Stella keep picking. The bushes are so heavy with berries that they fill boxes quickly. Cynthia still has a cotton bandage over her stitches and it flashes against the blue sky as her fingers pull berries from the branches.

On the way home Stella thinks Granny seems better, but still, she is inattentive, her gaze wandering up to the sky. Three times Cynthia grabs the wheel and pulls them back into the lane. Granny hardly notices. "Dear, it's dangerous to interfere with the driver," she says.

Back at Cedar Grove Granny sprinkles sea salt in a glass of water and gulps it down as she walks away muttering to herself, leaving the girls alone in the old kitchen. The enormous house is very still and Granny's voice echoes and ricochets as she climbs the huge staircase, and then fades away as she reaches the landing on the second floor.

Cynthia ignores this and shows Stella how to put blueberries in plastic bags. They fill up a rack in the upright freezer in the corner of the kitchen. Then Cynthia scurries around, cleaning up with trembling hands, her face red and her eyes tearing up. Stella watches her but doesn't know what to say. The Seabury pain is flooding her being and she can hardly stand it. They ride to Stella's with blueberries in containers in the baskets at the front of their bikes. Her father isn't home — still out for his walk, Stella thinks. An epic walk. There isn't an upright freezer at Stella's house, so they pour some blueberries in plastic bags and put them in the fridge freezer, leaving the rest on the counter for eating. Cynthia knows the recipe for blueberry muffins with rose petals and lemon by heart. She has regained her composure. Now her face is placid, as if nothing at all happened with Granny Scotia. Her backpack is on the chair in the hall and she's wearing an old apron she found hanging on the back of the kitchen door on a hook.

Stella's father returns while they're baking. He has a satisfied smile on his face as he puts his hands on his hips.

"Girls, I have a special announcement. I finished my paper."

Cynthia claps her hands. "Congratulations. That's super."

Stella forces a smile. Why did he wait until Cynthia was here? He finished it in the morning but didn't say a word. She had to sneak into his office to find out.

"It's a relief. It's so hard to work at home. But I managed! So, how was your morning? Cynthia, you are remarkable. You can cook just like your grandmother. I haven't smelled anything that good in this house since my mother was alive."

Stella remembers her mother's peach jam. Her mother's lemon loaf.

"I think it's the same recipe, Mr. Sprague. Granny taught it to me. She said it was one of your mother's.

From her recipe book. We looked for it but we couldn't find it. I knew it off by heart though."

"I'm sure they'll be delicious."

The muffins are delicious. Stella's father eats five of them, one after another, slathered in butter, washed down with a cold bottle of beer. Then he invites Cynthia to come with them to the Jericho Centre tomorrow, to see the old foundation of the poor farm on the property and then the old graveyard. And then he might take them to Halifax to see the harbour. He seems to forget that he has promised Stella he would spend time with her, alone.

Her father goes out back to smoke and Cynthia and Stella clean up. Stella leaves Cynthia in the kitchen sweeping. In her father's office she finds his paper, all neatly stacked on the desk now. She takes it and walks down the hall. She can hear the water running in the kitchen sink. Cynthia must be finishing up the dishes. Stella quickly shoves the paper in Cynthia's backpack, under her pink cotton sweater. Stella's hands shake as she closes the zipper, but only partway. She leaves the backpack on the chair unzipped...just enough.

Stella's father walks in from the porch, squinting in the kitchen after being outside in the bright sunlight. A car pulls into the driveway, the door opening and slamming shut, feet quickly crunching over the dirt driveway, rushing in through the back porch, the door opening.

"Hello, Sprague Household." Frank pokes his head in the kitchen door. "I was talking to Granny, Cynthia, and she sounded a bit confused. I thought I'd go check on her and pick you up. She called me in the middle of a meeting," Frank said, "rambling away, as she does nowadays, a bunch of nonsense. We're trying to finish up the details for the backwoods weekend for some colleagues, at the old lodge at Mercy Lake, before we turn around and close up for the season. It hasn't been used much in years, so lots of last-minute details. Tommy's looking after it so I can check on Granny."

Stella sees her father tense up.

Mercy Lake. Granny mentioned Mercy Lake. Had warned Stella about it.

Cynthia crosses her arms and eyes her father. "What's wrong with Granny? She was totally fine when we left, right, Stella?"

Stella doesn't answer.

"Sorry to hear that, Frank. Maybe it's the afternoon heat." Stella's father opens the fridge and takes out another beer. He holds it out to Frank, who shakes his head. Her father twists the beer cap off and takes a swig. As Stella listens to him guzzle, she thinks about the flinch that rippled across his face when Frank mentioned Granny rambling.

"Come on, Cynthia, let's get going. I have things to do. Put your bike in the trunk." Frank is impatient so Cynthia hurries to get her bag. Stella wraps up a few muffins. She gives them to Frank. "For Granny Scotia," she says. Frank is delighted. "How thoughtful, Stella, dear."

Her father nods. "Actually, Cynthia made them. But that's nice of you to get them ready, Stella, to share. Maybe you can learn to cook," he says hopefully, and reproachfully. Stella is too much like him and not enough like her mother, her aunt, her grandmother, all the dead Spragues.

"Billy, you said you found a book of your father's, on the history of the town. Do you have that handy?"

"Sure, in my study." Stella's father heads down the hall. He comes back right away, his face serious. "I can't find my paper."

"What paper?"

"My research paper. For the November conference. I've been finishing it up over the last week. I don't have another copy."

"I'm sure it will show up. Don't worry about the book. I'll get it another time. Cynthia, let's go. Take that apron off."

Cynthia takes the apron off and hangs it neatly over a kitchen chair. She disappears down the hall. Stella's father looks at Stella. "Did you see it, Stella? Were *you* in my study?"

"Dad, I was wrapping up muffins."

Just then Cynthia comes back into the kitchen. She has the backpack in her hand and throws it over her shoulder. The paper falls out, all sixty pages of it spilling over the floor.

"Cynthia?" Frank's face flushes red and his eyes bulge. "Jesus Christ, Cynthia. What's wrong with you?"

Stella says nothing. She looks at Cynthia, who holds her father's glare. "I wanted to read it," she says.

Stella can't believe she's not even denying it. She waits for her father to get angry too, but he says nothing. He runs his hands through his greasy hair and raps his chin with his fingertips.

Frank starts gathering up the pages. He barks at Cynthia to get on her knees and help him. "There will be hell to pay when we get home. You can't steal people's work. What's wrong with you? It's that boarding school we put you in. And your grandmother ranting and raving. There's going to be changes around here, that's for sure. I'm not going back to New York and leaving you behaving in this way, with no one in charge."

"Frank, I think you're overreacting. Let's ask her why she took it. Cynthia, why on earth would you steal my paper? I cannot even fathom."

She looks straight at Stella's father. "I wanted to read it, Mr. Sprague. Stella's always talking about how interesting your work is. She says you've been working day and night. She's so proud of you."

Cynthia doesn't say that Stella has been complaining day and night.

"I wanted to read it, that's all. I know I should have asked. I'm sorry. I thought you'd say no. I thought when you finished it that you wouldn't look at it for a few days, that I could sneak it back."

"*Sneak* is the word. I have a mind to tan you with a cane just as I did when you were five years old."

"Frank, there's no need for that. It's actually kind of flattering. Stella isn't interested in reading my work. I talk too much about it, she says."

This is not going anywhere near what Stella had planned.

"I'm so sorry, Mr. Sprague. I hope you'll forgive me."

"I accept your apology. So how about it? Will you accept our invitation for the day trip? We'd be overjoyed if you came. Right, Stella?"

Stella says nothing. She shrugs and jiggles her head, trying to shake it, to remind her father it was supposed to just be the two of them, father and daughter. But her father decides this means Stella thinks it's a brilliant idea. Cynthia looks so happy that Stella wants to slap her.

FRANK COMES BACK OVER that evening as Stella is eating her bedtime snack before going upstairs, a glass of milk and some toast. Frank calls from the back porch where he's having beer and pretzels with her father: "Come out and join us for a few minutes, Stella." She sits in the old Morris chair in the corner of the porch.

Frank has an ancient tackle box with him. He says that her father should go off fly fishing for a break, the way he did as a boy. Stella can stay with Cynthia over Labour Day weekend.

Her father fiddles with the exotic-looking flies. Stella has never seen her father do real physical labour or anything mechanical. The boy her father had been was waking up—Billy, who made things with his hands. But then Stella wonders if he's been pretending helplessness his whole life.

Her father explains the parts to Stella: the head, hook, tag, hackle, and tail, holding them up so she can see them from her chair.

"Like old times, Billy. It's good to have you and Stella here. I wish you all had come to visit earlier in the spring."

"You don't know how many times I've wished that myself, Frank. But I couldn't convince Catriona to come. I tried. But she refused to come back to Nova Scotia. I reminded her how many years had passed since she had seen her brother. Catriona said they talked on the phone. When I called to tell Isaiah she had died, he said they had spoken every week, every Monday. He asked for her ashes to be sent to Nova Scotia, so I guess one way or another she's ended up back here."

Stella's father seems to have forgotten her sitting off in the corner, in the faint light, just outside the circle cast by the floor lamp. He holds a blue feather, studying it as he speaks. "Isaiah's an odd duck. The family were Believers, an offshoot of the Shakers, who created intentional societies. There's still a community east in the Valley. They came up from Kentucky, way back, Catriona's father's people. Her mother's people came up from North Carolina, but originally from the Island of Islay, in the Old World."

"Well, at least she had you and little Stella here. Tragic. I had a car accident once. I still remember skidding on the road, the car overturning. Do you have any memories of it, Stella? Has anything come back, now you've been able to relax in Seabury?" Frank has not forgotten she's there. Frank is as alert as he is insensitive. Her father is normally oblivious, but Frank is something else entirely.

"No," she says quietly. Stella wonders why her father doesn't intervene and tell Frank not to talk about car accidents. She still remembers the squeal of the brakes, her mother crying out, the sound of the windshield breaking, and then shadows, a dense shadow, and then nothing. The dark shape grows in her memory. It seems larger, with defined edges, wide and thick. Her answer doesn't stop him from asking again. "Any idea of what happened?"

"No," Stella says again, in a louder voice. It's strange how he keeps looking at her. And how her father keeps quiet. Her father yawns. Stella thinks this is his way of masking his annoyance at Frank for pushing Stella. He yawns but says nothing. They both know the doctor said she might remember, she might not. Stella's brain may have created the memory and stored it, or maybe not. Only time would tell. Or not.

Stella's father takes a sip of beer, licks his lips and looks at Frank. "She doesn't remember, okay?"

Frank purses his lips as he looks at Stella's father. She watches Frank take a sip of beer and then smile. "Remember how much salmon there was when we were boys, Billy boy? Did you do much fishing in Ohio?"

Stella finds Frank's folksy way of talking, of changing the topic, off-putting. He's a rich, New York–based business man but pretends to be something else.

"Oh, on occasion, Frankie. A bit of smallmouth bass, quillback and channel catfish."

This is news to Stella, but maybe her father had gone fishing when she was really young and she just didn't remember. Stella has no way of knowing if her father is concocting a story in his brain or recalling something true.

Stella leaves them there, without saying good night, and they don't call after her. She bounds up the stairs and as she reaches the top, she hears something clatter to the floor in front of her dead aunt's bedroom. A skeleton key. It must have been hidden on the ledge at the top of the wooden casing around the door. Stella can't resist. She turns the key in the lock. Click. Her sweaty hand on the glass doorknob, which twists without a sound. The door glides open. She feels along the wall for a light switch. It snaps on with an echo in the empty room. Only her father's memories inhabit this space. Stella stands on her tiptoes and puts the key back. She slips into her bedroom and between the covers.

Later, she wakes up when she hears a bang. The inside kitchen screen door from the porch. It swings closed again. She hears low voices, male voices. Her window is open. She gets out of bed to close it and hears her father talking. *Violette. Stella Violette.* And Frank's voice, threatening, intensifying as he delivers a harsh sermon. *Debt. Repayment.* She can't make out much more: Frank menacing, her father meek, subdued, compliant. She doesn't put the old window down for fear it will make noise, that her father will hear. *Frank* will hear. And think she is listening, which she is, but not on purpose.

She crawls back into bed and pulls up the wool blanket from near her feet, covering her ears. She imagines riding her bike on the road through the marsh towards the water, the horizon. She realizes she is in a dream when she sees she is walking on the water, her feet wet, but not sinking. Out in the offing, someone is calling her name.

Seraphina and Aurora.
Age Demolishes Them.

Now

LOUD, THROBBING ENGINE NOISE and blaring music cut through the cemetery quiet. An old green pickup truck emerged from behind the bushes on the bumpy lane in between the graves. Distorted violin and strings, guitar and bass, blared from the truck.

"Oh no, oh no," Dianne said. "Not that one. She's a crazy one. Don't we know it."

Seraphina screeched with the music and stopped as she shut off the engine and hopped out. Seraphina— unhealthily skinny, chain-smoking as she stood in her hiking boots and her jewel-toned flowery sundress.

"Are you planning on sitting there all day or are you going to get out and pay your respects?" she said to the person in the passenger seat.

The passenger door opened and a very pretty girl got

out, slamming the door behind her. She was probably about thirteen or fourteen, Stella thought, amber skin, long brown hair, lanky, a wise face, too much weight on the brow of someone so young. Her daughter. Stella remembered Grace at the hospital saying Seraphina had a daughter. In foster care. Dianne coughed and smacked her lips.

Seraphina spun around. She didn't seem surprised at all to see them, as if for all the world she was a frequent graveyard visitor and at ease with whomever showed up. Seraphina bowed, a wild look in her eyes. She spoke on high speed. "Well, hello, ladies. It's always a bitter-sweet symphony at the graveyard, isn't it?"

Dianne looked around at the graves and then at Seraphina. "I reckon so."

Seraphina smiled. She started singing again.

The girl crossed her arms. She was wearing a petal-pink tank top and very short denim shorts. She held a phone, the same as the ones the workers at the centre had and kept in the basket they ran to at their breaks. "God, Mom. God. I keep telling you you're stuck in the nineties. I hate that "Bitter Sweet Symphony" song. How many times do I have to tell you? It's all emo and angsty. So. Embarrassing. How about Beyoncé?"

Stella watched the teenager twirl as she sang about halos.

Seraphina was on overdrive. She answered the girl, speaking very quietly, but with her voice racing: "Time doesn't really move, you know... Time is a state of mind... *This* is what most of you don't understand. I. Aim. To. Have. You. Understand. Now look who we have here — Stella and Dianne, my friends from the Jericho Centre. We were just going to visit my mother's grave. I thought maybe she might try to give me a sign but probably not. The dead aren't much help, are they?"

It was exhausting trying to keep up with Seraphina. Stella was sitting on the ground and Dianne reached down to put her hand softly on Stella's head while Seraphina foamed on: "My mother did try to help me. She had a hard life. She thought it all stopped in her generation. I don't know why. She just turned and looked the other way. She hoped they would go away. They never do. Not until they're stopped once and for all. They say Lucretia will soon appear again, over by the bay. It means it's time. They're coming for you, Stella. And maybe my daughter. She's thirteen now. They came for me. They never stop."

Dianne cleared her throat, checking behind her, narrowing her eyes. "What do you know about that?"

Seraphina continued to speak quickly, but now her voice rose: "I know that those fucking cocksuckers are on the loose. Back trying to clean stuff up. No one else remembers what happened forty years ago, but I do. It happened to me too. That's why I picked up my daughter, to keep her safe. I tried to make her the potion, but she wouldn't drink it."

The young girl stared down at Stella with her hands flecked with pine needles, sitting in the red clay dust, as if Stella were a statue or grave marker. Then she started to whimper. "Mom, you're scaring me. Who's coming for me? I don't want to drink that stuff you brew up."

"You did when you were little."

"I didn't know any better. I would have done anything you said. You were my hero, Mom. I was just a kid. I'm *still* a kid. You're off your meds. You aren't making sense. You aren't sleeping. I only came with you because I'm afraid you'll have an accident. There's no one taking care of you." She let out a cramped scream and pounded her fists on her bare thighs. "I'm just so mad at you, Mom!"

Stella watched the thirteen-year-old wipe her nose on her arm, and then her eyes, trying not to cry. Seraphina didn't acknowledge the girl's distress.

"Aurora, this is Dianne and Stella. They live at the Jericho Centre just outside of town, in Blossomdale. Stella used to spend time over in Lupin Cove at Periwinkle Cottage with her uncle, not far from where we live." Seraphina's face gave no sign that her daughter didn't live there anymore. "I heard he died. So sorry. It's so peaceful here. You'd never know how much danger is about."

"Only place you can find true peace and quiet, yes it is," Dianne said softly, playing with her silver necklace.

"Dianne is just cracking the one-liners today." Seraphina lit a cigarette and handed it to Dianne, who took it without hesitation. They smoked in silence.

Seraphina closed her eyes. "That's how it used to be. Now they call it forest bathing and therapeutic gardening, for fuck's sake." She groaned.

Seraphina is not as she was when you first met her. Stella looked around. There was no one else, just the three women and the girl. Age was demolishing them all. Seraphina's voice was fast, as it was in the hospital lobby. She was ramping, ramping, ramping up. Stella remembered the hospital. Tests. Tests for something, something caused by something bad. She wasn't sure when it was. She waited for that whisper again, to tell her secrets, but there was only a dull ache behind her eyes. She brushed her palm over the soft tips of grass and picked a wild rose from a bush at her side.

Aurora lifted up her phone. Stella thought she was going to call someone but she held it up in front of her. Seraphina twirled her arms like a windmill. "You can't film them. You can't post pictures to Instagram all the time," she shrieked. "They're human beings. They're the kind of human beings who are close to the edge, close enough to peek in and see the mystery that is behind that thin piece of rice paper we call life. You can't just go making art out of everything you see. There's something called privacy. Something called permission. And we have to hide them."

Aurora slid the phone in the back pocket of her tight jean shorts. "Whatever. Jesus Christ, Mom. I just want you to go to a hospital. There's no one after them. There's no one after you. Or me. You're paranoid. Can't you see? No one wants to get you. And who would be after *her*?" The teenager pointed at Stella.

"Except maybe the police would come for you... for kidnapping me. I'm supposed to be at the foster home. You're not supposed to even see me until you get some help."

Seraphina's face crumpled but she shook off her shame as quickly as it had come. "I'm sorry about that, you know, dreadfully sorry. Sorrysorrysorrysorry-SOSOSorry."

Stella studied Seraphina's face. Age seemed to have trailed behind Seraphina and, when she wasn't looking, leapt out and settled into her skin, as it has done to Stella. Only Dianne seemed younger than her age, although today her years were showing more than they ever had.

Dianne didn't care about their mother/daughter problems. She was slowly walking in a circle around them now, her legs stiff. "Got any water, Serrie?" Dianne opened her mouth and pointed inside. Stella thought Dianne was worried Seraphina might not understand English.

Seraphina walked to the truck and came back with a glass bottle of water. "I'm only using glass now. For the environment. They say microfibres are in the sand of every beach on Earth."

Dianne passed the bottle to Stella and Stella took a drink, knowing Dianne would insist even if she refused. She then passed it back to Dianne. She guzzled the water, gave Seraphina a wide, toothless smile and wiped her lips.

"The two of you should get back to the centre. You'll be safe there. I can drive you."

Dianne looked at Stella and Stella shook her head. She would rather take her chances with the people who were supposedly after them than go back to the centre. They were going to send her away, and send Dianne away. Stella would gamble with running through the woods before getting into the truck with Seraphina.

"Suit yourselves," Seraphina said, suddenly giving up, cocking her head to the side, listening to something no one else could discern, receiving instructions. "Okay, let's go, daughter."

Aurora hesitated, but Seraphina was already making for the truck and didn't notice. Stella watched the teenager trying to decide what to do — to leave her mother to her own devices or to go with her. Aurora ran over to the truck, where Seraphina was throwing her hands up into the air, bellowing at the sky: "Hallelujah!"

Aurora dashed by the truck and down the narrow lane between the tombstones as Seraphina started the engine and followed, stopping in the road behind her daughter. Aurora kept walking as Seraphina yelled out the window. They shouted back and forth at each other.

Then quiet. A truce. The girl got in the truck and away they roared. A quiet settled in. The breeze dropped. One bird sang out.

Stella's stomach churned and her crotch felt raw. But she was not going back to the centre. The sun was over in the west now. It must be mid-afternoon. Maybe a bit later.

Seraphina was right — Stella had gone over to Lupin Cove when Isaiah was her guardian. They had spent time at the cottage with a fireplace made of beach stone, with pieces of amethyst, agate and jasper interspersed with smooth grey stones.

Stella began walking, wondering if some of Seraphina's energy had possessed her. Or maybe the drink of water had revived her.

"Stella, Stella, you're heading the wrong way!"

Stella knew she was heading the only way she could. North. She would walk to Lupin Cove. What she needed to remember might come to her if she went to the shore, to the cottage, to the Bay of Fundy. Dianne hopped behind, calling her name. They got to the top of the hill where the sidewalk began by the farmhouse at the edge of town. And Stella was out of breath. There were some bikes on the lawn. She picked one up and got on, stabilized herself, leaned forward and began pedalling.

Dianne shrieked, "Stella, Stella, you can't take that. We're too old for biking."

But Stella kept pedalling, her knees creaking, euphoria building—she was on a country road riding a bicycle and no one was stopping her.

Dianne came up behind, huffing and puffing on a squeaky bicycle. "You're not going alone, Stella. Not you. You're not acting normal. Not that I know what normal is. Time to go back. Now."

Stella knew Dianne didn't suspect they were going to send her to a nursing home and Stella to a group home in the middle of nowhere. Dianne would be in a locked ward for old people who wandered. And Stella would be trapped in that house in the woods way up on the South Mountain with David Jessome, the brand-new volunteer, miles from the nearest town, no walking trails, a prisoner.

The Disease of Melancholia.

Then

STELLA'S FATHER BEAMS AS they drive east to the Jericho County Care Centre. It's been three days since Cynthia got caught with the essay in her backpack. Stella thought her father wouldn't follow through with his promise of an outing but, of course, because Cynthia is involved, he has. He drives slowly, pointing out landmarks and such, all the way.

"Girls, I'm not quite sure what we'll discover when we arrive. I'll be Frank with you, okay?" He waits for them to laugh—only Cynthia does.

Stella wants to give him a slap, make him stop behaving like a teenaged boy. She wishes it was Cynthia she wanted to slap, but any way Stella looks at it, she knows Cynthia is just being polite, with that adult understanding of men she has.

They drive with the car windows down and a sweet

wildflower breeze blows in from the meadows beside the highway, Cynthia in the back and Stella in the front. Swirls of clouds frost the sky into an upside-down blue cake. Her father constantly looks in the rear-view mirror at Cynthia, speaking with her for almost the entire drive. She's just had her stitches out and her scar is a bright red line on her tanned skin. Stella knows they've forgotten she is in the car. When she coughs they both jump, and then go back to their conversation about poor farms and lunatic asylums.

"The main purpose of our research expedition today is to visit the old graveyard and see if it's even there anymore. It's supposed to be on the banks of the Cornwallis River. If we have time, on the way back we'll stop to see the sanatorium. It closed in 1975 but there are still a few buildings left. Tuberculosis was a terrible disease and no one even remembers it anymore. We so quickly forget."

Stella scribbles and doodles in her sketchbook. Her father turns on the radio, twiddling the knobs until he finds a station playing something old-fashioned. She thinks her father is too sentimental. He is the *melancholic type, the nostalgic kind*, her mother always said. "You're listening to *Jazzland*," the announcer says as the song finishes and another begins. Stella's father begins humming and drumming on the steering wheel. He's showing off for Cynthia, who is smiling and humming with him from the back seat, as though nothing at all had happened to her in that grand old drawing room at Cedar Grove. As if the attack... the assault had never happened. Stella can't stop thinking about it, but it seems Cynthia has forgotten. Or is able to secret things away inside her mind in a way Stella doubts she ever could.

They pull off the main highway and drive on a secondary one that Stella's father explains was the old post road, the stage coach road. *Jericho County Care Centre.* The sign is simple, discreet. Stella's father drives down the narrow road and at the end they see a modern hospital sort of building, not something out of his pictures of Victorian brick hospitals or Edwardian cottage-style hospitals, although it is set in a sprawling acreage.

"You see, Cynthia... and Stella... back when they built hospitals in the country, they believed fresh air and nature, a view, could restore. It's a misperception that it was all about isolating patients and hiding them away." Stella has heard this so many times and now she has to listen again while he tells Cynthia how the poor farm was a place of servitude and poverty-shaming.

Stella's father has the strangest look on his face, his voice quiet and thin. As he parks, he consults a fold-out map. "Now this would have been where the original cottage hospital was. They made it into a nursing home after they built the new hospital. And then they tore it down."

The road continues to the west and then disappears behind some high bushes. He points to the left. "That's where the poorhouse would have been."

They get out of the car and walk down the road. It dips north. "I'm sure it's this way." Stella's father pulls out an old compass. He's out of sorts, oblivious to the North Mountain, a man without his bearings. "This was my father's. He was the same as Frank's father, always out at Mercy Lake, avid outdoorsman. He wanted me to be tough and hardy. I bet you didn't know I could use one of these." Her father shakes the tarnished brass instrument like it's a tambourine. "Judas Priest, it's supposed to show us true north. Maybe it's broken."

Neither Stella nor Cynthia point out that he has probably just broken it now. Stella sees Cynthia wink at her and she tries not to giggle.

Birds chirp and butterflies flit about like bursts of confetti.

"Well, I'm sure it's here somewhere," Stella's father says as the dirt trail gets even narrower, ending in a meadow at the bottom of a hill. There is another trail through the high grasses. The blades ripple and shake, a whispering, louder and louder. Her father forges ahead and the girls follow. Stella hears the river but she can't see it. At the top, the grass is trampled down. "I imagine the residents come out here for enjoyment and peace. They're the only ones who remember it, aside from us."

Stella doesn't point out that most people in the centre probably don't walk this far back into the woods. There are no plaques. Stella follows her father and Cynthia to the sea of short, numbered concrete markers. At the north side, through the leaves, there are bits of blue water, the red muddy riverbank half exposed.

Stella has wanted to confront Cynthia the whole day, to scream at her in front of her father that she's a liar, but of course she can't do this, because she's the one who started the lie in the first place. Cynthia is also so sincerely kind to Stella, trying to bring her into the conversation. "I wouldn't have known anything about this, Professor Sprague, if Stella didn't talk about your work all the time. I wish my father was a historian."

What bothers Stella is that she believes Cynthia. Her sentiment is absolutely genuine. If it is a technique she's learned to wield for watchful adults — she has perfected it, probably from carefully hiding for safety, hiding to trap them. But how, at such a young age, Cynthia is so seamlessly able to blend fact and fiction, Stella has no idea.

Seaward.
Periwinkle, Shell and Flower.

Now

THEY DROVE UP THE Mountain, the bicycles in the back of the cab, the four of them squished into the front of the truck. Seraphina twiddled the radio knob until "O Fortuna" poured from a classical music station. There was no way they could have biked, let alone walked around these switchbacks. She and Aurora screeched as if they were on stage at an opera house. Stella put her hands over her ears as they kept belting it out. They both seem to know Latin. *O Fortuna. Velut luna, statu variabilis, semper crescis, aut decrescis* — Seraphina singing the Latin and her daughter in English. *O Fortune, like the moon, you are changeable, ever waxing, ever waning.*

Stella observed how this was the first time Seraphina and her daughter seemed happy together.

Seraphina snapped the radio off. "That's all about fate and gods. Enough of that."

"That was awesome, Mom. Super-awesome." Aurora smiled at her mother, who lit two cigarettes and handed one to Dianne. Stella's stomach lurched from the smell. They drove by an old boarded-up house surrounded by outhouses.

"My father collected those old shithouses. That's where I grew up," Seraphina said, glancing at Stella but not at the house, and then crossing herself as they passed by, slowing down. Stella watched Seraphina's lips move but no more words came out. Then Seraphina pressed on the gas and her childhood was left behind them.

Stella watched the teenaged girl with her cellphone and its shiny screen. Aurora was tapping away on it, missing the view. "I lost the signal. For fuck's sake. This stupid place. Why did I ever get in the truck with you, Mom? Fuck. What kind of fucking place doesn't have fucking-cell-fucking-phone reception?"

Seraphina cackled and sucked back a mouthful of spit, swallowing it as she spoke her garbled words: "Well, the North-Fucking-Mountain. That's the kind of place. The land we speed across now, in my holy pickup. This place resists change. It adapts slowly, and there are some things it never relinquishes. Amen." Seraphina was ascending to her pulpit.

How many years was it since Stella had been up

here? She couldn't remember the years but she recalled beach barbeques and seagulls and looking out over the bay at sunrise and sunset, walking on the beach, Isaiah building a fire. She knew the fireplace, a room upstairs that looked out over the bay. The mantel where Isaiah put a scented candle in the evening. The Bay of Fundy crashing on the shore at night. The cry of the gulls in the purple hour. The salt water loon in the morning.

"Are you from around here?" A finger poked Stella in the rib. She pulled away from Aurora. The bay was ahead, frosted with heaving whitecaps. The tide was coming in, a cool breeze with it. Stella's heart quickened, thudding. She put her hand on it. Stella refused to look at this young girl. Stella wasn't in charge of her. She was hardly in charge of herself, had never been in charge of herself. This quiet truth seemed to perch on the top of Stella's head, miniature but heavy, weighing down on her skull, on her neck, drilling into her core.

"Stella doesn't talk, Aurora," Seraphina said.

"Oh." The girl's voice quivered. Stella felt sorry for this teenager stuck in the truck with this strange sisterhood of mentally ill old women. Aurora seemed to think Stella was the sanest of the lot. But it wasn't her job to provide this Aurora girl with comfort. That was Seraphina's responsibility. Stella's singular responsibility was getting to Periwinkle Cottage, disappearing into the grey beach and the fog.

Dianne looked at her cigarette. Stella wondered if

she found it more comfortable to talk to it than crazy Seraphina and her daughter. "It's God's truth. Stella don't say a word. Never does. Some people says they remember her talking, but I've known her for years and she's not said a word in all that time."

Seraphina pushed in a CD. Startling piano music, then a woman's voice singing about being a mermaid in jeans. Seraphina turned it up loud, singing along again, Aurora singing with her as they flew over the road towards the silver-blue bay, the mighty Bay of Fundy.

Stella looked straight ahead at the sea. The highest tides in the world. A body of water that was sometimes soothing and calm, sometimes deadly and raging. Always wild and untamed. Waters that can smash you against the cliffs and suck you far away. There was a slight ache behind her eyes, a pain she hadn't had in years. It seemed a rigid starfish was lodged at the centre of her head, wiggling its arms, poking at her eyes, now jabbing the little seahorses in the side of her head. Her plan was to go to the cottage. No one would think to look there. No one would even think they had the ability to get there. They would look in the woods. In the river. In ditches. But not at the shore. Stella could get them to the cottage, and she and Dianne would be safe. She wouldn't need to remember, if they could just get out of the Valley, away from that place closed in by mountain and shadow. Stella could see the island far offshore, the island her people had lived on.

"I'm hungry," Aurora complained. "We didn't even eat dinner, Mom. You never eat when you're crazy. But I need to eat. So do you. I'm literally starving. How come I have to be the grown-up here?"

By the time they drove down the hill into Lupin Cove, Seraphina and Aurora were arguing in earnest. Aurora talked about her father, about how it wasn't fair she never knew him, or even who he was, why did Seraphina have a baby when she was forty anyway, she had no money, no family to help, that it was all her fault. It seemed to Stella that Aurora, stuck in this truck with a bunch of crazy old ladies, was thinking maybe the foster home was the better option. Or a group home, which was where they would put her next. Stella understood having Seraphina for a mother wasn't the same as having a regular mother. Aurora was crying. For the first time in years, Stella wanted to scream. There was nothing she could do for this girl. She was fifty-four and helpless. She put her hands over her ears and rubbed, to brush away Aurora's young desperation, the knowledge that it would just keep coming up over the girl's life, an unstoppable tide in a world where Aurora did not belong, until it turned and sucked her back out into relentless currents, pulling her so far from shore she could never come back, pulling her to the place where Stella floated and Dianne floated, lost at sea with so many others.

Dianne kept checking the rear- and side-view mirrors, patting Stella's knee. And Seraphina carried on. "I have to keep you all safe. And Aurora. They'll try to get her too. Danger is coming. Danger! Stella, you need to remember. That woman from California got in touch with me. By accident. I went and found her. She was in the historical society. What I prefer to call the Hysterical Society. She was talking to Jillian at the archives. She was asking questions. Don't you know who I'm talking about? The Black woman. Well, she's not just Black, but she sure isn't white. Her mother's people go way back here. She's in trouble too. I don't know why she's here. I don't know how to protect her. I knew her mother. She was smart and went away. Stella, what do you know? What do you have? I have been forewarned."

"Mom, you are totally fucking insane."

Stella felt Dianne take her hand and squeeze. Why was this woman from California after them? And what did they all think Stella was hiding? Seraphina's hypomania was swollen up now, spilling out the windows of the truck as they roared over the bumpy old road. Stella felt sorry for all of them.

Seraphina almost tipped the truck coming around the bend, over the bridge, barely missing the signpost that said *Lupin Cove*, and below it *Petal's End*, with an arrow pointing west, and then barrelling into the driveway of a house right on the road by the river that ran into the harbour. Stella assumed it was Seraphina's house but she didn't really care whose house it was. It was rundown, once a lovely place, but shabby with neglect. Stella wanted out of the truck. She balled her hands into fists. The water flowed into the harbour and the air reeked of rotting fish and rancid mud, seagulls shrieking as the four women clambered out of the truck—Dianne very stiff, moving slowly, turning back and taking Stella's hand, helping her down from the truck cab to the stone driveway—Seraphina's voice was a gale, rising and falling, gusting, talking about the meaning of life and secrets being revealed to her. Aurora was cursing her phone because there was still no reception, and then holding it up at her mother. It looked so strange, this black rectangle with a round circle at the corner. "Don't you take any pictures of me!" Seraphina screamed. "No movies. Don't you break my right to privacy, my own daughter. Those pictures last forever. You have no right. And that's how they hunt us, with those stupid things."

It was then that Stella slipped away, back across the bridge they had just driven over, Dianne following. The other two—on a stage in a play with no ending—didn't even notice them leave.

Stella's body knew the way, her feet guiding her.

"Stella, do you remember, even a tad, coming over before, when we were younger, with your uncle back when he was alive?"

Stella did not. But she understood now that Isaiah was dead. Isaiah was dead as a doornail. The Covid killed him. Who didn't it kill? Her. And Dianne. They were spared.

Stella turned left by the east wharf, with Dianne beside her now, still talking. "Do you think coming here will help you remember? Or do you just want to hide? I wish you would let me know, Stella. At least at the centre we were safe."

Stella was happy she couldn't talk—otherwise, she would have blurted out that they weren't safe at the centre because Nurse Calvin was going to have them kicked out.

The island was gone from view now, completely obscured in the mist moving in over the water. They were on a laneway lined with firs, and then on an overgrown path through the woods. Stella had a flash of memory of two parked vehicles, a green car and Isaiah's blue truck. And the path clipped and neat. Isaiah always trimmed it, she recalled. Bits and pieces coming to her. It was not an extensive walk but they were not young women. Dianne huffed and wheezed and Stella wished for the sea air to do her good, to do them both good. She heard her mother's voice, telling her how people came over to the Fundy shore to take the sea air to cure what ailed them. Once upon a time people would carry out children with polio and stricken limbs and hope the salt water would heal them.

They came through the woods to the blue cottage near the beach. The front had a covered verandah that faced north, out over the water. On a hot day the breeze could be chilly. At the back there was just a stoop with a few steps to climb to the door. It was August and there should be a screen door, but of course there wasn't because Isaiah was dead. He had not put the screen door on after the winter, as he had done for years. Stella's eyes watered and she sniffed back her tears. Beside the door was a square mirror, the glass dull. Stella's hair was tangled and streaked with more white than she remembered. There was a thick border of periwinkle and mint all around, the flowers an unearthly purple.

Stella gazed out to the beach, the island gone in the fog. Had it even been there to start with? No one else had mentioned it. Stella's cheeks were wet and she couldn't tell if it was tears or mist billowing in from the water. She was thirsty, terribly thirsty. There was a spring in the slope behind the cottage. Stella's need for a drink pushed her forward. Borage plants rose up from the sage-green beach grass, the blue, star-shaped flowers resting on the thick blades. The spring ran into a pool. Stella knelt and lapped out of it. She sat up and looked back at Dianne through the branches. She was on the verandah, yawning, her legs stretched out, rubbing her knees with one hand. Stella drank a bit more and then wobbled back to the cottage where

Dianne dozed against the peeling wooden shingles. The curtains were pulled shut. Stella knew there was always a key under the steps, in an old metal cough drop box. The box was there but no key.

Dianne snored as Stella considered what to do next. Her hands trembled, part of her sensing the younger woman who used to come here with her uncle and part of her feeling a thousand years old, wanting to walk down the beach and lie down on the rocks, letting the tide cover her, take away her breath, fill her with brine, wash her out to sea. Dianne grunted in her sleep and rubbed her nose, smacked her lips.

On the verandah there were some grey beach stones. Stella used one of them to smash the window by the door. The pane shattered and a jagged piece of glass pierced the tendon at the base of her thumb, slick warm blood running down her wrist, smearing over her hand, her fingers slippery as she reached inside and undid the window lock. She pushed the window up enough so she could fit through. Stella managed to get her legs in the opening, her belly pressing against the window ledge as she moaned.

Dianne lurched awake. "Oh, Stella, I dozed off. What are you doing stuck halfway in the house there? Sky's heavy. We should take cover. Take a rest. My land, look at your hand. We need to give that a wipe."

Dianne pushed the window open a bit more, and Stella slid in and landed on the wooden floor where she lay taking deep breaths. The cottage smelled of wood and spice, as it had when she was younger.

"Stella, let me in." Dianne pounded at the door.

Stella flicked the lock and Dianne looked around as she stepped over the threshold patting her grey hair.

"That mirror give me a terrible fright. Wish Isaiah had taken it down, for Christ's sake. Got a look at myself and almost had a heart attack. We're not dressed up for no party, that's for sure." Dianne wheezed out a bray of a laugh. "But still, weren't nothing coming over my shoulder." She eyed Stella. "Remember why it's there?"

Stella did remember; she knew how people here put a mirror beside the door to see if the dead had followed them home.

Dianne looked around the kitchen and eyed the copper kettle on the antique cook stove. There was a napkin folded on the counter and she wrapped this around Stella's bleeding hand. "Ain't nothing but a scratch, Stella. Don't fret."

But Dianne looked worried, and very tired. *She's an old lady, you know.* Stella was not sure who had spoken in the quiet voice, not quite a whisper, as though the person it belonged to was outside, speaking in through a window. She looked around but there was nothing through the windows but beach, a tinkle of wind in the silver birches. Her heart thumped in her chest. Had they been found? Dianne didn't seem to have heard.

"Goddam wind. Can hardly get any shut-eye around here," she said, behaving as if they had rented an expensive cottage and she was disillusioned.

Stella pointed at the old red sofa and Dianne lumbered over and stood by it. "If I wasn't so tired I'd go upstairs and take a rest but that crooked, twisty staircase might be the end of me." Dianne must have been here before, Stella realized.

Dianne seemed to read her mind. "But I don't reckon you remember when we come over here for a little holiday?" Stella wanted to say, *yes, yes, of course*, to not let Dianne down. She shook her head and Dianne sighed as Stella helped her lie down. She covered up the exhausted old lady with the black wool blanket on the back of the sofa on the ocean side of the cottage, across from the petite loveseat on the opposite wall.

"Just a short rest, Stella dearie, and then I'll be right as rain. My mother always said that. Funny what you remember. What's right about rain? Been asking myself that for years. If only it'd rain. Endless dry summer. Oh, my legs. I'm the original Tin Lady. Get me an oil can." Dianne closed her eyes as she mumbled. "I'll just rest up and then go down to the shore and get some snails and seaweed and make you supper. And a cuppa tea."

There was a knick-knack shelf over the sofa. The top shelf was covered in figurines—a few handmade wooden trinket boxes sat on the second shelf, and a row of china fishermen on the bottom. Stella didn't recollect

specific times but general times, quiet days spent reading and walking on the beach, Isaiah making soup
and tea, simple days, everything the same except the
weather. There was still a circle of armchairs crowded
in front of the fireplace, and a rocking chair, the table
beside them by the west window looking out over the
beach. A dark blue vase in the centre of the mantel over
the fireplace made of gemstones and basalt. Lace sheers
in the windows, the pictures on the walls.

There were still glasses in the cupboard by the sink
and a glass pitcher, everything left as it had always been,
waiting. More knick-knack shelves, with a collection of
salt and pepper shakers: a pair of starfish, two lobsters,
two lighthouses, a pair of seals. They all had round
eyes, even the starfish. Stella took the pitcher and went
out to the spring to fill it, and when she came back into
the cottage Dianne sat up, taking a glass of water and
gulping it down before falling back to sleep.

Stella sat in an armchair by the fireplace looking
at the empty woodbox. She wondered where the
matches were but was too tired to stand up and look.
She thought about the snacks in her backpack but her
stomach was queasy. She considered her brain, that the
seahorse in her head would restore itself now they were
by the ocean. Or maybe not. But perhaps she could
navigate without it. Stella wanted to take a nap but she
needed to pee. The floor creaked as she stepped carefully, not to wake Dianne.

It was then she saw the book on the shelf against the wall beside the red sofa. By itself on the shelf except for a photo in an elaborate frame made of seashells. Stella crept over the floor, carefully, and looked at the picture. It was her and Isaiah, standing on the beach around a driftwood fire, the sun setting on the bay behind them, the island low and dark in the background, a silhouette. The island was real. This was confirmation. And Dianne, sitting on a log, her head back laughing as she roasted a marshmallow. Stella did not remember that night. She closed her eyes and waited. She pictured the mind shells guarded by the seahorses. But they didn't move.

The outhouse was in the woods and full of cobwebs. But Stella didn't mind cobwebs. She left the door to the outhouse open and sat on the cold wooden seat. Nothing came out, and then a gush. She kept sitting, waiting, thinking about the photo and who had taken it, not who was in it. There was old toilet paper, damp from age. The cottage had been a year-round house when it was built, for some ancestor who was a fisherman. But Isaiah had only used it as a cottage in the warmer months. When they would open it up in the spring it was always neat and dusty, as it was now.

Stella wiped and saw blood on the toilet paper. She thought about her test at the hospital. She couldn't recall if they had given her the results. She was quite sure they had not, but not sure enough. Through the branches the sky was orange. Sunset. Evening.

DIANNE WAS STILL SNORING as Stella poked around in the kitchen. There was no food, of course, except what she had in her backpack. Her routine was gone, the routine that framed and shaped her life. Stella wasn't sure what day it was. There was no Fireside Friday. No Seaside Saturday. She knew she should try to light a fire but her body felt weighted down. It seemed the rocky beach had come in through the floor and the rocks had fingers, curling around her ankles. She looked at the photo again, and then at the black book. She took it to the window for the last of the dying light. There was a silver flower on the spine, the stem running to the bottom, delicate petals near the top. She opened the book, turning the thick, yellowed pages until she came to the title page: *The Commonplace Book of the Offing Society.* The rest of the book was blank. Must be one of Isaiah's antiques, she thought as she set it on the coffee table and curled up on the loveseat, across from Dianne. Stella kept looking at the book. There was something familiar about it but she couldn't quite figure out what.

The light was dark grey now. She heard the breakers. Almost high tide. A breeze came in through the broken windowpane, blowing the curtain. The ocean was calling her name. Her thumb throbbed. It seemed a lady in alabaster had come through the door humming, holding a gauzy shawl she whispered was made of sleep, and it fell down upon Stella, a spiderweb covering her, taking her away to a place where there were no dreams, and no sound, no words or wind or ripples.

A VOICE. DRONING ON. It was hard to wake up. The air was cold in her nose. Where was she? Who was speaking? The air smelled different, familiar, but it was the reminiscence of a scent, comforting, a scent of another time.

"Rise and shine."

Stella's face was crushed into a musty pillow, a hard pillow, cotton stuffing dense from years of resting heads. Her eyes were crusty. Stella was at Periwinkle Cottage. Her thumb burned and she pulled her hand out from the blanket. It was swollen and red.

"Going to sleep all day, Stellie? Must be almost noontime from the looks of the sky. We're safe here, I reckon, for now. Awful stiff today. But nothing like sleep to fix you right up."

Dianne was eating crackers at the kitchen table, mushing them up with her gums. She sipped from a glass of water and ate a few blackberries and raspberries that she must have picked outside. Sunlight streamed in through the windows. "Come and get your breakfast. Can you move yourself, Stella girl? Lots to look at here. Bringing back any memories for you?"

Stella shook her head. Dianne was in no hurry, relaxed and comfortable in the way people are when they have always lived in a place. "We could put on a fire and have a cuppa tea. Better than this old water." She rattled a tea tin on the centre of the table. "Found this in the cupboard. Bags inside. Tea gets better with age, my nana always said."

There was a croaking sound outside and a crow flew by the window. Stella fell back to sleep.

When she woke the next time, her thumb still ached. Stella opened her eyes. Dianne was sitting up on the sofa, an iron fire poker across her lap, the knick-knack shelf with the figurines and boxes and shells directly over her. Stella worried for a moment that it might fall. But she could see how expertly it was attached to the wall. Isaiah was exacting and particular. Everything at Periwinkle spoke to this.

The sun was coming in from the side and front windows, the west and the north. It was late afternoon. They were at the cottage. There was a fire in the fireplace. A bit of driftwood in the woodbox. Stella pushed herself up. She had been in a dead sleep and hadn't heard Dianne get up and leave, make the fire. The tide was coming in. The water was a silvery golden quivering thing advancing on the land. Dianne pointed at the black book on the coffee table. "See you found that. Remember what it is?"

Stella did not remember *what* it was. But she did have a feeling it was important. Stella knew Dianne was watching her face carefully, looking for a change in Stella's expression, any sign she might be recalling just what the book was. Stella felt a pulse in her arm, in her chest. Something inside of her was festering its way out, whether she wanted it to or not.

Poetry Night.
Private Matters.

Now

THE POETRY READING WAS in the old courtroom in the Jericho County Museum and Mal was the first one to arrive. She sat on a wooden bench at the back of the room. She hoped she would get more out of Grace than she had from the strange old woman on the Flying Squirrel Road and from Seraphina. Mal wondered if Grace might know who these women were, but it sounded so ridiculous when Mal tried to prepare a question: *Do you know that old lady on the mountain who lives on a dirt road, by the run-down house with the strange fountain? She ran away into the woods when I questioned her.* Mal tried to figure out what to ask. Grace hadn't exactly been welcoming, but at least Mal knew how to talk to her.

"Malmuria?"

Mal jumped.

"Sorry. You were a million miles away, as they say. I didn't mean to startle you."

Mal stood up. Grace looked like her author photo in her book, which Mal had bought at the stationery in Bigelow Bay — her hair down, a flowing blouse. The stationery store had a whole gift section and a post office, a book section in the back, as well as a toy aisle, a puzzle aisle, and a table in the corner with a sign that said *Tea-Leaf Readings*.

Mal wanted to ask Grace if they could go for coffee, if Grace could tell her what to do. She needed a friend here. A big sister. Instead, Mal said, "Thanks for not calling security on me at the centre."

"Thanks for coming to my reading."

"I still want to speak with Stella Sprague."

"I'm on holiday this week, Mal. And I really can't talk about residents. I'd lose my job. You understand that, right? Privacy. Stella's had a lot to deal with. She doesn't need someone trying to pry into her past."

"I'm not trying to pry. I'm telling you I interviewed someone in California who said she had been abused when she was young, by this group of men, Sodality, and that it went back for decades to some secret place at Mercy Lake. She said these men were worried there was evidence that could incriminate them." Mal sighed. "Listen, I know this sounds crazy, but I want my work to have meaning and I can't let this go."

"I don't think you're crazy, I really don't, Mal. You should go to the police. Most people my age know stories about Mercy Lake, but they're the kinds of stories we told as kids to scare each other. If you're doing research, you need to know how quickly fact gets mixed up with fiction. If any of this is true you could be in real danger. I don't mean to sound motherly but I really think you should let this go. I know you talked to Stella's friend. Dianne mentioned you came by. She seems to believe you. And one of the nurses on her unit said she saw Dianne talking to someone . . . who looked like you."

"You mean Black?"

Grace smiled. "Yes, that's what I mean."

"I'm sure she didn't put it that way."

"No, she didn't. This isn't California. It's a white place. It's an English place. Some of my heritage is Acadian and they don't like the French either. It's the Georgia of the north here. You need to be careful if anything you're saying is true."

A woman at the front of the room was introducing Grace. She turned to go. "I read some of your stories online, Mal. The *Paris Review. American Short Fiction.* Impressive. And I listened to some of the episodes on your podcast. You have a lot of talent, you know. Your work already has meaning. You don't have to be an investigative journalist on top of that."

Maybe it was the strangeness of the setting, the old courtroom. And the fact that Grace and Mal were both writers. Whatever it was, Mal knew Grace understood the absurdity of the situation, and its seriousness, and the peculiar obscurity of a short-fiction writer and poet.

Grace read from her latest poetry book, which was about the murder of a woman in the early twentieth century that the husband had been hanged for. The trial had taken place in the same courtroom they were in. It was packed. Mal thought it had probably been packed back when the trial took place too. It was strange, poetic, being in the same space once for law and now for art.

There were three older Asian women in the front row, but almost everyone was white — white and middle-aged — except for a row of Girl Guides in their uniforms sitting with their leader and a few chaperones, one who wore hijab. Mal thought of California. Of her mother in Big Sur. Her eyes watered. She wanted to go home. Grace's voice rang out, each word washing over Mal. She leaned back and looked at the wooden ceiling. The poetry was incredible. She thought about her old boyfriend, his shaman journey, the poems he rattled off. There was no comparison.

Mal was not going home now. She needed to talk to Seraphina again and ask her what she knew about her mother. But how was she going to find her? If Mal asked Grace or Jillian how to track Seraphina down, they would think Mal too was off her medication. If she called her own mother, interrupted her retreat in

Big Sur, she would be able to figure out things much faster. But then she would have to admit she'd lied. And the real problem was not Mal lying—it was what her mother had omitted from her childhood. Mal was beginning to realize her stories and memories had been carefully curated—details and people and places selected as though her mother was picking apples, only the safe ones for her daughter.

Big Girls Don't Cry.

Then

STELLA SITS AT THE breakfast table eating soggy cereal, thinking about what the neurologist called *circadian rhythms* and how hers seem all out of whack from the car accident and probably the change in geography. Her father is at work for the morning in his new office at the university so he can get oriented with the campus.

Stella jumps when Cynthia calls out, coming in from the back porch, the screen door slamming behind her. As Cynthia strides into the kitchen, the black book on the bookcase between the table and the counter falls to the floor. Stella looks at it and then at Cynthia who smiles, her eyes bright red and watery in the way eyes get from lack of sleep.

"I'm just finishing breakfast. Don't people knock around here?"

"No one knocks in Seabury. Haven't you learned that by now?"

What Stella has learned by now is that Cynthia will keep appearing and reappearing, no matter what Stella does. They are bound by secrets, and something else Stella only senses. It doesn't matter if they have fun. It doesn't matter if Stella even likes Cynthia. She'll never get rid of this beautiful, gregarious, kind girl with the impervious face, this girl who brings out a swell of shame in Stella, followed by a gush of seething jealousy, chased by the highest wave, one of icy remorse. She wants a best friend but she has compromised this friendship. Cynthia lied to protect her, the stolen paper never spoken of between them, the act of framing Cynthia only drawing her closer.

Cynthia picks up the black book from the floor. She looks at it and opens her mouth, about to speak. But she doesn't, and sets the book on the counter. Cynthia begins tidying up the kitchen. "Granny's hoping you can come over today. She wants to show you some of the plants in her garden."

Stella takes her plate and glass over to the sink and Cynthia washes them. "Is this the book Granny was talking about? It's got that weird title but the pages are blank." Stella holds the book out.

Cynthia dries her hands and takes the book, flipping through the pages, not surprised. "My grandmother will know. Yes, I think it's the missing book the Offing

Society used. We can ask her, okay?" Cynthia stuffs the black book in her backpack as the girls head outside.

THEY SPEND THE AFTERNOON helping Granny in the garden. She sits in a chair and tells them what to do. They are digging out a garden for her in the shape of a maze. It's hard work, digging, but she wants to move some plants into it. She's very serious, and speaks in hushed tones. She's acting strange and Cynthia is acting strange by pretending that everything is normal. Stella wears sunglasses and a hat so the light won't bother her eyes, but she gets tired and sits beside Granny Scotia both of them watching Cynthia dig. She never seems to tire. Stella is overcome with loneliness, wishing she had her mother to fly home to in Ohio, or her own grandmother, or that she could live with Granny Scotia and Cynthia, and not have to pretend anymore with her father that they are a family. Stella keeps wanting to cry. Her father was always irritated by her mother's tears. Her mother's tears frightened him. *Big girls don't cry*, he would yell. What would have happened if her mother hadn't died, if they hadn't gotten in the car that evening?

Not much progress has been made on the maze. They head inside, out of the heat. Stella feels Cynthia is humouring Granny Scotia now, that she knows this is foolish, to put in a garden in September. If Stella knows that, and she's an American from Ohio, surely they must know it. They drink iced lavender lemonade and eat ginger cookies in the shade of the verandah. Cynthia disappears inside and comes out with the black book, which she hands to Granny. Granny Scotia sets her glass down. She looks at it, closes her eyes and strokes it. She then opens her eyes and the book. Stella thinks maybe now the pages will be covered in words, that it was her concussed head that couldn't see them, that Cynthia had just played along, as she seems happy to do, only pretending the pages are blank, and that now Granny will read her a story and everything will be okay. But Granny Scotia just runs her hands over the thick yellow paper. "I wish I could read this. I wish I could see the words and read it. Girls, the weather is changing. Things are not as they were. I feel so tired now. This was your grandmother's book, Stella. She brought it over from the island when she left. Morgana kept this secret. She kept it safe. I can't remember how to read it anymore." Then Granny leans back in her chair with her eyes closed once more, and her breathing slows and her hands relax. The book slides down her dress. A seagull flies overhead in the peerless blue sky.

CREAMY SEAFOOD CHOWDER AND warm scones for supper. Granny says grace, a short, quick one, with a moment of silence and then a few words Stella has never heard before. "Praise to Holy Mother Mercy. Praise the salt and earth, the fire and water. Bless the vulnerable. Bless the fragile. Bless the courageous. Give us strength. May the gatherings of the earth and the sea nourish us and sustain us. Praise be. And forgive us, Holy Mother Mercy, for any of our failings, if we have not served you properly. Praise be."

"Praise be," Cynthia echoes, in what sounds like a habit. Granny looks at Stella through the steam rising up from her chowder bowl.

"Dear, you look as though you've seen a ghost. I wouldn't wonder. You're the same as your grandmother. She had a way about her. My way is what I can find in the garden."

Cynthia doesn't say a word—her sole focus is eating. Stella thinks she's wondering if Stella will decide Granny is completely senile, which she might be. Or maybe not. It's hard to tell.

Granny's mind is sailing around in time now, only gently tied to the shore of the present in which Stella met her, but the knots are already loosened, letting go. Stella remembers her mother once said that there comes a time when the body gets frail, older, weaker, when life wears on it, and that the mind will either follow the body or it won't. But once it starts down the path of the failing body, it rarely comes back. She believes now, as she thinks of her faceless mother, that Granny is far down this path.

"So...how did my grandmother die, Granny Scotia? My dad never told me. He just said she died after Stella

Violette drowned. Did my grandmother have tuberculosis? Is that why my father is so interested in old
institutions?"

"My goodness, Stella, *no one* had tuberculosis. Your
grandmother fell down the stairs. Just tumbled down.
She was grief stricken, after Violette drowned. Didn't
your father tell you any of this? It almost destroyed him,
so perhaps his approach, as it is with many people, is
not to talk about it, to hide it away and pretend it never
happened. He had to take a year off school when your
grandmother died. And Franklin could never forgive
me when his father died. He fell down Seabury Gorge.
I was the one who found him. Franklin insinuated I'd
pushed the man down there myself." A look ripples
across Granny's face and is gone before Stella can decide
if it was a smile or a frown.

Stella is still sorting through what Granny has said
when the old woman bursts out with more family
history Stella had no idea about. "Your *father* was
in the institution, not your grandmother, for land's
sake." Granny thumped her cane. "Nobody got put
into an institution but your father, and I don't think
it was humane. He goes on about the old days of
moral care but those days were gone by his time. His
father didn't even visit him, to my knowledge. We
went down once on a Sunday. He couldn't even speak.
I don't know what they did to him. That's why he
ended up studying these hospitals, the philosophies

and theories of buildings and healing. Well, I'll have you know that the mind is a structure, and when you compartmentalize and create rooms in it as your father did, it never goes well. But at some point he needed to face reality and make some choices. Instead, what does he do but lose himself in his work, wishing that there was a morality to healing and caring, that the mentally ill were not seen as pariahs but as the prophets he believed they were. You see, his work is his message. You really should know this. We need to know our family history. I can't believe he's kept it a secret. I expect your mother didn't even know. Your grandfather just had a heart attack in his sleep. No one even knew he had heart problems. I had Frank take him over some special tea, to help him sleep deeply. He was having nightmares and that was no surprise, after the terrible life he led. Did your father tell you anything about that?"

"Just a bit. He said that my grandmother was married off to him after the lighthouse, that she was young and didn't really have much choice."

"Yes, that's the truth. We were all married off in those days. My own family had me marry into the Seaburys. We were out of money, except for the land."

Granny gazes over their heads. Then she looks at Cynthia and next at Stella, then back at Cynthia. "Cynthia, I think it's time to take Stella Maris upstairs and show her our sitting room, don't you?"

Stella climbs up the stairs behind Cynthia. She has said nothing about any of this shocking family story. She let Granny Scotia tell it without even a comment, only stirring to pull the black book from her backpack.

The stairs open onto an imposing landing with windows facing all four directions. Stella can see stars in the sky. It's a widow's walk, Granny explains as she leads them to an old door beside the western window. She takes out a skeleton key from her pocket and opens it. The house is quiet, so quiet Stella thinks she hears the beams creaking, the sound of the waves and the wind at the windows, murmuring, speaking to her. For once Stella's head doesn't hurt. She feels light-headed, emptied. Then her hands and feet break out in a sweat. Her panic and anxiety feel alive, a beast pushing its way up through her.

Granny claps her hands and they are just three people in an old house. "Stella, come back to us," she says. They go down a skinny back staircase and Granny opens another door, at the rear of the house. The sitting room is an alcove with poufy chairs by an oval window looking over the gardens and out to the water. Granny turns on a lamp. The air smells savoury, aromatic—overhead, hanging from hooks on the ceiling, are thick bundles of dried herbs and flowers. Stella doesn't know what these herbs and flowers are, or if they are freshly dried or have been hanging here for a hundred years. There is a wall-to-ceiling cupboard that runs the length of the room, the shelves lined with books and glass jars of dried herbs and flower petals, powders and salts, several mortar and pestles, made of marble and slate. There are glass bottles with unguents and liquids.

"This is where the Offing used to meet. The men have the Sodality and we have the Offing Society. They don't pay attention to these things, you understand, Stella Maris."

Cynthia sets the black book down on the wooden table. Granny holds her hands over it. "That's right. We'll keep it here. Better than at the Sprague house. It did well to avoid being discovered, except now, by you, Stella. I'll see if I can remember how to use it. So much time has passed and it was something Morgana Llewellyn understood. She brought it from the island."

Stella wants to linger in that old comfortable room with the pungent air, air dense with secrets, but Granny hustles them out right away, maybe worried Stella's father might arrive while they are in this special room, that Frank might suddenly appear. "Girls," Granny says, "the key is to keep a man's attention diverted. It isn't that men don't pay attention — they sometimes cannot have their attention diverted when it's drawn to a secret."

They come downstairs just in time to see head-lights turning into the driveway. Stella says goodbye to Granny and Cynthia. She goes out to the rental car and as she buckles her seat belt, she looks back at Cedar Grove. Granny and Cynthia are illuminated in the doorway, their arms linked. Stella's father honks as he drives down the lane, away from the warm glow of the house.

Aside from a bit of catch-up, Stella and her father don't talk. Stella wants to ask about her grandmother, about her aunt, about her father himself. If Granny mixed it up, if only her dad could just clarify, if he could just make sense of everything that had happened since the spring, how they had gone from a predictable life in Ohio to living in this weird village of Seabury where nothing seems quite right. She doesn't know who to turn to. She wants to talk to Cynthia but she can't. Stella has been waiting for Cynthia to confront her about the stolen paper, to ask why Stella did it, but it never comes up. It seems Cynthia hasn't wondered at all. Maybe it doesn't matter to her, as if at thirteen she's already chewed on enough life to know that people do strange things. Either way, it's disturbing.

That night Stella dreams of the verandah on Sunnyside Drive, the night sky, Polaris fixed in the muted ebony overhead. But then it is dusk. Her mother driving without the seat belt, surprised it didn't work, that it was jammed, but not worrying about it. There is a flash. There is a shadow but it seems displaced, a broad shadow looming over everything. A flash outside the window before they leave the house. A man, a squat man, hurrying over the sidewalk. Turning towards the house, to the window, where Stella pulls back the curtain.

The Path.
The Rain.

Now

MAL SAT ON THE lawn chair on the deck of her Sun
Valley Motel cabin drinking coffee. The air was heavy
and it was either going to start raining or the sun
would blister through the clouds. Mal hadn't bothered
checking the weather or listening to the news. She
worried about her phone now, although she suspected
Seraphina was just ranting in the way manic people
sometimes did.

This was all a very, very bad idea. Mal saw that now.
She knew she was trying to prove to herself that she
could do something of value. Grace had put it in plain
words, the way her mother would have, and in the same
non-judgemental way, an observational way. Maybe
painters and poets had the same sort of brains, Mal
thought. All of this was in response to the texts she

got from her ex-boyfriend in Vancouver, just before her mother had started talking about going to Big Sur. He even wrote his text messages like he thought they were awesome poems.

Hey Mal Nice podcast

He had listened to her podcast. He thought it was nice. *Nice.*

Soothing like tea & strawberry jam on tea biscuits
The kind the Empress Hotel served for their high tea
Remember?

Of course Mal fucking remembered. That was part of the problem. She wanted to forget her poor judgement. Scott had been a geophysicist before he was a writer. He had decided to study creative writing after he started writing short stories when he was up in the Yukon working in the gas and oil industry, bored. They both loved cycling. That was their connection: meeting at a party, sex and mountain biking. And talking short stories. It was her first and only relationship aside from a few hookups. It lasted for a year. Then her father got sick. She went back to California. He was vaguely supportive, sending her ludicrous poetry texts, FaceTiming her before and after his mountain biking. Then that time she heard someone giggle, a female giggle, from behind a tree.

Mal couldn't talk to her father about it because he was dying. Her mother told her not to waste her time on a man who clearly wasn't serious. Heartbreak devastated her. Mal worked herself into anxiety tornados trying to analyze every feeling, ever single decision, every failing, until she was just a hysterical, useless lump on her bed in her parents' apartment above the garage.

Mal's coffee was cold now, but that didn't take much, as the coffee maker in the cottage only brewed it warm. She drank it anyway. She had been waking up every hour during the night to check the parking lot, to see if the black car was following her. Mal set the coffee cup on the copy of *Midnight's Children*. She was paranoid, exhausted, and alone — the same way she'd felt when she left Vancouver. Just looking at the novel on the arm of the lawn chair evoked her dad. Mal wished he was here with her, having cold coffee.

After he died, Mal had gone back to Vancouver, and Scott was happy to see her. But he was on a shaman diet. A shaman's path. He was going to hike the Pacific Trail and live in a tent, eat and drink out of one bowl, with one spoon, a bland diet without spices. He was going to write a memoir. He would be one with the trees. He was also almost forty. He was having a mid-life crisis, her mother said. He was all about the swagger. There were other fish in the sea, stars in the sky, flowers in the garden, shells on the beach. Blah blah blah. Mal knew all that, but it didn't make her feel better. She couldn't believe she had ever found him attractive. Self-loathing wrapped around her in a cold, clammy squeeze.

When California issued a shelter-in-place alert because of the coronavirus, Mal's mother insisted she come home again, immediately. *Mal, just let it go. It's okay. We all make choices we regret. It's not falling down that's the problem. It's getting back up you need to do. And none of it matters right now. There is a pandemic.*

It was like listening to a hockey coach. Mal dropped out of university. To make it worse, her parents never pressured her to be like them, but to make the most of her high-strung nature. They never got angry when what she tried didn't work out. There was so much less opportunity for her generation — it wasn't her fault. Their kindness and patience made Mal feel crazy with failure.

A truck engine. A loud engine. Mal stood up as the old green pickup came revving into the parking lot. Seraphina drove over and parked in front of her deck. There was a girl in the passenger seat. She gave Mal a little wave with such a look of longing on her face that Mal wanted to ask if she needed help. But the young girl looked down and by then Seraphina was standing in front of Mal.

"Hi there. So how did you find me?"

"There aren't a lot of places to stay around here. I figured I'd check out the motels first. And here you are. Not so good at hiding."

"I'm not trying to hide."

"Well, you should be. I can't protect so many of you." Seraphina reached out and put a cloth bag in Mal's hand. "This should help a bit. It's some flowers and herbs. You're on a dangerous path, girl. Too bad there's no periwinkle here, around your cottage, like where those other two are."

"I see." Mal didn't see anything except that Seraphina was what her gramma Grant would have called *touched*. "Just who is Lucretia? It would really be nice if someone would tell me who the hell she is."

Seraphina laughed. "You do have some life in you. Well, let me tell you, I used to think Lucretia was dead. Or just make-believe. But now I believe there's always some old woman named Lucretia who starts walking by the shore when danger comes, who understands the currents and knows the old words and ways. We're all related to her, way back."

Mal exhaled. "I see."

"Oh, you don't fool me. I know what people think of me. But I understand. I can read the signs. It doesn't matter if they think I'm nuts. Your mother knew— that's why she left. You get on a plane and go. They'll try to get rid of all of us, don't you understand?"

The car door opened and slammed shut and the girl came over. "Mom, we need to go. You're scaring her. And me. Don't you see that?"

"What I see is that everyone is trying to get me to just shut up, trying to be helpful. But—"

"I know, Mom, danger's coming. It's going to be the police coming. You know they'll call and report me missing."

Mal watched the girl walk back to the truck and get in, her head down again. Seraphina stomped back to the driver's side and hoisted herself into the seat. She started the engine and looked through the windshield at Mal. She didn't smile but she didn't look angry either. Her face was still and her mouth was set in a thin line. Mal recognized this expression. It was one of realization, that moment where things fall into place, and with this, resignation coming down in a soft and unstoppable rain.

Seaweed and Salt Water Stew.

Now

THEY GATHERED DRIFTWOOD ON the beach in the afternoon. The cottage was just behind the beach, only about twenty feet back from where the grey rocks started. Stella collected sticks for kindling. Her hand ached where she had cut it on the window glass. Dianne carried a few bigger logs. They hobbled back over the beach after piling the sticks in the wood box. "Got to find some dulse. We can eat that. Used to do that with my nana, down that way." Dianne pointed west. She gathered some seaweed left behind by the tide, also picking up hollow pieces of straw and putting those in the pocket of her dirty blue dress, now smudged with soot from the fire. Dianne walked slowly, more stiffly than normal. Stella felt a tightness in her chest as she listened to Dianne wheeze. "Out of smokes, Stella. Just as well but not the time I'd pick to quit smoking."

A high-pitched squealing came through the fog from down near the water. Dianne and Stella looked at each other. With the second shrill squeal Dianne stiffened. "Might be seals," she said hopefully.

Stella considered this. Seals grunted, barked — sea dogs, Isaiah used to call them. Surely Dianne knew that. In her mind, Stella saw herself as a young woman on the beach near Periwinkle Cottage. Sunset, the bay crimson-stained, a hot summer evening. The man beside her, Isaiah, her uncle, the dark shapes on the luminous water, seals chasing fish on the incoming tide.

Then children's laughter pulled Stella back to the hazy August beach on a day of the week she couldn't remember, the idea of a week almost dissolved, with time measured in daylight and nightlight, and the times in between. Dianne smiled and Stella wondered at how foreign the laughter was, how these young creatures were so remote and unknown to them. There was the clinking of rocks as the children came up the beach and emerged from the white, the older one with dark hair saw them first and stopped, putting her arms around the other two, both much younger.

Cynthia. Was it Cynthia? No, it couldn't be, Stella thought, as she looked down at her hands, her old hands, and the sudden twist of her gut, the ache. She was not a girl. She was not middle-aged. She was not old. She was lost in between ages, no different from that time separating night from day. It was Dianne before her with her hands on her hips, trying to stretch her sacrum by leaning back, her hair loose now, moving in the humid breeze. She and Dianne might be washed out to sea and no one would ever know what had become of them. No one would ever be there at her grave or Dianne's grave except for banshee seals and whales and keening winds.

"Hello, girls," Dianne called to the children. She smiled, but without her teeth she looked menacing. Her hair was matted, like long pieces of bleached seaweed, streaks of soot on her cheeks. For all Stella knew, Dianne had drawn them as part of a ritual while she was making a fire, evoking forces Stella couldn't even imagine. Stella smoothed her dress, running her fingers over the stains from where she had slopped the tea and onion soup the day before. Or was it the day before that? The mist blocked out the sun and sky. A perpetual twilight. All Stella could see were her hands, the misty faces of the girls, the back of Dianne's head, a few dark rocks. But she could hear the breakers. The water was higher on the beach.

"Girls, we're looking to know the time. Do you have the time?" They didn't say a word and then the two smaller ones giggled, and the older one pushed them up the beach, over the rocks in their bare nimble feet. "It's suppertime soon," the older one called over her shoulder as they vanished into the mists.

The blue cottage had been obscured but now it

peeked out as they came onto the lawn. Stella saw Dianne stumble with her seaweed, putting out a hand and steadying herself on a rock. She pushed herself back upright and Stella noticed a bit of blood on Dianne's hands. Stella took in a sharp breath and Dianne smiled. "My land. We both got cuts now, battle scars. Don't you worry about me. I'm tough as these old rocks. You're not looking so good, Stella. Let me cook you up a camp supper." Stella was feeling very warm, even with the damp breeze.

There was a crunching, the sound of feet on the rocky beach. Dianne whirled around, wincing from the effort. A wave crashed through the mist. The tide was close now. "If they come for us, you go in the water. You'll be safe there." This made no sense to Stella. The footsteps on the rocks became louder and louder, closer and closer.

"Well, for God's sake. Look who it is. Are you two following me?" Seraphina clomped out of the white, over the rocks in her uniform of hiking boots and sundress. Stella thought that they too must look in uniform with their house dresses and running shoes.

"Serrie! For the love of God, what do you want? Scared the life right out of me."

"There are worse things that could happen. I've come to warn you again. That journalist still wants to find you, but I said I didn't know where you were. And it was true. I thought maybe they got you and then

I thought maybe you were saved. Then I thought maybe you were both shivering away in that blue cottage not knowing what to do. I'm here to help. There's no point in calling the police. They're just covering up all of this anyway. You can't trust anyone. Do you understand? Someone already did call the police and then took Aurora away. I told her she wasn't safe either. She's got eyes the same as yours, Stella. They'll look for her too. I told her that, I yelled it at her when they took her away. They wanted to take me too, back to the hospital, but there was no way I was getting in that police car. I know my rights, my patient rights. They don't care because it's just one less person for them to deal with. Aurora told them she ran away, that I didn't take her. It is to weep. I told Aurora to tell them I was about to head down to Seabury, to tell them that, so they wouldn't look for me here. I whispered it in her ear when I hugged her. She was bawling away but I think she heard me." Seraphina's voice was very loud; she was singing, then chanting and finally wailing.

"I don't know the right words. But Stella does. If only she could remember. Don't you remember being in Seabury? Don't you remember Granny Scotia? Your eyes, Stella Maris. You have the gemstone eyes. It must be in you still. Granny Scotia only knew the teas and herbs, the things of the land. But your people knew the salt water cures, the salt water spells. Dianne, you know."

Stella waited for Dianne to laugh and roll her eyes, but she was listening very carefully, with her head cocked to the side. "I do," Dianne said.

"My mother was a lost cause, God bless her soul." Seraphina bowed her head. "All I know is what Granny Scotia said: *Keep watch. You keep watch.*"

Stella's head felt full, those beach pebbles, shifting from side to side, pouring back and forth with the slightest movement of her head. She parted her lips, making an opening to the cave of her mouth. But no words came. Her throat was so dry and her arms trembled.

Seraphina pointed out over the water. Stella could see strange gleaming peaks. "It's the three sisters," Seraphina yelled. "Three waves coming together. You don't normally see them this close to the beach—it's something offshore. Surely you know that, Dianne? You should too, Stella, if you could just wake up. What's wrong with you two? Why does it all fall to me? I don't have any power. I'm just the prophet. But no one listens to me. Oh, there goes Crazy Serrie. There goes the madwoman. They just don't want to hear my message. There are powers who will destroy us. They have everything to lose and we have nothing to lose."

Dianne beckons at Stella to come up off the beach, which she does just as a wave breaks on the rocks, the surf stretching up and over her feet, soaking her running shoes, gushing ten feet ahead of her to Dianne, who loomed cliff-like in the spray. A spiralling twist of green water broke, the sea swirling around Stella's knees, the force of it knocking her over as the salt water sucked back into the bay. Seraphina pulled her up, her manic energy unbelievable. "The salt water will revive you, Stella," she said, as their faces and hair were soaked. She carried Stella up the beach to Dianne and plunked her down. Dianne carefully took Stella's uninjured hand and led her off the rocks while Seraphina turned to greet the last rise of glassy green sea water that shattered on the beach in a white foaming veil stretching forward over Seraphina's legs as she walked into the ocean, her head lost in the fog, only her shoulders and black hair visible, a strange painting—*the headless sea girl of the Fundy*, Stella thought, clutching her abdomen. There were no more high breakers, just steady crests moving in to the high-water mark, the mist lifting a bit, and Seraphina's voice out in the bay where she was splashing, singing a song Stella didn't know.

"Don't worry about that one. Couldn't drown her if you grabbed her by the neck and held her under the surface. She'll live forever," Dianne said.

But Stella did worry. She worried about whomever it was coming after them. She worried about Seraphina being right. And she thought about the earnest young woman in the sunshine-yellow dress, who worried her most of all.

Various Sorts of Glory.

Now

MAL REACHED AN AUTOMATED answering service at the Jericho Centre. She had to press a bunch of buttons to get put through to Grace. It went right to voicemail—Grace was on the other line. Mal sat in her car in the graveyard looking at Isaiah Settles's tombstone while she kept pressing redial.

"Grace Belliveau speaking."

"Hi, Grace. This is Mal Grant-Patel."

Pause.

"Mal, I told you I can't talk about residents." Grace's voice was quiet.

"I know, I know, but I just—"

"But I am going to because something has happened. Stella has gone missing. I was going to call you. That card came in handy. You only had one of those email contact forms on your website."

"What?"

"And Dianne has gone missing too. They can't be far. They could be dead in the woods. They could be injured in the forest. Someone saw them in the graveyard."

"That's where I am now." Mal coughed.

"What are you doing in the graveyard? Mal, you sound sick. I think you should go back to California. Can't you research this from there? The police are looking for Stella and Dianne now."

"It's this group, Sodality," Mal said. "They could have them. Or they'll find them first. I'm telling you, Grace, they think Stella has some incriminating evidence — something they thought burned up in the fire at Mercy Lake. They prey on young girls. And, apparently, the occasional old woman. If they find Stella and whatever she has, that's pretty much it. They've been following me around."

"For real? Mal, if that's true, we need to go to the police."

Incredulity was gone. Grace believed her, Mal could tell. She was speaking quietly. The way Mal's mother did when she was alarmed.

"What would I tell the police? They're going to think I'm crazy for coming here in the first place."

"What you need to focus on is your own safety, Mal. Right now we have to find Stella and Dianne, especially if some crazy person is following women around. Stella has a history of wandering off. Dianne doesn't, so that's worrisome. Stella doesn't remember anything about what happened at Mercy Lake, so how do you think she'll know where this so-called evidence is?"

"Stella's grandmother was related to some lighthouse keepers out on an island in the Bay of Fundy. The Llewellyns. They came from Wales. There was some sort of story about them, you know, having some strange ancestry?"

"That's just a story, Mal. When you live here you know all the old stories, the weird woman by the shore, stuff like that."

"Grace, you know what I'm saying is true, even if it sounds crazy."

Just then there was a loudspeaker announcement in the background, a page for Grace.

"I do believe you, even though, yes, it sounds totally crazy."

"And I am looking into Sodality. But I'm also looking into this Offing Society, this group of women who used to meet. It came from the Old World, coastal communities, island cultures."

"Mal . . . why don't you call Lark Collins? She can better advise you than I can. She hosts the morning news show. Have you heard it?"

"I've been listening to it a bit while I'm here. Do you think she knows anything?"

"She'll be able to tell you who might. It's just history

and stories getting turned into fairy tales and myths. You have to understand how vulnerable these women are. We can't even find them."

"That Seraphina woman came and found me. Maybe she would know?"

Grace was quiet. She appeared to be hesitating. "Did Seraphina say anything about Stella and Dianne?"

"She was talking about keeping people safe, and danger coming. She gave me a bag of dried herbs and stuff. She was talking periwinkle. And a cottage." Grace was silent but Mal could tell she was listening. And Mal knew deep inside that Seraphina, despite her strange clothes and loud voice proclaiming various sorts of glory and evil, wasn't crazy at all.

Periwinkle Morning.
Lost in Time.

Now

STELLA WOKE UP ON the loveseat. The toilet paper in her panties felt stiff. Her thumb was festering where the window glass had pierced it. It was red and hot, half her hand puffed up like an inflatable glove. Dianne sat in the chair across from Stella. The fire had died down and only the tiniest glow simmered in the hearth. "Not feeling too good, are you? I think you got an infection in that hand of yours. You got a fever. I felt your fore-head. I'm not feeling so good myself, but I don't have no fever." Dianne wheezed as she went into the kitchen.

Stella had hoped a good night's sleep would make them both feel better. She missed the centre, the struc-ture of the days, the weeks, her walks with Dianne. Cat. They had come all the way to Periwinkle Cottage, but Stella hadn't remembered enough. They had hidden themselves away—that's one thing they did. Stella missed the institutional smell of the centre, what it represented. The predictability. The halls. The people. Fred and Bob. Charlotte Pacific's visits. Yoga Mondays and Crafting Tuesdays. The paths and bench by the river. Her Queen Anne chair and her clock. Her photo on the bookshelf. This cottage was full of echoes and silhouettes, flickers, the way an empty space is a reminder of what is gone, Stella thought. The centre, for all its strangeness, was a reminder of life, the strangeness of it, the worthiness of it.

Dianne came back from the kitchen and set down a cup of steaming tea in front of Stella. "Sure you don't recollect anything, Stellie, my girl? Remember your uncle—he always said you needed to go looking in the shells. Remember even that? He told me to tell you that and so I am, for what it's worth. He said he thought what you needed to know was hidden back in 1980. I know, girl. I know it's forty-some winding dark years past."

Dianne walked to the window and peered out. Then she lumbered to the sofa, stretching and settling into raspy, slow breath.

Stella sipped the tea. It was salty and sweet, and the pungent steam tickled her nose and sinuses. She thought of Granny Scotia, of Cynthia. She rubbed her temples. Deep inside her head an ache fluttered about. It was quiet in the cottage, except for Dianne's breathing and the sound of the surf outside.

Late-Night Visitors.

Then

STELLA AND HER FATHER are in the car, heading over to Granny Scotia's. He's going fly-fishing, alone, and then spending a few nights at the Faculty Club at the university, while Stella stays at Cedar Grove.

"Dad, you never told me what the moving company said. We've been here for two weeks. I just want to know." She wants to see the photos, ones of her mother, of her with her mother.

Her father stares ahead at the road. He reaches for the knob on the radio and then stops himself. He clears his throat. "Stella, I wish you'd stop asking me. Do I remind you of a truck driver? I told you to take anything you really wanted with you when we left."

The dull vibration deep in Stella's head starts to pick up pace.

"Didn't you do that?"

"Sure. I mean, I packed stuff I needed. It was hard to decide."

"Okay, I'll tell you the truth. I decided we didn't need anything from our old life. I told the landlady the Salvation Army was coming to get everything. It was all donated."

Stella bites her lip and tries not to cry. Her mind is noisy, her brain pulsing, her heart beating in her ears.

"Don't give me a hard time about it, okay? We can get new things, Stella. It's only stuff."

It's all gone. She only has what she has stored in her head. She knows why he did this—because he wants no reminders of the past. What is out of sight is out of mind. Granny is right when she says that her father stores things away in rooms in his mind. It's how he navigates his mind, like it's a building and he controls all the space.

It's almost noon when she gets out of the car, slamming the door, crushing his words. He reaches over and rolls down the passenger window. "Stella—"

"Leave me alone, okay? I just want you to leave me alone." She stamps towards the house as she hears the car engine idling and then driving down the lane. He beeps and beeps the horn. She gives him the finger. Inside, she takes a sharp breath, smoothing her hair, trying to compose herself.

Stella finds Granny and Cynthia inside making blueberry jam with late-summer berries. Granny intently screws lids onto the glass jars. Then Granny wants to go outside. She's flushed and her hair is messy. She looks how Stella feels inside. The girls follow her out to the garden where she sits in a chair beside the abandoned attempt at the Celtic knot garden she had them working on a few days before.

"Why don't I make some sandwiches, Granny?"

The old lady doesn't look at them.

Cynthia takes Stella into the house to make ham and lettuce sandwiches. "I'm sorry your mom left," Stella says as she spreads mustard on the bread. The old house seems extra creaky today, in sympathy with them, Stella thinks.

"Yeah. Whatever." Cynthia takes the knife and hacks away at the cold picnic ham.

STELLA AND CYNTHIA ARE in their nightgowns having cinnamon toast and milk at the kitchen table. Granny is not yet ready for bed but she's making a pot of sleeping tea, she calls it, from mint and passionflower and chamomile. Granny sits at the table while the concoction steeps under a tea cozy. It smells lovely as it brews, and for a moment Stella convinces herself that this is all for the best, the two motherless girls here. That maybe she can convince her father to let her live at Cedar Grove, and he can live at the Faculty House. The only problem is Cynthia and her impervious face. Stella wonders now if her seemingly devoted friend might turn on her. What if she knows that Stella was outside the window when Tommy Jessome attacked her? What if she is planning revenge for the stolen paper?

There is a strange knock on the back door. One knock followed by three shorter knocks, repeated three times. Granny doesn't move or speak. The knocking repeats, Cynthia watching Granny. The air in the room feels alive, heavy and thick, and the overhead light seems to dim for a moment. Stella puts her head down. She looks at her socks and wonders when they became grey. When Stella lifts her chin up, Granny is looking at her. "You're one of us, you know, Stella Maris, star of the sea." Then she points towards the back door. "Cynthia, see who it is."

Cynthia opens the door to the porch where a woman stands, bags under her eyes. She looks older than she is, fatigue pulling her mouth down, early middle-aged but an old lady at the same time. At her side is a young girl, about Cynthia and Stella's age. She has dark braids and tattered jean shorts. It's chilly and she has only a green T-shirt on, her arms covered in goosebumps. They both stare at Cynthia, with her black dress and eyeliner, her teased wild cloud of hair. Cynthia stares back. The curiosity of two strangers in Seabury knocking at the door in the purple hour.

Granny picks up her cane. "Martha. Goodness. It's late for you to have come all this way from the Lupin Cove Road. I haven't seen you in years. And who is this?"

"This is my daughter, Seraphina. Say hello." The middle-aged woman named Martha pushes the girl forward. She doesn't seem afraid, just nervous, shifting from foot to foot. "Hello, Mrs. Seabury."

"Ah, your daughter. Named for a fire spirit." Granny looks at Martha, who stares back.

"I need to speak with you."

Granny shoos Stella and Cynthia out of the kitchen. "Go to the front parlour, please, girls. Close the back door behind you."

They leave and close the door but the girls do not go to the front parlour. Cynthia and Stella hide behind the door to the kitchen listening, Stella looking through the keyhole.

Seraphina turns her head towards the kitchen door and Stella sees the girl sniff the air. Seraphina keeps looking at the door, blinking, cocking her head. Stella is sure Seraphina knows that she and Cynthia are on the other side.

"I need a tea for my daughter. I need something to keep her safe. She's thirteen now."

"I see. And why don't you go to the Flying Squirrel Road?"

"Because Lucretia is in prison. You know very well why."

"Yes, I suppose I do."

"Can you help me? I'm afraid for Serrie. I'm afraid for myself. It's desperate times. They have that stupid

Sodality. Just when you think things have fallen away. They'll never stop."

"And what is it you think I can do for her?"

"I know you still know the old ways. From the sea."

Seraphina hasn't spoken. She stands quietly while Granny and the other woman talk.

Stella hears the thump of Granny's cane, and through the keyhole sees her shuffle across the floor into the porch. Cynthia opens the kitchen door and takes Stella's sweaty hand as they creep into the kitchen and peer into the porch. Granny with a silver tin, measuring something into a paper bag. Muttering something into Martha's ear. It isn't any language Stella recognizes. Martha's eyes are closed and she bows her head as Granny whispers. Martha opens her eyes and Granny Scotia strokes her cheeks. "You understand, Martha? You must keep her safe. I know you're tired. I know how long the years can be. Keep watch. You must keep watch. Lucretia will come back. She always does."

Stella sees Seraphina in the porch with Granny and Martha, looking cowed. Seraphina sniffs again and then looks through the opened porch door into the kitchen at Stella and Cynthia. Her face is implacable, her dark hair casting her eyes into shadow.

The girls scurry back through the kitchen and down the hall to the parlour. A few minutes later they hear a car leaving and Granny thumping down the hall and into the parlour. She bangs her cane three times before turning and leaving the room.

Cynthia whispers very quietly, but Stella hears her: "We're not like other people, Stella. And neither are you. Granny did something she regrets. Something that brings her terrible pain. But I don't know what it is. She has a secret. Sometimes secrets are bad."

THE NEXT MORNING THEY find Granny in the garden. She's gathering up flowers in one arm, magenta phlox and late daisies, and lamenting: "Girls, you can't go to Mercy Lake. Don't go to Mercy Lake. That's where Stella Violette went. She should never have gone. She could swim. I don't see how she drowned. Don't go to the lake, girls. You'll drown there. That's what happens at Mercy Lake. I can't remember how to keep you safe. What has resided in me, it left this morning at dawn."

Then Granny Scotia goes wandering towards the marsh. They jump when Frank calls from behind them. They hadn't heard him drive up. He must have been listening. Frank doesn't say so, but his face says so. Frank tells them that Granny is having a spell, that she's having them more and more often now and they shouldn't pay attention. "I'll just follow her out to the marsh and see how she's doing, girls."

Stella looks around and then up at the sky, fantastic-ally hopeful a flock of birds might pass by and swoop down to her rescue. She doesn't know what to do. Her bicycle isn't here. Her father is away. Cynthia sits down in the grass and Stella sits beside her. For once, Cynthia's smooth calm face is troubled.

"Your aunt died at Mercy Lake. Granny said your father blamed himself. So did my father. They were with her in the boat. She could swim. The Sodality back then, back in 1940, was still weird, you know—a cult, I guess, some strange religion. And when the church helped you, you had to pay them back with something. My grandfather was dead by then, and Granny didn't really know what was going on. I mean, only men could join Sodality, go to the meetings in that old hall in the village. They didn't go to church anymore. It was just this weird fellowship. But your grandfather owed my grandfather's family money. He never took care of his debt. Now your father owes my dad money. Because now your grandfather's debt is your father's debt. They *never* forget."

"What? What do you mean they had to pay them back? With what?"

"Well, your grandfather had to pay them—"

"With what? What did he—"

"He had to pay them with…"

"Yes?"

"With your aunt."

Stella feels her breath draw back over her tongue, drying out the inside of her cheeks. She picks a dandelion from the lawn and blows it, and lets the empty wishes float away.

"Something about purity. That's all I've been able to figure out when Granny goes off the rails. I think Violette had to marry someone."

Finding her voice, Stella said, "But she was only thirteen years old!"

"I know. They took her to the lake. It was summertime and there were men visiting on a backwoods hunting trip, rich American and European men who came up. They went out in canoes and back into the woods with guides. She didn't want to go. I don't know it all, Stella, only bit and pieces."

Cynthia reaches for Stella's clammy hand and pulls her closer, dropping her voice, looking over her shoulder and then back at Stella. "Your father would know. He was there, Stella. He and my dad took Stella Violette out. At first she didn't want to go, so the men got our dads to take her. They tricked her. They were only fifteen. She was thirteen. They didn't have much of a choice. And then she went into the lake. Your dad tried to rescue her. But it was twilight. And your grandmother was very upset. They had tricked her as well. She hadn't even imagined that could happen. Your father was sent to boarding school. While he was there, your grandmother tripped and fell down the stairs. Your father, he came home for the funeral but he went crazy. They put him in the Nova Scotia Hospital. He wasn't the same afterward, Granny says, ever. And then he went back to boarding school."

Frank and Granny are walking back towards the house now, Granny leaning on Frank's arm. She seems better. After she goes inside, Frank tells them he is taking her to see the doctor.

The house is quiet after they leave. Granny didn't even protest, and got in Frank's car without a word. Cynthia is reading and Stella takes a nap. Her head has filled with a tedious pain. Her brain is trying to tell her something. Cynthia has known the whole time what happened to Stella Violette. She wonders what other secrets Cynthia might be keeping from her, or assuming Stella knows. Maybe it isn't just Stella who has been hiding things.

The phone rings just before supper. It's Frank, Stella can tell right away.

"Granny isn't well," Stella hears Cynthia repeat. *She's gone into the hospital for tests.*

Cynthia tells her father there is food in the fridge, that she can get supper. There is a silence and then Cynthia says in a quiet, hard voice that they are *teenagers* and, no, Tommy Jessome doesn't need to come over and keep them company.

STELLA AND CYNTHIA WAIT outside for Frank, who said he would take them to see Granny Scotia at the hospital. It's Saturday and the air is warm, although a few early-September leaves are turning orange and yellow. Frank arrives but doesn't get out of the car, and the girls hop in back. They drive down the lane with Frank talking about the splendour of fall, how much Stella will appreciate it. They don't turn into the village but head out into the country.

"I thought I'd take you girls out to Mercy Lake. I'm having a group of men out for a get-together. You girls can come and entertain yourselves."

Stella says nothing. She doesn't want to go to Mercy Lake with Cynthia and Frank. She thinks about what Granny and Cynthia said the previous day. Cynthia doesn't seem to want to go either. She crosses her arms and frowns as she stamps her foot. Frank is changing the plan without even asking them, a slight menace in what he's talking about now.

"You said you'd take us to see Granny Scotia," Cynthia says. "How's she doing?"

"She's doing well, Cynthia, but she needs to rest. She might have a heart problem. She's not making a lot of sense and it would just confuse her to see you girls in there. We'll go see her in a few days, okay? I let your father know what's happening, Stella."

IT'S A LENGTHY DRIVE and Stella is completely disoriented. Frank cruises at Sunday-drive pace. They head southwest, passing a very odd abandoned shack on the side of the road with faded flowers painted on the little front window. Cynthia explains that this is the house where Maud Lewis lived and painted. Her husband was murdered in the previous year, and Maud died a decade ago. Stella's eyes tear up as they pass the minute house where this painter had lived but now was forgotten. Stella feels this way too, how no one even knows she and Cynthia are alive. They continue on and eventually turn off the main road and drive down a paved back road for what seems an hour before turning onto a dirt road, and then onto an even smaller bumpy dirt road for miles until finally there is a wooden sign: *The Lodge at Mercy Lake*. There are security guards at the gate. They look like forest rangers but they have guns. They wear explorer hats and mirrored sunglasses, faceless as they let the car in through the imposing gate. Frank whistles as they drive down a winding lane that twists and turns for a few more miles, and at last, there's the old lodge on the lake. It is a magnificent setting, with forest right to the water's edge, and Mercy Lake stretching far, far back. Stella had no idea a lake could even be this large, could disappear into the woods. There is one beach area. And some men with gas tanks and chainsaws.

Frank smiles in the rear-view mirror. "Just some fellows helping with the maintenance and such."

Loons call as they get out of the car. Stella has an urge to run into the woods, but that seems a dangerous thing to do. Frank is here and Cynthia is here. Security is here.

Frank goes into the lodge after pointing out some canoes and saying they should have fun. Stella has no idea how to canoe but Cynthia does, and she pulls one into the water from where it's been resting higher on the beach. Cynthia has a backpack and gives Stella a granola bar. She's starving. By the time they turn back there is a chill in the end-of-day shadows, the trees casting dark ribbons over the lake, the silhouette of the lodge against the sky. They pull the canoe onto the beach and gape up at the lodge. A fire flickers inside and dusky smoke coils out of the immense stone chimney.

Tommy Jessome appears with two glasses of juice. They are champagne flutes, the same kinds as the ones at Frank's house up at Seabury Gorge, crystal with a gold rim, goblets in this setting. Tommy smiles at Cynthia, acting like nothing happened a few weeks earlier in the dining room of Cedar Grove. He doesn't look at the scar on Cynthia's arm. And she doesn't behave as though it happened either.

"Lovely evening isn't it, girls?" Stella is immobilized. She tells her legs and arms to move but they don't, instead keeping her upright as a statue.

Tommy looks at Stella. "Have a drink. Fruit punch. Doesn't every girl love a drink of fruit punch? Helps keep it sweet. Stella, you look parched. This will fix you right up. I've spent time in Ohio — in Athens, Ohio — and they do have the nicest punches. And library."

It is, Stella thinks, an odd comment.

Cynthia puts her hands on her hips. "I thought my dad said the conference wasn't until next week?"

"That's right, it's next week. This is just the executive meeting."

"Where's my father?"

"He got called back to town. Your grandmother was asking for him. Poor old lady. I guess it was a heart attack. I know how fond you gals are of her. But old age comes for us all. Stella, your father understood when Frank said you were needed out here to keep Cynthia company. After all Frank's done for your father, he couldn't say no. I told him I'd make sure you get brought back into town."

Stella follows Cynthia towards the lodge. They carry their drinks. Tommy Jessome is gone. Stella isn't sure where he went. It's the purple hour and the light is fading quickly from the sky. Cynthia sets her backpack on the table near the lodge and puts her crystal glass beside it. She tells Stella to set hers down. But Stella is thirsty. "Put it down, Stella. Listen to me. Take mine," she orders, in a voice resembling her father's.

But Stella doesn't trust anybody now, especially someone who sounds like Frank, so she tips back her fancy glass and drinks her own drink. Cynthia won't tell her what to do. She won't let her shame over Cynthia guilt her into a worse mess than they are already in.

It takes only a few minutes before Stella's head is light and she can hardly feel her legs. Her stomach is on fire. She has trouble walking. Tommy comes back out and next thing Stella knows, she and Cynthia are in another room. The light is low and Stella is laughing. It's one of her dreams. She wonders if she'll see her mother here. But Cynthia is pinching her cheeks. "Stella, you have to snap out of it. Please, Stella."

There is a dress on the wall and a strange white hood. Cynthia sits Stella on a chair and then she puts on the dress and the hood. "You have to be very quiet. Stay here. I'll come back for you later." Then she pulls and pushes Stella into a cramped closet. "Stay here. And take this." She hands Stella a sachet, the smell of fresh mint and rosemary, crushed borage and lavender spiralling through her nose. Stella tucks it in her training bra, Cynthia's bra, once upon a time. Cynthia closes the closet door. The darkness encases Stella. After a few minutes (just seconds?), Stella doesn't know if her eyes are open or closed.

Stay quiet. Stella thinks it must be her mother talking, not Cynthia. She left. *Hush.* Or Granny Scotia. No, she's gone too. *Not a word, not a word, sweet child.* If only her head wasn't so heavy. It's dark and quiet. And then the door to the room opens. The door to the closet opens. "Lookee what we have here. Hiding, were you? That's what they say your aunt did. Well, someone has to pay your grandfather's debt. Debt is a terrible thing to inherit. Your aunt refused, so she was taken care of in the lake. And it would have been a whole lot easier if you hadn't decided to go to the library with your mother. You girls make everything so complicated."

Tommy puts her over his shoulder and brings her down a dim hall and into an open space. Stella tries to kick her legs, to punch him in the back, but her arms and legs feel formless. *Mommy.* She hears her voice. *Mommy.* She's screaming, but only in her head. Tommy Jessome is gone again. The light is so low. Stella crawls off to the side of the space as voices mutter: "Sodality first. All debts are paid."

The building smells of incense. It is dark in the lodge. It's surrounded by towering trees and the remains of the sunset can't reach inside the windows. Outside a coyote howls. Inside the men laugh. Their faces are shadows, masks. A very old man sits in a colossal chair woven out of twigs. There are twig crosses on either side of him.

The men are in a circle, about twelve in all. It's hard to see in the dim light. Stella hides behind an armchair and peeks around the corner. Stella can't see their faces. They're wearing dark dressing gowns. Tommy is gone. Cynthia is on the floor. The old man wears a bird mask with a curved beak. They all seem to move in slow motion. Stella's head spins.

The flames flare in the tremendous old fireplace, and shadows flicker up into the high ceiling. Stella sees Cynthia is on her back, her legs open. Stella hears a shuffling from above and looks up at a balcony. Men

are up there watching. Stella sees a man with a camera.
He is taking pictures of this ceremony, of this violation.

Stella has never seen a naked man before, not even
her father. The old man's penis rises out of a mass of
ashen hair, moving back and forth, coming closer to
Cynthia. She can hear Cynthia screaming, sobbing,
the first time Stella has ever heard her cry. Stella is too
dizzy to move. She calls out but her words are only
puffs of air.

STELLA IS OUTSIDE. ON the dock. Cynthia is there.
She is trying to get Stella into a rowboat tied to the
dock. Stella's hands are numb. She wants so badly to
help Cynthia, to take over, but she can't even do that.
Thudding. The dock shaking. Frank running over the
dock, his voice severe, hissing. "What were you doing?
I told you to stay *out* of the way. Jesus, Cynthia, this
wasn't supposed to happen to you. You *never* do what I
say." Frank is shouting. Frank is very angry. He is very,
very, very angry.

Stella throws up into the water. And now another
loud voice, more shouting.

It is her father. He's apoplectic, screaming as he runs
down the dock.

"Franklin. Jesus fucking Christ. Why are they out
here on the dock? You said it would be quick, the trip
out here, a new ritual, not like the old days. Frank,
you said would bring her back from Mercy Lake to

Seabury. *You lying bastard.*" The clouds blow back and darkness comes. Opal light glows on the dock. Stella sees Cynthia stand up. She has her backpack.

"It *already* was me," she spits out to Frank. "What do you think Tommy was doing to me the last two summers? What do you think? Are you that blind? Are you that much in debt to your fucking stupid brotherhood and business and money?" She's raging away, storm raging. "You took Granny Scotia. I'll never forgive you. I'll *never* forgive you."

Stella's father takes a step towards Frank, who punches him in the nose. He splashes into the water. Just then another man thuds onto the dock. "For fuck's sake, now is not the time for pictures, you asshole." Frank hits the photographer in the head and the man falls to the dock, his camera and camera bag rolling from his hands. Then there is silence. Stella throws up again. The photographer crawls a bit, and then gets up and lurches back towards the lodge. Clouds blow over the moon and it's dark and then they blow off into the midnight blue and moonlight dazzles on the lake. A breeze comes up. The coyotes keep howling.

Cynthia takes something out of her backpack. She holds it up. Frank takes a step back. It is the black book. But then the clouds blow over the moon again and Stella can't see. The clouds move away from the moon and illuminate Cynthia and the blank pages of the book she holds open. There is a sound in the lake.

Water rippling…stirring. Stella lifts her dizzy head up and the sky swirls, the moon a bright glowing marble, rolling through the night. And then the moon again anchors in the sky, steadies Stella. The dock is empty. She doesn't know where everyone is. Cynthia gone, Frank gone, Stella's father gone—only Stella and the lonesome warning of the loons and coyotes on the pine-scented lake air moving in over her now in warm drafts. The silvered wooden dock is marbled by moon and clouds in a strange rhythm, Stella sprawled on the dock now and looking up at the twinkly stars, the rushing clouds, revealing the round lunar face gazing down on Mercy Lake.

Hallelujah.

Now

THE SILKY LIGHT OF day slipped in through the curtains
in the cottage window, turning the lace a phosphor-
escent white. Stella had been dreaming of floating in
a still ocean, but not an ocean she knew. The water
was warm, bath-water warm, soft as satin on her body,
gentle undulating heaves. Dianne slept on the other
sofa in the early grey dawn. Stella remembered they
were up late. Her eyes were swollen and she gently
rubbed them. Crying, yes, these eyes, tearful in the
night. She remembered what she was dreaming, and
then what she was awake remembering. Mercy Lake
at night. She was coming back to herself.

It was quiet in the cottage. Dianne's arms by her
side on the sofa, her heavy breathing and random
fuzzy snores and gulps of air. The fire was almost out,
warmth still from the hearth and a few dull embers.

Stella breathed this strange lovely air in through her mouth, tasting it on her tongue, this strange elixir.

The bay lapped on the beach—she heard it through the thin wooden walls of Periwinkle Cottage, through the warped windowpanes. Her hands clasped together in her lap. A radiant beam of light cast in through the glass, filtered through the sheer lace curtains, falling on the floor. *Home*, the curtains whispered. *Hallelujah*. But the sheers were still, not a rustle or swish, still in this moment of ceremony. Stella felt very warm. She might have a fever. Her lips were very dry and scuffed together. Only Stella's lips moved. Just a whisper but her voice nonetheless. Stella was speaking.

"Hallelujah."

STELLA DIDN'T NEED TO close her eyes. She was in her mind, and the room at Periwinkle Cottage receded. She was in her mind with the shell-lined shelves. The seahorse quivered and turned. A shell opened. It was 2005. It took no effort—the top shell gliding back, the story coming out in pictures and sounds. Stella finding her way into the pictures. At the beginning of the summer of 2005 she went with Dianne to Kingsport to stay with Sorcha. Stella smelled the salt water of the Minas Basin. And then a cooler sea air, a rockier beach. Lupins by the side of the cottage. Summer flowers. She was at Periwinkle, in Lupin Cove. Laughter inside the cottage. Almost a hee-haw. Dianne.

Stella stood outside the screen door. If the screen door was on then it was deep summer. Isaiah only put it on in May and took it off in early October—he stored the door at his house down in the Valley. The screen door was on. The mirror beside the door. Superstitious. They were superstitious people, the Llewellyns and the O'Clearys. The Spragues. Who said that? *Nurse Calvin*. But she was not here. She said that before they left. That's right. For the weekend. To Periwinkle. In Isaiah's truck.

Stella saw someone over her shoulder. Blue eyes. Bald. Sunken face. Is it a man or woman? Is it neither? The face was still. It was the dead. The dead smiled over her shoulder, in the mirror, a soft smile, putting her hand on the back of Stella's head, a trembling hand but the pressure firm and steady. *In this head is all you need to know.*

Cynthia. *Cynthia.*

Cynthia alive then, but soon to be dead.

They were inside Periwinkle. It was clean and warm and smelled of fresh bread and cinnamon.

"How was the plane trip from Florida? Big flight for you, Cynthia," Dianne said. Dianne was here too—she was on a weekend pass with Stella and Isaiah.

The shell was emptied. Oh, but not quite. Stella waited. She has been patient for years.

An ebony pearl rolled out, expanding into an opalescent wall, a projector, the kind Stella's father used for his lectures. But these were not his photos. This was a movie, an old kind, Super 8 — Stella and Cynthia, Isaiah and Dianne, all together in the cottage living room, Dianne in the old rocker, Stella and Cynthia on the red sofa. Isaiah standing by the mantel. But she can't remember. She won't remember.

"I will remember every blessed thing," Dianne said in her gummy voice. She was toothless that weekend. "I'll remember for you, Stellie. Until once more you can. I know the old ways. Me and Sorcha come from the Offing too."

They put it in a wooden box. What is *it*? Dianne and Isaiah clasped hands. The box was locked.

They were outside on the beach. The sun low. They boiled clams and roasted marshmallows.

The water was glassy peach as Stella held Cynthia's hand. She had a cane like Granny Scotia — Granny Scotia for tired old bones, Cynthia for bones riddled through with cancer that burrowed down from her breasts.

Sally flew up with Cynthia for the weekend. They came back to see Stella. Sally never knew what Frank was up to. He hid it so well. Sally was distracted by her own sorrow. Sally's face is lined with decades of remorse. The regret and grief will never leave her side. Cynthia has so little time left, and so much pain. *How can you be here walking and talking, and then dead?* Stella asked. Cynthia replied: *Death is never what you think it will be.* And she wants to return to the sea. Her ashes. Did Stella understand? Part of her in the earth and part in the sea. And she would be complete. *Stella, do you understand?*

Stella did not.

They were back out on the beach, roasting marsh-mallows. Cynthia roasted two on her stick, a thin, pale scar on her thin arm.

Dianne on the log with her banjo. Isaiah and Stella, who didn't talk and didn't remember but who stored things away, in her mind shells.

Sorcha there with her fiddle.

Dianne and Cynthia sang now, filled up her head:

I know dark clouds will gather 'round me
I know my way is hard and steep.
But beauteous fields arise before me
Where God's redeemed, their vigils keep.
I'm going there to see my Mother
She said she'd meet me when I come.

Roasting marshmallows. Cynthia, sitting on a log, taking the photo that's on Stella's bookshelf at the Jericho Centre, that time they gathered by the sea and laughed, a gathering of poor wayfaring strangers together one last time as the sun slipped into the horizon and a darkness came high over the bay except at the line where the water meets the sky, where an extraordinary eye of lavender and red deepened slowly into the night and sank into the ocean.

What Comes Forth from the Water.

Then

STELLA WEEPS ON THE dock in the dark. She can't find her hands. Her body is numb. When she does find her cold hands she claps them together to warm them but they won't fit, too stiff. The moon is covered by clouds. Her head is fuzzy from the drugged punch. She is wet. She fell in the water—she slipped and fell in the lake. The lake water was warm but she crawled out and onto the breezy dock. She wanted to find Cynthia. Cynthia had said she needed to get something. Cans? Is that what she said? Stella can't remember. Then steps on the dock, the dock swaying, heavy steps. Frank and Tommy. Where is her father? The clouds blow away from the moon and the light beams down. A stocky shadow falls on the dock. A shadow from her memory. Tommy takes her by an arm and hauls her to her feet,

Frank grabbing her other arm, at first saying they're so sorry, whatever could have happened to poor Stella Sprague. She must be on drugs the way city kids are these days. Stella squirms and they shake her. *We will not have you ruining everything, young lady. You will do as you're told.* They snigger. Stella wonders how they can be so heartless but she knows now that theirs is a heartless world, a world of owning and buying and selling, a society once bound in religion and now just bound in perversion, the vestiges of their strange cult used to justify whatever they want, empty rituals. That there is no god they believe in — there is nothing but power and personality, jesting and vying. That they'll prey on each other as fast as they'll prey on young things.

The wind has picked up and it blows through the hemlocks and brushes over the water, rippling the surface, water cresting, splashing against the dock, a briny smell rising off the water as it licks at the dock. The men holding her by the arms, bracing themselves, and the clouds blow over the moon and the light shines down on the lake and there are dark shapes in the swelling water, and Frank and Tommy push her. Stella is on her knees, the splintering wood piercing her skin, a sharp burning, and she grabs the oar out of the rowboat heaving up and down at the end of the dock. It's so heavy. She clenches her fingers. Her arm tingles and then her whole body. She can move. She stands up. Stella smashes the oar into Frank's knees and he crashes onto the floor of the rowboat that rocks and tosses him into the lake and Tommy grabs her by the hair, no different than a fish he's hauled out of the water, and he shakes her, holding her by her neck over the water, the wind howling, and strange sounds, whistling sounds from the lake. She swings the oar and whacks Tommy in the neck. He drops her in the lake and falls in on top of her.

Silence under here and darkness, waterwaterwater. Stella sees her mother swimming towards her but then there is nothing but bubbles as Stella lets out the air in her lungs. There are shapes in the lake, moving quickly, grasping Tommy, swimming away as Stella is crashing up from the water, propelled upward, smashing down onto the hard wooden dock, the lake water streaming from her hair, the wind cold now on her rippling skin, the lake surging. She looks over and sees the men far away from shore now, splashing and screaming, a flash of moonlight on their waving arms, and then darkness, shrieks, and they go under.

That Bright Land.

Now

STELLA SAT UPRIGHT. SHE was covered in sweat, wet all over, and her hand was a swollen, scorching club. Her mouth a shrivelled leather pouch. At Periwinkle. She knew this. But when? Summer? Yes. What year? Dianne over there on the sofa, still sleeping. Old lady Dianne. Middle-aged troll of a Stella who must get water. She didn't want to wake Dianne but she needed help. She called her name. Stella spoke her name: *DianneDianneDianneDianne.*

Stella felt the name leap off her tongue. It filled her ears with warmth. No answer from Dianne. Stella clenched her muscles, willing herself to sit up. She took a deep breath and pushed herself to her feet. "Dianne?" No reply. Stella lurched over and gasped as a short old woman watched her. Stella put her hand to her mouth and the lady did as well. It was Stella, in a mirror, Stella whose hair was now pearl white. Stella dropped down on the sofa beside Dianne. Stella touched her wrinkled hand. Cold, so cold against Stella's hot fingers. Dianne still.

Stella recalled a dream. Or was it a conversation? Dianne telling her to remember, to remember where it was hidden, that she had kept it safe, that Isaiah had given her the key and she was keeping it safe. Dianne was not breathing. No breath coming from the mouth of this old lady, her hair hanging cape-like down over her shoulders, her necklace resting between her breasts on this chest that did not rise or fall, the swell and fall of breath gone now, a tide receded forever. Thin salty creeks coursing down Stella's hot cheeks, scorching on her cracked lips, wet and salty on her leathery tongue. Dianne hadn't stood a chance, not with her efforts to care for Stella taking all she had left. Stella's tears dripping on Dianne's fingers, yellowed from her years of smoking, her wild, steely hair matted and tangled around her shoulders. Stella knew this was a sleep she would not awake from. Dianne would never again walk at the centre, or sit on the bench on the bank of the inscrutable river, the paupers' graveyard behind them. Stella would never hear this strange, splendid old creature sing again, but even as she thought this, Dianne's voice filled her mind. Her banjo, her low, gruff, sweet spirit of a voice:

I'm travelling through this world below
There is no sickness, no toil, nor danger
In that bright land to which I go
I'm just going over Jordan
I'm just going over home.

STELLA DIDN'T KNOW HOW much time had passed
when there were footsteps outside, on the back verandah. One knock. Three more. Then the door opened.
She heard a high loud voice and Seraphina loomed over
her. And behind her Grace. And behind them, men in
uniforms who approached Stella and she screamed. She
clung to Dianne, stiff now, cold now, silent.

Seraphina wept. "I'm so sorry. I had to get help. I told
them the angels were calling out from the sea and from
the sky. It was my duty to save you and I can't save you
and you can't remember and so I had to go to Grace and
Mal for they will try to help you. I have failed. I hope
you'll have mercy on me, Stella. I don't have the words."
Seraphina's head dropped and her arms flailed at her
side, fanning dark broken lines of shadow on the floor.

Stella in her delirium was roused by a ripple of anger,
reviving her enough to croak and spit at Seraphina in a
slow voice: "They'll find me now. And I have betrayed
Cynthia by not remembering. But why is it my job to
remember?"

Seraphina rocked back and forth. Grace put her
hands to her mouth.

Stella *speaks*.

Stella *roars*.

Fire raged in Stella's throat and in her gut, and flames shot from her fingertips. Her eyes were glowing embers. Grace shrank back and Stella roared again and again and again until a dark curtain fell over her, extinguishing the blaze in her eyes and in her body, enveloping her words, filling her mouth, and there was nothing but deep thick quiet as Stella fainted and fell to the floor at Grace's feet.

Part 3

Go warn the children
of God of the terrible
speed of mercy.

—FLANNERY O'CONNOR,
The Violent Bear It Away

Goodbye Uterus, Farewell Cervix. The Fierce Old Lady Within.

Now

I DON'T KNOW HOW long I've been in the hospital. I do know that Nurse Calvin does mean well, in her own stiff, deformed fashion.

Nurse Calvin clears her throat once, twice, three times. I have never seen her so nervous. She licks her lips and speaks: "You've certainly had good care here. The Valley Regional is a good hospital. They had you on intravenous antibiotics for a whole week, Stella Sprague. You're a wreck. Look at your hair! You could have died from that infection. What were you thinking, breaking into that cottage?"

I don't explain, even though I could now. Periwinkle is my family cottage. It's *my cottage*. All those years of wondering where my voice was, and it was there, inside, still needing to be coaxed out, but it's here now.

But what good is it? It doesn't matter if you can speak. It doesn't make any difference. Words don't make it better. It's easier to just listen to Nurse Calvin, exhaling all her proclamations, until she's emptied out, an empty bag that will refill again, and again and again.

Nurse Calvin points to the windowsill. There is a banjo beside a potted rose. "I brought you Dianne's new banjo. It finally came. I thought you might want it. And I put some cards there from Fred and Bob, and Charlotte Pacific. I see Grace has been in with some flowers and a card." Nurse Calvin's voice breaks and she looks away, patting her hair, composing herself. "Fred and Bob have been very upset with you gone. They mope about all day with that cat. I had to delay my retirement for a few months to keep things steady, what with all the uproar. What a shock to the system this all is. The boys don't seem to comprehend that Dianne isn't coming back. It's a pity. And speaking of, that box of things over there that Dianne kept for all those years, she left for you with your name on it. We had to clear out her room, you see. She surely didn't have much. But she had a will, of all things. Never estimate an old lady. Anyway, what's yours is in the box, a bunch of junk. And you know you'll have to go to the group home. It doesn't have to be Mountain Top but you'll have to go somewhere. We couldn't hold your bed for you. I know Eugene has been in and told you. I just felt it was my duty, before I retire, to come and tell you myself. To say goodbye, seeing you missed my farewell barbeque and all. I appreciated the table decorations you and Dianne made. I kept them."

"I understand."

That's all I say.

Nurse Calvin's eyes widen. She's thrown off her game. Despite Dianne dying and me almost dying from my blood infection, and then having surgery for my cervical cancer, Nurse Calvin is put out that we ruined the barbeque, her swan song, her grand farewell. And so she has come here to the Valley Regional Hospital to let me know that when all is said and done, she forgives me, in her own fashion.

Everybody was shocked. No one ever thought we would make it so far away. Nurse Calvin says Dianne's funeral was terribly sad but her time had come. And of course it saved them from having to tell her that her cousin, Sorcha, had passed too, some time ago. I was still unconscious so they had to proceed without me.

Nurse Calvin says she just knew that manic, Seraphina Sullivan, had to be behind most of our shenanigans, that she was off her medication and if she would only take her medication, but it was the bane of Nurse Calvin's existence that patients would just not be compliant.

"They took her daughter away, probably permanently. She has no one to blame but herself. Going on and on about the evil group of men coming to get her and to get you, and that no one is safe, that there are people in high places, people in power, all out to get her, to silence her, that only Stella Maris Sprague knows the salt water cure. Gone off her rocker right into the deep end, Seraphina has. What a pity, and a good thing her parents are dead and gone so they don't have to witness it."

I don't point out that maybe someone *is* after us, that something bad happened many years before. Maybe we do have evidence, and these middle-aged mental patients might know something—maybe we aren't just drunk mermaids ranting and raving.

The shock of hearing my voice has her somewhat subdued, although I can tell from the gleam in her narrowed eye how she is sure that I probably talked all along, and even now I'm just stubborn. For I remember so much now, but there are still holes. And I know that memory is more alchemy than science—that what comes back and what recedes, what is permanently lost and what finds its way back is a great mystery. It is not one that brings me any comfort.

And then Nurse Calvin surprises me. She comes to my bedside and leans down. "There was a man at the Jericho Centre looking for you. I sent him away and said I'd call the police if he came back again. I didn't like the looks of his eyes, all watery blue and round, like some sort of rodent. I told Grace and she seemed to know something about it. Lord, I'm too old for this.

Anyway, you stay put. You'll be safe here." She pats me on the cheek and then turns, but as she does I can see a tear trickling down her cheek.

Nurse Calvin has left me a vase of deep magenta asters she must have picked from the path out back to the graveyard. Now I can't stop myself from blubbering. Dianne is dead, and because of me. What a burden I must have been to her at the end, although she never complained. I wish she was here. She's been protecting me for years—I can't manage without her.

They say they got the cancer before it spread. It was a vaginal surgery, which is why I don't have an incision on my abdomen. The surgeon is a nice young man. The other surgeon with the turban has retired, was retired, had just been filling in. Silence, my old friend—she swirls around me.

The doctor says he understands. Silence speaks well for me but she can't take over now.

"I know you've had some mental health issues and traumatic brain injury, Stella. Call me any time, if you have any questions. No lifting or exercise for at least two weeks. But I think you'll heal quickly. All your walking has you in good shape."

"Thank you."

He smiles. He says he'll see me any time, not just for my follow-up but if I want to discuss my health, menopause, all these things that seem to have avalanched down on me. *How can it be I was twelve and now that time feels oceans away, and I'm fifty-four, in a hospital bed, with my uterus gone, my cervix gone, my shrivelled oyster ovaries left alone inside?*

THE NEXT MORNING I wake up and feel a bit sore but more alert. I remember the doctor's visit. And with my clearer thinking, I remember that someone was out to get us. Was it real?

They bring me lunch and I eat it sitting in a chair, a bowl of soup and some applesauce is all I can manage. I've lost so much weight my skin hangs on me, my flesh an old dress that no longer fits. After I eat, a terrible exhaustion comes on and I fall asleep looking out the window of the hospital at the brick wall of another wing. I think of my father and his misplaced and idealistic desire for moral treatment, for beauty and healing, and I think of him at the centre that day, with Cynthia and me, when we were young and full of life, with Cynthia already captive to Tommy Jessome but hiding it, of Cynthia who must have known I was in the window that day. My tears leak from the corners of my eyes into the hospital pillow, which smells of bleach. This is all my fault. For not doing anything when I should have, for not speaking up, for being a coward, for being so weak and spineless when I should have helped. And no matter how I try, I can't remember what Cynthia told me to keep safe, what Dianne told me to do. Dianne's banjo lies on the window ledge.

I feel gutted. They're all dead now, and it's just pathetic Stella left behind. I close my eyes and wish I was back at Periwinkle, listening to the surf pounding on the rocky beach, with the light falling in the window, listening to Dianne snore on the sofa across the room. I would settle for the graveyard, listening to the crows call, or the museum bench by the rebuilt Maud Lewis house with Charlotte Pacific telling me that sometimes the blank pages say the most. But I'm down here now, away from the ocean, in the Valley. Dianne was my last key to the past. My tears can't keep sleep from approaching and I fall into its warm, tangled fingers.

When I wake up there is a woman by my bed, a woman who looks familiar, but I can't place her. She has frizzy black hair and she wears a lovely green dress and running shoes.

"Stella. I've been waiting for you to wake up. My name's Mal Grant-Patel. We met once before, on the lawn at the Jericho Centre?"

There are no visiting hours after lunch, when it's quiet time. Mal must have snuck in. I point at the *Visitor Hours* sign taped to the wall.

"Can you talk now?"

I nod.

She waits.

I say nothing. Mal looks confused. It's understandable. I am too. Silence stands up and extends her arms. She's so beautiful as she dances in the room while

I look at this visitor. Yes, I know her. The woman in the yellow dress. Except it's a stylish green dress now. And a black cashmere sweater. Does it matter what colour her dress is? It's early autumn—I can tell from the maple outside the window.

Silence is waving, blurry, disappearing.

I clear my throat.

"Can you talk to me, please, Stella?" Mal speaks quickly, quietly. "Cynthia's mother talked to me. Sarah Windsor. The painter. You knew her as Sally Seabury. I went to Florida. She said that Cynthia had given you the evidence against Sodality, against Cineris, when she came in 2005. Do you remember? Do you know where it is? Do you even know *what* it is?"

Just then a nurse breezes into the room and looks at Mal. "No visitors—Stella needs to sleep." She points to the visitor sign.

The woman in the green dress looks at me and I say nothing. Not because I can't speak but because there is nothing to say. Nurse Calvin is wrong. A sea of change has come, and being able to speak for myself has done nothing to prevent it. There is no mercy for me, or if there is, it is a mercy that comes too late. This eerily insightful young woman is trying to help but there's nothing I can do to assist her. There is only danger.

I'VE BEEN IN THE hospital for two weeks, Eugene said yesterday. This I remember. They hope I will be discharged soon. Eugene says he thinks the group home will grow on me. He was worried if I kept sobbing that they might send me to the psychiatric wing—or worse, they'll send me to the NS, where my father was all those years ago. I don't know how my father died, or when. And no one has told me. It's been many years. Will I remember?

I read the get-well-soon cards on the window ledge beside the box Nurse Calvin brought. There is a card from Eugene, and a card from everyone on the Willow Unit. One from Charlotte Pacific in the mail from Vancouver. She writes that she was terribly worried, that she looks forward to coming out next summer and drawing with me. There is a card from some other social workers, from Karen, our yoga teacher, a card from Grace. And a card from Seraphina in an envelope that has been duct-taped shut, top secret, from her paranoid mind. I must destroy it after opening it, she has written. She's put her name and her phone number on the card with a vintage image of a blue wave.

Eugene's been with me for many years and has never given up on me. But this just reminds me of how many people I have let down, Eugene now one of them. I can't tell him about Frank Seabury or Tommy Jessome, about Seabury. If I tell him even he'll think I'm crazy and then I will get sent away. I will be medicated right into outer space.

AFTER SUPPER A MAN stands outside my room in the hallway. He doesn't seem to know I'm there. He's looking at the other side of the hall. It takes me a moment to remember him. It's David Jessome from Mountain Top. He's not wearing casual clothes though. He's dressed in a dark suit, looking official. Every pore in my body releases drops of sweat. Part of me has wanted to believe I'm crazy, or that Seraphina's crazy has infected me—that Dianne was just a senile old woman and that the woman in the green dress with all the questions about "evidence" is also deluded. And Cynthia, when she came to visit, was delusional from her cancer, that maybe it was in her brain, that what had happened in 1980 died in 1980, in Mercy Lake that early September night.

A young nurse approaches him. "Excuse me, can I help you?"

"Yes, I'm looking for Stella Sprague. I'm a friend of her father's. From years ago. I can't remember her room number."

"Well, you're standing right by it." She points at my open door and David Jessome turns his head and looks into my eyes. He means me harm—there is no doubt, even as he smiles. This young nurse can't see his face but she must not appreciate his tone. "Well, sir, visiting hours are ending soon and the doctor has limited Stella's visitors. We're very strict about this. Stella's very tired, and while people think visits are helpful, they really do wear the patient right out, so you'll have to come back tomorrow."

I roll over on my side and pretend I'm asleep. All is truly lost now. It's just me, the only one left, sick and tired. Even now I doubt my mental stability. I have learned to respect the shattering power of trauma and the equally deep power of the subconscious to protect us, to seal off the world around us, allowing us to be in the world but not of it. I'm wary of my own self, wary of this Stella inside who must be watching, waiting to emerge, this Stella who kept the shells lined up for so many years. But for now, I lie still, my hands trembling, clasped together, listening to the man in the hall insist on a quick visit, the fiery petite nurse having none of it, annoyed now by his persistence, by his tone, his expectation.

"And look at that, she's asleep already! Me oh my, as the old ladies say! No one can sleep like the sick, except for the dead. So you'll have to come back another time." The nurse shuts the door to my room.

For now, I'm safe. I fall asleep. It's the only place I can hide now. When I wake up, it's dawn. But I'm back in the cottage. Dianne is talking as I wake up on the sofa. She is talking about the box. The necklace she wore, that Isaiah gave to her. Yes, he gave it to her. At the beach. When Cynthia was there.

"Yes," Dianne says, "the silver necklace. It turns into a key. It looks all swirly and ornate but if you just turn it this way, and then that way, and then this way, you'll see. It was crafted by Irish silversmiths in the Old World, Isaiah said. Clever, hey? Don't you remember, Stellie?"

"Yes, Dianne, I remember," I say. Dianne smiles her toothless smile. "Such a pretty voice. I could always hear it loud and clear. But you always knew that, Stellie, you always knew it. My own daughter, you were to me. You get those film canisters out of that box and you get them developed and to the girl in the yellow dress. Understand? Isaiah and me, we kept the memories for you, until you could hold them again."

Then the sun is shining in and Dianne is gone, and it's full morning. It's not Periwinkle but Valley Regional Hospital. The September leaves shiver but the window doesn't open and I can't hear their sound, what it might be telling me. I don't know where this box is with the film, or Dianne's necklace, which was probably buried with her. I close my eyes and get caught in a sticky sleep.

A seagull cries as it drifts by the window and I sit up. Napping makes it hard to keep track of time. The bird flaps its wings and disappears and I look at the cardboard box on the window ledge, the one that Nurse Calvin brought. What could Dianne have left me? She hardly had anything. I bring the box back to the bed and turn my back to the open door. They must have come in to check on me. There are a few empty wooden boxes inside, a few old sweaters, an old ivory hairbrush. Dianne's false teeth are in the box. Maybe there will come a day when I can wear them. Her nana's apple blossom teapot. Something rattles inside. I take the lid from the pot. Inside, her antique silver necklace. My eyes fill with tears as I hold it. I twist it three times this way, and then that way, and then this way. A key. If only Dianne were here now, now that I can talk, and she could answer me. I close my eyes. I have no idea what to do. *Useless*. Without Dianne, without that fierce old lady, I am nothing.

The Speed of Mercy.
Then and Now.

Now and Then

SILENCE UNDER HERE AND darkness, water. I see my mother swimming towards me and I reach out to her, her gentle face blurred by the water, but still her face, her hands reaching out, but there is nothing but bubbles as I let out the air in my aching lungs. And then I am crashing up from the water, propelled upwards and smashing down onto the hard wooden dock, the lake water streaming from my hair. Frank and Tommy swim back through the choppy water to the dock, their arms flailing. Cynthia is on the dock, dry, standing, her backpack at her feet, holding a book, the *Commonplace Book of the Offing Society*. Tears bead down her cheeks and fall on the pages. She kneels down beside me and an illuminated text appears in the moonlight, her tears of regret pouring onto the pages. *Chaidh na geasan a chur oirnn.* Cynthia speaks the words, a language I have never heard before, and yet one that sounds familiar. She sings. The rising wind is cold now on my rippling skin, the lake surging. *A Bhana-phrionns' a' chuain shiar.* The men are far from shore now. *A bheil sgeul agad ri luaidh?* A flash of moonlight on waving arms and then darkness, screams, and under they go in the inky black water. The same waters where Stella the Original perished.

We run then towards the lodge. Cynthia has gasoline — the tanks we saw by the chainsaws when we arrived, although that seems years ago now. She has matches and she lights one and hands it to me. She lights another and we ignite the gas canisters. The timber lodge so old and dry. We stand back as it blazes, Cynthia holding the straps of her backpack, me with my hands at my side, demon flames leaping up, rumbling groans of rage emanating from the fire.

What happened returns in pieces: Running through the woods. The hospital. The news that my father died at his parents' house, out back, in the sugar maple — a young boy climbing to fasten a swing, but not a young boy anymore, a tired man engulfed in cowardice and shame. And later, Granny Scotia escaping the seniors' home to the tidal currents of Mercy River. Presumed drowned.

Aurora.

Now

I WAKE UP WITH the silver necklace around my neck. I have to do something. There is no one left. Then a submerged part of me remembers: Seraphina. But I have no phone. Maybe the nurses will let me make a call.

A knock at my door. I don't say a word. The years of silence remind me that there is safety in it... sometimes. The door opens, a dark head peeking around. Aurora.

"Stella?"

Who else does she think it is? She comes in and closes the door. I didn't realize how petite she was, a mere child. With her mother over in Lupin Cove, arguing in the driveway, they both seemed larger than life.

"You have to help my mother. You have to do something."

I lower my head. She thinks I can help because I'm old. I lift my chin up. But the words I speak contradict my thoughts. "You're asking the wrong person, girl. I can't help you."

Aurora's eyes widen then, and she takes a step towards the bed and leans over. I pull back against the pillow. Her eyes are similar to mine, one a dark green and the other brown.

The door opens and a nurse comes in. "Stella, you should have a shower. I can bring you a chair to sit on, if you want. I think that's a good idea. And Miss, it's not visiting hours yet. Why don't you come back later?"

Aurora doesn't say a word. She looks at me and then out the window. I take her young hand. "Okay, we'll just finish up with our goodbyes. Then I'll have a shower."

"Okay, hon. Buzz if you need any help."

She leaves and Aurora looks at me, her lips quivering. She's crying now. "I can't tell if what my mother says is true or just made up. You know, the crazy stuff. She sees things that aren't there sometimes. She thinks she's a seer. When I was little I believed everything she said. She keeps saying that you will know what to do." Aurora throws her head back as she rolls her eyes through the tears.

I don't know what to do. She knows this — a fifty-four-year-old lady, thin stringy white hair, sagging cheeks, has no idea. She has no faith in me. I am merely a confirmation of her mother's illness. A confirmation that adults are helpless children in wrinkled bodies.

"Call Mal," I whisper.

"The podcaster?"

"Yes," I say.

Aurora weeps as she leaves.

The shower revives me. I don't need a shower chair to sit on but I lean against the wall, hold the metal support bar, and turn my face up to the shower head. The water pours over my hair and skin, warm and soothing, settling my mind.

I walk down to the nurse's station and they seem surprised to see me. Serrie's card is back in my room, but I have her number in my brain now. I worry I might forget it but when they pass me the phone and tell me to press 9 for an outside line, it comes back right away. The phone rings and goes to voicemail. My head is a bit dizzy. There's been so much trauma, so many types of medication, so much upheaval, so many knocks on the skull. I try her number again. Someone answers but doesn't speak.

"Seraphina?"

"Who is this? Aurora? Is that you? It's loud in my head. You'll have to speak up," Seraphina shrieks.

"It's me." I'm whispering. One of the nurses looks over at me. I fiddle with my hair and let out a fake laugh. "It's Stella," I say, as loud as I can without shouting, my raspy voice hissing into the receiver.

"WHO?"

I say again, "It's Stella. Stella Maris. You know."

She's almost in full mania now. "Why, yes, it is. It's Stella with the eyes. Same as my daughter's eyes. I've never heard you talk. Not even when we were young girls in Seabury that night. When my mother thought Granny Scotia could save us. The tea was just to keep us strong, to fortify the young. It couldn't stop bad things from happening."

Her voice is very fast. She's still on her high. The shock of my speech has only brought her down for a moment.

"I want you to come and get me. And take me back to the shore. I know what to do."

"Hallelujah," Seraphina squawks. It hurts my ear so I hold the phone away. The gaggle of nurses look over at me, not moving their heads, but their eyes, their eyes all on me.

"Get ready, right away. I'm in town now. I'll be there. But come downstairs, to the entrance outside, because if they see me in there, I'll never get out. Never, ever, get out."

"How do I get downstairs?"

"Stella, Stella, I don't know. You have to figure that out yourself. I'm trying to eat a sandwich. I'm arguing with angels. You're all making it hard for me to have my dinner. Don't flap those wings at me. Sorry, Stella. I have more important things to do than tell you how to go down the stairs." She hangs up.

I don't have any clothes to get dressed in so I tell a nurse I'm walking in my slippers to the canteen. Eugene has left me some vouchers. All they need is one look at me to dispel any thought of flight. I think about the silent Stella, running away into the woods, off on trails, the Stella who got locked on the unit, who could only go on outings with Dianne who never once let me run away, until the end, the run that killed her.

I take the stairs to the ground floor lobby where the canteen is. The lobby is full. I'm not the only one in hospital clothes and a housecoat. I see the canteen at the far side of the lobby. I have never been down here before, not that I remember. I make my way through the people sitting in chairs waiting to register, people standing talking on their phones, children whining, old ladies with walkers, doctors whizzing by in lab coats, technicians, a few ambulance attendants. I keep shuffling through the crowd to the door. I look over my shoulder and see David Jessome. He doesn't see me at first but he turns his head, almost in slow motion, and his eyes widen. I shuffle out the automatic doors just as Seraphina pulls up in her green truck.

We roar away and Seraphina's ranting and raving about the salt water, and seals and the podcaster and her mother, all of us from the shore and the sea.

"Could you slow down, Seraphina?"

"I can't go slow. We have to get there." She presses her foot on the gas and goes faster.

"No, I mean can you speak more slowly. It's hard for me to follow you. You're speaking on fast-forward and you're yelling."

"Oh Holy Mother Mercy, it talks. Praise be. Who would have ever thought that you'd speak. All that time. It must have been the salt water cure. The teas. You know, I always thought those potions and brews didn't work, but now I see they were supposed to make us buoyant, to help us weather the shit-storm of life, until we could reunite."

I don't point out to her that the salt water cure in the Bay of Fundy with my sore hand, and sleeping in wet clothes, almost killed me. Seraphina doesn't need to know that, and right now she wouldn't listen. She's holding forth and speaking so quickly I give up trying to follow.

We soar into Lupin Cove, down the hill and over the road by the east wharf. She pulls right into the path, driving until the mirrors on either side of the truck are jammed in the trees, so no one will see her vehicle.

The cottage is locked and there is a board nailed over the broken window. The key is in the old metal cough-drop tin though. Inside, I catch my breath. It smells of salt water and soot. The sofa must still be wet, without a fire to warm the place up, from our wet clothes. I touch the armchairs. They're damp, but it could just be the coldness of the cottage in September, that there is nothing left of my time here with Dianne.

Then I hear her voice in my head. *Hurry, hurry, Stella.*

And then Cynthia: *This is what you need to keep safe. They'll come back. They never go away. Someone survived. They'll come looking. They know I have them.*

Isaiah taking it from Cynthia.

The box. That handmade wooden box.

On the knick-knack shelf. Above where Dianne sat on the red sofa. *Every object has a story.*

I step up. My stomach is a bit sore but I push through and take it down. Seraphina is watching out the window. She leaps, almost flies across the room, like a unicorn, and steadies me. She sits me down in the rocking chair and I hold the box.

"And?"

I look at her. I look at the box.

"What do we do now, Stella? You said you knew."

I rock. Dianne. I touch the necklace and pull it out from underneath my green hospital gown. I take it off and twist, twist, twist. A silver key.

"Wow!" Seraphina screams.

"Be quiet, be quiet."

"Sorry," she whispers.

I turn the key. In the box are four old film canisters.

The Purple Hour.
Princess of the Western Ocean.

Now

SERAPHINA HAS BEEN GONE for hours. I know this because the sun has slipped over in the sky and started to lower. She left to take the film to Mal and Grace. She was convinced that if I went too, they might make me stay. Seraphina said, *You are the one who knows.* That I'm safer here by the sea than anywhere else. What it is I know, I have no idea, and she doesn't seem to know either. Seraphina thinks I'm a holy relic. So I wait for her here. Seraphina says she has called the mother of Mal, the young *podcaster* asking questions, that she's in danger too.

If there is anyone who can help us, it is Grace. There is no one else left who would believe me, especially believe Seraphina. But with a bad feeling in my stomach, I realize this is probably too much for even Grace to believe, that her kindness and goodwill and open-mindedness have limits too. And Seraphina could be completely delusional by now. She might have tossed the film out the window. But Mal knows. Mal believes.

Seagulls fly overhead, squawking. It's very cold inside. The surf rolls on the rocks. I'm a nervous mess, wringing my hands, wishing for medication, wishing for the return of my hazy mind, full of gaps and holes. And wishing I could stop the tears. I walk over the path to see if Seraphina might be parked back at her house by the bridge, or if she parked near me but got distracted. Anything can happen to her when she's in a manic phase. It's easy for her to go off track.

But what I see is a black car, an ominous black car. And I think of Fred and his devotion to John Wick, and I'm blubbering, wishing that John Wick would come and save me, that he would burn down New York and all the horrible men there. Then car doors open, and it's David Jessome and someone else, someone younger, with a mustache. They see me before I can duck back onto the trail. I run to the cottage and lock the door. But I know I'm not safe here anymore. I go back out and there they are.

"Stella, Stella, just calm down. Do you remember me? From Mountain Top? Eugene sent me. He asked me to come and find you. You took off from the hospital. You can't be doing that at Mountain Top because there's nowhere to go but the woods."

He must think I'm stupid, that a real counsellor would talk this way.

I remember what the woman in the yellow dress said: *They're watching you. They know you have something. It isn't safe.*

The other man speaks. "I'm a doctor, Stella. Just stay calm. Just stay relaxed. You've had a very hard time. A very hard time. Let's everybody stay calm. You need to come with us. I can help you. You need to rest."

"And we need to know what your friend Cynthia gave you. If you can just tell us that."

He's holding out his hands the way he thinks a hostage negotiator does, moving them down every time he says "calm." He's getting closer. They both are, not stopping, just taking one step after another, closer to Periwinkle. I open the door, slam it shut behind me and lock it. I will go out the front door, to the verandah and then down over the beach. I rush across the room and then I see it, there on the shelf, the *Commonplace Book*. I grab it and see the blue vase on the mantle. I know what's in it now. It is an urn, not a vase. I take them, both clutched to my chest, high on adrenaline, and pull at the door. It sticks. I haul one more time and it opens up. And then I'm through the verandah, and over the lawn, and onto the rocks.

"She's around front," one of them yells. And David Jessome comes out the front door I just rushed through, the other man around the side of the cottage. They aren't used to a rocky beach and they both fall as I continue stepping from one rock to another, moving faster and faster. *Fly, fly, fly, Stellie, fly.* And I hear Granny Scotia now too. Other voices, voices I have not known but have always known. *One foot after another, one foot after another. Look to the offing, look to the sea.* The men are still behind me, stumbling over the rocks, but coming faster now. I turn from the water. Behind them a flash of yellow, someone else coming. A few drops of water fall from the dark clouds overhead.

It's too hard to run. It doesn't matter how many miles I have walked with Dianne in the preceding decades. My joints are tired, my knees worn out, hips swollen as I rest atop the steep beach on the grey rocks. The towering waves of the incoming tide crash and roar. Cynthia to me: *Open the book, open the book.* And I do, putting my head back and looking at the rolling clouds, the sky dark in the east and glowing in the west. I feel my tears trickle down over my temples and into my hair, soaking my scalp. I look down at the blank yellow pages and weep onto them, all my regret and sorrow, my tears of love and loss, my tears of childhood, and the salty strange tears of the older woman I have become, the curious minuscule seahorses in my brain swimming and rocking. I hear the men now, on the rocks. So close. The speed of mercy is not slow. It is not fast. It is timeless. The old ancient words burst

from the shells. *Chaidh na geasan a chur oirnn* / Spells
were laid upon us.

I hear the young Cynthia at Mercy Lake speak:

Rè ar beò bhith le luchd-fuath / During our human lives
by foes —

And a chorus of voices singing from all the seas:

'S ged a tha sinn snàmh nan caol / Though we now swim
the strait.

Sounds coming from my mouth as the words
illuminate on the paper, the meaning swimming in
my blood and my tears:

A Bhana-phrionns' a' chuain shiar / O Princess of the
Western ocean,

The old exhortation flowing from my lips:

A bheil sgeul agad ri luaidh? / Do you have a tale to
weave?

I hobble over the rocks to the water and throw the
blue glass urn onto the beach where it shatters, the surf
rushing over it, pulling Cynthia's ashes and glass shards
away, the power of the bay sucking back, the sound of

410 | Christy Ann Conlin

rocks rumbling and crashing, and then another wave washing in, surging over my ankles, up toward the top of the beach as I wail out over the ocean and the mist billowing in, the two men following, hear them tripping, falling, yelling.

The mists gust in a castle of clouds and the beach is enveloped. My chanting is done, the words I've called out. I turn and hurry down the eastern beach, the stretch that will be flooded by the relentless ferocity of the stormy bay and the moon-driven tides, the mighty sea pounding and crashing against the sheer vertical cliffs.

Stella Maris, Star of the Sea. Under the Arbor.

Now

THE SKY WAS OVERCAST, the clouds a dull amethyst over the silver-grey sea as Mal drove down the steep hill into Lupin Cove. She had called Lark, the host of the morning radio show, who had promptly said the police should be notified, that she would take it to her producer and an investigative reporter. Mal should stay put. Mal had tried to do that, for about ten minutes. She wasn't a journalist — she knew that now. She was also a woman who had descended from the people by the bay. There was nothing more for her to do than to try to help Stella. The call from Aurora was the turning point. A girl so young with no one to turn to. This was about all their lives and Mal would see it through to the end now, however it played out.

The rain started as Mal parked on the east wharf. There was a black car already parked there. She hurried over the path Grace had told her to look for on the right, and came upon the blue cottage on the beach. The doors were open and the wind swirled through as Mal walked into the living room. She went out the front door onto the verandah, zipping up her long yellow raincoat. The wind was gusting and the bay was covered in whitecaps breaking on the steep rocky beach. It was evening now and the light was already dim from the clouds.

A crack of thunder boomed as Mal walked onto the beach. It was rocky and uneven and she had to place her feet carefully, as did the two men she saw up ahead, hopping from rock to rock, their hands held out to their sides for balance. There was another boom followed by a flash of lightning. Far down the beach, Mal could see Stella sitting on the rocks, her head bent down and then thrown back, Stella's pearly hair whipping through the air. Another crash of thunder, and lightning ripping through the blackening sky. The tide was coming in now, and the rain began to smash down, bouncing off the rocks. A tremendous lip of water curled forward and Mal leapt from rock to rock to the upper beach but the frothy surf swelled around her, up to her waist, pulling her seaward, under water where the roar of the water over the rocks was dimmed, distant, a sound coming through time, coming from her mouth.

Postcards.
The Starlit Sea.

Now

A FLOCK OF GULLS pass overhead and land on the rocks, cackling and crying, waking Stella. The smell of fresh bread wafts out from the screen door onto the front verandah at Periwinkle Cottage as Stella stirs in the chair. Her appreciation for this home built once as a year-round residence, and then a holiday cottage, and now a year-round home again is immense. Quiet footsteps stop at the screen door.

"Stella, we'll be eating soon, when Seraphina gets here with Aurora. The dinner rolls are cooling. I just took them out of the oven."

"Thank you, Grace. I dozed off."

It's Friday. Stella is tired from her early-morning shift at the bakery run by the Alzoubi family who have immigrated here and set up a shop in Bigelow Bay.

They live in a house in Lupin Cove and four mornings a week they arrive at dawn to pick Stella up. Stella goes to bed early, rising and setting with the sun. She is a natural baker, with her reverence for routine and ritual.

Stella turns and sees Grace through the grey mesh of the door. She smiles at Stella, who laughs and looks back out over the bay where a thin veil of haze hovers over the surface — through it she sees where the skyline and waterline merge in all their shades of blue. Inside, Stella opens the fridge and gets a glass of lemonade. There is a postcard of Elizabeth Bishop's home in Key West, where Grace went on a two-week poetry residency in February, stuck to the fridge with a magnet. Beside it is a postcard from Colorado sent from Eugene when he was on vacation in the early summer. And next to it, a postcard of Lombard Street in San Francisco. Mal promises to take Stella there if she comes out to California. She's going to Vancouver to interview Charlotte Pacific for *Under the Arbor*, her now hugely popular podcast. Mal is also writing a book, a memoir.

Stella remembers when Mal woke up on the upper beach, near the cottage, shivering and cold as the rain came down. Stella is still not sure of just how she'd made her way back — memories of swimming, of singing, of many cold hands pushing her, pushing Mal. And then the rain had stopped — the storm clearing, the sound of ambulances. Later, the bodies of two men washing up on the shore of North Haven Island in

Maine, found by a writer out for a walk with her dog in the early morning.

Grace is outside now, bringing in laundry from the clothesline off the back porch. She and Stella will fold it after supper, as they always do, taking the fresh piles to their rooms and the linen cupboards. Stella walks across the creaky wooden floor, past the red sofa, the gemstone fireplace, and sits on the verandah again. The seagulls are gone now. Whitecaps dot the sea as the tide makes its way in.

Stella hears the screen door at the back slam shut. Grace is inside now, back in the kitchen, turning on the old radio. She always listens to the six o'clock news. The familiar jingle-jangle of the opening music, the announcer's voice. The lead story is about the ongoing trial of an international sex ring dating back well over a century, a story broken by following a lead from a California blogger named Malmuria Grant-Patel. Photographic evidence introduced last year was indisputable, implicating powerful business figures—generational groomers, generations of abuse. Grace turns off the radio.

They'll eat inside at the kitchen table and then walk on the shore to watch the sunset. When the purple hour comes, Stella's visitors will leave and she will go to bed. Seraphina will take her daughter home for the weekend. And Stella will look through her window and see the starry sky. She will see Polaris shining, and then, as she closes her eyes, Stella Maris will fall asleep in her room with framed photos of her family on the walls, her bookshelf with the quartz stone from Isaiah on the top, the window facing the bay open a crack and the ocean breeze slipping in—a soft motion on the bed, Kitten jumping up, curling into a ball, purring into sleep beside Stella as she slips into a dream. Dianne is on the beach with her banjo, bowing her head as Stella walks by barefoot, slowly stepping from rock to rock. Stella swims in the starlit sea, all around a chorus of voices on a still summer night.

Not Possible Without

Strange finishing a book in a pandemic, the illusion of certainty turned to dust, each day unknown terrain. This novel was possible because of a gleaming crew of compassionate people, places, and things. Thank you to the Woodcock Fund through the Writers' Trust of Canada for support when all seemed lost. Fathomless salty admiration and appreciation to my editor supremo, the tireless Michelle MacAleese, who bravely leapt on the deck of this novel and brought it out of the fog.

Thanks to my publisher, Bruce Walsh, and to all the amazing people at House of Anansi Press, especially Maria Golikova, Sarah MacLachlan, Janie Yoon, Joshua Greenspon, Debby de Groot, Laura Chapnick, Zoe Kelsey, and Curtis Samuel. To Alysia Shewchuk for the exquisite book design. To Linda Pruessen and Chandra

Wohleber. The Banff Centre for the Arts, where I had the fortune to work with Cherie Dimaline and Liz Howard. Thank you, Cherie, for telling me to re-read *The Stone Angel*. Liz, for your grace with poems. Gratitude to the society of writers I met in Banff (I'm here for you, always). To Zsuzsi Gartner for her brilliant mind and for endless encouragement from the West Coast.

Kinnie Copeland, 1961–2020, rest in peace: For teaching me how to swim in the Bay of Fundy when I was a child. To the hearts of Rhys Copeland-Swift, Phillip and Crystal Copeland, and Janice Lutz. Miranda Hill, for keeping me on the splintery log hurtling down the crazy-wild river of what is more commonly known as the final draft. Keiler Roberts, for the hilarious and moving letters, photos, genius comics, and all around sisterhood. Gillian Sircom, for having me at Crosstrees, where I briefly escaped the gerbil wheel of everyday life to work on this book by the wintry sea. Love to the Sircom clan, for kindness and incomparable zest for life. Betsy and Ed Holtz, for hosting us in Madalyn's Cottage at Salty Pines, where I finished the novel. My dad, who taught me how to rockhound on the Fundy shore. My mum, who taught me how to hear the spirits. My dearest cousin, Eileen Fred Roberts. Thanks to Sarah Berman at *Vice Magazine* for journalism and cult consultation, and to Portia Clarke for her expertise. My agent, Marilyn Biderman. Intrepid Trevor Corkum who carefully read numerous early drafts. Marianne Ward, for her meticulous insight on my continuing work.

For the abiding friendship of Silmy Abdulah, Millie LaPorte, Shawk Alani, Marie Cameron, Sarah Emsley, Amanda Peters, Gwenyth Dwyn, Jennifer Paterson, Kim Kierans, Sara White, Helen Burns, Catherine and Peter Nathanson, and Joceline Belliveau Doucette. Thanks, Sue Goyette, Megan Leslie, Dr. Mike Rudd, Dr. Jaspal Singh, Dr. Beverly Cassidy, Jan Tait, and Heather Morse for Ohio days. Thank you, Kim Barlow, for your banjo and gospel music. Robyn Carrigan from Cape Breton, for *An Ròn/Ann an Caolas Od Odram*.

Gratitude to Sylvia Hamilton, a lodestar, and to Andre Fenton, for such generous editorial input, for discussion historical, contemporary, and personal. To Casey Plett for such insightful and empathetic editorial perspective and notes. Katherine Collins, for inspiration, honesty, and a friendship of a lifetime. Beloved Olivia Purohit for carefully reading and sharing insight. The Canada Council for the Arts for support on an early draft.

Biggest briny love to my wonderful children, Milo, Silas, and Angus, for understanding that when I'm staring at the waves I'm really hard at work. To my incredible lighthouse of a husband, Andy Brown, whose presence transforms the stormiest days into magic. To Marshie, rest in peace.

To the misfits and miracles in the world, I love you. Keep healing.

Some Notes

This novel was touched and shaped by: *Hysteria: A Memoir of Illness, Strength and Women's Stories Throughout History* by Katerina Bryant; *Down Girl: The Logic of Misogyny* by Kate Manne; *The Shaking Woman or A History of My Nerves* by Siri Hustvedt; *Salt on Your Tongue: Women and the Sea* by Charlotte Runcie; *Meander, Spiral, Explode: Design and Pattern in Narrative* by Jane Alison; *The Erotics of Restraint: Essays on Literary Form* by Douglas Glover; "The Development of the Lunatic Asylum in the Maritime Provinces" by Daniel Francis in *Acadiensis*; Nova Scotia Hospital for the Insane, Halifax, NS, Sixteenth Annual Report of the Medical Superintendent (1874); *On the Construction, Organization, and General Arrangements of Hospitals for the Insane: With Some Remarks on Insanity and Its Treatment* by Thomas Story Kirkbride (1854); Dorothea Lynde Dix, 1802–1887, advocate for indigent mentally ill; *Gracefully Insane: The Rise and Fall of America's Premier Mental Hospital;* stories from old ladies in waiting rooms and lobbies; "Psychiatry in Canada a Century Ago" by V. E. Appleton, *Canadian Psychiatric Association Journal*; *A Wholesome Horror: Poor Houses in Nova Scotia* by Brenda Thompson; "For Them but Never Really Theirs: Finding a Place for the 'Aged' within State-Funded Institutions in Nineteenth Century Nova Scotia" by Cheryl Desroches, *Journal of the Canadian Historical Association*; *Celtic Women: Women in Celtic Society & Literature* by Peter Berresford Ellis; "The Backward" in *The Collected Neil the Horse* by Arn Saba (Katherine Collins); *Poems* by Elizabeth Bishop; *Elizabeth Bishop: A Miracle for Breakfast* by Megan Marshall; *Echoes of Elizabeth Bishop, Elizabeth Bishop Centenary* (2011) *Writing Competition* edited by Sandra Barry and Laurie Gunn; *On Elizabeth Bishop* by Colm Tóibín; *The Mapmakers' Legacy: Nineteenth-Century Maps of Nova Scotia* by Joan Dawson; *The Glory of Woman, or Love, Marriage, and Maternity* by Monfort B. Allen and Ameila C. McGregor (1901); *Creative and Sexual Science: or Manhood, Womanhood and Their Mutual Interrelations* by O. S. Fowler (1875); *The Spinster and Her Enemies: Feminism and Sexuality 1880–1930* by Shelia Jeffreys; *Reviving Ophelia: Saving the Lives of Adolescent Girls* by Mary Pipher; *Historic Black Nova Scotia* by Henry Bishop and Bridglal Pachai; "Slavery in English Nova Scotia, 1750–1810" by Harvey Amani Whitfield in *Journal of the Royal Nova Scotia Historical Society,* Vol. 13, 2010; "Searching for the Enslaved in Nova Scotia's Loyalist Landscape" by Catherine M. A. Cottreau-Robins in *Acadiensis*; "The Canadian Narrative about Slavery Is Wrong" by Charmaine A. Nelson in *The Walrus*; *The Hanging of Angélique: The Untold Story of Canadian Slavery and the Burning of Old Montréal* by Afua Cooper; *And I Alone Escaped to Tell You* by Sylvia D. Hamilton; Dan Conlin, curator (brother), National Museum of Immigration at Pier 21; *Brain Pickings* by Maria Popova; *Camera Lucida* by Roland Barthes; *Relational Frame Theory: A Post-Skinnerian Account of Human Language and Cognition* by Stephen C. Hayes, Dermot Barnes-Holmes, and Bryan Roche; *Where Moose and Trout Abound: A Sporting Journal* by Mike Parker; *Seashores of the Maritimes* by Merritt Gibson; words from my psychiatrist; David Lynch; stories from grandmothers; stories of old women; stories from girls; artwork of Marie Cameron, Mary Pratt, Emily Carr, and Gathie Falk; *The Union Street Café Cookbook* by Jenny Osburn; music of Tori Amos, Karl Orff's "Fortuna Imperatrix Mundi"; Kate Bush, Beyoncé, Joy Division, the Verve, P. J. Harvey, Dolly Parton, Amanda Palmer, Rachel's; wind and sea sounds; "Wayfaring Stranger" (traditional); Brian Stokesbury; Burial Grounds Care Society; Kings County Museum; Kate MacInnes Adams; North Mountain United Tapestry; Burlington; Harbourville; *On Being with Krista Tippett*, with Resmaa Menakem,

"Notice the Rage; Notice the Silence"; *What the Ocean Remembers: Searching for Belonging and Home* by Sonja Boon; *Under the Sea-Wind: A Naturalist's Picture of Ocean Life* by Rachel L. Carson; *A Field Guide to Trees and Shrubs* by George A. Petrides; *A Field Guide to Wildflowers: A Visual Approach* by Roger Tory Peterson and Margaret McKenny; Karen Roberts Yoga; Yoga with Adriene; *The Nova Scotia Atlas*, Fifth Edition; *Charlotte Sometimes* by Penelope Farmer; *One Flew Over the Cuckoo's Nest* by Ken Kesey; *All the Light We Cannot See* by Anthony Doerr; *The Age of Creativity: Art, Memory, My Father, and Me* by Emily Urquhart.

KATE INGLIS

CHRISTY ANN CONLIN is the author of two acclaimed novels, *Heave* and *The Memento*. She is also the author of the short fiction collection *Watermark*, which was a finalist for the Danuta Gleed Literary Award and the Forest of Reading Evergreen Award. *Heave* was a national bestseller, a *Globe and Mail* Top 100 Book, and a finalist for the Amazon.ca First Novel Award, the Thomas H. Raddall Atlantic Fiction Award, and the Dartmouth Book Award. Her work has appeared in numerous literary journals including *Best Canadian Stories*, *Brick*, *Geist*, *Room*, and *Numéro Cinq*. Her short fiction has also been longlisted for the Commonwealth Short Story Prize and the American Short Fiction Prize. Her radio broadcast work includes co-creating and hosting CBC *Fear Itself*, a national summer radio series. Christy Ann studied theatre at the University of Ottawa and screenplay writing at the University of British Columbia. She was born and raised in seaside Nova Scotia, where she still resides.